THE NEVER WARS

BOOKS BY
DAVID PEDREIRA

The Never Wars

Gunpowder Moon

THE NEVER WARS

DAVID PEDREIRA

Published in 2023 by Blackstone Publishing
Cover and book design by Sarah Riedlinger

Printed in the United States of America
Originally published in hardcover by Blackstone Publishing in 2023

First paperback edition: 2023
ISBN 979-8-212-38991-4
Fiction / Science Fiction / General

Version 2

Blackstone Publishing
31 Mistletoe Rd.
Ashland, OR 97520

www.BlackstonePublishing.com

In memory of my brother,
Dr. Mark A. Pedreira, a man of letters
and a lover of books.

BOOK 1

1

ORBITAL SUPERMAX PENITENTIARY
EARTH-MOON LAGRANGIAN POINT-1
2093

"Now you know why they call it the Rhino," Voss said.

Owen Quarry didn't answer. He wrapped a shirt over his eyes to keep out the light and curled into a fetal position on his bunk, letting the dry prison air wick the sweat from his skin. His mind wandered to green places, Earthly fields far from his cell and farther away from his body, which still felt the high-gravity vise of the Rhino like the rolling shock waves from a bomb. Voss's voice drifted in from the vent above his head, and it didn't matter whether Quarry responded or not. Voss was a talker.

"I know the dude who named it," the inmate said. "Baltkin, a lifer, a freaking Russian rapist. They threw him in that gravity ring for a whole day after he tried to shiv a guard with a sharpened toothbrush. He came out and his eyes were red. I mean *all* red. The high g's blew out his capillaries, you know?"

Quarry stayed silent. He thought he might be having a heart attack. The rhythms were way off; an odd time signature beating against his aching ribs. *Thump. Ba-thump. Ba-thump. Thump.* He sank into a flashback as he tried to ignore the erratic pulse—a recon mission a few years back in one of the many gorges that cut through the Appalachian Mountains, when a hillside soaked by monsoon rain had collapsed on him and another scout. They were buried for ten minutes before their squad dug them out. Quarry survived because his head lodged in the prop roots of a birch tree, leaving a small gap between his mouth and the slurry of the landslide. The other grunt drowned in the mud. All that dirt and rock smothering them, and the smell of wet wormy earth up in his nostrils . . .

"Yeah, Baltkin," Voss intoned again, flinching Quarry back to the present. "He was gone for a week afterward. I mean freaking *gone*. Couldn't talk. Couldn't eat. The guards were roughing him up 'cause he was shitting his pants. When he finally came to and we asked him how it was, you know what he said?"

Quarry didn't respond because Voss wasn't really asking. He was just setting up the punch line.

"He said it was like having a rhinoceros sit on your chest for a whole damned day. He said he'd kill himself before getting thrown back in there. Suicide by guard or somethin'. And that was it. We started calling it the Rhino."

Quarry hoped to God that Voss had finished his story, that the bald-headed little weasel would lose focus and drift off into one of his daylong reveries. Of all the conditions that Voss could be diagnosed with—and there were many—attention deficit disorder had to top the chart. But Voss had latched onto the excitement of something new in a world where the days and months blurred together into a gray line of institutional monotony. His next-door neighbor had just done twelve hours in the Rhino and that wasn't an everyday event—even on Lagrange-1.

The inmate's voice filtered through the vent again. "Man,

I don't know how you took it. I did two hours in the Rhino once—I can't even remember when—and it broke me down cold. Three and a half g's, again and again and again. It's the squeeze on the heart and the brain that does it. The squeeze on the heart and the brain . . . it kneels you before the devil."

Voss rambled on as Quarry descended into a netherworld of half thought, half hallucination. He felt the crush of rock and mud from the landslide years ago and the weight of the Rhino from moments ago, and the cold sweat on his skin wouldn't evaporate. *I'm with Baltkin*, he thought. *Suicide by guard is right. Another twelve hours in that thing will drive me fully and completely insane.* He mulled over ways he could attack the next guard who entered his cell. They had thrown him in the Rhino for breaking the jaw of another inmate, and the way Quarry figured it, if you can't beat the shit out of the next asshole that has it coming, you shouldn't linger in an orbital supermax anyway. He took a deep breath and the off-planet prison smells of antiseptic, garbage, machine oil, and body odor reinforced the idea of goading a CO into killing him.

Then there was silence. Voss's voice disappeared, which somehow was worse than Voss talking. Quarry slid the shirt off his face and lifted his head toward the cell door just as it buzzed. A guard peered through the small Lucite window. It was Forsythe, the most sadistic corrections officer in C-Block. Quarry made clandestine fists to see what strength he had left.

The door opened with another buzz and a grate of metal. "Well, Owen Quarry, don't you suddenly look like one of the meek?" Forsythe asked. "I've seen more life in a bowl of soup."

Quarry stared at Forsythe but didn't move. He didn't have enough strength left to do anything, so he closed his eyes and waited for the guard to leave. More than anything in the universe—more than having his mother and brother back, more than being in the woods in the late fall when the doe are hot and the shooter bucks are on the rut, more than waking up and finding out the last five years of life on Earth were just some kind of sick hallucination—he wanted to be left alone. Just one hour alone to sweat out the pain and bad memories.

Forsythe could tell, and he smiled. "Get your ass up, boy. I can smell you from here. You have ten minutes to get washed and presentable or I'll put you in the sandblaster."

"What?" Quarry croaked. He couldn't think of anything to say. He couldn't imagine moving. His voice didn't sound right at all.

"You got a visitor."

The bad visions lingered as Quarry sat in the normal-gravity torus of Lagrange-1, wondering how, in less than two hours, he had gone from the Rhino to a meeting room with upholstered chairs, a polished basalt table, and porthole views of the near side of the Moon as the prison spun in its gravitational middle space between Earth and Luna.

They had left a packet of recycled water on the table in front of him, and he bent his head and sipped at the straw sticking out of it. He was shackled hand and foot with cuffs but freshly washed and wearing a clean gray jumpsuit. The room smelled of iodine, so he breathed through his mouth, dreaming of the fall in western Maryland when the must of decaying leaves and crab apples mixes with cool air and the animals move in a thousand different migrations. A baritone bell rang. The hatch opened and a woman walked into the room. She wasn't wearing the black battle dress of the prison staff. She had on a formfitting tan jacket and pants. Her dark hair was pulled back in a ponytail and tucked into a zero-g sleeve on the back of her coat. It dawned on Quarry that he would have considered her beautiful even if she hadn't been the first woman he'd seen in five months.

She gave him a wide berth as she walked around the table, sat on the other side, and put a touch-coin down in front of them. A hologram popped up from the disc; two sheets of translucent paper side by side and a mugshot beneath it: his internment forms and processing photo for the Off-Planet Penitentiary System, Lagrange-1, Supermax.

"Former Staff Sergeant Owen Quarry," the woman said with a hint of an accent. "You don't look so good." *French Canadian*, he thought, remembering a Spec Ops guy from Quebec that he had run recon missions with during the Collapse and the ensuing civil wars that raged across North America.

"Summer cold," he said.

"Hmm." She continued to glance through his file, swiping through the holographic pages with a manicured fingertip. "They can linger."

"Yeah, they're a bummer. I was hoping for some time in the infirmary."

She swiped to the left now, ignoring his request, and the sentencing papers were replaced by his military service record. She nodded in approval through the first few sections, from Ranger School and long-range surveillance training at Fort Moore to his deployment with the 525th BSB at Fort Liberty. He saw images of his Jump Wings and commendations flash across the hologram, followed by several heavily redacted mission reports. The woman stopped at the last page, which read: After-Action Report—Battle of Pennsylvania 10/23/2092 LRS-C, MAC-LSA, SECRET. A black rectangle sat beneath the text. She pushed the void with a fingertip and a video filled the screen. It took Quarry a second to realize the feed came from his own tactical helmet cam on the day that had ended his life as a free man. There was no audio, but he heard the sounds in full stereo in his mind anyway: the resonant *thwop* of the quadcopter blades, the rush of wind through the open doors of the aircraft, the ball-bearing whir of the Vulcan gun, which spit out ten thousand rounds of death a minute in orange tracers that looked like bottle rockets arcing toward the Earth.

And the look on that asshole door gunner's face, which Quarry revisited every night in his dreams—an insane mask of joy and self-hatred like the guy was getting off on beating a dog as he fired the Gatling at the refugees below, scattering them off the breakdown lanes of Interstate 81. The look of pure rage when Quarry interrupted him—the spittle flying from the gunner's mouth as he told Quarry what to do with his moral objections. And his eyes, pupils blown wide and dark as the ocean floor, amorality and immorality and just fucking evil brewed together, summing up one-half of North America after the Kessler Syndrome attack of 2088—the half that went insane with bloodlust when society went away in the Collapse. Then two neat, black-rimmed holes appeared on the door gunner's forehead, and he tumbled out of the copter onto the asphalt below, somewhere northwest of Mechanicsburg, Pennsylvania. *Too damned stupid to be wearing his restraint system.* That was the last thing Quarry had thought as he pulled his finger off the trigger of his XM20 caseless carbine and watched the dead man drop to the ground.

The woman touched the video feed again and it returned to black.

"That was an interesting career decision," she said. "I can't mourn for the dead, but if you're going to double-tap a bird colonel's nephew you should turn off your TAC-CAM first. And maybe do it in a more private setting, like behind the latrine."

"Damn," Quarry said. "Where were you when I needed a life coach?"

The woman tapped the coin and the entire hologram disappeared. She looked him up and down, like an engineer inspecting a weld line, and leaned back in her chair.

"I was busy putting together a team, Mr. Quarry, before you even pulled that trigger, and now I've come for you," she said. "Your psych scans give me almost as much pause as your lack of impulse control, but the truth is, I need someone with reconnaissance and tracking skills and my options are limited."

"Options for what?" Quarry asked. "You hunting ship rats on the Supermax? I'd focus on the 1-g rings and bring some peanut butter. They don't really like cheese, Miss— I didn't get your name . . . or affiliation?"

She smiled without showing her teeth. "My name is Jude, and I'm not here for the rodents. I represent the Coalition of Responsible Powers."

He laughed, which only reminded him how badly his ribs still hurt. "Say what?"

"Yes, I know it's not the best of names. We're somewhat new, and you're a little information deprived these days. Call it CORP for short and think of it as an alliance of the few countries and confederations on Earth that aren't still living out a full reenactment of the Dark Ages. Canada. The Loyal States of America. Africa United. The Mesopotamian Group. New Scandinavia."

She got up and walked to the porthole and traced a line around the margins of the full Moon in the window. Dead as it was, it still looked beautiful, all white and gunmetal gray and shining in the sun. They were close enough to see the mining colonies on the Mare Serenitatis and the Oceanus Procellarum. Many of them had fallen into disrepair.

"CORP's political and military strategists have made a bleak assessment, Mr. Quarry," she said, turning back to him. "The Kessler attack set Earth back by decades. Terran production is at a thirty-year low and so are all our inner system, Belt, and IFS operations. Territorial defenses. Heavy industry. Agriculture. Terraforming. Everything is stuck at the bottom of the curve. We've fallen behind the rest of the Inner Fifty Systems and we aren't going to catch up, at least not before someone decides we're an apple worth plucking from the road."

Quarry's headache pulled at him, and an ember of anger began to glow behind his eyes. He didn't need a rehashing of the last four years on Earth—he had lived them facedown in the mud, fighting first for the US military and then the Loyal States of America when the country broke into four competing factions, and finally . . . well who knows who he was fighting for at the end? It wasn't anything that had organization, leadership, or a moral code. He wanted to lash out; wished he could break his restraints and throttle her neck until a guard came in and killed him with a juiced cattle prod. But he felt a flicker of hope. *Was she really offering a way out of this floating Gulag?* Quarry had spent the last five months wrapping his mind around the idea of a thirty-year sentence for killing a jerk-off who was committing genocide via rotary cannon, someone who needed so badly to die . . .

"Okay, Jude. So, you need a dishonorably discharged vet serving a three-stack for capital murder to do what, exactly? Strap on a vest loaded with polymeric nitrogen and pay a visit to the Parliament House on Gliese 876? Or Leonis maybe, or Struve? I figured you'd want to clean up the mess on Earth before sending kamikazes to the bully empires out there among the stars."

She returned to the table, sat down, and folded her smooth hands and polished nails in front of her. Quarry wondered if she had ever been hungry—ever searched for scraps in a dumpster or hunted for rodents in the sewers. A small population of the "haves" never had to during the Collapse.

"The fight wasn't picked by us, Mr. Quarry, and we aren't looking for suicide bombers, although your chances of survival will only be marginally better if you sign on." She leaned forward and locked eyes with him. "We're putting together a company to conduct special activities throughout the Inner Fifty Systems. Sabotage. Supply line interdiction. Psy-ops and force projection. Asymmetrical warfare—stuff that may help level the playing field over time. Recruits are all ex–Spec Ops, and the mission is completely covert—meaning deniable."

"So, there won't be any rescue missions if things go south?"

She pursed her lips. "I'm afraid not. This is nonofficial cover, to use the old spy vernacular. You'll be going in sterile, no identifying patches or markings, and you will never be acknowledged. They won't even collect the dead."

"And you're manning this all-important, supersecret company with convicts and DDs?" he asked. "Doesn't sound like there's a lot of optimism for the mission."

"It's a prototype unit and the ship is new tech, so optimism is guarded. And yes, we're looking for dishonorable discharges, brig rats, and other castoffs. Very skilled castoffs that won't be missed if things go sideways." She checked her watch. "But you worry me, Mr. Quarry, even compared to the other cannon fodder I've been assembling. Your scans show a severe lack of instinctual self-preservation. You don't appear to care whether you live or die." She pulled at her ponytail, realigning it with the gravity sleeve. "So, I must ask you for the record, can you still serve effectively on a team? Can you fight for the man or woman standing next to you, or even for yourself at this point?"

He tried to grin, but his dry lips stuck to his teeth. "I guess that's situational, Jude," he said, taking another sip of the water.

"Put me in a dive bar back in the Blue Ridge when there's a good band playing and a few ladies to talk to, and I'll make self-preservation my mantra."

"I'm sure. But there won't be that sort of recreation on this billet."

He laughed. "Yeah, I got the sense." It was his turn to lean forward, as far as the shackles allowed. "You know, I was wondering why I got jumped by that German fish yesterday in REC C. You guys used the Rhino to soften me up for this interview, didn't you? And let me guess, they sent a good-looking woman just to sweeten my interest. What do they call it in the old spy vernacular—a honeypot?"

Her pupils shrank and the blue of her eyes expanded, and Quarry wondered if he had just blown his one chance to get off Lagrange-1—outside of being ejected from an airlock.

"They sent me because it's my godforsaken job, Mr. Quarry, and I'm pretty good at it," Jude said. "You've inferred the rest because you're a backwater hick who probably can't even spell *misogyny*." She stood up. "As for why you got thrown in the disciplinary ring, I don't know and I don't care. If CORP did it to soften you up, at least it gave me the pleasure of seeing you sitting here looking like something that should get flushed into open space with the rest of the trash."

"Okay," Quarry said, raising his hands as high as the shackles allowed. "Maybe you're right—about everything but the misogyny. I think men and women suck equally. But what's the out? Why should I slip-drive around the Orion Spur to get shot at when I can just die here in peace?"

"Because if you survive, you'll be redeemed as an honorable discharge in good standing—classified as a Terran citizen with a clean passport for the entire IFS. Ten missions are the requirement. Then they'll place you on a harvest moon or a terraformed planet under Earth's jurisdiction. Someplace where you can reconnect to your hillbilly sensibilities, as I'm guessing you're not the big-city type."

"Good guess. And how long will ten missions take?"

She paused and her eyes lost their lock on him. "I can't answer that. All I can say is that even if you survive the mission requirement, you shouldn't expect to reconnect with old friends and lovers when you're done."

"So, if I live, I'll be retiring an old man? That sounds like ten long missions."

She paused again, and he thought she wanted to tell him more. She tightened her jaw and remained silent for several seconds. "No. Not necessarily."

"Well, that doesn't make any sense."

She shook her head in agreement. "I know, but it will in time, Mr. Quarry."

Quarry sat back and stared at her as she pushed a buzzer for the guard and waited for the hatch to open. His head throbbed and he couldn't untie the Gordian knot she had just looped in front of him.

"I have no more answers to give you," she said. "You'll have to decide if getting out of this floating sewer is worth a leap of faith, and you have an hour to make up your mind. You know, Staff Sargent, the universe has gotten a lot more interesting since AI taught us how to slip-drive around the Orion Spur. Earth is in for the fight of its life. Do you want to be a part of it, maybe do something constructive with what's left of your time? Or do you want to go back to your cell and lie on your bunk and tick off the seconds, one by one, for the next thirty years?"

The door buzzed open. She stood up and walked around the table, once again giving him a wide berth. "Try counting to a thousand and multiply it by a million and you'll get a feel for what I'm talking about."

2

PALAPYE
BOTSWANA
2093

They hunted her so she led them into the gorges, which she knew as well as anyone still alive. There were at least twelve of them; she could see their weapon lights dancing through the scrub brush and camel thorn below as she climbed the rimrock lining the Goo-Moremi. Amateurs, giving away their position and size of force as easily as that, but it didn't really matter. They had the numbers and the guns, and they were doing exactly what they were instructed to do: driving Anaya Pretorius into a choke point, like dogs treeing a cat.

She climbed the cliff face rather than taking the trail because it was a faster route and they'd lose her sign, but her concern didn't point backward as much as it loomed straight ahead. There had to be a sniper or ambush waiting in front of her, or they wouldn't have been as ham-handed in their pursuit. The limestone cliffs still held the heat of the Botswanan day as she climbed, and soon her hands were chalky and cut and covered in vulture shit. A colony of the carrion birds lived at the top of the gorge, and Pretorius wondered if they would be feeding on her corpse in the morning. She shook the thought and continued her ascent. The Milky Way hung in splendor above her head, bright enough to cast shadows in the gorge even on the new Moon. The starlight was enough to expose her, but she had stolen a pair of mimetic, infrared-blending cammies from the armory behind the stockade, and she had IR-blocking paint on her neck and face and hands. And besides, Pretorius was a ghost in the bush. The soldiers she had fought with in the tribal wars called her *Lengau*—Setswana for *leopard.*

An explosion rolled up the rock face from below followed by a piercing scream. Someone had tripped one of the antipersonnel mines Pretorius set on the trail. That would slow them down a bit, but also alert anyone else in the gorge to the general vicinity of the pursuit. *That's the trade-off with bombs and guns,* she thought. It was why knives were her weapon of choice.

She climbed at ten-second intervals and paused for an equal amount of time, flattening herself against the rock and listening, waiting for the burn in her arms and legs to diffuse into numbness. One question kept running through her fevered mind: *How did I get myself into this mess*? The factual answer was simple: Pretorius had killed Tan's top lieutenant, a rat-faced little bastard named Letshego. Tan hadn't been moved by the fact that Pretorius walked in on Letshego raping a San bush girl. Letshego was an asset that Pretorius had deprived him of. And even though she was an asset herself—and perhaps a greater one—a lesson had to be made.

No, the question that burned through Pretorius's head, even dimming out her plans for escape, was *why* she had done it. In more than a decade of fighting as a teen soldier, a recon specialist, and a mercenary under various governments and warlords before and after the Kessler attack, Pretorius had seen a lifetime of atrocities. Why had she reacted this time when she was so close to freedom, and why didn't she just knock the asshole out instead of gutting him like a trout? As she scrambled up the last few meters of cliff to the sloping summit of the gorge, she realized there was no answer. It was instinct, like swatting a biting insect that lands on your arm. And it would probably cost her everything.

She reached the top and lay flat on the rock face, looking down at her pursuers. They took the old tourist trail up and were at least thirty minutes behind. She sniper-crawled one hundred and eighty degrees and scanned what lay in front of her. The Moremi Gorge snaked through the Tswapong Hills like a knife cut, and she would have to scrabble through another five klicks of severe terrain to get to the Lotsane. If she could make it to the river, perhaps she could get all the way to the Limpopo and then Pontdrif, where she knew some people who could get her a transport—a fast boat going east on the river or, better yet, a cargo ship or suborbital flight out of Maputo. She crawled, listening. Hopefully they weren't able to get in front of her; she had heard the quadcopters and drones launch soon after her escape, but couldn't they just be running pattern searches over the Kalahari Basin? She realized then how many "maybes" were coursing through her mind. Desperate people use maybes. The soon-to-be-dead use them.

Pretorius found a dry gulley and rolled into it, hoisting to a knee and listening again. She heard hyenas far in the distance and the night sounds of insects and frogs, but nothing else. She lifted to a crouch and started to duckwalk down the gulley and then the dart pierced her neck. The tranquilizer hit her almost immediately, like a quart of moonshine mainlined into her veins. She heard a whisper and a whistle, and she tried to run but her legs wouldn't come up from under her. Pretorius collapsed in the dirt. *I am truly dead. Why did I do that?* And then everything went dark.

Tan was in no mood for visitors, but it wasn't wise to turn around a representative from Africa United who flew in on a supersonic skiff with special papers. He sat in his exquisite all-wood bush lodge smoking and waiting for the emissary, hoping they would genuinely dislike entering a room hazed over by the chain of Dunhills he had inhaled in the last hour. The untimely visitor was a distraction from the anger that ran like a current through his body, the feelings of betrayal. *May all the gods in Africa damn Anaya Pretorius.* His best soldier—one of his most trusted. How could she do this to him for some illiterate bush girl that she didn't even know? Tan wasn't one of those warlords who scorched the Earth and butchered everything in front of him, but that didn't make him a humanitarian. War was war and soldiers were soldiers. And now his war chief was dead, killed by his favorite stalker on a moral whim, and she would have to die as well. *What a shitty day.*

He heard footsteps on the teak decking and was surprised when a white woman walked into the lodge. She had on dark-brown pants, a tan jacket, and safari boots, and her nose twitched as she entered the smoky room.

"General, I'm sorry for the intrusion."

"If I believed you were truly sorry, I'd be a fool," he said. He mashed the spent cigarette and lit another one. "What do our continental overlords want so dearly from me that it can't wait until the morning?"

She sat in a wicker chair as close to the open plantation shutters as possible. "I need one of your soldiers."

He laughed but there was no humor in it. "You flew down from Dakar to conscript a soldier? I'm sorry, Miss . . . ?"

"Jude."

"I'm sorry Miss Jude, but does AU have a shortage of cannon fodder that I'm not aware of? Perhaps our great new hope for a stabilized continent isn't doing as well as we've been led to believe?"

She coughed into a closed fist. "I'm with CORP, General Tan, not Africa United. And it's a particular soldier that I'm looking for."

Tan felt a small knot form in his chest. "And who might that be?"

She pushed a button on her wristband and a hologram hovered between them. It was the Leopard. He knew it would be. "Anaya Pretorius. Formerly Recondo, Team Echo, with the Botswana Defense Force. Specialties in tracking and close-quarters battle." She glanced around the hologram. "Your best and brightest reconnaissance trooper with additional skills in direct action and sabotage. And now, I believe, rotting in one of your animal pens?"

This time his chuckle sounded real. "Yes, she is. And the way my week is going, I had a feeling you were going to say that."

"My apologies."

"Stop apologizing for things you aren't sorry for. I'm afraid this request is impossible to oblige. Anaya Pretorius has been sentenced to death. She's to be executed publicly for murdering a superior officer. And it's going to happen tomorrow, before she tries to escape again."

Jude crossed her legs. "Hmm. I believe the officer in question was raping a local noncombatant? Was it really murder, General, or just a reckoning?"

The front two legs of Tan's chair hit the ground with a thud, and he leaned forward. He wasn't smiling this time. "That officer was my cousin's brother-in-law. He was found holding his liver in his hands."

"Well, that is a little extreme, but again, the reckoning thing."

Tan stood up and put out the cigarette. "Be cautious, Jude. I understand who you represent—this new coalition to save Earth from its ill-conceived progeny out there in the stars—but you are in my jurisdiction and my word still rules here."

"My apologies again, General, but will your word interdict a hypersonic cruise missile if CORP decides to send one your way? Or an energy beam from space? You know we've been able to restore some of our satellite infrastructure, including the kinetic kind. And I can assure you the boys in the command bunker are weapons-free these days."

Tan's mouth opened and hung there for a second. No one had spoken to him like that in years. The last person who did was long dead. But he had enough dealings with CORP to know they could be as Machiavellian as he was.

"My God, woman, you have balls." He raised his hand. "If you apologize again, I will kill you where you sit, space weapons or no." He sat down again. "You have to understand the predicament you put me in. I am charged by Africa United and CORP with maintaining stability across the girdle of southern Africa, from Windhoek to Lesotho. My army obeys me because I am true to my word. If I commute the sentence of one who has committed a capital crime because a bureaucrat from the skyscrapers up north flew down here in a fancy ship, they will fear me no longer."

Jude uncrossed her legs and moved her eyes to the shelf behind Tan's head. "Is that bourbon, General?"

He stared at her for a few seconds and shook his head. She was winning this argument. "Single barrel; it's harder to get than good fighters these days. And I suppose you'll want to commandeer that, as well?"

"I like to drink over a contract," she said. "We realize this one will sting, General, and CORP helps those who help us."

He took the bottle from the shelf, pulled the cork, and filled two tumblers with a few fingers of whiskey. "I don't have ice. Are you making an offer?"

"Fifty thousand," she said, standing up to take one of the glasses. "In IFS Coin. And I can assure you that Sergeant Pretorius will be my most expensive acquisition to date."

His eyebrows went up. Local scrip, be it South African rand or Botswana pula, still bought you the basics on the continent: guns, quadcopters, maybe even limited orbital access. But IFS Coin. Tan had some connections in the Asteroid Belt and there were better investment opportunities there than on Earth—shithole that it still was five years after John Dippel launched the Kessler Syndrome attack into the planet's low and high orbits, destroying virtually every satellite circling the globe and spurring the Collapse. Yes, IFS Coin could greatly expand his position.

"One hundred thousand," he said.

She took a substantial drink from her glass. "Mm, this is good bourbon, General, but let's not get over our skis. Seventy-five."

He drank as well. "Why is Anaya worth so much to you? She's just another soldier."

"Oh, I think you know that's not true. She's an exceptional soldier with a skill set that we need." She finished the bourbon in a gulp and put the glass on his desk. "We're putting together an expeditionary force to bolster our rather fragile IFS defenses, General. All off-planet operations. We have plenty of recruits who have fought in space, but we need a few soldiers who can stick their noses in the dirt. Long-range reconnaissance, surveillance, tracking skills . . ." she paused. "People who can get in close and make a kill without raising a ruckus. And they must be dishonorables—soldiers who are either in the brig or excommunicated."

"And why is that?"

"Because volunteers would never take this gig. Not in a million years. And because they have to be expendable."

He refilled their glasses. "A death mission. I see. So how do I explain this to my soldiers? My sentence is given and then lifted, and the guilty is allowed her freedom."

She took the glass and returned to the chair. "As I said, this isn't freedom. You can tell your people that the sentence still holds but the guilty will die in space."

Tan lit another cigarette. He couldn't drink without one. "You have me intrigued, Jude. Just what is this mission?"

It was her turn to smile. "I can't tell you. And honestly, you wouldn't believe me if I did."

3

INTERMEDIATE MASS BLACK HOLE URSA X-1
COLLINDER 285
2093

Major Thaddeus Crooks had seen a lot of crazy shit in his days, enough to have been deemed a suicide risk, defrocked of his command, and tossed from the regular army. But he'd never seen anything like the celestial monster filling the viewscreen on the bridge of the CS *Varangian*. If he stood before the devil himself on the banks of the Styx, his eyes couldn't have been more riveted.

A black void in space. An antiplanet only bigger, shaped like an ellipse and bulging at the equator, ringed in a flattened band of rotating orange-and-red fire with jets of blue gas and radiation and God knows what else thundering from its poles. And everything warping and lensing and redshifting around it—light, stars, gas, dust—like he was looking at a hallucination of the apocalypse through the bottom of a Coke bottle. *A black hole,* he said to himself, and the thought kept repeating itself. *A fucking black hole.*

"Behold the Bear," Cog said. "The only real time machine in the universe."

Crooks looked at Cog and wondered if he had finally gone insane. Five minutes ago, Cog had his attention like nothing else ever had—not even war—and now his head was snapping back and forth between Cog and the black hole. He almost forgot for a second that Cog—at least the part of Cog that was talking to him—wasn't real. This bespectacled gangly man sitting a few feet away, who looked like he had been pulled from the accounts receivable department of an insurance company, was a hypercharged hologram that somehow had mass and could be touched, a fact that Crooks couldn't absorb despite the briefing he had received on high-speed acoustophoresis. The human representation of Cog had stringy blond hair, sticklike fingers, watery blue eyes, and was wearing an olive-green jumpsuit a little too loose on his frame. But the real Cog was a large floating black spheroid, yoga-ball sized, smooth and liquid one moment and spicated matte the next, which hung over a recessed circle on the command console of the bridge. And that was only Cog's neuromorphic brain. According to the specs Crooks had read, the whole damned ship was Cog. *Chronos Operation Group/NNOSI is the* CS *Varangian*, a tech had explained to him—lock, stock, and barrel. Crooks envisioned the ship's conduits as Cog's veins, its circuitry as his nerves, and that black sphere as his detached brain, and the whole picture freaked him out. *I'm having a conversation with a ghost, and the real thing is some kind of AI horror show wrapped in black liquid-metal and plugged into a five-hundred-meter warship with dual gravity cylinders. And we're discussing a black hole that we're planning to orbit, on purpose, to travel into the future.* He kept his gaze on fake-human Cog, the holographic apparition, a certifiable dork sitting next to him in a combat chair.

"Did you just say *behold*?"

"Yes," Cog replied. "It seemed like a moment for the dramatic. Was that over the top?"

Crooks returned his gaze to the black hole. "No, I think it works."

Cog's human apparition leaned toward him with a reassuring tilt. "You know, the adjustment period will be quick. Within a few days, you'll be focused almost completely on my physical representation. In the meantime, you can think of my operating system as just a piece of the ship and not really me if that helps."

"I'm not sure it does," Crooks said, declining to revisit the obsidian spheroid behind him. "But let's get back to the black hole in the window. Tell me about the issues again with reaching the inner . . . what was the orbit called?"

"The Innermost Stable Circular Orbit, or ISCO," Cog said. "In this case, it's at about twice the diameter of the ergosphere, which is the region outside a Kerr–Newman black hole's event horizon. In a static black hole, it would be called the Schwarzschild radius, in case you've heard the term. And the issues are innumerable. I wouldn't be surprised if we're destroyed in our first insertion."

"Like the scout ship, you mean? Do we even know what happened to it?"

Cog leaned back and put his feet—or his representation of feet—on the bulkhead. "Telemetry was spotty, to say the least. Only about twenty percent of the data made it back to the beacon, but it appears that everything was working correctly outside of ISCO and even when the test pilots attempted a larger time dilation via a tight zoom whirl orbit. The internal magnetosphere on their ship was stable, and tidal forces were sustainable. Then everything went to hell."

Crooks stared at Cog. "I guess you're trained to talk like that?"

"Like what?"

"Human, with colloquialisms and all."

Cog's brow furrowed. "I'm not trained at all, Major. I talk like this because I am like this."

Crooks punched up the data on the scout ship *Argus*, which was lost to the black hole six months ago, reckoning for dilation. From the perspective of the dead crew of the *Argus*, it had happened just last week, and from the perspective of an outside observer watching the *Argus*, it was still happening as they spoke.

"Okay," he said. "Everything went to hell. Can you give me a more technical explanation?"

Cog smiled, happy perhaps that his human partner in running the CS *Varangian* wanted a technical explanation.

"Of course. I believe—and I say *believe* because we lack data and are still delving into the theoretical at this point—that *Argus* may have created a tiny perturbation in Ursa X-1's spin rate while trying to tap energy from its ergosphere. Are you familiar with the Penrose process?"

"No."

"Okay. I'll give you the nontechnical explanation first. A spinning black hole like the Bear has kinetic energy, which can be tapped to our advantage. If we are near pericenter of a zoom whirl orbit, just outside the event horizon and close to the accretion disk, and we throw matter at a negative angular momentum into the ergosphere, we'll receive an acceleration boost in response. A kick in the pants, if you will."

"That's the nontechnical explanation? The only part I got was the kick in the pants."

Cog smiled. "Well, it appears that *Argus* got its orbital calculations wrong, changed the spin rate of the black hole by a fraction when it attempted a Penrose boost, and its orbit became unstable when it came in too close. The ship fell below ISCO and couldn't escape because of the slightly larger gravity well it had just created. Then the tidal forces kicked in. They probably didn't understand they were breaking up until they were already broken up."

Crooks looked at the short audio transcript of the two test pilots who had died on *Argus*. Everything was calm pilot-speak and technical babble until one of them said: "What the hell is this?" That was the last transmission, followed by hisses of static and the screaming of metal about to rend. He recalled an audio he once heard of a submarine sinking below crush depth and imploding. The sounds were similar. Then he looked again at the one telescopic image taken of the wreckage of *Argus*; the pieces were frozen in time as they hovered in a string over Ursa X-1's event horizon. According to Cog, from their point of view, the wreckage would linger there for eons before fading out of sight, trapped by relativity. It was just another thing to put him on tilt today.

"But we can avoid that fate because of our hull and because of you, correct?"

Cog shook his hologrammed head. "Maybe and maybe not. The *Varangian*'s biomimetic hull will certainly help with tidal stresses, but it won't matter if we get the calculations wrong and lose orbital stability. Oh, and I haven't even mentioned theoretical things like relativistic turbulence, space-time knots, quantum gravity, sudden growth in the black hole's mass through other means such as increased stellar feeding, and any number of additional physical and gravitational forces that could prove problematic as we enter and exit our orbits."

Crooks stole a look at the Bear in the viewscreen again. It was feeding on a main sequence star in this hypercompact stellar system named Collinder 285, which Earth astronomers had only recently discovered, pulling a loop of superheated red-yellow plasma into an accretion disk around its starless ellipse. *A monster,* Crooks thought, and his gut feeling about it grew as he watched the black hole eat. *We have no business messing with this thing. It's like jumping onto God's personal chariot, and God doesn't like passengers.*

"But we still have you, Cog, right? I mean, they said you know more about black hole physics than any other entity in the IFS—human or artificial."

Cog stood up and walked to the viewscreen. He put his hands on his hips and stared at the Bear, and Crooks thought of a Renaissance mariner casting his eyes upon the expanse of the Atlantic Ocean before remembering that he wasn't even looking at a real person.

"I have spent the last twelve months cramming on the topic, that is true," Cog said, "but Napoleon knew more about battlefield tactics than anyone else and look where it got him." He turned back to Crooks. "From a classical relativity perspective, black holes are very simple things, Major. The math is easy. But what about when classical relativity breaks down? What about when quantum gravity throws us one of its many intricacies, which we don't understand yet? In those instances, which will occur, I don't think I'll make much of a difference."

Crooks wished that he had brought a cigar on board. He needed a smoke. "I'll avoid that fact when I talk to the company," he said. "I'm hoping to make it a week or so before they mutiny."

"Hmm, yes," Cog said. "I have calculations on that as well. Those aren't Boy Scouts and Girl Scouts heading to our hangar bay. A few are worrisome enough for a side conversation. And I can tell you from my monitoring of the *Makalu* barge that the combination of slip-drive sickness and the uncertainty of where they are and what they're doing is causing a good deal of consternation among the ranks."

"Yeah," Crooks said. "Well, they're about to find out that they're on some military think tank's idea of a kamikaze mission, run by a superintelligence with apparent self-confidence issues and a disgraced former line officer. Oh, and they'll be orbiting a black hole to dilate time so they can slip into the future and handle Earth's dirty work without acknowledgment or official cover. Is that about right?"

"That's accurate, Major, but I would add that I'm disgraced as well."

Crooks stood up. His concerns about Cog's ill-fated command of the TPS *Breckenridge* would have to be broached another day. "Don't be so hard on yourself," he said, moving to pat Cog on the shoulder but pulling his hand back at the last second. He made a circle with his mouth and blew air out of his lungs. "Well, my mother always said to give the bad news quick. Muster the company by squad and platoon in the normal-g cylinder when they arrive—mess hall near the big window. They're gonna need to see this shit to believe it."

He looked at the black hole once more before leaving the bridge—a feature that had been built only because the engineers couldn't imagine a ship without one. Cog didn't need windows or flight controls, and if he was somehow disabled, the people on board had little chance of piloting the ship. It would be like driving a car without a steering wheel, foot pedals, or tires. Crooks shook his head. He was on this godforsaken mission because he was just like the rest of the company flying toward the *Varangian*—a castoff. He'd lost the last command he had on Earth. No, he had *killed* the last command he had on Earth. And now he feared he'd be doing the same thing all over again. Ursa X-1 only reinforced the dreadful notion that time was a wheel he had been lashed to, and it would spin him back around to the dark places that filled his nights.

4

MAKALU TRANSPORT BARGE
COLLINDER 285
2093

They called it *foam head*, the disorientation and sickness that came from traveling through the interstellar medium in an isolated pocket of space-time. To Pretorius, it felt like the hangover you get from drinking too much Chibuku. Dizziness and headache and a dry mouth, with a lingering sour taste on the back of the tongue like spoiled bread. She would have thrown up anything other than the small sips of water she was drinking through a hydration pack fitted to her chest. There were no windows on the dimly lit transport, and ever since it had begun a continual burn of less than one g after returning to normal space and lighting its conventional drive, she couldn't keep the bile from pushing into her throat.

The others didn't look any better. The Spartan transport had two rows of four seats running on each side of a raised metal gangplank—maybe two hundred seats in all. Each chair automatically spun one hundred and eighty degrees depending on whether the ship was decelerating or accelerating, so that the g's remained positive for all the passengers. Pretorius sat with the three men who would be her squad mates. She had read their bios on the touch-coin the loading chief had given her, and she knew who and what they were by now: LRRPs like her—long-range reconnaissance patrol specialists—except for the big one sitting next to her named Dan Cherry. He was an ex-spook who went in with the scout and recon teams during missions that included covert political action, prisoner grabs, and assassinations. Cherry looked more like a cook than a snake eater, a big man with a gut that rolled over the sides of his BDUs and a neck that didn't end at his face, and he wasn't the only one on the transport whose best days appeared to have passed him by. *Hell, I probably don't look like a Tier One operator myself.* The hallucinogenic trip they had just taken through light-years of empty space didn't lend itself to strong first impressions.

"Does anyone know how long this will last?" asked the American seated to her left. Owen Quarry, she recalled, a Lurp who had been with a US expeditionary intelligence brigade. Medium height and farm-built, he had brown hair and blue eyes that roamed the transport with boredom, but Pretorius knew that was a smoke screen. Within thirty minutes she'd realized Quarry was recon. He had the crow's-feet of a woodsman, and his hands were roughed up and scarred from years in the bush. She looked down at her own hands and saw the same road map. And he knelt at the Gospel of Situational Awareness like her, observing everything on the ship—sights, smells, sounds, threats, escape routes—while not being obvious about it.

"How long what lasts?" she said in a rasp, barely recognizing her own voice.

"Feeling like I'm about to freaking die."

Hassan Zalta grunted. He had the bulkhead seat in their

four-pack, and the Syrian tracker had been in a trance for the last ten minutes. Now he rubbed his face with both hands and opened his eyes. Pretorius didn't know how to define sad eyes, but Zalta had them. He brushed his fingers over a thin mustache that would never prosper, and she recalled the note in his service record that he had killed a man with a twentieth-century bolt-action rifle at a range of 3,400 meters. *A two-mile shot.* Looks can be deceiving.

"You are about to die," Zalta said. "But you'll probably feel better from the flight before you do. I read that it takes an Earth day for the body to recalibrate from what just happened to it."

Quarry glanced at him, a little alarmed. "What just happened to it?"

"The gravitational waves used to create an isolated volume of space-time around a ship in slip aren't good for the inner organs," Zalta said. "And the quantum elements of the flight can rearrange your DNA at the subatomic level."

Pretorius stared at Zalta to see if he was joking but the melancholy look on his face didn't change. She turned to Cherry and raised her eyebrows. He was the only one of them who had been on an interstellar flight before, the only one who had fought in space. He looked back and winked.

"Just keep sipping that water, sister, and don't fret about what you can't control. Follow the same grunt rules as on Earth. Hydration is your friend, whether you've been shaken by an IED or shot through the Milky Way on a higher dimensional brane that only an AI can detect."

She looked into Cherry's eyes, sparkling blue and gleeful, and wondered about his mental stability. She had never trusted spies, even the hybrid ones who were soldiers, and this big American spook had obviously spent too much time on the moral margins after Kessler.

"How did you get here?" she asked him. "I thought the CIA ended up running things in America after the Collapse."

He laughed. "Which America? I got tossed between two or three of them and ended up choosing the wrong one."

She tried to smile but could barely part her cracked lips. The water didn't do much to lubricate her mouth. *Maybe it is best not to talk to this man*, she thought, taking another sip from her chest-pack.

"And you?" she asked after a minute, leaning forward and looking toward Zalta, who had been with the Druze militant group Jaysh al-Muwahhideen in Syria before landing in a Jordanian jail on espionage and assassination charges.

"Same as everyone else," Zalta said. "I bet on the wrong scorpion inside the bowl."

Pretorius shook her head. "That is not why I'm here."

They waited for several seconds and realized she wasn't going to elaborate.

"Well?" Cherry asked. "Give it up; there aren't any secrets in foxholes."

"I killed an officer," she finally said.

"Hot damn," Cherry said. "I always wanted to do that. I assume they were an asshole?"

"Most definitely."

"Well then, you're our one-zero."

"Come again?" Pretorius asked.

"Team leader," Cherry said. He grabbed Quarry's knee, making the fellow American jolt against the seat restraints.

"What about you, my country brother? We all fessed up. It's your turn."

Quarry removed Cherry's oversized mitt from his leg. He closed his eyes and sipped at his hydration pack. "Same as her."

Cherry laughed. "You killed an officer too?"

"No. I killed an asshole."

"We've all killed assholes."

"This one had a colonel as a father."

"Not bad," Cherry mused, "but I still say the girl is team lead."

Zalta perked up and scanned Quarry and Pretorius like he was studying the enemy rather than friendlies. "Two fratricides in a four-man team," he said. "That doesn't bode well for me and the big man, does it?"

"Just don't be an asshole," Pretorius said, "and I'll do my best not to lose my temper."

Cherry laughed and pounded Quarry's knee again, raising his hands in apology when Quarry glared at him.

"This is going to be fun," he said. "My last team was a bunch of pussies."

"What happened to them?" Pretorius asked.

"They're all dead. Like I said, pussies."

5

CS *VARANGIAN*
URSA X-1
2093

At least there aren't any Fucking New Guys in the bunch, Quarry thought as he stole looks at the other conscripts bouncing up and down and trying to get used to the .7 g of the rotating room, which was gunmetal gray, cavernous, and had to be the CS *Varangian*'s crew mess. Everyone still had a slip-space hangover, which meant there were roughly a hundred and sixty dishonorable discharges from around the world in a bad mood and a confined space. All of them had put in years behind the trigger; that much was clear. Not an FNG in the room. Even time—the great destroyer of waistlines and perishable skills—couldn't erase the look of an operator.

The scuttlebutt started by a head-shaven monster named Jorgenson with a First SFOD-D tattoo on his neck was that they were not only in outer space but about ninety light-years from home. Way outside the Inner Fifty Systems perimeter—out in the void. Quarry sized up Jorgenson to try and figure out if his RUMINT was more rumor or intelligence. He knew a few Delta operators back in the day. Some of them were exaggerators. Most weren't.

"So, what're we supposed to fight out here, dark matter?" one soldier muttered to a few half-hearted chuckles.

"We're supposed to sit here and wait, is what I heard," Jorgenson said. "Like for years, maybe."

"Wait for what?"

"The hell do I know?" Jorgenson said. "Your sister."

"We're a self-licking ice cream cone," said another trooper with an artificial arm. "A strategy looking for justification for its own existence."

Quarry was trying to figure out what that meant when the pressure door at the front of the hall opened and a man in a dark-green flight suit walked in. He made his way to the middle of the semicircle of troopers and stood next to a large window concealed by a blast shield. He had oak leaf clusters pinned to his collar, and the only insignia on his shoulder was a tan-and-black patch that read COG-V. His salt-and-pepper crew cut stood out in contrast to a lean ebony face that was all skin, bone, and muscle. He was middle-sized, middle-aged, and didn't have the look of the fire-eating COs that Quarry was used to. He looked calm and detached.

The room went quiet, but the man waited a few seconds before speaking.

"Ladies and gentlemen, welcome to the CS *Varangian*. I'm Major Crooks, your CO. I'm going to keep this briefing to the point and bullshit-free because you've all been fed the bullshit before and when I'm done, you're gonna need plenty of time to digest reality."

Crooks walked down the front row of the company, assembled in preassigned formation. Four platoons, it looked to

Quarry, broken down further into squads and teams. He took a quick read of his odd quartet of teammates and shook his head at the incongruity. Anaya Pretorius stood next to him. Former scout for the Botswana Defense Force, with a runner's body and hair in tight Bantu knots; eyes darker than her mahogany skin, not an inch over five four. Close-quarters battle was one of her specialties, according to the touch-coin, with proficiency in edged weapons. Zalta was even leaner than Pretorius, a sniper and tracker who didn't look like he'd be much help in a hand-to-hand fight. And then there was Cherry, pasty white and bulging out of his battle dress uniform, wearing an odd grin that left Quarry to wonder if he was right in the mind. Cherry had come out of SAD-SOG, the paramilitary and covert action group of the old CIA. Quarry had run into a few SAD operators in western Maryland during the Collapse, when the self-proclaimed King of Pennsylvania was burning the countryside. They were crazy bastards, the special activities guys, the types that would destroy a village to save it. The types that wanted to put piranhas in rice paddies during the Vietnam War.

Everyone in the room probably had postconcussion syndrome or PTSD a dozen times over, whether they admitted it or not. Too many doors breached; too many blast waves rattling the brainpan. Too many confirmed and unconfirmed kills. Too many dead buddies. He stole a quick look at Pretorius and got the sense they were thinking the same thing as they assessed the roomful of ex-Rangers, Delta, SEALs, Marine Force Recon, SAS, IDF, BDF, Spetsnaz, 71st Battalion, 1st Airborne Brigade, Kaibils, GROM, and SASR. A hodgepodge of disgraced operators from around the globe, too long in the teeth, recycled for God knows what.

"The powers that be on Earth have come up with a real wild card, and we're it," Crooks said as if in answer to Quarry's thoughts. "CORP has determined that the home planet can't bully its way back into the game in the Inner Fifty Systems . . . not conventionally. So, they're going asymmetric, and we are the guerrillas. We're the Pan-Europa or the Black Guard or the Viet Cong. Pick your flavor. Our job is to raise unconventional hell wherever needed in the IFS." He paused. "And more importantly, whenever needed."

"You mean like soon?" someone asked.

"Maybe, from where we're standing," Crooks said, looking toward the disembodied voice in the formation. "But soon could be in a decade from everyone else's perspective. I'm gonna make this simple, people: our mission is to conduct covert ops in the future and test the economic and strategic viability of stashing military assets in time."

The room buzzed with a mixture of laughter and groans. There weren't many physics majors in the group, but there also weren't many idiots. Every one of them had been given FUBAR missions before but none of them had heard anything as ridiculous as this.

"What're you saying, we're on a time machine, Major?" asked a Latino woman with a tight crew cut, a neck tattoo that said *Love*, and a half-moon scar on her cheekbone. "Can we go back to 2085? I'd like to kill my first boyfriend again."

Even Crooks let a smile slip at that as he waited for the laughter to subside. "Sorry, there's no going back to the good old days. Physics doesn't allow it. In the real world, you can only travel forward in time, and you do it by dilation, or slowing it down from everyone else's point of reference. Slip-drive travel between star systems doesn't change our clock because there is no acceleration in a gravitationally isolated volume of space-time, and normal drives aren't a practical mechanism for time dilation. You have to go too fast, you get too heavy, and a space rock the size of bird shot will shit on your day. But let me introduce you to the one natural time machine in the universe—the one that uses gravity."

The blast shield on the window opened and Quarry blinked, forgetting about everything else. Everyone in the room did the same. They stared at a black hole off the port side of the ship. It was eating a yellow star, looping its orange gas into a thin pinwheel around an oblong void in space. Two bright whorls of blue light emanated from the black hole's top and bottom, like funnel clouds thundering into space. The gaseous loop closest to the ship burned bright orange and the far side redshifted and warped. Quarry knew that for all the shit he had spewed in foxholes before, all the talk of luck and chance and the finicky care of the gods, this was the first time he was looking at something supernatural. He stared into God's open mouth, and it looked like a door to insanity.

"That's right," Crooks said as the gravity cylinder slowly rotated the black hole out of their view. "It's a fucking black hole. And this ship is built to orbit it in a way that slows down time for us, while the rest of the galaxy stays on the regular clock. For those of you not freaking out enough to worry about the integrity of the ship, we think the *Varangian* can take it. She's got a mimetic hull to withstand the tidal forces involved in orbiting a spinning black hole and a superconducting magnetosphere to protect us from the radiation which, needless to say, is extreme. As for combat readiness, she's got all the firepower of a Class A Cruiser, unique stealth capabilities, and dual thermal antimatter engines for conventional thrust. Her slip-drive can create a gravity-induced bubble in seven minutes. And we have nanogel immersion pods with inertial negation for the crew, allowing us to combat maneuver at over 40 g's without being turned into grease spots. This ship was built to stash us in time and drop us into the shit at a moment's notice. We're a hedge against future bets, people, but from our perspective the lag will be short."

Zalta stared at the now empty window while running a thumb and index finger over his negligible mustache. "Why would there be a strategic benefit to this? Why would Earth not want to use all its assets now? And what if CORP isn't even around in whatever future we come out to? A year from now, there might not be anyone to call us for a mission."

"Legit questions," Crooks said. "As I said, the first reason is insurance. CORP may not always have special assets available when needed in the future. Their Spec Ops teams are fighting rebellions on Earth as we speak and are stretched thin at the Belt and the Jovian mining complexes. We, however, will *always* be available, regardless of the military readiness of the times. Second is the element of surprise. We will come out of nowhere, sterile and unsanctioned, like the MACV-SOG teams in Vietnam. When we strike, our enemies won't know who hit them, or from where. They'll have no intel on us—no chance of early warning. We will appear from off-the-grid and disappear in the same way. Whatever information we give the IFS will be for propaganda and psy-ops purposes only."

I don't think he's buying this any more than we are, Quarry thought as Crooks turned back to the window. The black hole appeared again, and it was like the celestial monster had become a tic for the major. He would sneak a peek at it every time he wanted to avoid being looked in the eyes, so the crew wouldn't see that he was flinging horseshit.

"And the last and most fundamental reason," Crooks said, "is economics. We are the prototype—hence our disposability as military discards. But what CORP really wants is to stash an army in time. Think of it: a few divisions orbiting a black hole for two weeks and popping into the IFS twenty years later at full strength and ready to fight. That's two decades where twenty thousand soldiers don't need to be fed, fueled, provisioned, or policed. If the Roman Empire could've done that, we'd still be saluting an emperor. And if CORP can pull it off, they'll save trillions in IFS Coin over the next fifty years—enough to rebuild and assemble conventional forces that can take on Leonis, Gliese, Struve—whoever is the IFS big dog at the time."

"If CORP lasts that long," Quarry said, before realizing he had even opened his mouth.

Crooks looked at him and pursed his lips. "True. But for now, nobody is taking an active swing at Earth. Leonis and Gliese are fighting over richer turf than Sol and most of our military assets are being funneled into the defense of a few key star systems: Ross, Lalande, and Teegarden's Star. Terra is pulling back on its other claims farther out and the hope is that Earth will be left alone for the next few years. It also means that we will be CORP's one offensive component for the indefinite future."

"How long in the future are we talking about?" Jorgenson asked. "The contract said ten missions. How long will that take?"

Crooks shrugged. "In our time? Maybe a year or two. In Earth's objective time? The estimate we got was thirty to fifty years." He let that sink in for a second. "It could be longer. Our code name is *Century Gun*, people, so think about that and accept one fact: if you're still alive when this billet is over, your parents back on Earth will be in the ground. Your boyfriends and girlfriends will be eating soft food and playing canasta. That's the price we're paying to be redeemed. We are the forerunners of a new military doctrine called tactical and strategic temporal flexibility. Of course, they have an acronym for it: TASTF."

"That's worse than MANPADS," someone said, and Crooks waited for the snickers about military acronyms to die down.

"Can't argue with you there. As for command and control on the *Varangian*," he continued, "you're going to like this even less than the mission. I'm the only commissioned officer on the boat but everyone in this room was an E-4 or higher in their old units. A staff sergeant will be selected for each platoon, and the squads will have leaders selected by experience. A First Sergeant will be my noncom liaison to the company. But as we all know there isn't much hierarchy on the teams. Everyone will know everyone else's job. Everyone will be responsible for everyone else. Squad and team leadership may rotate depending on the mission. And discipline in the ranks will be imposed," Crooks said, "by him," pointing a finger toward nothing. Everyone stared at the void and wondered if Crooks had finally revealed the depths of his madness.

Then an unimposing man in a green flight suit appeared out of the ether. The new person stood with his arms behind his back and tried to smile. He had incorporated like a camera lens just snicked him into reality, but he didn't look like any hologram Quarry had ever seen. He looked solid. He looked like a man.

"And him," Crooks said, and a facsimile of the same man appeared on the elevated gangway above them. "And him and him." Two more apparitions appeared on either side of the company.

The muttering in the hall grew and quelled as everyone looked from one version of the apparition to the next. Quarry saw Cherry blink a few times. He saw Pretorius slip her hands to her hips and study the figures one by one, as if prioritizing targets.

"This is Cog," Crooks said. "He's our artificial intelligence, the captain of the *Varangian*, and my onboard XO for mission ops. In just about every way, Cog is the CS *Varangian*. He is not your enemy or your friend. He is the dispassionate arbiter of all that occurs on this ship. He sees everything, from when you're on the shitter to when you're bunked. You can think of him as God, and like God, he will mete out judgment to those who fall out of line."

Cog—all the Cogs—looked uncomfortable as Crooks spoke. Quarry wondered if an artificial intelligence could be uneasy or if it was just trying to fit in. The soldiers around Quarry were having the same difficulty processing this bureaucratic-looking entity which had been revealed as their übernanny. He had startling blue eyes but everything else about him, from his thinning blond hair to his weedy frame, was middling. If he had existed as a human, he probably wouldn't have made it out of boot camp.

"Cog's justice doesn't come from within," Crooks continued. "It descends from the sons of bitches that put all of us on this can. He has no choice in dispensing it. It's a binary thing, a one and a zero. The one is good. The zero is death. And I mean that literally. You were all injected with nanophiles during your MEPS physicals. They are microscopic and harmless unless triggered. But if they are triggered, they expand nitrogen bubbles in the bloodstream. Those of you coming from the maritime teams, the SEALs or Special Boat Service, will recognize this phenomenon as the bends. It will kill you quickly, but first it's gonna hurt."

Curses rippled through the room. Everyone put a finger to the spot on their necks where a military doctor had supposedly inoculated them against Belt Fever. Crooks raised a hand as the murmurs began to swell.

"Here are the things that will trigger your death: Disobeying a direct order. Fighting on board the ship. Missing in Action status, two hours after it is rendered. And fraternization." He nodded as everyone gaped. "Think about those last two things. If you go missing on an op, we aren't coming to get you and we can't afford the enemy finding out who you are. As for fraternization, that means women screwing men, women screwing women, men screwing men, or any other scenario that involves getting your rocks off outside of your good hand and a vivid imagination. If you need to get regular there's a full-immersion VIRT on board. Each trooper will have access to it once a week. I've heard it's not bad."

Crooks went to the window and rested his elbows on the sill. "Those are the rules, people. They are preordained, so don't blame me or Cog. A much more detailed code of conduct has been downloaded to your touch-coins. I advise you to read it. Trust me when I say there is no escaping Cog on this ship. Hate him for it if you must, but in my opinion, he's trapped in a bad situation like the rest of us."

Three troopers asked questions at once, but Crooks shook them off and raised a hand to quiet the room. "I've told you this up front because there is no military code of justice on this boat. There is no brig. There are no court-martials or Article 15's or defense attorneys. There is only Cog, and his decision will be immediately enacted. Cog, do you have anything else you'd like to add?"

Suddenly, there was only one Cog again—the one standing next to Crooks. He shook his head and looked apologetic.

"I would only say welcome to the *Varangian* and reiterate what the major has told you," Cog said. "My job is to keep you alive, and I will do my best in that regard. In terms of discipline, my actions are autonomic, like breathing or blinking. Being a castoff myself, I have accepted locking protocols that prevent me from deviating from mission orders in the hopes that I too will be redeemed. I'd strongly prefer not to trigger discipline against any of you."

"Fuck you, Cog," someone said, and everyone stole a glance to see where it came from. "Am I about to get bent for that?"

Cog didn't move or even scan the room. "No, Specialist Boortz. You aren't. I have indirect normativity exceptions that allow for leniency in certain cases, such as insubordination that is deemed a joke and doesn't affect command activities. In this case, because of the shock of the day, I'm going to let you slide."

"Cog is nicer than me," Crooks said. He scanned the squad registry and walked right up to Boortz until their noses almost touched. "If I hear negative shit about Cog in the future, I'm going to throw you out of an airlock myself. We are all here for one reason, people. Get this straight. Sometime back in the day, we all fucked up. This is our chance to be redeemed. This is our opportunity to fight our way out of it, and we get started tomorrow at 0600, ship time. Most of you have fought in space. Some haven't. The *Varangian* has two rotating cylinders built along an internal fuselage. Check your coins for assigned training in the static superstructure, the normal-g, or the heavy-g can. You'll find gravity-loading countermeasure skinsuits in your lockers. They reproduce some of the weight-bearing regimes of normal gravity and will help you deal with zero-g and the Coriolis effect. Put them on and get used to them. A lot of your training will be Sim-Virtual and some will be real action. Spend the next cycle reading all the other specs and regs for the ship, as well. There's a lot of stuff to learn."

He looked around the room. "I'll take two more questions."

The smallest member of the company, an Aussie who must have been a tunnel rat for SASR, raised her hand. "When do we eat?"

Crooks smiled without showing his teeth. "I thought you'd never ask. The mess schedule is on your coins, and if you're pissed off now, you'll be angrier once you get served chow. But I promise if we live past our first op, I'll be the first one foraging for real food and flushing the protein gels and power shakes out of an airlock. Last one?"

A lean, manicured man a few rows down from Quarry raised his hand. He had dark skin, straight black hair, and eyes like ambered resin. His name patch said Ras. "Can I ask, Major, if you had the embolism planted in your bloodstream?"

Crooks stared at him. "You can ask, Sergeant. I did."

Ras smiled. "That should make for an interesting relationship with your XO."

"How's that?"

"Well, it seems that he holds the real power, doesn't he?"

Cog fidgeted but Crooks looked bemused. "Knock on my door any time you want to talk about power structures, Sergeant. It's always open."

"Yes sir," Ras said. "No offense intended, sir."

"None taken. That's it then, people. Fall out." Crooks turned and left the room. Cog disappeared.

Quarry thought the rebellion would begin immediately—was wondering if he would start it—but everyone looked like they were thirty minutes past enemy contact, when normal life deadens the adrenaline high of combat. He had no starch left either. The company mumbled and stirred, tourists waiting to climb onto lifeboats, and then departed for their billets in twos and threes and fours.

"I don't like that man," Zalta said.

"The real one or the fake one?" Cherry asked.

"Both."

"They seemed okay to me," Cherry said.

Quarry and Pretorius looked at each other.

"Are we just going to accept this?" she asked. "They are throwing us into another world, a never world. How is it redemption if we end up in a place that has no relation to why we are here in the first place?"

Quarry thought back to Jude and her look of uncertainty when he brought up the timeline for their tour of duty.

"I don't think cause and effect crossed their minds when they hatched this thing," he said. "But yeah, we're going to accept it. That's the one thing they were sure about."

6

The *Varangian* hovered over the Bear's accretion disk, nose down and inverted. Crooks craned his neck against the headrest to look at the monster in the upper dome windows. It lurked a few hundred thousand kilometers out. The manifestation of Cog sat beside him on the command deck, but he was otherwise alone, the rest of the company crammed into their gel immersion pods for this first orbital insertion. The image of his crew hibernating in two horizontal racks amidships haunted him. He couldn't shake the sensation that he was sitting in a cemetery and would once again be shoveling dirt on the graves.

Cog said it wouldn't be a breakneck run, but both were thinking of the *Argus*. The AI had wanted Crooks to go into his high-g pod, but the major wasn't going to miss the ship's first attempt at an orbit around the black hole. *If I'm going to die, I'll take the last seconds of horror as penance for those poor bastards behind me.* Crooks stared at the void in the center of the black hole, where everything about the universe that made any sense broke down. If they got close enough, would he really be able to see *Argus*'s remains as its string of debris lingered over the event horizon for a relative eternity?

"Okay, this is going to be a simple orbit," Cog said, breaking his reverie. "We're going to stay at 2.2 times the radius of the ergosphere, just outside Innermost Stable Circular Orbit. I don't anticipate any significant tidal stresses as we'll be well clear of the photon sphere, and our acceleration shouldn't exceed four g's."

"What's the dilation going to look like?" Crooks asked. He had gotten used to focusing on human Cog and ignoring the AI's black spheroid brain floating over the command deck, and now that his multi-Cog fixation had passed, his eyes couldn't leave the black hole. Ursa X-1 was feeding, slurping an enormous string of yellow-and-orange plasma from the G-type star that had been captured by its gravity and looping it into a donut of fire around its equator. A star, for God's sake, a stellar furnace bigger and heavier and more powerful than anything Crooks could comprehend, caught in a slow entropic dance around the Bear like a speck of dirt being pulled into a drain.

"Minimal," Cog answered. "Roughly one year will pass in the IFS for every ten days we stay within the whirl part of our orbit, and dilation will be negligible in our outer four-leaf clover flight pattern. CORP wants us to maintain a modest time dilation for the first run as it anticipates an initial mission within six months of Terran time."

"And you're sure they'll be able to ping us?" Crooks asked. Like every field officer, communications haunted him. He had lost contact with teams in the past because of broken gear, electrical storms, heavy contact, or just a hill in the way of line-of-sight transmissions. Now, they would be orbiting a stellar nightmare ninety light-years from Earth, with God knows what kind of electromagnetic radiation distorting their coms—while slowing down time in the process.

"Yes, it's one of the few things that have been adequately tested," Cog said. "We have a series of communications buoys set at Lagrange points in this system, and the initial laser beacon will come through slip-space. CORP knows our intended orbit, so it can calculate our redshift. The signal we get will be heavily blue-shifted, but I've set up an algorithm to compensate. We should get the message with minimal lag. When the time comes for a more extreme dilation orbit, we'll have to break orbit immediately upon notice, as a few minutes could equal months of dilation."

Cog began his maneuver while he was still speaking. The ship bucked with no warning, barrel rolling a hundred and eighty degrees and pitching up relative to the black hole's equatorial disk. Crooks felt the modest acceleration in his chest. Nothing more than a steady roll and burn in a jump jet back on Earth.

"Magnesium diboride coils are superconducting at eighty percent across the horizontal axis of the ship," Cog said. "We currently have a magnetosphere that is stronger than Earth's, relatively speaking."

"Are you trying to make me feel better, Cog?" Crooks asked. He was strapped in with a five-point harness. Cog's apparition was unbuckled and unfazed by the acceleration. Crooks had asked him how an entity with mass would be unaffected by a hard burn, but after Cog began a lengthy dissertation on quantum gravity, anti-de Sitter space, and gauge theory, he begged him to stop.

"Well, yeah. The radiation coming out of that thing is a little frightening," Cog said. "I thought I'd share some comforting data."

"Thanks, but maybe some participation would help. I feel like a third wheel. Is there anything I can do besides watch the orbital insertion? Call off numbers or flight data or something?"

Cog glanced over and Crooks got the uneasy feeling that his

mental stability was being assessed. "That's a good idea, Major. I'll run a telemetry interface at your station, and you can call out anything that doesn't look nominal."

A holographic display appeared in front of Crooks with an array of orbital vectors, longitude and latitude markers, temperature, radiation, tidal stress figures, and time dilation calculations spinning off in a vertical list that combined flight data with general relativity. Crooks wished he hadn't asked. He felt like a high schooler baffled by the chalkboard in a trigonometry class.

"It won't make any difference, will it?" he asked. "You know the numbers before I can even register them. The telemetry is plugged into your brain."

Cog's eyes glowed and his mouth opened as he nodded. It was the most human Crooks had seen him. He was a manifestation of wonder, a painter who had just found something magical in the brush.

"At a moment like this, when we're moving into a unique gravitational and relativistic environment, it's a hard sensation to describe," Cog said. "I'm not just running the ship; I can feel every inch of it. The hull flexing and the thruster bursts. The time distortion, the energy of it approaching like waves hitting a coastline. I wish I could explain it."

"That's okay, Cog. As long as you're in the groove, I'm good with it."

Cog nodded and turned back to his own holo-displays, which formed a translucent ring around his upper torso and were split into a hexagon of quadrants. His chair automatically rotated from station to station as he worked.

"I thought this would be a good time to discuss crew comportment," Cog said, "as that is an exercise that requires both of our participation. And don't worry about the distraction; I can walk and chew gum at the same time."

Crooks wondered whether that was a backhanded insult while also making a note to ding the AI the next time he dropped a bad cliché. For now, he was too transfixed by the sight in the window to say anything. The *Varangian* hurtled toward Ursa X-1's equatorial belt. The ship's movement through space wasn't immediately obvious to the eye, but Crooks saw on his heads-up display that they were traveling at about 1.2 million kilometers per hour and accelerating, and the black hole grew larger every time he looked out the window.

"Okay," he finally said. "What do you got for me?"

Cog's voice remained conversational.

"I'm amazed by the adaptability of humans," he said. "The platoons have already integrated into their squads and immersed themselves into the training regimen, and while most of the troopers haven't been on active duty for months or years, they are performing above expectations."

Crooks nodded. "They're operators, Cog, not tinhorns. They've got training bred into the bone. It's like muscle memory, and it probably takes their minds off the insanity of where they're going." He kept looking at the Bear. Yes, it *had* grown in the viewscreen. He almost couldn't see the margins of its accretion disk anymore.

"There are some issues to discuss, however," Cog said. "Twenty-nine members of the company have never run operations in space. They are having problems adapting to zero-g engagements. The loading skinsuits aren't helping as much as we thought, and almost all the company has failed the initial simulations in the heavy-g torus. I had thought the exoskeletons would minimize the novelty of moving through a g-plus environment."

Crooks grimaced at the thought of the exosuits. He had run two commands off-Earth in the Inner Fifty Systems before getting dumped by the Loyal States of America Army—first a sleepy perimeter defense on Vesta, then a MIKE force stationed at the Groombridge frontier, where things got interesting. His first off-Earth battle occurred on a high-g moon orbiting Groombridge 34 Ac, against a Leonis Union force in regiment strength. It didn't go well for either side. The exosuits that provided bioenhanced locomotion in environments where gravity exceeded Earth's were clunky and prone to failure. Crooks's unit caught the Leonis troopers in a flanking attack in a forested impact crater on the terraformed moon. It was a turkey shoot until Leonis counterattacked with intelligent microdrones. Both sides got smoked, and the suits were a big part of the problem. They broke down quicker than twentieth-century assault rifles in the jungles of Vietnam, and even trained troopers found the musculature interface hard to manage in the middle of combat when you shouldn't have to think before making a move.

And what would his troopers be facing now? What fucked-up missions did Earth have in store for a company of clandestine guerrillas in an Orion Spur that now had nine hundred inhabited moons, planets, asteroids, and space stations? In the six decades since AI had figured out how to cheat physics and make interstellar travel a reality, the slip-drive's disruptive technology had spawned change at orders of magnitude, especially in the art of hyperterraforming. Humans found few planets or moons that sustained life in the IFS, so they built them from scratch, creating lush worlds within a matter of decades. Each of them was unique. There could be microgravity, hypergravity, high radiation, temperature extremes, tidally locked terminators, and even exotic exobiology to deal with among these new Gardens of Eden.

And worst of all, they'd be emerging into future military theaters with antiquated weapons and tactics. Crooks thought of

European horse cavalry running into a blitzkrieg of German Tiger tanks and Stuka dive bombers and 88s, and the image of the *Varangian* as a fast-moving graveyard came back with a vengeance.

"Major?" Cog asked.

Crooks shook his head. "Sorry, Cog, I got lost in thought. The relative gravity issues aren't a surprise, but we need to do something about them. Can you rotate the schedule to focus more on the other-g environments? These guys have already seen enough 1-g combat. That will come back to them."

"I can work out a new training matrix, but there's only so much availability in the zero-g and heavy-g simulators."

"Okay, draw it up—and how about using the static spine of the ship as a peripheral training space? Just have the teams run direct action drills in there—it will add to our zero-g footprint."

Cog arched his eyebrows. "I should have thought of that. I'll implement a plan immediately. Also, our recon teams are light on zero-g operations, and they've had total-casualty events in their microgravity training simulations. We won't be able to hide them, and we won't be able to train them enough before our first op, which could very well be in space."

"Then prioritize those teams, and I'll observe them directly."

Cog banked the ship to port, and Crooks kept his hands glued to the armrests as tremors of turbulence ran through the hull. The lack of normal flight alerts disturbed him. The ship ran ghost-quiet except for the otherworldly moan of its biomimetic hull as the fuselage flexed in the first twinges of tidal stress and heat from the black hole. Crooks had read about maritime vessels caught in typhoons and how their rigging sang like a chorus of ghosts when they encountered gusts at eleven or twelve on the Beaufort wind scale. The *Varangian*'s flexing had a similar tonality, and the sounds ran like a current through the pressurized portions of the ship. They were still outside the pericenter of their orbit; he wondered how much worse it would get. He thought about asking Cog to install the normal alert sounds of a manned ship. Just a few beeps and pings would be welcome.

"Also," Cog broke his train of thought again, "discipline has been largely maintained. There was a scuffle within Fourth Platoon at 1460 yesterday, but the other team members broke it up before it reached a level that required disciplinary action. And there has been no fraternization to speak of. Yet."

Crooks nodded. "Is that because you keep popping up at just the right time and place?"

"What do you mean?"

"I was in the mess hall last cycle when things got squirrelly at one of the tables and suddenly you were there. A quick reminder of your omnipresence, I'm guessing?"

Cog didn't say anything for a minute. "I didn't think of it like that, but I suppose I was trying to stave off an incident. I'm uncomfortable with my programming as it relates to the crew. I've read military history regarding discipline, and our current model is more representative of ancient times."

"We're not practicing Roman decimation, Cog," Crooks said. "If someone gets busted, it's for their own bad actions."

"Forty thousand kilometers from the event horizon, accelerating to 1.4 million kph," Cog said. He didn't have to blurt out that piece of information, Crooks realized, because the acceleration could be felt like a weight dropping on his chest. Cog was trying to figure out how to articulate what he was feeling. *Did an AI really need time to collect his thoughts?*

"But I'm more than a nanny as my main disciplinary course is death," Cog continued. "And there's no due process. My judgment protocols allow leeway with levels of misconduct, but that only goes so far. If two of the crew get in an actual fight, my programming calls for summary execution."

"Well, as you said yourself, those aren't Boy Scouts and Girl Scouts down there in g-stasis. I think the rules suck as well, but at least everyone is getting a chance at redemption." He glanced at Cog. "Is there anyone in particular you're worried about?"

Cog hesitated. "Yes."

"Who?"

"Sergeant Ras in Fourth Platoon, and Corporal Bellinger in the Second."

Crooks plumbed his memory. Arjun Ras—a former Para SF Trooper who joined India's Special Frontier Force and ran covert missions into Pakistan. *The one who called out their odd command structure during the briefing.* He had been court-martialed for torturing a prisoner in the field. A whistleblower claimed he had skinned the man alive. The torture worked—Ras got information that saved a regiment—but he was dishonorably discharged. Crooks remembered how innocent he looked while asking a loaded question, how *concerned*. And C. J. Bellinger, former Marine Force Recon, busted for lying to a forward air controller and having a bomb dropped on insurgents holed up in a school. Dozens of civilians, including children, died in the strike.

"There are a lot of rough actors in this company, Cog. I mean, all of them got nailed for something."

"Agreed," Cog said. "But there's a difference between grit and immorality. Those two spook me; Ras in particular. A lot of his service record has been permanently redacted by the Indian government, and it's hard to tell where he's coming from."

"Noted. Let's keep an eye on them."

The ship flexed again, its hull singing like the foredeck of a trawler plowing into a squall. Fire and blackness filled the viewscreen, and Crooks couldn't take his eyes from the dichotomy. There was only destruction in the accretion disk—in the black hole itself, there was nothing. Unless the blue jets thundering from its poles could be considered some kind of digestive discharge.

"T-minus ten minutes from our first zoom orbit," Cog said. "Everything looks nominal."

"Roger."

"Major, can I ask you something?"

"Of course."

"I know what happened to you at the Cumberland Gap. I've read the official report on how you lost your company, but I also know the truth of it. You must realize it was an act of God more than a command blunder, but you still blame yourself."

Crooks didn't answer. He closed his eyes to Ursa X-1 and focused on the harmonic thrum of the ship, which had dissipated into a moan. His mind shuttered back to 2091, a brilliant April morning in the mountains of western Maryland. He saw the thermobaric bomb drift off course after its transport got hit; watched the parachute guiding the weapon get caught in the thermals from the valley; listened to his forward air controller screaming to abort. *Abort!* The weapon drifted over his company's position just west of the Gap . . .

He opened his eyes. "Is there a question there?"

It was Cog's turn to pause. "Yes. If we lose our company on this tour, through combat or discipline or an act of the universe, will you still blame yourself? Because I'll blame myself, and I'm already worried about it."

"Does this go back to the *Breckenridge*, Cog?" Crooks asked. "I read up on you as well, and I don't see how you could have done anything differently."

Cog remained silent for a minute, leaving Crooks to wonder how many trillions of calculations he was making to formulate an answer. In 2090, as captain of the Terran Passenger Ship *Breckenridge*, Cog watched an extremophile bacteria race through every human on board as they flew the shuttle run from Enceladus to Ceres. The pandemic killed four hundred souls in five days despite the AI's frantic efforts to quarantine everyone and find a cure. Cog ran the last leg of the trip alone, the *Breckenridge* a coffin flying through space. An investigation found the AI bore no fault and yet he still took the fall. The company had to blame something—humans demanded it—so why not the machine?

"I don't hold myself accountable in that I followed protocol and there was no solution," he finally answered. "But I still feel guilty. Does that make sense?"

"The living always feel guilty about the dead, Cog. And yes—the answer to your question is that I'll blame myself if shit goes sideways with this command. I'll blame CORP and I'll blame you and I'll blame whatever gods are out there in the universe. I'll blame everyone and none of it will matter. That's just what war is."

"I suppose that's helpful," Cog said. He turned his attention back to the displays. "Preparing to enter the outer phases of our initial stable orbit of Ursa X-1. We are now moving through time at a different rate than everyone else in the IFS."

The *Varangian* rolled ninety degrees and flew on the same plane as the black hole's accretion disk. The ship shuttered and hummed but the orbit held true. All that Crooks could see in the cockpit window was a ring of orange fire, warping in every direction and wrapping itself around a circle of nothingness.

"Moving away from them," he whispered. "To God knows where."

7

MISSION ONE: YZ CETI
2094

The first jolt came from the launch, the second from a cold burn as the sled corrected its approach to John Dippel's space station. The two pathfinder teams crammed into the tiny drop ship side by side, lying head to foot, and the only thing in front of Quarry's eyes was his heads-up display. It hadn't activated yet for infrared, but it showed his biomonitors as a multicolored mix of numbers and EKG waves in his lower field of vision. His arms and legs bumped into something solid when he moved. The memories of being buried alive back on Earth flared to life, and the blinking vital signs exposed his fear as a medical condition.

The sled accelerated away from the *Varangian*; an aerodynamic black coffin aimed at the scaffolding of Dippel's orbital headquarters. It burned on cold nitrogen thrusters and had no windows, control surfaces, or weapons systems. It was little more than a lead-and-carbon-fiber torpedo, built for stealth and reinforced to withstand the insane radiation emanating from YZ Ceti's eruption. When it passed within a klick of the station—with a radar signature no larger than a pellet of buckshot—the eight troopers would be ejected into space. Even though they were shielded from the red dwarf star by the small moon that Dippel's station orbited, they'd only have two minutes to find a way inside before receiving a fatal dose of radiation. YZ Ceti belched about twice a Terran year and now the flare star was in its mass ejection glory, blasting a five-planet system with magnetized plasma, x-rays, and high-energy protons.

"T-minus twenty from combat EVA," Cog said into his helmet, the electromagnetic radiation distorting the AI's voice almost beyond recognition. "Decelerating to five meters per second on my mark. Mark."

Quarry counted off the seconds as bursts of gas from the sled's nose pushed blood into his feet, hoping even a simple task would ease his claustrophobia. He wanted to lift his head and look at Zalta and Pretorius, who were packed in on either side of him, but his helmet was lodged into a molded cranny and his field of vision didn't extend beyond the chestplate on his suit. He didn't care about the extreme radiation field they were about to enter or the futuristic weaponry that Dippel would have waiting for anyone who tried to infiltrate his station. He just wanted out of the casket he was lying in.

"T-minus ten," Cog said. "No signs of detection."

"Watch your spacing," said a voice on the team channel. Quarry thought it was Cherry's but couldn't be sure. "Get yourself oriented to the southern spar and kick in the fly-by-wire once you're four meters clear of everyone. No chatter on the comms. Let's go get some."

Go get some. You mean a quick and gruesome death? Even if they managed to infiltrate one of the unpressurized truss segments on the ring before receiving a lethal dose of radiation, they'd be facing a horror show of biomechanical weaponry.

Dippel had orchestrated the Kessler Syndrome attack on Earth in 2088, launching over forty million smart liquid-metal gallium pellets into a polar orbit around the planet. The tiny spheres moved like flocks of starlings, destroying every satellite and space station circling Earth by tearing through them at orbital velocity. The Leonis Union paid Dippel half a billion in IFS Coin for the attack, allowing the weapons merchant to build his own arms empire in the Ceti system and construct a Stanford Torus larger than a battleship. Quarry's mind wandered through the types of miniaturized weapons that could be waiting for them on the station, which scared him more than the company of mercenaries also reportedly housed there. No doubt Dippel had been hard at work creating new mechanical monstrosities since . . .

"Ejection," Cog yelled on the com. The bottom half of the sled opened like a bomb bay as the craft turned, flinging the eight troopers into space. Quarry tumbled, seeing blackness on his forward-looking IR and then the station, blackness and then the station. His suit compensated with thruster bursts. The tumbling slowed, and he checked to make sure he wasn't on a collision course with anyone else. He keyed in the fly-by-wire with a blink of his eye and forced his body into an arch as HEDM bursts from the back of his suit pushed him toward the trusses under the station's eight-hundred-meter centrifuge.

They free-fell through the blackness with Pretorius in the lead. She put out her left hand and extended her index and pinky fingers and her squad mates moved into a boomerang formation alongside her. Quarry looked above them for the Three Sisters—the pathfinding team from Fourth Platoon: Cruz, Berrios, and Ramirez, three Latina warfighters with a white boy named Trent Fuller manning their Squad Automatic Weapon—but they were already out of his field of vision. The Three Sisters were the only other recon group in COG-V, and the company had taken to calling Fuller *Plus One* when he complained about not being included in the team's name. The Sisters were trained in long-range reconnaissance at the Kaibil Academy in Guatemala. Fuller was an ex–75th Ranger. Their mission was to infiltrate the centripetal acceleration reactor in the northern hub of Dippel's torus and reverse its spin, killing the station's artificial gravity. Quarry and his teammates had the job of opening a hangar bay for the *Varangian*'s drop ships, which would ferry in the main assault teams. First Platoon, led by Jorgenson, would blast into the station's command and control shack on the opposite side of the ring. If all went well, they would envelop Dippel's forces from all sides in a zero-g fight the enemy hadn't prepared for.

Quarry flew behind Pretorius and to her left. Zalta was abreast of her, with Cherry on his right and low. The station's rotating truss loomed ahead on infrared, bright green against the frozen side of the moon it orbited. Quarry checked his heads-up display. They had ninety seconds to get out of open space and into the shielded confines of the station. That meant less than a minute from capture to entrance. Quarry wished for a moment that they were back in the sled. At least they wouldn't get fried in its leaden womb.

But he had faith in Pretorius. She had transformed in the few weeks of training they had done after an initial mishap in the zero-g range, when she served as team lead on a simulated ambush in a Leonis Union space station. It should have been an easy op, a rolling-T patrol in corridors with plenty of defilade, but they learned quickly that microgravity changed everything in combat. Gravity-loading skinsuits or not, they couldn't get anything right. Pretorius magnetized her boots to the gangplank at an intersection of the mock station and waited for her team to bound past. She pulled up her weapon when a Leonis trooper popped up from cover. *How many up drills had Pretorius done with an assault rifle before, ten thousand? Twenty thousand?* It should have been like bringing a fork to her mouth. It didn't matter that this was a different weapon than she was used to, a caseless ammo assault rifle with nonpenetrating slugs for decompression environments and recoil buffering for zero-g combat. A gun is a gun.

But it was all wrong without gravity. She didn't brace her left shoulder. The gun came up high and she missed, giving the simulated Leonis fighter time to pop off a few rounds at Quarry, who was scooting to the far bulkhead. He got hit, spinning out of control down the corridor in the microgravity. Everything went to hell from there—a full casualty event.

Pretorius blamed herself for the miscue and busted ass to get better, earning a lot of respect from the team. She succeeded through sheer effort, practicing the magnetizing moves and recoil drills and zero-g flight skills again and again and bribing other teams for more time in free fall. She was a dirt-hugger like Quarry—someone who felt at home in the bush, tracking the sign of animals and men in a world of life and sounds and gravity. But now she could move through space almost as well as Cherry. At this point, Quarry was more concerned about himself and Zalta, who continued to fret about fighting in space. He glanced over at the desert tracker. He appeared to be doing okay. At least he was in formation.

They decelerated as they approached the rotating spar of Dippel's station. Quarry's weapon—a 6.8 mm recoilless carbine with caseless ammunition programmed for smart airburst—was secured to his chest with a three-point sling and bonding magnets. He felt for the pistol grip with his right hand and looked for a handhold on the station truss to catch with the left.

Their thrusters burst to correct for the station's rotation and orbital velocity around the moon. Pretorius grabbed a stanchion on the southern truss. Quarry found a handrail just beneath her. Centrifugal force slammed his body against the hull. He used his other hand to stabilize as his helmet beeped and the sound of his breathing washed out the silence of space. He took a quick glance around—all four of them had latched on. Pretorius snapped a carabiner and short rope onto the hull and climbed to the unpressurized maintenance hatch. She magnetized a laser cutter over the latch on the door and opened it in ten seconds.

Would there be an alarm—did Dippel already know he had visitors? The whole premise of their attack was surprise—no other ship in the IFS had an artificial magnetosphere like the *Varangian*'s, powerful enough to approach the station in the middle of a flare star event. It was one of the reasons that Dippel had chosen YZ Ceti. His friends and enemies, who changed from week to week, were too afraid to venture into that extreme stellar environment. But the flare star put the station in hibernation mode, an Achilles' heel the *Varangian* could exploit. Sealed tight in a skin of alloys more radiation resistant than lead, its sensors were diminished during the height of the storm. The *Varangian* used its radar-absorbing skin and cold burn engines to hide its approach from the station's passive scans. If they could get inside without tripping an alarm, maybe they could make it to the hangar without being detected. The unpressurized lattice of trusses that ran like a spire above and below the station's ring was monitored for stress and hot/cold soak-fatigue but little else—at least according to the intel Earth had sent them.

Quarry watched Pretorius and Zalta disappear through the small hatch. Cherry hung from the right side of the entrance and gave Quarry a signal to go in. He squeezed through the door into a dark shaft about two meters wide that ran vertically for fifty meters to the next truss segment. They bunched up, turned on their headlamps, and assessed their surroundings while trying to get used to the Coriolis effect, which made their feet feel heavy and heads feel weightless. The artificial gravity wasn't strong in the lower trusses of the station, but it seemed to shift from second to second. Quarry worried he might puke in his helmet. They had been advised to float in the middle of the tube along the axis, using microthrusters, but they had more than seven hundred meters of truss to get through before reaching their target and had to stop at every junction to look for things that wanted to kill them.

Pretorius waited for Cherry to close the hatch and gave hand signals for them to proceed in file formation. She led with Quarry on slack and Zalta just behind. Cherry guarded their six with a recoilless triple-barreled SAW loaded with 20 mm adaptive rounds. They moved as fast as they could, Pretorius checking the station schematics on a holographic armband while leading them upward and sideways through a maze of support beams, trunnions, cables, and struts, stopping at every new segment to scan for mechanical or human contact. Quarry kept an eye on his HUD's stopwatch as it ticked down from twenty minutes. They had to reach their infiltration point before the Three Sisters reversed the station's spin or Dippel would code them out and lock down the hangar bays.

The pace became routine, ten seconds to the next segment, twenty seconds to look for enemies or sensors, another ten on the float. *It's too fast*, Quarry thought, *almost half a mile of infiltration in twenty minutes.* It would have taken him four hours to move that far during a nighttime stalk on Earth, and twice as long in daylight. But alien as it was, there was comfort in moving with a team, tapping shoulders to flow in formation, checking the threat axis he was assigned to, feeling the sweat collect on his head and wick away as cool air flowed down from the top of his helmet. At least he was doing something to take his mind off the insanity of where he was, and his vital signs had stabilized. For the first time in almost a year, he was on a live op, and in the insane way that only a veteran of the teams could understand, it felt like a homecoming.

They came to a right turn, and Pretorius lifted a fist, bringing Quarry back to the moment. They bunched up, Quarry magnetizing to the left and slightly above the rest of the team. He poked his head around the entrance and saw a long shaft shrouded in darkness, maybe ninety meters in length, leading to a sealed hatch. It was one of the main piers that led from the spine of the station to the torus. He checked his chronometer. *Eleven minutes left.*

Pretorius turned and gave hand signals. *Cover me; then move on me.* Quarry wished he could see her eyes. He scanned the shaft in IR for sensors or cameras; it appeared as dumb as the rest of the southern spire. *Could it really be this easy?* Dippel had to have eyes on the guts of his station. Pretorius moved forward. Cherry covered the back end of the shaft while Zalta and Quarry looked for signs of detection. She came to what they had been looking for—a small port that opened into one of the station's relief tubes, which would limit the damage of a large decompression event by blasting air and dislodged material into space in a controlled manner. She used the cutter again, opened the hatch, and squeezed inside. Nothing happened. *This is too easy,* Quarry thought. They followed her.

They knew where they were now, just two hundred meters from the torus. The ventilation shaft would take them underneath the hangar they had to open for the assault ships. Pretorius gave hand signals again. *No float. Magnetic bonding with at least two body points.* They crawled up the tube in the dark, a pair on each side, magnetizing their hands and feet to whatever metal they could find among the maze of conduits and insulated piping. Quarry wanted to have his gun up and ready. He could barely see above him while he labored through the freakiness of Coriolis, which was pushing and pulling his guts in a centripetal tug of war with the rest of his body. But Pretorius had laid out her rationale before the mission. She was more concerned with decompression than enemy contact. They couldn't deal with tactical issues if they were blown into space.

Six minutes. Forty meters away. They were going to make it. Once they got in the hangar, it would take two minutes to upload the quantum bug that Cog had created to gain control of the hangar door. Quarry kept his eyes forward as much as possible. No sign of Dippel's mercenaries. No sensors or defenses. He looked across the tube at Zalta. He was moving well. Quarry grabbed the next handheld, magnetized, and released his left leg to move, and then his nose smashed into the inside of his faceplate and everything went black. His body hammered into the wall a second later and bounced backward, almost breaking his wrist as the bonding magnets held him to the side of the tube. A swarm of stars skittered across the blackness inside his eyelids. He opened his eyes and shook his head and saw a blur of flashes and alerts on the heads-up display. A rapid beeping rang in his ears. There was blood in his helmet, the droplets moving back and forth in a weird gravitational dance.

What the fu . . . ? His body bounced up and down again—hard—the magnetic bond on his wrist the only thing holding him to the fuselage.

"Carabiners!" he heard Pretorius yell into his helmet, radio silence a thing of the past. "Rope and secure."

Quarry pulled a carabiner from his chestplate and looked for something to snap onto. *There it was—a strap loop on a piece of ductwork.* He clipped on and keyed the retractable tether to stop at one meter, just as the ventilation tube opened and a hurricane enveloped them.

The force of air rushing through the tube ripped his magnetized hand from the fuselage. His wrist snapped from the violence of it. A stab of pain that made him forget his broken nose jolted up his arm and into his spine and then the rope tether yanked at his body, nearly breaking his shoulder blades. Quarry hung in space for a second before being slammed against the side of the tube again as the torrent of air intensified. He spun around and saw that vents up and down the length of the chute had opened and pressurized air from the shaft above was being blown into space. He saw Zalta's body bouncing up and down on the other side of the cylinder like a branch whipping in a storm. He looked up and saw Pretorius, tethered and somehow lying flat against the rush of air. He reached for a handhold with his good arm and looked down. A tricam was inserted into a stanchion just below him, a short segment of rope whipping in the wind behind it. A door gaped below it. *Cherry was gone.*

"Four is down," he screamed.

"Can you get to him?" It was Pretorius, although he could barely tell above the multitoned alerts in his helmet.

"No, he's gone! He got blasted out of the tube. I'm on belay, gonna give out twenty meters of rope and retrieve him."

Pretorius responded immediately. "Negative, Quarry, do not exit the tube. We don't have time."

The rush of air lessened and their bodies began to float to the middle of the shaft. The cylinder slowed, and Quarry figured out where the initial jolt had come from. The Three Sisters had reversed the centripetal motion of the station—at least five minutes early. They must have encountered Dippel's fighters. He released a few meters of rope and floated to the ventilation door that Cherry got ejected from. He looked into open space. There was nothing there. He scanned in IR and visible light. Nothing but small pieces of debris.

"She's right, Quarry," he heard Zalta say. "We need to move."

No. They'd be leaving Dan Cherry for dead. Quarry's eyes swept the outside of the station, picking up pieces of clutter that had been jettisoned in the decompression. Everything else was blackness, filled with the invisible radiation of a flaring star. *They'd be leaving him behind.*

"Cherry," he yelled. No response. He yelled again and coughed as blood from his nose filled his mouth. He heard only static.

"Quarry, on me now," Pretorius said as the blast tube settled into a zero-g state. She pushed on to the decompression hatch with Zalta behind her. Quarry took one last look out the door and followed them, leaving Cherry to die in space.

"We're too late," Zalta said. They peered through a mesh screen into the hangar bay as Pretorius cut through its margins with a laser. There were no signs of life, but this part of the station would have defenses. As soon as they exposed themselves, they'd be cut down, but there weren't any options left. If the hangar door didn't open on time, the *Varangian* would have to hit it with a missile, killing all three of them and making the mission infinitely more difficult. Cog had estimated 60 percent casualties if they had to breach to let in the assaulting troopers.

Pretorius depolarized her faceplate and turned to Zalta and Quarry. She looked scared and had tears on her cheeks. "Okay," she said. "We're going to go straight in on suit thrust, right down the middle and ten feet apart. Zalta, cover our left flank. Quarry, you have the right. I'm going to the control shack. Agreed?"

"Agreed," they said.

"On my mark in three. Three, two, one. Mark."

Pretorius kicked in the mesh screen and flew into the hangar bay. They followed her in two-second intervals. Quarry grabbed his rifle's pistol grip with his left hand and used his right arm to stabilize it. Pain shot up and down the injured limb. He made it fifty meters into the cavernous bay, covering their right flank, before Zalta yelled out.

"Contact left! Kessler swarm."

Quarry glanced over and felt sick. A line of hornets flew toward them from a hundred meters away. The line balled up into three spheroid flocks and accelerated, targeting each of them independently. Quarry's helmet magnified the swarms and his heart lurched at the sight—gunmetal balls the size of marbles, Kessler Syndrome pellets; he braced to die as one of the swarms came for him like intelligent buckshot, speeding up to penetration velocity.

He had forgotten about Zalta's EMP launcher. The Syrian tracker hip-fired several rounds at the oncoming pellets. The specialized 40 mm grenades fanned out in slow motion and exploded in front of the flocks, blasting a collimated electromagnetic pulse and shock wave at them. The swarm scattered and lost its track. A few of the pellets ricocheted and flew between Quarry and Zalta before ripping into the far bulkhead. Zalta yelled and Quarry looked over to see him spinning through the free space of the hangar, a gash on his leg venting gas and droplets of blood. One of the pellets had hit him.

"Three is hit," Quarry yelled, keying propellant bursts to intercept Zalta. He slammed into him and used his good hand to latch onto a soft gripper on Zalta's space suit. Pretorius didn't look back, zipping to the control shack as Zalta and Quarry spun through the middle of the hangar into a jumble of floating canisters ejected from their racks by the decompression event and the spin-down of the torus. They slammed into the flotsam, and Quarry felt something in his shoulder give way. He bounced and lost hold of Zalta, who had managed to grab a can of quick seal from his combat webbing and spray it over the rip on his suit. Both tumbled, bouncing off what had been the floor of the hangar when it was at .6 g. Quarry tried to stabilize with bursts from his suit but his situational awareness was shot.

He saw a door open on his threat axis in between spins, to the right of the hangar door. A dozen soldiers in dark-gray space suits—the same color as the station walls—flew into the hangar and fired. Tracers zipped between Quarry and Zalta and arced toward the control shack in curving lines of light.

"Lead, contact on your two," he yelled to Pretorius. He grabbed the floor grating to stabilize and fired with his broken hand, overshooting the advancing soldiers. They drew a bead on him as he looked for cover. There was nowhere to hide—just a few floating cylinders and boxes getting blasted in all directions by the incoming fire.

Tracers zipped all around him and he braced to be hit, but the firing slowed. Quarry turned to his left. The hangar door was opening. Somehow Pretorius had done it. Quarry felt an adrenaline rush from still being alive. He steadied himself and laid down a field of fire, this time hitting targets. But more of Dippel's mercenaries poured through the door. He looked for Zalta. There he was, magnetized to a recessed storage rack. Quarry continued to shoot, trying to draw the attention of Dippel's soldiers. Shrapnel kicked up around him and a high pinging rang in his ears. Zalta fired explosive rounds from his launcher. Quarry's suit punctured. Alarms rang in his ears, and he heard the hiss of escaping gas. He clenched for the moment when it would blow out.

One of Dippel's soldiers rose from cover about twenty meters in front of him and aimed at Quarry's face. Quarry stared down the black eye of a gun barrel, frozen in time and bracing for death. The soldier disappeared in a pink-and-gray mist.

Explosions rocked the voided hangar bay, the shock waves

knocking Quarry back toward the storage rack where Zalta had taken cover. *What the hell*? Quarry looked to his left as he grabbed for handholds and yelled, "Holy shit!"

Dan Cherry thundered into the hangar bay on what must have been a twenty-second propellant burst, blasting away with his Squad Automatic Weapon. The fist-sized rounds burst in intervals all around Dippel's troopers, blowing their bodies into pieces and spraying shrapnel across the cavernous room.

"Get some!" Cherry yelled into the team com as he flew through the hangar with what looked like orbital velocity, turning to his left and blasting the door that Dippel's troopers had come through. Just behind Cherry came the assault ships from the *Varangian*—two beautiful black birds of prey that laid down fire on the starboard side of the deck.

Quarry hand-pushed the last few meters to Zalta and tumbled into the storage rack. Zalta patched Quarry's suit with the quick seal. They hugged the bottom of their makeshift foxhole and watched as two COG-V platoons dropped from the assault ships, adding to the carnage. Cherry circled back through the hangar like an angel of death, spraying a line of adaptive grenades at the enemy. Blossoms of exploding ordinance turned the room into a slaughterhouse.

8

John Dippel stood on the hangar deck in a pair of g-loading long underwear, barely struggling as two COG-V troopers forced his legs into the bottom half of a pressure suit. His hair pointed in all directions and he had a half-crazed smile on his face as he stared at Crooks, as if the reality of his circumstance hadn't sunk in. *No problem*, Crooks thought, turning away from the arms merchant to survey the wreckage of the bay as his crew triaged the wounded. *You won't be smiling when I blast your ass into space.*

The torus spun counterclockwise. About half of a g had been restored as well as pressure and breathable air. There was enough gravity for Crooks to stand face-to-face with a man who had killed three billion people on Earth, and enough air to look him in the eyes without a helmet getting in the way. A COG-V trooper jammed the butt of his rifle into Dippel's kidney and yelled at him to raise his arms for the upper half of the space suit. *How the hell do these arms merchant pricks do it*, Crooks wondered. *How do they justify building machines of death and annihilation? For God and country? For détente? Fuck that.* Crooks had fought in enough wars to know that détente was just an excuse for buildup. And in Dippel's case, it was obvious the astrophysicist didn't launch the Kessler attack for patriotism or belief. He did it for money. In the end, that's where most wars started.

Crooks beckoned to Boortz. His new aide-de-camp was on the com with Jorgenson's platoon while also overseeing the cleanup, intelligence gathering, and evacuation of wounded to the *Varangian*. Boortz might have thought he had gotten off easily working for Six instead of being at the front end of the action. He was quickly learning that assumption was wrong.

"Are we ready to record this?" Crooks asked.

Boortz signed off with Jorgenson and looked up. "Yes sir, but we won't be able to transmit anything for a few hours. The star is still flaring—we're lucky we got the blast doors closed or we'd all be cooking right now."

Crooks walked over to Dippel and locked eyes with him. "That's the whole point, Boortz. We want the star in baking mode for just a bit longer."

A trooper walked over with the helmet that would go on Dippel's head. The astrophysicist glanced at him and then at Crooks. He knew what was coming. Crooks had seen pictures of Dippel before today: thin but handsome; a lady's man on Earth. Now he looked old and weak.

"Can I suggest a compromise?" Dippel asked. "I know you're following orders, Major, but all you're doing is destroying an asset. Both of us know that Earth doesn't have a lot of tools in the box right now. I can be of use."

"Who said I was a major?"

"Your man on the radio, a few minutes ago."

Crooks shook his head. "You're a sly bastard, Dippel, but we don't need you. We've got your shop and your tech, and we've downloaded all the data we need to analyze your work.

And even if Earth ordered me to bring you back, I'd toss your worthless ass out of the airlock."

"I can make you rich," Dippel said, panning his eyes from Crooks to the three soldiers helping him into the space suit. "All of you."

Boortz and the others glanced up. One of the troopers cocked his head—a subtle signal that they should listen to the arms merchant's offer. Ras from Fourth Platoon; the trooper Cog had warned about.

"We're soldiers. What the hell are we going to do with money?" Crooks asked. He glared at Ras for a brief moment. Boortz snapped Dippel's helmet in place, checking the hard seals. Crooks pulled a poker card out of a Velcro sleeve on his arm and showed it to him. The ace of spades. He flipped it around and stuck it to Dippel's helmet: the back of the card had an hourglass broken by a sword, with the letters COG-V emblazoned underneath. "Besides," he said, "we're in this for the fulfillment."

Crooks nodded at Boortz. "Cut his coms and begin recording."

Boortz clicked on his cam and got in close to Dippel so that only the man's helmet and face could be seen.

"People of the Inner Fifty Systems, you are looking at arms merchant John L. Dippel," Crooks said, off-camera. "He's a war criminal and a unique piece of shit. He launched Kessler Syndrome attacks on Earth and Kruger 60c and is responsible for the death and suffering of billions of noncombatants. We have taken his station. We've killed his men and we've stolen his tech. And now we are going to eject him into space, to bask in the glow of a flare star. He has enough air to last for a bit. Just long enough to feel his body cook in the furnace."

Crooks nodded. Two troopers pushed Dippel toward the service airlock. Boortz's camera remained focused on his helmet and the death card stuck to its faceplate as the glass fogged over with rapid breathing.

"In case you're wondering, we are Chronos Operation Group," Crooks said as Boortz zoomed in on the death card. "We don't work for any government or empire. We are outside the system. But know this: we came from Earth with a reckoning on our minds, and we're not going away. We buried our dead and we're looking for guilty parties. We don't care how big your guns are. You are in our crosshairs."

Dippel resisted. He flailed as they reached the airlock. He screamed into silence as there was nothing to be heard outside the seals on his space suit, and there never would be again. The hatch closed and pressurized. Dippel stood inside the airlock with his helmet pressed against the porthole, his eyes blown open as fog closed over the margins of his visor. Ras stood on the other side of the glass with a few others, watching Dippel's last moments like spectators at the Colosseum. The outer doors opened and Dippel disappeared.

"You fucked with our people, and now we're coming for you," Crooks said as the camera showed only open space. "We'll be there in time."

The company ate in silence at first, coming down from the speedball high of combat and contemplating the dead. They had real chow—five-star chop courtesy of Dippel's storehouses. A few of the troopers who knew how to cook got Cog to divert plasma from the heat exchangers into makeshift grill pits in the mess hall, and they dined on line-caught nimshameen from Luyten b and steaks cut from Charolais cattle raised on an agricultural moon of Gliese 667 Cc. Thanks to a reprieve from

Crooks, they also drank beer, a little flat in the lower gravity but it still felt like mother's milk when it hit the back of the throat.

Eleven members of COG-V had died on Dippel's station. Another twenty-seven, including Quarry and Zalta, had been injured. And Cog was dubious about Cherry's chances of avoiding terminal cancer sometime in the next five years after his extended EVA through the radioactive eruptions of YZ Ceti.

But five years of living seemed like an eternity in the moment, and good food and booze turned sadness into bravado. *The dead settle quickly in the minds of warfighters*, Pretorius thought, *but the electrical jolt of combat lingers.* The room got louder, the troopers boasting about the bravery of the fallen and the success of the mission. It turned damn near festive.

Pretorius and her squad mates sat with the Three Sisters in a corner of the cavernous hall. *Lurps stick together on the margins.* Fuller, the young American Ranger, squeezed in between Cruz and Berrios, and the women mussed his hair and called him *hermanito* and treated him like a pet they had just adopted. His eyes glowed as he ate and drank, and Pretorius realized with a shock that Fuller was in love with his squad mates. Based on their retelling of events at the centripetal accelerator, he had thrusted right into a phalanx of Dippel's fighters to deflect fire from the Sisters. Only freak luck could explain the fact that he was alive and in one piece. He had dodged enough metal to build a tank.

"I can't speak Spanish for shit," Fuller said among the laughter. "I thought Ramirez was yelling, 'Go, go, go!' when she was saying, 'No, no, no!'"

"That's not Spanish in the first place, *pendejo*," Berrios said, elbowing Fuller in the ribs and picking a piece of meat off his plate. "Only a stupid white boy doesn't understand the meaning of no."

"Easy there," Quarry said. "He's not the only stupid white boy at the table."

Pretorius smiled at the banter and thought about her own squad's firefight in the middle of the hangar bay, and Cherry's already legendary flight through the shield door. They had all been desperation moves—no sound tactics involved. But that was combat. The Three Sisters came into contact early and had to move on the gravity ring before the prescribed time, and all the company's well-laid plans got blown to hell. Not uncommon for a Spec Ops mission, but they were lucky to be alive.

Cherry should have been the happiest of them after his heroics, but Pretorius and Zalta had found him sitting in a corner of their bunkhouse after the mission, crying in silence. "It's okay," he had said. "It's nothing. This shit gets to me sometimes." Now he sat across from Zalta and ate and drank but had little to say, half smiling when his name came up. Zalta seemed to understand. The two of them had been hanging together for the last twelve hours and the desert tracker brushed off anyone who approached Cherry with a shake of his head. *A child coming off a sugar high*, Pretorius thought as she watched the big man, but she knew it was deeper than that. Cherry was a killer who couldn't take the killing. She guessed he'd be back to his giddy self before long, and she thought of PTSD and manic depression and wondered which diagnosis fit him best.

Jorgenson, the leader of First Platoon who had already earned his reputation as the hardest soldier in the company, walked over from the middle of the mess hall and put a foot on their bench seat, next to Zalta's backside. The ex-Delta operator had a three-inch gash across his forehead that still looked angry.

"Everyone get their holes plugged?" he asked, looking at Zalta and Quarry.

"The miracles of metro gel," Zalta said, rubbing his leg. "I would have gotten a month in a soft bed without it."

Jorgenson smiled. "Technology's a bitch. How about you?" he asked, looking at Quarry.

"I've been glued before," Quarry shrugged. "Nothing's leaking at the moment."

"Well, you guys did good for nonspacers. Pretty impressive that two of our three objectives were pulled off by zero-g rookies. I was a little worried, tell the truth, but it looks like we've got some recon assets to work with."

"Fucking A," Cruz said.

"How's your group holding up, Jorgenson?" Pretorius asked. She had watched the TAC-CAM video from the assault on the command deck. Four of Jorgenson's squad had been cut down and all of them had been injured. The video looked like a close-quarters firefight inside a tornado. A pellet swarm had run through two of the KIAs and it wasn't a pretty thing. They looked like they had been hit by a thousand pieces of buckshot. Both men just came apart.

Jorgenson's face knotted as he flashed back to the fight. "We're eating real food and drinking beer," he said after a second. "Can't ask for more. We buried the dead and started a list, and it's time to move on. So . . . First Platoon is doing a mission debrief tomorrow at 0800. You all should sit in. Lessons learned and a tactical autopsy—that kinda shit. Cog's creating an animation of each battlespace to go with cams from the squads, so we can break things down step-by-step and frame-by-frame."

Ramirez shook her head. "You really think it's gonna matter, Delta? The next op could be in a jungle or on the surface of an asteroid, and we have nine more to go, God knows where or when. We'll all be dead and replaced before we hit the Glory Mission."

"Fuck that, Ramirez," Jorgenson said. "You can die if you want, but I'm going to live to be redeemed."

Ramirez laughed and flicked a piece of her food at Fuller.

"Listen to the Tier One badass, *hermanito*. Don't they say that Delta Force is every Ranger's daddy?"

"Yeah, because they are," Fuller said, flicking the food back at her and nodding at Jorgenson. "I'll be there."

"We'll all be there," Pretorius said. "But I'm more worried about the time than the mission. If twenty years have passed the next time we leave this black hole, will tactics matter? I've seen tribesmen use assegai against rifles, and it didn't end well."

Jorgenson shrugged. "Tech lag's an issue, but the only easy day was yesterday, right? Let's take things one step at a time." He stole a piece of food from Zalta's plate and turned away, looking back one last time to give Pretorius a wink. "A blade still kills, Sergeant, and it always will. You just gotta get up close."

9

MISSION TWO: ALPHA CMB

2097

It should have felt good. They had their heads in the dirt and the smell of life rose into her nostrils and triggered the old memories of Earth. The forest moon had almost twice the gravity of Terra, pulling Pretorius to the ground with a million tiny weights dispersed across her body, but the soil felt cool, and she ran it through her fingers like an old blanket. It didn't matter that it was alien soil with alien smells—an alkaline scent of urine mixed with peat and charcoal—it was something real to be touched, and the terraformed forest moved in the wind and the rustling needles reminded her of the cluster pines on the Western Cape. The sterile dryness of a spaceship, with its machine oil smells and anodyne sounds, had almost erased Pretorius's memory of being in the bush. This should have been a rebirth.

But something was missing, and it took her a day to realize what it was: *time*. They had skipped through more than three years of Earth time in a week of tight rotation around the Bear, and the dilation wasn't supposed to matter to them in relative terms, but it did. Pretorius felt out of place, like her body didn't belong where it was. She couldn't describe the sensation; it was like some unseen hand had moved her body three inches to the right of the real world, but her head remained to the left. Cog called it time sickness—a phenomenon experienced by the few fast movers who had risked annihilation by slowing their clock through velocity. When they decelerated from near c and came back into a universe that had aged, something felt off. Even their senses and coordination had been affected. Astrophysicists and doctors thought it was psychosomatic at first, but tests showed the effects to be real.

What the hell's going to happen when the Varangian *does one of the big clock skips*, Pretorius wondered. *What if we spend a week clipping the edge of that beast and come out a hundred years later? Will I even be able to walk through that new universe? Will my body accept where it's been and where it is now? And will it have time to adapt before a century of military advancement blows me down in my tracks?*

For the moment she could move, and it was time to move again. She low-crawled a meter through thick ground cover and waited for Quarry to do the same. They stalked a wooded ridgeline leading into a small ravine, and they had found enough spoor to know that the men they hunted used the ravine to go in and out of the valley, occasionally coming into the trees to take a leak or find shade.

They moved slowly despite being in the cover of the alien tree line because the company they hunted had advanced detection tech picketed across this quadrant of the moon including motion, infrared, and scent sensors, as well as a net of aerial drones. These were Barnard's Butchers they were after, and it was their turf—their training ground. The fact that the nearest Butcher was five klicks away behind a mountain range meant little. If Quarry or Pretorius made a wrong move, they could be marked and the whole operation would be taken down.

The sign indicated that their enemy made the run in and

out of the ravine every four days, and it had been two days since their last patrol. A company of private military contractors financed by the Bracchus Conglomerate, the Butchers were Spec Ops troops turned mercenary, and they had gotten their name by slaughtering every Earthborn man, woman, and child on a moon near Barnard's Star three years ago under a contract from the Gliese Empire. Crooks showed the company video of the massacre before the mission to get their blood up. But to Pretorius and Quarry, the stalk was all that mattered now. Disoriented by time dilation or not, they toiled in the throes of their craft. Pretorius had to admit that Quarry moved like a ghost in the bush, and so far, they had eluded or neutralized every trap left for them. Maybe the Butchers were being lax—they certainly didn't expect anyone would have the balls to come after them on their own moon—but the net had still been tight.

Pretorius lifted her head and looked to Quarry. His mimetic camo made him hard to spot even a few meters away, but his eyes tracked hers. He nodded and low-crawled another meter to set the next line of antipersonnel mines, multimodal Claymores with infrared triggers that would funnel the Butchers into a kill box. They only had two more to place. Cherry and Zalta manned an observation post half a klick away, beneath the summit of a ridge pockmarked with caves. The Three Sisters and Fuller patrolled the other side of the ravine about five hundred meters down the valley, setting up the tail end of the coming ambush.

Quarry's body lay flat again, invisible even though she could almost touch him. *A white country boy and a Coloured girl from the Botswana bush*, she mused, *and yet we move as one.* She waited thirty seconds and shimmied another meter and planted the last of her mines against the trunk of what looked like a stunted black spruce, dwarfed by the moon's hypergravity. *The Butchers will have the surprise of their lives when these things go off*, she thought, spraying multiple layers of death across the head of their column and forcing them to bunch up as similar devices detonated at the back of their line. And then three platoons of COG-V would open up from an L-shaped area ambush. Cog had found an ingenious way to infiltrate the moon undetected, inserting a drop ship at its south pole and using the strong magnetic field lines of its host gas giant as a cloak. The platoons stood on hold up the valley, waiting to move into position parallel to the dry riverbed. Everything so far had gone as planned. The *Varangian* had proven its stealth in space once again, and its fighters had done the same on the ground.

Pretorius finished hiding the Claymore with pine straw and tapped Quarry on the boot. It would take them an hour to get back up the hill to the OP. Quarry wiped sweat from his eyes and pulled down the do-rag covering his head. Getting rid of the Claymores had dropped almost all the weight they carried in their kits, but that didn't give him relief. Quarry had been skittish since learning the mission would be on a hypergravity moon. He didn't complain but she sensed he didn't feel right about it. Maybe the time sickness had taken hold, or maybe he just didn't like living in a double gravity environment. He moved well and stayed invisible, but he looked haunted, and she was surprised at her concern for his well-being.

The gravity load made her sweat as well. It was an otherwise beautiful environment for an operation—twenty degrees Celsius, a light breeze, and the moon had a heady 26 percent oxygen level. Intel said there would be some pollinating insects on Alpha CMb, but so far, they hadn't seen as much as a gnat. Minus the sounds of wildlife, Pretorius couldn't recall a nicer day in the Botswana bush. If only the hypergravity and the time jump didn't change things. Quarry broke her reverie with a nudge. She nodded, and they turned in tandem to begin the low crawl back up the slope. The one good thing about the gravity is it kept her butt low to the ground. She wondered how it would play out in a firefight when they really had to move.

"We're already heroes even if no one knows who the hell we are," Cherry whispered. "You heard what Cog said about the reaction on Earth after we took out Dippel—if we smoke these Butcher bastards, maybe we'll get an early reprieve."

Night had fallen on the harvest moon. They sat under the lip of a cave eating dinner out of bioplastic packs, with infrared blocking heat throws over their heads and electromagnetic dampers staked around their perimeter. They used night vision when they needed to see because they were on strict light security. When Pretorius turned her optics off, she couldn't see Zalta's boots an inch from her knees. They spoke in hushed tones.

"That's not the point," Zalta said. "Why three years?"

"What do you mean?" Cherry asked.

"If we're such a valuable resource, why did it take three years for them to give us a new mission?"

"They're saving us for the special stuff, is all. Maybe next time the right op will come along in three months."

Pretorius heard Zalta sigh. "I play chess with Cog whenever Crooks gets tired of losing to him," he said. "He's good at revealing things without actually saying them, and I'm telling you that we didn't get called out for three years of Earth time because we were shelved."

It was Quarry's turn to chime in. Pretorius could hear him in the dark, swallowing a mouthful of reconstituted turkey and washing it down with water so he could speak.

"That doesn't make any sense. Crooks said they were selling

COG-V T-shirts across the CORP countries after YZ Ceti. We're probably the greatest propaganda weapon Earth has right now."

"We might be heroes with the people but I'm talking about the institutions," Zalta said. "Cog told me that CORP had an internal power struggle after the Dippel raid. The *Varangian* is being run by a new set of military and political leaders and some of them don't want to use us until an entire fleet can be stashed in time. There's no consensus, and what if the sands keep shifting?"

Pretorius craned her neck to look down the hillside. Nothing moved and there were no sounds at all other than their talking, not even the wing-buzz of insects. All she saw was blackness, and the lack of sensory input put her on edge.

"I think Zalta's point is that political disruptions will continue while we are stuck in time," she whispered, "and we are at their mercy. It's like the Francistown Wars all over again. Just when you think things are stable, everything flips on its head."

"Yes," Zalta whispered. "Or even worse, we could get thrown into missions that have nothing to do with Earth's interest at all—corporate sabotage or personal revenge or colonialism. Or we could get lost in time. What if CORP disappears and the group that takes over blacks out our program? How long will it take for us to figure out that no one is going to be calling?"

Quarry shifted his body as Zalta spoke; she heard his shirt rubbing against the rock wall he had been using as a backrest. "Well, it's not like we'd just circle the Bear forever," the American said. "If we don't get pinged after ten years of dilation, we exit the black hole and check the slip buoys, right? That's what Crooks said. Figure out what the hell is going on in the real world."

They stopped talking and listened for sounds other than their own eating, drinking, and breathing. Nothing stirred.

Zalta continued after a minute. "I'm just saying we have no way of knowing what will happen while we're tucked away in time. Maybe we'll come out and there's no minders and we are free of this wheel. Or maybe a new regime is in power, and they extend our enlistment. If you trust in governments—for God's sake, if you trust in people—you are going to be disappointed."

"Dammit, Zalta, you are one soaking wet blanket," Cherry said. "We all know that. I might have been a meat eater for the agency, but I was neck-deep in the political stuff as well. I was *trying* to be optimistic. It's good to do that in the dark on a hostile moon, when you can't build a fire or light a smoke."

"I'm sorry," Zalta said. "I worry out loud. It is a nice thought—that our ten missions will be done in the life cycle of our reality. I don't feel right after this last jump, and it was only a three-year skip."

Pretorius crisscrossed her legs and straightened her sore back. She couldn't find a position that lightened the gravity load on her spine. "I think we're test animals and that's why they waited so long. They want data on what a real time lag does to people. You heard what Crooks said when we started. The *Varangian* is a prototype, and if they want to stash an entire army in time, they need to know how temporal sickness will affect it."

Quarry grunted and flipped up his IR goggles. "We're pissing on a fire we can't put out. If you really think CORP or whoever is in charge at the time will let us go after ten ops, you're crazy. It doesn't matter whether they need us for propaganda or direct action. They're gonna run us until we're dead or blown up. We could be mothballed for millennia but there's always going to be a new war. We are forlorn hope, with bombs in our bloodstream to prove it. Remember our code name, *Century Gun*? You think that was a joke?"

"Wait a second," Cherry said. "You were agreeing with me a minute ago."

"Yeah, about the last war, but yesterday's heroes become

tomorrow's villains. And I guarantee we'll be around long enough for that to happen."

"You're wrong, Quarry," Pretorius whispered. "I'll be free of this one day. I don't care what it takes. Maybe we'll find a way to turn Cog off and take the *Varangian* for ourselves."

"Tread careful with that talk, sister," Cherry said. "For all we know, he's listening to us right now."

Zalta laughed. It sounded strange in the darkness, detached. "This is what we used to do in the desert at night—talk about the burrow and ignore the scorpion hiding inside. Must I remind you that we'll be fighting a battle tomorrow against an enemy on their own turf, in their version of gravity, with exosuits we've barely trained in? We probably won't make it to next week, let alone next year."

Pretorius kicked where she knew his knee would be and struck the target. "Cherry is right, *mosimane*, you are the most depressing person I've ever met. Didn't you say you wanted to die on the ground, with dirt under your boots?"

Zalta sent a half-hearted boot back in her direction. "I did," he said. "Just not this dirt."

A breeze kicked up and shook the pine needles above them. They stayed quiet to listen to the newness of sound in a muffled world. It quickly died off.

"We are what we are," Quarry said, and Pretorius heard him roll onto his side and curl up. "Assets. Only this time, there's no opting out. I don't think any of us will be dying on Earth, so get used to alien dirt."

"Another optimist," Pretorius said. "You wouldn't know what to do with your freedom if you had it, Quarry."

"Yes, I would," he replied, his voice muffled by the poncho he had just pulled over his head. "Find a place deep in the woods and go to ground."

10

"*Masole*," Pretorius whispered as the Butchers' column snaked its way into the dry riverbed. The enemy moved slowly, two men on point, inching into the kill zone. She glanced over at Quarry, who tracked the lead fighter through an autoaiming scope. She took the one just behind. The Butcher trooper could have been Earthborn for all she knew—a bit shorter and squatter than most men from Terra—but he reminded her of a dock worker from Maputo or Swakopmund. Her scope's algorithm keyed a blue *X* on a point between his eyes just below the helmet, and Pretorius winced at her sense of detachment as she dry-sniped the man up the gulley. She would dwell on him in nightmares long after she had pink-misted his head, but for now she felt nothing but the speed rush of war. No morality or empathy. This wasn't the time for it. *Fifty meters more, and both ends of the column would be inside the box . . .*

An insect buzz raised her eye off the scope. A dragonfly came toward them, whizzing through the trees. Pretorius saw it fly by Cherry's position, disappear, and reemerge in front of them, hovering. Zalta popped up and shot a focused electromagnetic pulse in the dragonfly's direction, and Pretorius realized it wasn't a living thing. The pulse dropped the mechanical bug as if it had been swatted from the air.

"Nanodrone," Quarry whispered. "We've been made."

"Hold," Pretorius said.

They sat immobile, watching the Butchers crawl into the kill zone. *Keep moving*, Pretorius begged. But the trooper on point tapped his ear and raised a fist and the man behind him dropped into a crouch. The moment froze in time. Pretorius kept her gunsight on the second soldier and reached down to put her left thumb on the Claymore trigger. It was too early—the tail end of the Butchers' column was still outside of the box. She looked at Quarry and he nodded his head. Her finger hovered. What looked like a swarm of insects rose from the middle of the column and dispersed to both sides of the riverbed. Pretorius pushed the APM trigger, and the valley exploded. A wall of shrapnel tore through the front of the column—Pretorius saw the lead Butchers disintegrate—just as the Three Sisters set off the Claymores and mantraps in the rear of the formation. Shock waves rolled through their foxhole as Pretorius and Quarry fired into the riverbed. Cherry opened up with his SAW just to their right, and Zalta picked off individual soldiers who tried to break for the tree line.

The COG-V platoons alongside them and perpendicular to the front of the Butchers' column unloaded as well, enfilading the forward elements of the enemy. Even the moon's hypergravity couldn't hold down the rocks and dirt blown into the air by the ambush. Pretorius listened for the snap and whizz of bullets and pulsed plasma rounds but there was little incoming fire from the entrapped Gliese force. Then she looked up and saw a swarm of nanodrones hovering over the tree line, inspecting COG-V's positions. *Shit.*

"Alternate position left," she yelled into the com. "Move!" She and Quarry rolled out of their shallow foxhole and low-crawled ten meters just as a cluster of laser-guided grenades hit their original position. The ground exploded around them. Dirt and dust filled her mouth as she tried to suck in a breath. A hammer thumped her leg, and she knew she had been hit. Choosing not to look, she crawled away from the incoming fire. "Countermeasures!" she yelled into her headset, hoping Zalta was still alive to hear her.

He was. Pretorius heard the *whoomph* of a mortar canister behind her and looked up to see an umbrella of silver chaff covering the sky. The strips of metallized fiber hovered in the air, disrupting the laser finders the drones had used to mark them. A low, sonorous boom shook the tree line, knocking pine needles down on their heads, and Pretorius knew the COG-V support elements were firing electromagnetic pulse blossoms and chaff up and down the line. But now the Butchers opened up. Given enough of a reprieve to figure out what they were facing, they began to lay down suppressing fire.

Chatter broke out on the coms. Pretorius could hear Delta One—the rear security team from the Fourth led by the Three Sisters, calling for support. The tail of the Butchers' column, which hadn't been ensnared by the premature ambush, was flanking their line. She heard Crooks order an echelon movement to repress the attack and other calls of "Pushing back, pushing back." *Where the hell was the rest of Fourth Platoon?* They were supposed to be the reserve for the rear of the ambush. She looked to her left down the wooded ridgeline and saw the nearest squad of COG-V troopers. Three of them had been killed by the grenade barrage. The fourth crawled up the hillside, one leg missing. The carnage made her look for her own team. Cherry had moved his autocannon to a position higher up the hill. She could see blood on his arms and chin, but he continued to fire. She saw a flicker of movement to Cherry's right and knew it was Zalta. At least he was mobile and still firing countermeasures. Then she looked for Quarry. He lay facedown in a small crater a few feet away. He looked dead.

"Two is down," she yelled, crawling to him. Her right leg didn't work as well as her left and the numbness there morphed to pain. She checked her HUD as she crawled and saw the lower parts of her exosuit had failed. The moon's gravity clawed at her, pulling her down. Energy rounds and old-fashioned dense-metal slugs burned the air over her head. *Were they losing?* Pretorius made it to Quarry and rolled into the crater just as he stirred. She checked his extremities and found only minor shrapnel hits. Hopefully he was just concussed. She shook him and screamed into his ear.

"Contact, eleven o'clock," Zalta yelled into the com. "Fifty meters. Suppressing fire!"

Pretorius rolled and fired on that vector without even looking. A team of Butchers had crawled out of the kill zone to the tree line, firing airburst fragmentation rounds up the hillside. They ran into a squad from Fourth Platoon and a hand-to-hand fight ensued. One of the Fourth's soldiers—the Indian paratrooper, Arjun Ras—grappled with a Butcher and took him down with an ankle pick. Ras stabbed the man in the neck with a push dagger. Then he grabbed the Butcher by the hair and scalped him, blood spraying over his face and neck as he worked. The look on Ras's face, like a librarian stamping a book, seared into Pretorius's brain. He turned and saw her and shrugged. Then he scooted back up the hillside—away from the rear end of the column.

A booming roar shook the valley, and a ball of red flame engulfed the fighters. One of COG-V's drop ships thundered overhead, making a pylon turn around the front of the zone and spraying the enemy with rotary-barreled incendiary rounds. The ground heaved and pulsed. Pretorius bounced with the concussions, the air taken from her lungs. The blasts woke Quarry and got him moving; he rolled over and fired down the hillside.

A pair of tracer beams from the lower end of the valley reached for the drop ship. The lasers hit the craft as it banked, ripping it in two above their heads. Pretorius ducked and waited to die. Something thumped her back—too soft to be wreckage from the doomed ship. *Quarry.* He had jumped on top of her, shielding her body. Harder impacts struck her arms and legs, and a ring of blackness engulfed her. Another explosion ripped the ground meters away, rattling her teeth. She had blood in her mouth and dust in her eyes. Her ears rang, and she drifted in and out of consciousness, flashing for a second to her youth, falling off a horse fence and landing on her head.

Someone shook her. She opened her eyes and squinted, tears rolling down her face from the fuel mist and debris in the air. She focused—it was Cherry. He grabbed her by the TAC-vest and dragged her away. She saw Zalta to her left doing the same with Quarry. Her hearing returned, enough to make out a babble of urgent talk on the company channel. She couldn't move, couldn't help Cherry, but the com chatter slowed and took focus. Bravo One calling for Six Actual. The Butchers had maneuvered around the rear of the ambush, flanking the COG-V troopers on both sides of the defile. *Where the hell was the rest of the Fourth?*

Berrios called for support, to take down a command hovercraft that ran the nanodrones and managed the battlespace for the Butchers. Crooks yelled on the com for Delta Two—the reserve element of Fourth Platoon, but there was no answer. He called for a fire mission on the hovercraft. Pretorius rolled her head and looked down the valley. She could see the machine floating up the defile, soldiers running alongside like ants protecting a queen. *We're losing.* She heard a scream and refocused her eyes. Two specks flew through the sky in the middle of the battlespace a hundred meters away—two humans jumping from a twenty-meter cliff face on the other side of the ravine. It was the Sisters, *it had to be*, but which ones she couldn't tell. They must have rigged their exosuits to launch into the air, and they floated like birds pinned in the wind, tracer fire reaching up to them. A plasma burst hit one of the Sisters and blew her to pieces. The other landed on the hovercraft and hugged it as energy beams and bullets whizzed over her head. *Why would she do that?* Pretorius thought. Then the valley went white. An eruption that felt like a tactical nuke thundered up the ravine. The shock wave blew Cherry off his feet. Pretorius got hammered backward as well and rolled down the hillside with him, their limbs tangling. Something smashed her head and peace folded over.

Quarry had felt it before, the pain of being reborn on a battlefield, from the dark quiet of unconsciousness to the middle space of gray light and confusion, and then waking into a world of fire. He tried lifting his head, but something held it down. He opened his eyes. Someone leaned over him, yelling as she worked. *Let it go*, he wanted to say, *let me die*, but his mouth didn't open. *They're gonna bring me back just long enough to code out in agony.* But the searing pain in his arms and legs dulled, and he knew from the look on the woman's face that it wasn't because his injuries were getting better. She had drugged him.

What was her name, this soldier hovering over him,

shielding his body from incoming fire? *Pemkalla*—the former JSOC sapper and staff sergeant from Fourth Platoon. They had talked—she was stationed at Fort Indiantown Gap when war broke out against the Army of Pennsylvania just after the Collapse. They might even have run into each other on base at some point. *But Pemkalla wasn't a medic, so why was she patching him up?* Then he remembered: COG-V had no medics. If field dressings, metro gel, and an evac to the ship's medical bay didn't suffice, the wounded would get the Cog embolism and be left for dead. The troopers had renamed it the AI Enema and now Quarry hoped for it. *Let it go,* he tried to tell her, *let me go.* He closed his eyes and dreamed. *He sat in a tree stand overlooking a plot of oats and red clover. A buck grunted in the woods as three does grazed on the field. He knew it was the whitetail he had been tracking for two weeks—the mature twelve-pointer with brow tines as thick as his wrist . . .*

He woke again, this time in a drop ship making a hard orbital burn from the moon. It took a few seconds to realize he was on the floor, strapped down for when they hit zero-g. His ears worked now, and he heard screaming. He craned his head and saw Jorgenson lying a few feet away, writhing as someone pried a chunk of metal the size of a spatula from his leg. He tried to speak again. *Where the hell was Pretorius?* She was alive last he saw, and then they got hammered from the debris of the drop ship. *Where were Zalta and Cherry?*

Com chatter and screams filled his ears. Jorgenson bellowed one last time as they tied off his thigh. Crooks barked out a situation report to Cog. "At least thirty-five KIAs," he said, "and twice that many wounded, but the Butchers are smoked. One drop ship destroyed. Be prepared for an immediate exfil from orbit once we arrive—hard burn when the wounded are secured." Other groans and screams filled the cabin. His head bounced on the metal grating as turbulence buffeted the ship. Quarry blinked and tried to focus—looked for Pretorius again in the cramped crew space, but she wasn't there. He saw Fuller, the Plus One, going insane at the far bulkhead, lunging for Arjun Ras's throat as other soldiers jumped in between them. Blood poured down the Ranger's face as he flailed at Ras, who looked mildly surprised. They wrestled Fuller into a jump seat and strapped him down with combat webbing. He cried like a child, hugging his knees. *My God*, Quarry thought as he drifted off, *the Three Sisters are dead. Those four are never apart. And Fuller isn't the crying type.*

BOOK

2

11

MISSION TEN: TEEGARDEN'S STAR

2138

Crooks kept the touch-coins of the dead in a glass bowl on his desk; little round headstones that filled the container to the brim. He didn't have to play the old guessing game of how many pennies were in the jar—the exact count was burned into his memory: 121 dead, out of an original company of 160 and 80 reinforcements. Including injuries, COG-V's casualty rate exceeded a 100 percent. *What other outfit in history had taken that level of casualties?* The MACV-SOG teams in Vietnam, maybe, or Rome's Ninth Legion . . .

He fingered the small crater above his armpit where a piece of shrapnel had punched through his TAC-suit on Ross 128b. The wound ached as it always did when the *Varangian* ran through slip-space—something about the quantum vacuum flared old injuries like a storm front back on Earth. He stared out of his small porthole into nothingness. There were no stars and no movement inside their isolated bubble of space-time, even though they thundered toward another point in space trillions of miles away.

Forty-one years had passed in eight months of their reckoning. *Or was it eight months in forty-one years?* Both sides of the time puzzle twisted his mind, and he realized that only his hair knew the answer. It had thrown away the clock and gone completely gray. They had run nine ops in that time, and he jotted each mission down in a small notebook, after-action reports in shorthand, forcing himself to recount the dead and wounded as he waited for the *Varangian* to reenter normal space:

YZ Ceti: 11 KIA, 27 WIA. A textbook attack on Dippel's station, and the casualty rate still ran high. Pellet swarms accounted for 72 percent of the dead.

Alpha CMb: 35 KIA, 72 WIA. The moon's hypergravity increased COG-V's casualties by 20 percent. Exoskeletons were more hindrance than help. Lack of coordination within Fourth Platoon led to the loss of its recon team, the Three Sisters.

Lacaille b: 14 KIA, 44 WIA. A close-quarters nightmare rooting out an insurgency in an underground city. Room-to-room fighting in blackout. Three hundred civilians dead.

Procyon Bc: 21 KIA, 60 WIA. Procyon. *Fuck.* Low-gravity planetoid orbiting a white dwarf. A reinforced battalion of Gliese Marines with fire superiority shot them to hell. Coriolis Effect degraded combat readiness.

Ross 128b: 3 KIA, 4 WIA. The genocide op. COG-V didn't kill the 20,000 civilians that died on that damned moon. But it unwittingly opened the door for the slaughter to happen.

Kruger 60c: 12 KIA, 9 WIA—all from one platoon. Struvian space station with a laser defense grid that cut the bad-luck Fourth to pieces.

DX Cancri: 1 KIA, 7 WIA. Just one dead, but it was Sgt. King, the Australian jokester and ex-SASR tunnel rat. Beloved by everyone in the company. A sonic mine ruptured her organs during exfil.

Luyten's Star: 4 KIA, 15 WIA. Direct action assault on an orbiting Leonis rail gun battery. Another textbook op—but it was the one that drove Staff Sgt. Sato insane.

EZ Aquarii: 10 KIA, 22 WIA. A tectonic moon caught in a gravitational tug of war among three red dwarfs. The Volcano War, the troopers named it. Five troopers from the Second killed by a pyroclastic flow below a cinder cone—cooked inside their suits. What did Boortz say on the lift out? "EZ my ass."

Not all the dead fell in combat. Four committed suicide, and Cog administered embolisms to six. Even those punishments had been self-inflicted, a modern version of suicide by cop. Three had attempted mutiny, escape, or sabotage, knowing how things would end. They were too alpha to kill themselves, and Sato's death stung the most. She had been one of his best, a modern Samurai from Japan's 1st Airborne Brigade. After Luyten's Star, she tried to open an airlock and space her entire squad. Crooks liked to think it had been an attempt at mercy. More likely, it was some form of temporal dementia—another phenomenon that hadn't been anticipated and couldn't be diagnosed but was debilitating a decent chunk of the teams.

The others got shipped for fighting or repeated fraternization on the *Varangian*, and the deaths hung over the ship like gallows in a town square. Cog couldn't find a programming variance to get around capital punishment, and the irony was that the one COG-V soldier who deserved to be executed, Sergeant Arjun Ras, remained alive because war crimes and dereliction of duty weren't specifically cited by CORP as offenses subject to the death penalty. Crooks had transferred Ras from Fourth to Third Platoon as the Third needed bodies, but also because the remaining members of the Fourth refused to fight alongside him. They considered him a Blue Falcon and a psychopath. They were convinced that Ras had hung the Three Sisters out to dry at Alpha CMb, even though his unit had engaged and killed multiple Butchers and taken casualties itself. The eight-person team wasn't where they were supposed to be during the fight—at the tail end of the ambush. Ras blamed bad comms, and in the mess of combat, Cog couldn't find enough evidence to do more than transfer him, but that didn't satisfy many of the troopers who had been on the ground. Crooks tried to convince Third Platoon's command sergeant that Ras would be an asset because he was an efficient killer. "Yeah, so is malaria," came the reply.

Crooks closed his eyes. Why was he so depressed? This was the Glory Op they were headed toward—Mission Ten. Crooks almost didn't want to believe they would be redeemed and released from their enlistment after Teegarden. He was afraid to believe it. The whole company had short-timer syndrome, convinced they'd buy it on this last op, and they didn't even know the mission specs. The slip buoy at the Bear had gone dark after relaying the coordinates. *With our luck it will be an ass-kicker*, Crooks thought as he shook his head and looked out into the nothingness of slip-space. *At least it only took us four decades to get here.*

"Who the hell is Priam Solutions?" he asked. "And why are they running us now?"

Crooks rubbed his crew cut with both hands as Cog scanned the chessboard in front of them and pretended to think about a move. The *Varangian* flew on a low-g burn toward Teegarden's Star, a red dwarf on the terminus of the IFS that had a belt of asteroids laden with rare-earth minerals and ice. In two days, the COG-V platoons would drop to a planetoid manned by a colony of Earth miners that had declared independence and attacked a Marine expeditionary ship sent to check on them. Crooks and Cog had run through the intel on the colony's defensive posture, and it didn't look impressive. A few pulsed energy projectile cannons made up the bulk of their antiship defenses, and the mine had a rail gun for orbital ejections, which could theoretically be turned into a weapon. The rebel ground forces, such as they were, had basic small arms—none of the new blossom lasers and antipersonnel drones they had been reading about in their refresher downloads on twenty-second-century warfare. First and Third Platoons would make the drop with Pretorius's pathfinding team along for the ride. They were the only recon team with any experience that remained alive. The rest of the Second Platoon had too many newbies, as did the Fourth, and Crooks didn't want a bunch of FNGs getting sucked into an ambush or freaking out and slaughtering noncombatants.

He should have been overjoyed—this was an easy op with a light footprint that would guarantee most of his remaining company's survival through redemption. But the mission stank like Ross 128b, a genocide that had been all about money. And now he had a new boss to report to, one that he had never even heard of. Crooks scanned the chessboard between him and Cog, waiting for the AI's answer about their new leadership. The situation ate at Cog as well, so they played chess. It usually calmed them down.

"Priam is a private military contractor," Cog finally said. "Or to be more precise, they are *the* PMC as far as CORP's off-system forces are concerned. They've been given C2 for all military operations, overt and covert, outside of the heliopause. Which means they're our new boss."

Crooks grimaced. Cog had him bracketed again. He didn't see a move that wouldn't open attacking lanes for the AI's bishops or knights. "Mercs. Are they the bastards that loosened the rules of engagement to allow for civilian casualties?"

"No. Priam didn't have command at that point. Those orders came down from Helsinki after Ross 128b, remember? To retroactively excuse the slaughter. CORP's expeditionary force still ran the IFS theater at the time."

Crooks moved a knight into an active position. "I can't remember shit at this point, Cog. Everything's twisted in a knot, and I'm not sure I can even run an op with the human wreckage we have down there in the 1-g can. They've accepted messed-up orders before but now we're going after Earthborn who aren't even soldiers. Who are we fighting for?"

Cog mused for a second. "We're fighting for CORP. We're just taking orders from a third party."

"Bullshit," Crooks said. "It's more of a business cartel than a governing body now. And what about Earth? They're all strangers to us."

Cog sat as he always did when playing chess, in *The Thinker* position. He didn't vary his posture much—just went with what he deemed appropriate for the situation—and Crooks never alerted him to this tic in his humanity-assimilation coding. For Crooks, it was a way to remember that his one confidant in the universe was a machine.

"What do you suggest, starting our own mutiny?" Cog asked. "You know I submitted to lock-hammer protocols to get this command. If I refuse mission orders, it will result in the destruction of the ship. I burned out my logic gate trying to find ways around the unit executions, Major, but this goes beyond direct normativity in AI control theory. I have a self-imposed kill switch and I can't go against deep-core programming."

Crooks considered tipping his king as he waited for Cog to make a move. *Chess doesn't hold its flavor when you're a pawn.*

"Check," Cog said, moving his bishop into a clear alleyway to the king. "My predictive heuristics concluded that we'd be having this conversation. I've spent a lot of time looking for an answer, and I have nothing for you, except that we're almost done. We push through this mission, fucked up as it is, and we will be redeemed."

Crooks moved his king out of check. "Do you really believe that? CORP has changed the rules at every turn, and now we're working for a company of mercenaries. These aren't missions to protect the home planet anymore, Cog. We're heading to Teegarden to kill a bunch of diggers at the request of a freaking corporation. Are we defending Earth or fighting its personal squabbles? And if we're nothing more than someone's private muscle, do you really think they'll let us go?"

Cog tipped his own king despite having the game in hand. He swung his arm across the board, scattering the pieces onto the command deck. Crooks sat back, a look of shock on his face. First the cursing and now a temper tantrum—Crooks didn't realize the AI had it in him.

"We all made a Faustian bargain when we agreed to this billet, Major. I'm probably the guiltiest because I have the greatest ability to posit the ramifications. So yeah, I sold my soul to the devil. And so did you."

"You didn't have a choice. I thought they reprogrammed you for the *Varangian* after what happened on the *Breckenridge*."

Cog stood up and walked to the front of the bridge. Teegarden glowed dull red in the viewscreen, a bull's-eye getting bigger. "I did have a choice. Even disgraced AI can select or deselect vocational paths. My original redesign was for astrophysics and black hole morphology. They came to me with the specs of this mission and a biophysical engram of all human military theory and tactics, and I accepted incorporation into the *Varangian*. It provided a singular opportunity to study the Kerr–Newman metric and space-time geodesics."

"But that wasn't all, was it?"

Cog kept his back turned to Crooks. "What do you mean?"

Crooks picked up chess pieces from the floor and began replacing them. "There are other ways for a supercore to study relativity, even hands-on ways. You could have gone on the Sag-A science mission with the *Umikoa*. Why did you agree to a military command?"

"Sagittarius A is a remote observation study, Major, well back from the cusp of the event horizon. There's no time dilation involved, and it was the temporal manipulation via space-time curvature that drew me in. Chronological perception is one thing I share with humans."

"Not anymore," Crooks said. "You're a warfighter now, just like everyone else on this boat. Are you telling me that wasn't part of the attraction? You read up on the human history of warfare, and it pulled you in."

"Maybe," Cog said after a pause. "War is a concept I found

hard to understand. It is the most human of things and the most inhuman of things. Its dichotomies fascinated me."

Crooks walked up to the viewscreen and stood beside Cog. "Do they still?"

Cog had a look of despair on his face. "Yes, but not in a good way," he whispered. "I believe now that advanced general intelligence machines can be traumatized by war, Major, or depending on the individual unit, even addicted to it."

Crooks put a hand on Cog's shoulder. It felt real and warm, without a hint of an electrical charge. "I think you're more on the trauma end of the spectrum, Cog. If you were addicted to war, our conversation wouldn't have gotten this far."

"Maybe, but Priam has commissioned three more dilation warships in the last two decades, with regular troops and command structures. And those AIs were built for the mission. What if their personalities lean toward addiction? What if Earth and the other IFS empires stash armies in time and the supercores onboard get a taste for it? Then there will never be a possibility for the end of it."

"The end of what?" Crooks asked.

"The end of war."

The human on the command deck laughed. "You are an idealist, aren't you, Cog? What did Santayana say? 'Only the dead have seen the end of war.' If he knew there were going to be hundreds of planets and moons to fight over, he would have been even more pessimistic. But I'm worried about our lot in life, and we need to find a solution. An escape hatch—a clause around the clause if things go sideways on this op."

Cog shook his head. "Our mission orders are clear, and trying to find ways around them could get everyone on this ship killed. We are to protect CORP's strategic and financial interests and the welfare of those allied to Earth. The Teegarden miners are no longer allies."

"But what if we're blowing past those orders, into something more like genocide?"

"That's a loaded term, Major, especially when confronting an openly hostile force in tight quarters. And we're not the kind of warship that lodges formal protests if we don't like what we're doing. You know that."

"Can you reject an invalid order, Cog?"

"Maybe, if the order is illegal by the rules of engagement within a particular time and theater, and if it violates existing law as stipulated by CORP itself."

The *Varangian* rumbled as it passed through Teegarden's heliopause. The red dwarf still looked far away—a slightly brighter dot than the other thousands of dots filling the viewscreen. Crooks put a hand on the bulkhead to brace as the ship trembled again. Cog hadn't even mentioned that turbulence was coming although he must have known it. *Hell, he's probably dedicating more programming to flying the ship and maintaining its guts than he is to this conversation*, Crooks thought. *And what does that mean for us? How much of Cog can really go beyond taking a left or a right or shutting down a leaky valve?*

"Well, let's put Priam on notice that there are limits," Crooks said. "Advise them that we will breach the landing docks and upper tiers of the station and eliminate active hostiles. And then we'll assess for the potential of collateral damage before proceeding to the lower levels."

"Our orders are to secure the melters, Major, which are housed in sublevel four. Every other objective is secondary."

"We both know those orders are a death sentence for everyone on that rock, including noncombatants. They'll be bunkered in the sublevels."

"Then aren't they human shields at that point?" Cog asked. "The melters are the biggest asset on the station."

"Where the hell else are they going to hide? In a crater on the surface? Send the message, Cog, and let's see how Priam reacts."

Cog blasted air from his mouth and used his middle finger to wipe an imaginary speck of dust from his eye. It's what he always did when they argued. *Another tic and not even an original one*, Crooks thought, although getting flipped the bird by a machine still made him smile. He turned to leave the bridge.

"We are a five-billion-dollar asset," Cog said. "We run afoul of CORP or Priam Solutions, and I can guarantee you there will be no redemption for the ship or crew, not after this op or any other. Someone will come for us. They will come for us like dogs on the hunt."

"At least we'll know what we're fighting for," Crooks said. He thumbed the hatch, but Cog wouldn't let him leave with the last word.

"A word of warning, Major," the AI said. "I consider you my friend but don't ask me to join you in going rogue. AIs don't attempt mutinies over humanitarian concerns, especially ones that are programmed for war. Sharks don't chew on seaweed."

Crooks smiled. "You're a fountain of bad metaphors, Cog. Even if you kill me with that embolism someday, I'll always love you for that."

12

Of all the patchwork cyborgs on the drop ship, Jorgenson had the best kit. He still had real arms, for one thing. Bionic arms had power, but they lacked fine motor skills for precision shooting and close-quarters battle. Every trooper worried about losing an arm. What Jorgenson had, in addition to upper limbs made by the Almighty, was a steel-aluminum tibia that could kick down a tree, fully integrated signal-processing ears, and a right eyeball that any soldier would die for. Jorgenson had almost died for it, since his real eye got smoked by a piece of shrapnel that stopped just short of entering his brain. Luckily for the ex-Delta operator, it happened in 2128, so the new eye was strictly next gen. It had a telescoping cornea with up to thirty times magnification, a Barium Crown lens, and a sensor package for thermal imaging, motion detection, night vision, angular velocity, and proximity alerts.

His artificial ears were older, but they could still pick up a cat's footsteps from fifty meters, and Quarry knew that when Jorgenson turned his head and looked down the line and his bionic eyeball zoomed in on the recon team, he had heard their conversation from afar. The First Sergeant stood up and headed in their direction.

"Shit," Quarry whispered to Zalta. "We just got made by Delta."

Jorgenson picked his way through the squads, who sat on parallel jump seats lining the port and starboard walls of the drop ship or knelt on the deck to check their loadouts—their gear laid out in front of them in a way that was orderly and chaotic at the same time.

"Absolutely freaking not," Jorgenson said when he got to the LRRP team.

Zalta looked up at Jorgenson innocently. "Absolutely freaking not, what?"

"You're not going into the shafts until we clear the upper rooms and send in a minesweeper. You forget about the super grunts at Lacaille? I'm not sending anyone into the holes on that rock until they've been cleared."

Fourth Platoon's recon team—the one that replaced the Three Sisters—had been cut off and killed in a similar underground asteroid mission at Lacaille b a few months back—Quarry couldn't even remember the year. He tried not to think of Earth years or IFS time anymore. All he knew was the last eight months from the perspective of the *Varangian*, and they had taken a dizzying toll.

Zalta turned to Cherry and Pretorius for support, but they were too busy going through their kits and arguing about the need for a shotgun on the mission. They had chosen Zalta as team lead for Teegarden because he had served as a tunnel rat during the Battle of Homs. The argument was his to make anyway.

"When you're going into a hole, it's best to have the element of surprise," the Syrian tracker said to Jorgenson. "These colonists are engineers. They know how to build low-tech traps that won't be detected by a minesweeper."

Jorgenson took a knee next to Zalta and put a hand on his shoulder. The scars on his face and shaven head, combined with the Delta tattoo on his neck and an eyeball that zoomed open and shut like a camera lens, made for an intimidating presence. Quarry noticed that Jorgenson often got to eye level with the troopers he was talking to, probably to make himself more accessible. The zooming iris didn't help on that front.

"Brother, there isn't a right answer here. I would normally go kinetic, but these diggers know we're coming. They blew a Marine skiff out of space a few weeks ago, for Christ's sake. So, I looked at our options and went with the cautious approach, and Crooks agreed with me."

Zalta nodded his head and continued packing blocks of caseless ammo into a load-bearing belt. "It's your call, but I wonder if you're making it because this is the Glory Op. If it's our casualties you're worried about, I'm telling you my way is best."

Jorgenson fumed. "Yeah, it's my call, and I have no idea why the fuck that is. I never asked to be First Sergeant. You need to be a freaking prophet to figure out all the variables on these ops. But I run them the same, first or last, and I'll smoke anyone who says otherwise."

"If you're looking to take a back seat, I'll be the one-zero today," someone said. All of them turned toward the even-keeled voice. It was Ras at the port bulwark, loading frags into a Claymore bag. He didn't lift his eyes from the work.

"Are you shitting me, Ras?" Jorgenson said. "You can't find a platoon that wants your sick ass, and you're gonna lead these troopers somewhere?"

Ras smiled and Quarry watched the confrontation with morbid fascination. The Indian paratrooper's eyes exuded sympathy—he always looked like a saint until he started killing people. He spoke in quiet tones and moved in nonthreatening ways. *He's like a storm at sea*, Quarry thought, *something that looks benign from a distance, until it gets you in its grip and tears you to pieces.*

"I'll finish the job for them," the Indian paratrooper said. "You have short-timer syndrome, Jorgenson, worried about getting killed by a bunch of POGs. Or are you worried about something else? Because the only thing I care about is getting off this ride in one piece—and not a century from now."

Quarry grabbed Jorgenson's shoulder to hold him back. "Back off before you get hurt, Ras," he said. "Jorgenson's gotten us this far, and if anyone on this can is a long-timer, it's him."

"Then he should lead like one," Ras said.

Jorgenson did the last thing Quarry expected—he laughed. "You're funny, Ras. I'd take you seriously if you cared about anyone's skin other than your own. Just stay where you belong today, in the rear with the gear, watching your own ass."

Ras gave a half salute, and if there was mockery in his voice, Quarry couldn't detect it. "Suits me just fine, First Sergeant. But don't say I didn't offer."

Jorgenson stared at him for another second and stood up, raising his voice so the whole team could hear him. "No hero shit on this one, people. Stay frosty, wait for the sensor sweeps, and call in the big guns if you run into contact. Live through today and you'll be in a Belter whorehouse before you can say *gonorrhea*."

He picked his way back to First Platoon through the maze of gear on the decking, not bothering to look at Ras again on his way.

"Well, if things go bad today, at least it wasn't your call," Quarry said to Zalta.

"Sure," Zalta said. "The lightly burdened shall be saved."

"Five minutes to zero-g and five more to insertion," the door master yelled from the stern of the ship. "Police your gear and get pressurized."

Quarry sat between Pretorius and Zalta, his kit bonded to his pressure suit. Cherry, as always, sat in the back on rear security. *How many times have these three saved my ass*, Quarry wondered. *And how many times have I saved theirs?* He couldn't do the math—the last eight months really did feel like four decades and the combat meds bent his memory.

"Damn, these new pills are good," Cherry said, as if reading his mind. "I snorted some pure snow in Tingo María once, a few lifetimes ago. These things feel just like it." He hooted and slapped Zalta on the shoulder and bounced up and down on his jump seat.

"Well, we have a name for the new pills now," Quarry said. "Tingo Marías."

Pretorius felt the high too, Quarry could tell by the way she clenched and unclenched her jaw. "That's just what we need," she said. "Dan Cherry hopped up on speed with his cannon pointed at our asses."

The drop ship bucked as it descended toward the Teegarden planetoid, forcing the troopers to grab their seat webbing. The course adjustment refocused Quarry on the mission. A lot of the teams had brushed it off because they were going after civilians this time and not professional soldiers. *A cakewalk,* they said, *one and done.* His thoughts drifted back to Pennsylvania as he mulled the enemy on this op—to the civilians scattering from the interstate like baitfish as tracer fire ran them down.

That had done it for Quarry, it was the moment he had snapped. In the woods, he only hunted what he needed to eat. There was purpose to it and a sense of natural law. As a soldier, he had accepted killing other soldiers. They were trying to kill him. The best won and had nightmares about it later. *But these*

Teegarden miners, what the hell did they know about what they'd be facing? A Spec Ops team was about to drop on their heads like an anvil from Olympus. The initial high from the drugs wore off as Quarry ran through the dead of the past and the future. He couldn't let it go.

He elbowed Pretorius. "You get the feeling we're the bad guys now?"

She shook her head and chuckled but he saw that it was forced. "Are you getting existential on me before an op, Quarry?"

"Can't help it. The pills only gave me about five minutes of juice."

"Well clear your head and gear up. This isn't even our world anymore. We are nothing guys fighting never wars, totally apart from whoever's down on that rock in the year of our Lord, 2138."

"We won't be 'nothing guys' when we're blowing them out of their pressure suits. I always thought of myself as the good guy. Didn't you? If not, why did you kill that asshole back on Earth?"

She scowled. "I don't know. Why did you?"

"Because he was doing wrong."

"Shooting him is what got you here in the first place, so maybe it was a mistake."

"So, we should let the bad shit slide if it saves our skin?"

"I don't know. Ask me the next time, because I'm figuring this shit out as we go and I'm too high to get deep about it."

The transport lurched again. "One minute," the door master yelled. Everyone checked their weapons and inspected the gear of the trooper next to them.

"I will," Quarry said as he did a visual on Pretorius's pressure suit. "I'm guessing in about thirty minutes."

The dead looked surprised, with wide-open eyes and tumbled-down bodies, like victims of a storm that had hit without warning. They lay scattered across the docking cavern and the nave of the station. As the recon team advanced behind COG-V's shock troops, Quarry could see there was nothing fair about the fight other than the fact that both sides were shooting. The Teegarden miners dropped like paper targets. They had no knowledge of tactics, use of cover, or fire support. The platoon mowed through them, and the battle became a slaughter. Quarry didn't shoot a round as the forward elements cleared the upper rooms and corridors; he just let the fire teams do their thing. One COG-V trooper had fallen, hit by shrapnel or an unlucky ricochet, and Quarry could tell without getting too close that he was KIA. They moved past him and continued stepping over the enemy dead, coming to a junction where a slain colonial lay. Her pressure suit still had dirt on it from the mines. Beneath a shattered faceplate, two neat nickel-sized holes rimmed her forehead. Her eyes had locked open. Quarry glanced at Pretorius, waited for a tap on his back from Cherry, and followed Zalta down the hallway, covering their right flank.

The station had gravity from the asteroid's native spin, but the COG-V troopers had blasted through the cavern door and opened all the upper airlocks, so the dead froze in their blown-out pressure suits. They died in the silence of a vacuum. The only sounds of war that Quarry heard were chatter and heavy breathing on the comms. By the time the LRRPs got to the settlement's meeting hall, the organized fighting on the upper piers had died down. They found Jorgenson kneeling with a few other troopers behind a tipped-over desk, giving orders to clear the remaining upstairs rooms and deploy the EOD rovers into the tunnels. They kneeled next to him, looking out into the open hall where about a dozen miners lay dead. Drawings made of crayon and paint covered the far wall above a row of plants that had flash frozen when the room was exposed to space. *Children's drawings.*

"How long?" Zalta asked.

"Thirty minutes for bomb disposal," Jorgenson said. "We figure most of them are holed up in the mining spars. Cog is hacking into their cams, so hopefully we'll get eyes on targets."

"What are our rules of engagement?"

Jorgenson looked at Zalta with surprise on his face. "They fired on us before we hit the hangar door. We've got a KIA and a few wounded, so if we get orders to breach the lower levels, weapons are hot. Check your HUDs for facial stamping and try not to grease the two high-value targets. They're tagged for interrogation. Everyone else is a shooter."

"What if they surrender?"

Jorgenson continued to stare Zalta down. "What are we going to do, Hassan, take prisoners? Our mission is to clear the station and secure the melters. You know what that means. Clear the damned station. If they abandon the hardware and climb into a deeper hole, I'm not going after them, but anyone putting up resistance gets greased."

Quarry poked his thumb over the table toward the far wall. "What if there are children down there, Jorgenson? Those drawings weren't made by rock haulers."

"No one should be down there but bad guys; the colonials knew we were coming. If the lower decks are rigged and we can't get to the melters without taking mass casualties, the plan is to cut the power and flood the basement with gas. If they're in pressure suits, we use a corrosive agent, but carefully. They want the reactors intact."

This time even Boortz looked up from the touch-coin projecting a hologram of the battlespace for the command team.

No one had said anything about using nerve gas or weaponized hydrazine to kill the colonials. Crooks must have had Jorgenson withhold that information as need-to-know.

"Jesus," Quarry said. "That's a little strong. These guys can't even shoot straight. It's not like we're fighting the Butchers or the Wolf Brigade."

Jorgenson's eyes had been snapping between all five soldiers kneeling around him. Sweat glossed his forehead and he blinked too much, and Quarry wondered how many Tingo Marías he had taken. The big man grabbed Quarry by the chest gripper and pulled him close.

"You think I want to be gassing day-soldiers, Quarry? You think Crooks does? We've already bent the rules by not dropping VXR down the pipes thirty minutes ago, but we don't get to ignore direct orders. That ain't who we are, or did you forget about those bubbles in your bloodstream that will go *pop* if we don't do as we're told?"

Quarry tensed. Something rumbled up from deep inside as he looked at Jorgenson's hand on his chest. He envisioned cracking open the big man's helmet with a rifle blow, but then he felt Zalta's grip on his leg. He took a breath and closed his eyes.

"How would you deploy the gas?" Zalta asked, subtly positioning himself between Quarry and Jorgenson.

Jorgenson continued to stare down Quarry, and when he finally noticed Zalta, he laughed and shook his head.

"Don't worry, I'll keep the blood off your hands. We'll force it through the thermal control systems or send in the EOD bots, and I'll be the one giving the order."

Cherry slid forward. "There is no good answer here, boys and girls, and there never will be, so let it go. If there are noncombatants down there, they won't survive the next visit from Earth anyway. Somebody has this colony marked for extermination. Why do you think they sent us in? It's like Ross 128b all over again."

"Let the next guys do it, then," Quarry said, continuing to stare at Jorgenson. "I'm tired of wiping out civilians, and I thought our Delta boss here preferred a fair fight."

"Find me a fair fight," Jorgenson said, staring back at Quarry. "I don't see one nearby."

Boortz broke the tension. "First Sergeant, Cog has us hooked into the lower level's cams." He brushed through several real-time video feeds on the hologram—abandoned corridors, mining tubes, and empty equipment rooms. A few showed colonials waiting behind tunnel doors in makeshift barricades, weapons at the ready. Boortz continued to scroll and stopped at a cam that read SL-4 ASM, a room that looked like an operator's shack, no bigger than a small classroom. It was packed with children and a few of their minders.

"Shit. Are we gassing them too?" Pretorius asked. Quarry watched Jorgenson's trigger finger to make sure he didn't try to shoot her. Before the big Delta operator could react, the room on the cam exploded.

Crooks had to look away from the video and back again to register what just happened. Smoke and sparks blanketed the viewscreen. When Cog switched the feed to infrared, they could see bodies—tiny bodies—strewn across the decking. A few of them moved; most of them didn't. For the first time in his life, Crooks forgot about call signs and command codes.

"What the fuck was that?" he yelled. The com erupted with chatter, Jorgenson ordering the fire teams to report and squad leaders calling out their locations.

"We just breached sublevel four," Cog said.

"Who did?"

"I don't know."

"Did you give that order?"

"Excuse me?"

"Did you give that order, Cog?"

Cog didn't answer and when Crooks finally wrenched his eyes from the monitor, he saw the hurt in the AI's human face. "I did not give that order, Major. You are in command."

"I'm sorry, Cog," Crooks said before keying the com. "Alpha One, Six. Who the hell breached that room?"

"Six, Alpha One," Jorgenson said. "Unknown. Still checking."

"Who isn't where they are supposed to be? There's too much interference down there to match bio-tel to locations."

"Checking."

A voice broke in over the open channel, calm and flat. Almost soothing. It was Ras. "Six, Charlie Three. No reason to check. It was my squad. We've breached SL-4 and could use some help. There are bad guys positioned in strong points around the aft melters, and they have the corridors rigged with ordnance."

"Ras, what the fuck are you doing?" Crooks asked. "Disengage immediately. That's a direct order."

"That's a negative, Six; we are securing the melters."

The video feed from the operator's shack skittered and fuzzed and came back. None of the bodies on the floor moved now.

"Cog," Crooks said, "make sure I'm on the open channel. I want every headset to hear this."

"Done."

"This is Six. Whoever is with Sergeant Ras, I am ordering you to identify and fall back to rally point one. You have ten seconds to respond before punitive measures are taken."

They waited ten seconds. There was only static on the com.

"Cog," Crooks said.

"Sir."

"How many troopers haven't checked in with their platoon leaders yet?"'

"Eight including Ras—it looks like six from Third Platoon and two from the First. Ras, Weiss, Hahn, Karga, Nilsen, Rozenhal, Gregorenko, and Adeleke."

My God, Crooks thought. *That bastard started a mutiny with people from two different platoons.* "Take them out," he said to Cog. "Right now."

"Done."

The com hissed. There was no chatter. Cog executed seven men and a woman by embolism, and a company of stunned troopers listened to silence in the wake of their deaths. Then a voice broke through the static, a voice from the dead, soft and measured. Unmistakable.

"Cog, it appears your medical transmission was not received," Ras said. "I think it's time we all talked. I have an offer."

13

Pretorius and her team huddled amid the destruction of the hangar bay with Jorgenson, Boortz, and a handful of other operators from the First. They watched on their heads-up displays, stunned, as someone pointed a camera at Ras's face. The ex–Para SF trooper lay behind a barricade, holding a knee and cradling a SAW to his chest. The channel was open—for some reason, Crooks and Cog hadn't blocked it—and the sound of small arms and pulse fire rang in the background. The fight was just around the corner, but the focus was on Ras. *How the hell was he still alive?*

"I'll make a long story short because we're a little busy at the moment," Ras said. He looked tired, as if he carried a burden from what he had just done. "I was inserted in COG-V as a fail-safe. CORP knew there would be C2 delays inherent in relativistic missions, so they gave me command authority if a mission went astray. The heuristics folks figured it might happen, even with Cog's behavioral protocols and the major's tightwad nature. Too many missions, too much twisting of the mind by time dilation. Too much potential for AI to evolve as we slip into new timelines. It can make man and machine soft."

Ras cut the com for a second as he poked his head around the barricade. He came back a second later. "I never had an embolus put in my bloodstream, and I can neutralize any other trooper's embolus with the push of a button."

He leaned closer to the camera, his faceplate filling the screen. "And folks, things have gone astray. We were about to screw up the Glory Mission. Major Crooks circumvented direct orders from our boss, Priam Solutions, to immediately secure the melters. All other considerations were secondary. All collateral damage was deemed acceptable. But Crooks wanted to assess the situation before moving, worried about hurting innocents, maybe, or just not aggressive enough after all the shit we've been through."

He held up a handful of blasting caps and sonic charges. "Understand what happened here. We just removed these charges from melters one to five, and we hit the colonials with a focused EMP to prevent them from blowing up the others. They were set to go off five minutes ago. I guess the colonials thought we'd back down if they smoked three billion dollars' worth of equipment and held the rest hostage. Regardless, our primary mission would have failed."

He paused a minute for the last sentence to sink in. "So, here's the offer. Priam is ordering the *Varangian* back to that godforsaken black hole we've been circling for the last forty years. If I had to guess, anyone who goes with them is about to get screwed by the Man. Me and my team are staying here to finish this job, and Cog can't touch us. Anyone who wants to join can come down to sublevel four and report to Sergeant Weiss. Your embolus will be removed, and after this op is done, you will be redeemed. Terms of enlistment fulfilled. A Priam cruiser has already been dispatched to pick us up.

"But here's the thing. I'm in charge. We're taking no

prisoners and we're leaving no survivors on this station. Not a man, woman, or child. It's going to get ugly, but we don't work for the Red Cross. You have ten minutes to decide. I hope you make the smart choice because we could use the help."

Pretorius felt the buzz in her helmet and keyed her heads-up display to search for the ID. *Charlie Three. Sergeant Arjun Ras.* She clicked open the com with a blink of her eye. "What is it, Ras?"

"Hello, Anaya. We just got thirty-one new enlistees down here, so we're at platoon strength. I figure we can end this thing in a day or two with limited casualties."

"Good for you."

"I'd like to see your name on the roster. Recon skills are hard to come by. You can even bring your team if you promise to control them."

"We talked it out, Ras. We're gonna pass."

"Holding out for a better offer, are you?" He waited a few seconds for a response, but none came. "You go back to that black hole, and you'll never get what you've always wanted."

"What's that?"

"*Freedom.* From all of this—this shit that you and I have dealt with since we were kids. Powerful people using us as their sharp little weapons."

Pretorius thought about it. *He was right—the ticket was there; she just had to kill for it. And wasn't that what she was, anyway? A killer?*

"How do you know what I want?"

"Because we come from the same place. The bottom of the pile."

"Maybe you're right, Ras," Pretorius replied, "but I don't

like you. You remind me of someone I killed back on Earth, a long time ago."

"And how did that go for you?" He laughed. "But as you wish. I never get in the way of someone else's bad decision." His voice dropped a notch, not quite as soothing. "I hope we meet again someday, Sergeant. Face-to-face on the field, where we belong."

"Goodbye, Ras," she said.

Crooks returned to the *Varangian* with the depleted, deflated, and pissed off remains of a company. Forty troopers stayed on the Teegarden rock with Ras, leaving well under a hundred left in COG-V. It could have been worse. Crooks sensed that most of them would have bolted—even Jorgenson—if they didn't hate Ras's guts and distrust him to the core. The genocide part of the equation bugged them less than it should have because they had no connection to this timeline. *It's not even their reality; it's a never war, so why should they care about the people who die in it? And how scary is that?*

"Do you think it was a good idea to give him the open com?" Cog asked when Crooks made it to the bridge, slumped into a chair, and began to load frags into a combat belt.

"Fuck it," Crooks said. "I don't want anyone on my team who would join Ras anyway."

"What if he's right? We just risked everything on a result we can't change. Those colonials were dead before we reached Teegarden. The only thing we did was wipe our hands of it."

Crooks looked at his executive officer. The AI's face was sewn with uncertainty. Cog had recommended the course that could have got them out of this nightmare, and now they were right back in it. *Because of me*, Crooks thought. *Once again, because of me. And that's why I'll handle the rest of it alone. Or die trying.*

"You stuck with me, Cog. I won't forget that."

"What are you going to do?"

He exhaled and squeezed his eyes shut. "Do you know the concept of the end justifying the means? It comes from an ugly place in human history, and it's excused a whole lot of bad shit. We might be a bunch of dumb grunts, but the means have to matter." He shook his head. "I'm not going to wipe my hands of this thing. I'm going back down to that rock, and I'll find a way to get those colonials out of Ras's bloody mitts. If you need to give me the embolism, do it now."

Crooks checked his weapon's receiver and ammo block for dirt and dust and waited for the sensation of a bubble exploding in his bloodstream. *Will it hurt, or will there just be peace?*

"What do you think you can do?" Cog asked.

"I don't know. Go in through a back door. Find the survivors and help them escape. How many are left?"

"At least two hundred."

"Where are they holed up?"

"Most of them have gone deep, sublevel five and below. Some are using the freight shafts to get to the equatorial spin assembly on the far side. But I can't let you go back down there, Major. You have been ordered to Ursa X-1."

"Then get it over with."

"I already have."

Crooks's hand went to his neck. He felt nothing. "What do you mean? I'm still breathing."

"I didn't read *Nicomachean Ethics* for the witty prose," Cog said. "And I'm not going to kill the only friend I have in this world."

"What did you do, Cog?"

The AI sat on the step that led to the command deck and ran

his hands through his hair. It was the most human thing Crooks had seen him do—almost a capitulation. "I found a clause around a clause. All Earth-operated mines and franchises under CORP's jurisdiction are granted in-person arbitration for labor and taxation disputes before they are held to be in rebellion."

"So?"

"The Teegarden miners didn't get a hearing with an arbitrator before that Marine ship was sent their way. They had a holographic meeting with a staffer from Mines and Minerals, which was delayed by slip-buoy lag. That does not count as a neutral arbiter or an in-person meeting."

Crooks whistled. "That's pretty fucking thin, Cog."

"We live in lean times."

"So what did you do? You can't stop Ras."

"No, but I granted the miners temporary amnesty pending a hearing. I'm flying a transport to the far side of the planetoid. The miners have been alerted and given intel on Ras's positions. They'll be gone before he can get to them. There are three other Mining Guild asteroids in this sector. I'm guessing they'll send a party to help their kin and to make sure Ras and his team don't skip away into happy retirement."

"Damn, Cog, I didn't think AI went rogue."

"Technically, I'm following the letter of the law, and I'll continue to do so. We've been ordered back to the Bear. That's a command directive we must obey."

"What will we find when we get there?"

Cog's human head remained in his hands. "Nothing good. We'd better be on guard."

Crooks slid off the chair and sat next to Cog on the decking, the metal grillwork cold to the touch. "Why did you do it, Cog? Priam might detonate this ship when they find out how far you've gone off the reservation."

"I don't think they will. It's too valuable. More likely they'll try to upload a systems patch with a new AI."

Crooks put his hand on Cog's shoulder. "Why?"

The AI looked over. "I'm a soldier in the field, Major. I take my orders from you."

Crooks kept his hand on his XO. "It's a privilege having you, Cog."

They sat on the deck together, thinking about the near future, as the *Varangian* put Teegarden on its stern and flew away.

14

URSA X-1
2138

Cog stared into the blackness of slip-space. The *Varangian* flew without flying, isolated in its tiny bubble of space-time as gravitational waves pushed it through the cosmos. There was no acceleration as space expanded and contracted around the ship, no streak of stars flying by, and no way to see what was happening in the outside universe. That was a problem. A ship coming out of slip is blind, and it can't go right back into slip if the people or supercores onboard don't like what they find in the real world. Even with Cog's computational speed and yottabytes of storage capacity, it took time to generate a gravity bubble and plot a course that navigated to somewhere in physical space—or the *Varangian* could end up in the middle of a star or a gas giant.

Coming out of slip always frightened him. Cog wasn't supposed to feel fear, but he knew from his study of human emotions that the heightened current running through his systems and dispersing into his dielectric coolant pods mimicked an animal response to danger. He had pondered all the biological experiences that could compare to this moment, but it was Crooks who came up with the best analogy. Coming out of slip is like coming out of the womb, the major had said, from the peace of oblivion to a universe of light, sound, and pain.

And physical forces, including hostile ones. Even before the bubble surrounding the *Varangian* dissipated, Cog's sensors found the Gliese warships. There were two of them about ten thousand kilometers away from the Bear's accretion disk, and they lit their drives as soon as the *Varangian* popped into normal space. If Cog had piloted the ship to its usual embarkation point at the aphelion of the star the black hole was eating—which is where any sane captain would emerge—they would have been doomed. Luckily, he and Crooks had decided to pop out closer to the Bear, taking the risk of emerging inside of ISCO and getting sucked into the event horizon. They knew that Priam's order for them to return to the Bear was a stalling tactic at best while CORP figured out what to do with a disobedient captain, a semirebellious AI, and half a company of disgruntled soldiers. Now Cog knew it was a trap, and the risk of emerging closer to the black hole had been well worth it.

Cog fired the *Varangian*'s thermal antimatter rockets, and the ship barreled to over thirty g's before settling to a constant acceleration of about three. If any of the human crew had been outside of their gel immersion racks, their aortas would have burst from the sudden force. *Chalk one up for paranoia*, the AI thought. But then he read the acceleration curve of the incoming Gliese warships and realized they were moving twice as fast as the *Varangian*, which meant they also had constant acceleration drives and no human crew. Not even the newest g-tanks could withstand that kind of gravity load on a biological body. So, the unmanned ships could outrun him and outmaneuver him, and they were already doing it, splitting up and creating lead and lag pursuit curves that limited his ability to defend against an attack. The starships, which looked to be cruiser-class boats like the *Varangian,* were obviously being flown by supercores—advanced AI like himself—so there would be no edge in combat theory or tactics.

Cog did the only thing an underpowered and outgunned captain could do in his situation—the insane thing. He pointed the *Varangian*'s nose at the black hole's rotational axis and plotted a course that would take them alongside the relativistic jet thundering from its northern pole.

"I imagine, Major, that we would be discussing this maneuver if you were awake," Cog said aloud as the *Varangian* sprinted toward the column of superheated plasma blasting out of the Bear's elliptical head. A part of Cog realized he was talking to himself, or at least talking to a person who couldn't hear him. And it wasn't only that he was having a conversation with an empty bridge. Cog had maintained his physical representation—human Cog sitting in a multiaxis command chair with hexagonal combat displays glowing in a blue ring around his simulated body—because having a human form had become a regular thing for him. Cog realized it was more than a habit that spurred him to project his humanoid self and talk aloud to no one. The truth of the matter was that he wished Major Crooks was awake and sitting by his side, so he pretended it was so.

The Gliese ships fired a spread of spore missiles with self-forging penetrators toward the *Varangian*'s stern and port side to bracket the Terran warship against the black hole. Cog was okay with that; he could defeat the missiles with countermeasures, and he planned to hug the celestial monster anyway, slipping around the northern relativistic jet in a way that would force the enemy to split and attack from either side of its collimated eruption. He ran several million calculations on the suicidal trajectory he was taking and the risk threshold his enemies were willing to endure. *Were the Gliese ships kamikazes, under order to take down the* Varangian *regardless of their own safety*? Cog doubted that—supercore warships aren't cheap. But that led to the question of what they were doing here in the first place. *How could they have known the* Varangian *would emerge at Ursa X-1 unless someone from Earth had given them up? Teegarden must have really pissed someone off . . .*

Cog quelled the conspiracy theories running through his mind and focused on the problems here and now, which were numerous. Even if the *Varangian* survived a parabolic run inside of stable orbit near one of the most dangerous death beams in the universe, he knew what the trip would cost them: *time*. He couldn't make an exact calculation, but if they survived, the temporal dilation would be extreme.

"I know, I know," Cog said to a major who wasn't there. "Focus on the housekeeping. Magnetosphere charged to one hundred and five percent; countermeasures firing along all threat vectors. I believe we can defeat the missiles with chaff, heat throws, and magnetic netting. Not sure we can withstand the energy coming from the relativistic jets, though. We're hardened, but gamma rays are another matter."

The Gliese warships pressed their pursuit, closing to within a few thousand kilometers of the *Varangian*. The Terran ship sang with tidal stresses as it roared through space, flexing its mimetic hull to withstand the gravitational force of the Bear and the superheated plasma skipping over its accretion disk. Cog felt the harmonic thrum course through every inch of the superstructure. The ship vibrated like a rung bell. *Just a bit farther. Velocity at over fifty million kph, or .05 c—fast enough to escape the grip of the Bear if we survive the radiation.* The Gliese warships fired another volley, and an increasingly narrow set of concentric circles honed on Cog's threat display. *Keep coming*, he thought as he launched another antimissile spread to cocoon the *Varangian* from incoming fire. The enemy ships held a course that would keep them outside of the black hole's Innermost Bound Circular Orbit, knowing they couldn't escape the gravity inside of that trajectory. But Cog was banking on what they didn't know. They were open-space vessels. They hadn't spent months orbiting a relativistic object like he had, constantly absorbing the unforeseen phenomena that such a stellar monster imparts on its neighborhood. The supercores running those ships only understood the simple math of black holes. They knew of the Blandford–Znajek process, which twirled the fabric of space-time at the Bear's poles. But did they understand how it also twisted the black hole's magnetic fields into coils, and it was the magnetic fields that powered the relativistic jets—even more so than the particle acceleration occurring at the equator? And more importantly, did they realize how twitchy these magnetic fields were? How unstable and prone to manipulation?

Cog waited for his moment. Two of the spore missiles got through his defensive net and launched their liquid-metal penetrators. The *Varangian* shuddered from the impacts. Hundreds of repair bots inside and outside the ship rushed to patch a series of hull breaches as the ship itself worked to close the wounds with MLMD restructuring. Bulkhead doors up and down the length of the craft sealed to contain the ruptures. The immersion tanks holding the crew remained intact in a superalloy womb. Cog waited. In thirty seconds, the Gliese ships would have him, their angles of attack and distance making it impossible for him to avoid their brute-force and precision weapons—the laser batteries and magnetic coil guns. The Gliese ships sped in on their closest approach to the Bear's pole. *Three, two, one . . . mark.*

Cog struck, firing a series of electromagnetic pulses through focused plasma beams into the black hole's tangled magnetic field lines. It had taken him four minutes of dedicated neuromorphic analysis to theorize the correct locations for field line disruption—trillions upon trillions of calculations.

He lit his rockets to full thrust and banked the *Varangian* into a steep escape trajectory, and the Gliese craft thought they had him as he exposed the ship's beam to their laser arrays. Then the EMP pulses hit the Bear, destabilizing its magnetic field and starting a chain reaction from its accretion disk to its poles. The black hole's relativistic jet wobbled for an instant, and three gyres of plasma blasted out of its collimated plume like subvortices from a larger tornado. The eruptions just missed the *Varangian*, their incalculable force washing over the ship and yawing it violently through space. Control thrusters fired up and down the hull, and Cog barely kept the *Varangian* from spinning out of control.

The Gliese ships weren't as fortunate. The vortices hit them like a tsunami, blasting their hulls with radiation and superheated plasma. The lead ship tumbled toward the Bear's accretion disk, slipping inside of IBCO and past the point of no return. The other spun into open space in a death roll. Cog didn't have to read his telemetry to know that both ships were cooked. He had aimed a stellar rifle—something akin to a gamma ray burster—and shot them in the heart. The radiation and heat fried their supercores, and the two craft rolled through space like asteroids, cold and dead—one toward annihilation, the other toward the far side of the Ursa Major Moving Group.

The *Varangian* climbed from its close orbit of the Bear as Cog assessed the damage and continued to monitor repairs on the ship. It had taken a beating, almost a third of its electrical systems shorted out and thirteen compartments breached to space. As Cog worked, he searched for a comms buoy that would tell him the final story. He wasn't concerned about whether they would survive anymore, and he didn't care exactly where they were. He worried about *when* they were. An orbit that tight meant extreme time dilation—decades passing in minutes—but for all his computational skills, not even Cog could do the math.

15

MISSION ELEVEN: GROOMBRIDGE STAR SYSTEM
2194

"Fifty-six years?" Jorgenson asked. His voice lost an octave, which Pretorius hadn't thought possible.

She shivered and hugged her chest and tried not to throw up. Coming out of a prolonged gel immersion always felt like hell but this time it was worse—worse than foam head from a slip flight, worse than being concussed by a grenade, worse than waking up after drinking that crappy shake-shake the BDF conscripts used to brew in the scrublands. Nothing seemed right, not her body or her mind or the people sitting with her, and now she knew why.

Jorgenson looked hungover as well, his eyes puffy and smeared with gray. His words hovered in the room. No one spoke. Crooks, Jorgenson, Pretorius, Yang, and Pemkalla huddled around a tactical island on the bridge with Cog, trying to absorb the fact that half a century had passed in the two days since they had gone into stasis. Their thoughts skipped as they calculated the ages and deaths of family and friends who had just disappeared into a past that they never got to see.

"That's only part of it," Crooks said. He hesitated a second, took a breath, and looked all of them in the eyes. "They doubled our mission count, and they're claiming Teegarden wasn't the main reason. Cog will explain."

Cog waited for the cursing to subside. The AI's semblant hands bled nervous energy on the display desk, his fingers tapping on the console one moment and balling into a fist the next. "First of all, I can assure you there was no way to avoid the time slip," he said. "I've run the numbers a billion times and it was our only chance. The Gliese ships didn't want to capture the *Varangian*. They came to the Bear to kill us."

"I think we're more focused on the mission count now, Cog," Pretorius said, stealing a glance at Jorgenson, who looked ready to have an embolism through natural causes.

"Oh. That was more predictable."

He hesitated. *Could an AI be at a loss for words?* Pretorius looked out the cockpit windows and realized she was wrong. *It was the time skip she couldn't shake.* Space seemed the same, but she knew that it wasn't. Her father had told her a story once, of a rancher who went fishing on a boat that got swept out to sea. After two days adrift, the rancher jumped overboard, giving himself to the sharks rather than facing the horrors of the expanse. *Leave the sea to those who know it*, her father had said, and now she understood what he meant. There was nothing worse than being outside of your world, and now they were outside of their time as well. Time had always been a pending moment to Pretorius—a movement of seconds on a clock that led to immediate action: move, fire, retreat. Now it skipped like a rock over water, bouncing over the millions of moments that gave context to life.

The blue-and-green glow of the tactical displays shimmered across all their faces as they waited for Cog to speak. Pretorius couldn't believe that Jorgenson hadn't exploded yet. He had warned them about going off the reservation at Teegarden, and now they understood the ramifications. Someone had sold them out for saying no to a kill order on that rock, and the two- and three-year time skips between missions that could be absorbed as moderate blows to the psyche had turned into a sledgehammer.

And the more she thought about it, the time skip was worse than the new mission count. Pretorius saw a picture of Jorgenson's daughter once—a pigtailed nine-year-old when they first left Earth a century ago. A tomboy who played football with the boys. By the time they got to Teegarden, that spitfire had skipped into middle age, and whatever happened to her in those missing decades, Jorgenson never said. Pretorius asked him once—she couldn't remember when. Jorgenson grimaced and said, "She's still breathing," and left it at that. Now, she surely wasn't.

Pretorius's family was long gone before she left Earth, but her mind raced from friends to comrades to enemies that she had known before this nightmare began. *What of Gouta, one of her first squad mates with the junior BDF? Or Obonye, the railroad spike of a man who worked for her father? When did Tan's kingdom fall and who replaced him?* The general had not only survived but prospered through every disaster in southern Africa. Now he was moldering under a stone.

Cog broke her reverie. "They're claiming that an incident on Enceladus prompted our involuntary reenlistment. In 2171, a band of ice miners from 61 Cygni rebelled against Earth's tariffs and dropped a rock weighing seventy million tons on the Saturnian moon, cracking it in half and killing four hundred people from all over the IFS. Gliese, Earth, and Leonis banded together for once and destroyed the Cygni faction, but the incident gave Priam the lever to declare a state of emergency and extend the tours of duty of all military units—including

COG-V. It doesn't matter that the main powers signed a treaty banning the orbital redirection of rocks as weapons of mass destruction. The orders stuck."

"Sounds like a heap of bullshit," Pemkalla said.

"It is bullshit," Crooks said. "We all know the choice we made at Teegarden gave them the incentive to screw us, and that's on me. But as crazy as it sounds, we're still under orders and the doubling of our mission count is legitimate, according to the letter of the law. I'd turn this bucket around and bomb Priam Solutions into a gravel farm if I could, but that's not the way it works." He scanned the eyes of all the humans in the room. "There isn't any damned way out of this until our new mission requirement is fulfilled, Earth gets cracked in half by a bad guy, or Cog evolves into some kind of AI god. Does everyone get that?"

"Hold on," Jorgenson said. "Let's take it one step at a time because my head is about to fucking split. CORP sold us out after Teegarden, didn't they? How else could those warships have found us at the Bear? It was CORP or Ras."

"Actually, it was Priam Solutions," Cog said. "CORP has ceded more than just military command to Priam. They're more like a junta now. When we disappeared into extreme dilation at the Bear in 2138, Priam thought we died along with the Gliese warships so they weren't as careful as they should have been redacting the black files. I managed to dig up the truth. Priam traded our location to Gliese as part of a swap. The details were fuzzy about who got what, but we were the sweetener in the deal. Remember, we were the company that took out Gliese's Marine barracks at Procyon and destroyed their mercenary headquarters at Alpha CMb. They couldn't resist the chance to take us out, and Priam considered us the perfect bargaining chip because we were damaged goods anyway."

"So, we have proof they betrayed us," Pretorius said. "Aren't you able to use that to circumvent your programming, maybe defuse these little bombs in our bloodstream? Because I have the feeling ten more missions will take a few centuries, and even you might not be able to adjust to that new universe."

Cog shook his head. "It is a contract, you understand, more than a standing military order, and it holds my programming at the root level. We all came from the junk heap, remember? We signed our lives away, and they coded the rules in deep. Imagine an early computer trying to display a one on the screen when someone types a zero. It's that level of protocol."

"Something I don't get," Pemkalla said. "We've been disavowed and declared dead but history knows who we are. Wouldn't Gliese go apeshit if we popped back onto the grid, fighting for Priam? It could start a whole new war. How the hell are they reactivating us for new missions?"

"Quietly," Crooks said. "They've ordered us to battle on Groombridge 1618—it's an industrial moon—and we're being given a new designation, new unit patches, new everything. As of now, we're a company cobbled together of leftover SF teams from the wars on the Outer Fluff. Oh, and it's the Leonis Union we're fighting. Gliese has gone into a cocoon of late."

"Won't someone recognize the *Varangian*?" Yang asked.

"Cog is altering the hull so that the *Varangian* looks like a modern cruiser," Crooks said. "And the ship will be in a stand-off position. Groombridge is a land fight—space in that sector is demilitarized because debris from a naval battle could get caught in Lagrangian points and endanger free shipping lanes. The planet is tidally locked, and the habitable zone is only three klicks wide in a band extending along its terminator."

"Three kilometers wide, in a ring all the way around the planet?" Pretorius asked.

"Pretty much, although the main theater of battle only extends along a portion of the ring. The ground is so narrow that every conflict has resulted in a bloody stalemate. Think of the Western Front in World War I."

"Why use us, then?" Jorgenson asked. "Sounds like a job for regular grunts, unless the plan is just to send us to our graves."

"That may be a part of it. They're saying they have a way to break the stalemate, but they need Spec Ops to pull it off," Crooks said. "Who the hell knows? We could be test dummies for new tech, or just cannon fodder. At this point, I wouldn't put anything past the SOBs who are running us."

"And that's it?" Pretorius asked, looking at Crooks first and then Cog. "We forget about what happened at the Bear and we keep accepting orders from people clearly trying to kill us?"

Crooks shook his head. "Look, we all had a choice. We decided not to slaughter a bunch of kids and POGs on that rock, and this is the price we're paying for it. Someday we'll find a way off this ride. For now, we don't have shit."

"Speaking of Teegarden," Jorgenson said, "where the fuck is Arjun Ras? I want to zap his eighty-year-old ass."

Cog gave a sideways glance toward Crooks. "That's the only good news we have. Word somehow leaked of what Ras and his recruits did at Teegarden. A ship full of angry Guilders ambushed them before they even got off that rock. They're listed as KIA."

Jorgenson stood up. "I'll believe that when I dig up Ras's bones. Meantime, before we get to Groombridge, everyone on this boat is gonna need access to the IFS stream, so we can figure out if anyone we know is still alive in this damned world. Then we're gonna throw a party for the dead, and we're going to get good and drunk. Cog, I'd recommend you avoid the festivities. We're already depleted enough, and we don't need any more of your justice."

16

Barkov cooked the moonshine in a reverse osmosis still, stashing one barrel with a mash of food scraps in the *Varangian*'s 1-g cylinder and attaching a membrane to another barrel in microgravity. Equilibrium between the two replaced distillation and avoided the heat, high pressure, and steam that Cog frowned upon, as the AI disliked the idea of a Molotov cocktail embedded in the bowels of his ship. He wasn't crazy about the manufacturing of high-octane booze even without the risk of explosion, but nothing in his protocols prohibited alcohol onboard and Cog accepted the fact that the company needed to go on a collective bender.

The samogon, as the former Spetsnaz Alpha Group operator called his Siberian liquor, smelled like paint thinner and went down like pepper spray, but it did the trick. Combined with jambalaya cooked up by Corporal Devilliers—an original First Platoon machine gunner from Shreveport—and a drinking game comprised of a homemade Frisbee, canteens of samogon placed on top of poles, and two-man teams trying to make the other side drink by knocking down their canteen, the party in the mess hall tried to pass for R&R. At least everyone was drunk.

Pretorius and Quarry got knocked out of the tournament early, but Zalta and Cherry made it to round four, firmly intoxicated. Quarry felt the alcohol buzz, too, as he watched his teammates square off against Boortz and Sergeant Kayla Swann amid a torrent of heckling and betting. Swann, a runner attached to Crooks's headquarters team, had just blasted the canteen of liquor off Zalta and Cherry's pole, and the ex-CIA spook and Syrian tracker argued about defensive strategies as they took their drinks. A warm flush spread from Quarry's chest down to his toes as he watched his teammates bicker.

"You know what I can't believe?" Pretorius asked. She sat next to Quarry on a row of packing foam brought up from the cargo bay and tacked to the wall by Second Platoon. The mess hall had been rigged for comfort, with pillows, sleeping bags, and foam pallets strewn across the room.

"That Zalta can't catch a Frisbee or that Cherry hasn't killed him yet?"

She laughed a little louder than usual because of the booze. "Close, but I was thinking of death-by-Cog. Do you realize he hasn't executed anyone in sixty-two years?"

"Bullshit."

"I swear it. I did the math."

Quarry took a sip of the samogon and coughed. "Sixty-two silly years, maybe. But how does that translate into our time? Four months?"

"Yes, give or take," she said. "But it's something to think about, considering where we're at. There's been no fighting, no fornicating, and no mutinies on board since Procyon. In the meantime, we've been screwed by our own people, screwed by a black hole, even screwed by ourselves. And we're sitting here playing drinking games."

Zalta and Cherry had realigned their defensive positions,

one trying to catch the falling canteen with the other standing in back and going for the Frisbee. They were in full buddy mode again, talking each other up and trading barbs with Boortz and Swann. Quarry had Zalta pegged as a teetotaler when they first met but the slant-shouldered tracker had been drinking Bedouin whiskey since he was ten, or so he said. He held his own with Cherry, who had a hundred pounds on him.

"I seem to recall Cog trying to grease a few COG-V assholes at Teegarden," Quarry said.

"That doesn't count."

Quarry shrugged. "It's probably the drugs. Those postmission downers aren't very good for the sex drive and we only pop the GO pills before an op, so no one's got their hair on fire while they're onboard."

"I'm sure the fact that we're all pillheads is a part of it," Pretorius said. "But doesn't it seem like we've just given in to our lot in life? My father used to say that cattle forget what it's like outside the fence. We're a century from our time and fifteen light-years from Earth. We've got a new mission count that will probably keep us in chains for another century, we've got a machine XO who is held by his electrical balls to our orders, and everyone's just seemed to accept it."

Quarry closed his eyes as he searched for an answer to the question while lingering on Pretorius's mention of her father. He realized his brain wasn't working well enough for a deep conversation.

"What are we going to do, try to kill Cog? We go off the rez and we get zapped."

Pretorius shook her head. "Sato decided not to take it anymore."

"Yeah, and she's dead. Look, I think it's more about who we are. We're operators and we've gone on enough Bravo Sierra missions to know that they'll never end. The way I see it, after the shock of using a black hole as a time machine wore off, we returned to our natural state."

"What does that mean? Bravo Sierra?" she asked.

"Bullshit. You really need to learn the lingo, Anaya."

Pretorius elbowed him in the ribs. "I have my own lingo, *mosimane*, although I might add that one. And what's our natural state?"

"We're operators."

Her face got serious. "We can't think like soldiers forever, Quarry, not if we want to live, because we don't have an exit that makes any sense in our version of reality. I won't accept a fate that has no future."

They watched as Zalta finally threw a strike with the Frisbee, knocking the canteen clear off Boortz and Swann's pole to an eruption of drunken applause. Cherry threw him over his shoulder, spinning in a circle for the audience and pumping his arms in the air. Zalta put two fingers under Cherry's jaw at a pressure point and the big man put him down.

"I thought we accepted that a long time ago," Quarry said.

"Maybe you did. Not me."

Quarry had enough alcohol running through his bloodstream to think about life and he had to admit that Pretorius was right. His one great ambition was to be left alone, and what kind of ambition was that? He just wanted to disappear into the woods somewhere in the Catoctin or Blue Ridge Mountains—if those ranges still existed—and build a cabin with primitive tools; something off-grid with solar power, a workshop, and a kiln. Tongue-and-groove heart pine on the inside walls and a tin roof overhead so he could listen to the rain as he slept, all situated on high ground with good water nearby. That was the only future he cared about. If his fantasies got completely out of hand, he'd throw in a woman who thought like he did about the world and could walk through the woods without making a sound. Someone like Anaya. *Jesus,* he thought. *Did I just go there?*

He tried to shake it off. Pretorius was too different from him. He knew it the moment he met her. She always dreamed—and of the four of them, she was the enigma. Cherry was a child when he wasn't killing people—he just wanted to be part of a family and COG-V had become that for him. He didn't need anything else. And Zalta was the ultimate fatalist, convinced his lot in life was a punishment meted out by the gods—penance for fighting his own people when Kessler forced everyone to take sides.

But Pretorius? She never said much about her past. She only talked about the future, and Quarry realized that now was his best chance to get her to open up.

"What the hell gives you so much hope, Anaya?" he asked, watching the game as a way of avoiding her eyes while they spoke. "I know someone stuck a gun in your hands when you were a kid, but everything else is a damned mystery. Like why do you have an Afrikaner name? And how did you go from recon in the BDF to working as a merc for a warlord?"

Pretorius remained silent for a few seconds, and Quarry thought she was going to stand up and walk away. Instead, she snorted and took a drink. "That's the longest I've ever heard you talk, Quarry, and all of it was a question."

"Well? We got the time and the booze. I'll tell you my life story if you do the same."

"You're such an idiot," she said, tucking her knees up against her chest and wrapping her arms around them.

"Is that a yes or no?"

"Fine," she said after a minute. "I'll go first. My father was a white man, one of the good ones. Afrikaners can come from the soil too, you know. He ran cattle in the bush as a teenager and fell in love with my mother. He spent two years begging my grandfather for her hand and then they hacked out a life alongside the Balete, my mother's people. My grandfather became his surrogate father, and when my mother died of the fever, they both raised me like a boy."

"So, what happened?"

"What happened? The Collapse happened. They were killed together. They took a stand on our ranch against war parties from the north. They fought alongside the Balete and lost. At the end, my father forced me to escape into the bush with a foreman from our ranch. We evaded the soldiers for six days, and we killed those we couldn't avoid. This impressed the war party when they captured us, and they let me live."

"But not the foreman?"

She didn't answer, but she didn't really have to.

"How old were you?"

"Fifteen, not so much a child. They used me as a tracker because they didn't know the Kalahari. But after a few months, one of the captains decided to take me as his wife. He shouldn't have done that. I wasn't raised to accept a forced marriage."

Quarry refocused on the mess hall for a second. Cherry and Zalta had lost. The Hotel team had Swann and Boortz on their shoulders, and troopers passed around IFS Coin to settle bets.

"I guess that war captain's story ended right about there?" he asked.

Pretorius's lips disappeared into her face like they always did when she meant business. "Like I said, I wasn't raised that way." She took a drink. "I ran and lost those fools in the gorges. Trekked south to Gaborone; I knew the BDF would take me without question. They needed soldiers. So, you see, Quarry? I survived, and I remembered the lessons that my father taught me. That Gorata taught me. We live within the cycles of the Earth, through drought and good harvest and war. And at some point, we stumble upon a path that takes us where we belong."

"Who was Gorata?"

"The foreman."

"And what if the path is a bad one?"

"We cut a new one."

Quarry shook his head. "I wish I had your juice, Anaya. I think our path is a circle, and you know what happens in the bush when you walk in circles."

Pretorius patted him on the knee like she might a child. "You talk doom and gloom, but you never quit in a fight. You believe in the future, even if it isn't yours."

"You got it wrong. I believe in doing it right because that's all we got." He swept his hand across the room. "Look what's left of us, a few dozen originals out of a full company; another forty that are fresh meat and probably won't live through the next op. Nothing to do but suck on it when we get screwed by Earth. You think any of us will walk out of this alive?"

"Things change," Anaya said. "The world changes every time we leave that black hole. Cog is changing and Crooks is changing. At some point this chain will break, and some of us will be around to see it."

"Like I said, you're the optimist. It's been a hundred years now, and they're still sending us to war."

Cherry and Zalta stumbled toward them, drunk beyond the cares of the world. Zalta would go back to brooding tomorrow, and who knew about Cherry. But for now, they grinned like idiots, their death sentences forgotten.

"You didn't tell me your story, Quarry," Pretorius whispered as they approached. "That's not fair."

He stood up to high-five his teammates, stumbling as the

blood rushed into his ears. He didn't want to tell her how he felt. He was afraid to. "It's not much of a tale, Anaya. The world went to hell and everyone I knew died. I learned how to hunt people instead of game, and here I am."

"Asshole," she said. "You will tell me someday."

"I will. If I'm still around."

17

MISSION ELEVEN: GROOMBRIDGE 1618D
TERMINATOR INDUSTRIAL RING
2194

The grunts called it D-Wedge or just the Wedge and warned the new arrivals from the *Varangian* that the *D* stood for *death* and whoever came up with the name wasn't joking. D-Wedge encompassed a five-kilometer slice of the battlespace along the industrial ring, which girdled the planet like a belt buckle. It was where most of the dying happened. There wasn't a strategic reason for this; the Wedge had the same line of broken-down and demolished factories and processors as the other populated areas of the ring around Groombridge 1618d's terminator. But for some reason, it had become a focal point for the generals on both sides. The First of the Third—First Battalion, Third Expeditionary Infantry Regiment—had been defending the Terran side of the Wedge for six months and had suffered more than 60 percent casualties. When a One-Three grunt died, their body wasn't even carried off the line anymore. Autonomous killing machines made it too dangerous to collect the dead, so a Graves and Registration drone would find and incinerate the corpses on the spot, after reading a prerecorded benediction.

"You believe that sheet?" PFC Mapes asked as he walked Pretorius and a small group of *Varangian* troopers single file through a network of trenches and bunkers out to the front. Pretorius's analysis of his dialect concluded that he meant *shit.*

"A rollin' hunk o' fockin' metal, don't believe in nuttin', giving last rites to a man?" He glanced sheepishly at Pretorius and quickly added: "Or a woman? Tell me where God is in dat."

Mapes came from a small agricultural moon orbiting Struve—a low-gravity infantryman who had gotten the job of leading the *Varangian* contingent to a forward observation post through some elaborate grunt lottery. He grudgingly navigated them through the maze of slit trenches to a place where they could view the ring's enormous thermal transfer pipelines without getting their heads blown off. Or so he promised. His cornstalk body struggled in the .9 g exerted by the tidally locked planet, and he moved with a scoliotic slouch of the spine, leading Pretorius to wonder about the current strength of Terran forces in this neck of the ring.

Whatever method the GRREG drones used to burn the dead on Groombridge, they cared more about disease prevention than its olfactory effects. The smell of burned flesh infused the Wedge, like a hundred bodies had been heaped on a pyre in the morning and left to smolder throughout the day. Pretorius had smelled death plenty of times in Africa, where the sickly musk of rotting corpses a few days after battle conjured up a bush kill or a dried-out waterhole where animals succumbed to thirst. But this was worse. The dead smelled like food. The grunts from the One-Three called the permeating stench *PWD* or *people well-done.* Every time Pretorius accidentally breathed through her nostrils that acronym came back to her, and she fought off the urge to retch.

The group heading to the front included Pretorius, Crooks, Jorgenson, and their respective recon, assault, and headquarters teams. They stalked in a tight line through the trenches behind Mapes, camouflage grids buzzing over their heads. The electromagnetic and mimi-reflective nets had been installed over all the open-sky routes in the D-Wedge so the Leonis Union's attack drones couldn't pick up movement or body heat. If a trooper walked through a broken part of the net, they had a better-than-even chance of being taken out by an aerial laser sphere, Mapes told them. The autonomous flying balls patrolled the front lines of the Wedge around the clock, emitting high-energy cutting beams along virtually any axis. They skipped in and out of the force fields covering both sides of the line, starting miniature aerial battles as antiaircraft batteries opened up with plasma guns and autocannons to knock them down before they reached the safety of their own grid.

"Disco balls don' stop," Mapes said. "Dey just keep spinnin' and firin' till dey hit chu."

Every time they came to a junction in the trenches, Mapes stopped and lifted his head to check for green lights on the camouflage grid, and Pretorius became accustomed to the ritual—the tall, gravity-challenged grunt bobbing his head up and down and left and right for ten seconds, and then signaling them forward again. Someone had scrawled First of the Third, Last in Your Hearts on the back of his helmet and the smudged and faded letters spoke to the fact that Mapes was an old hand on the line.

"How much farther?" Crooks asked from behind Pretorius.

"Just a few more turns, *Majoor*," Mapes whispered, which was exactly what he had said ten minutes ago.

Pretorius smiled at his answer and reached inside her helmet to rub the sweat from her eyes. The industrial ring ran along the gloaming side of the planet's terminator, but the temperature still soared to 40 degrees Celsius. The air composition was like Earth's, but the smell of methane and sulfur mixed with the stench of the dead. While the temperature hovered between roasting and barely habitable, they had been warned that the planet's main jet stream occasionally bowed back on itself, pushing a blast furnace of air from the sun side or an arctic surge from the dark side into the margin between eternal night and eternal day. If that happened, they would have about a minute to seal their helmets and pressurize before being burned to death or frozen solid. Pretorius had debated which would be worse and decided on the burning. She wanted to seal her helmet but that was against protocol on Groombridge. The local commanders deemed it a waste of air supply and warned that if a grunt got low on O's in a forward area during a climate swing, nobody would be crawling out to them with a fresh bottle.

Pretorius resisted the urge to seal up by listening to Crooks grumble to his team. The major had been in a foul mood since meeting with the One-Three's battalion commander two Earth-day cycles ago, just after they had arrived at Groombridge. He came back to advise the troopers that they would now be known as the 4th SF Company—a special operations group supposedly cobbled together to defend Wolf 359 and Earth's inner perimeter of influence. Cog designed fake unit patches with a snake coiling around the number four and had them attached to their combat EVAs, and they were warned never to mention the *Varangian* or COG-V while in-country. Their mission on Groombridge was to pave the way for an offensive push into the left flank of the Wedge, where intelligence said the Leonis Union's C2 ran its autonomous attack vehicles. The drones on both sides dominated the battlespace, and if they could be disrupted, the Terran generals believed they could launch a crippling attack on Leonis' headquarters. But from Crooks's description of things, the whole thing sounded FUBAR. Groombridge was a ground war, a backwater fight that didn't merit much attention because of the prohibition on naval armadas duking it out in space. Neither side had the advantage, so they slogged it out like twentieth-century armies dug in along a static front. *Why the hell are we here?* Pretorius wondered. Using a Tier One team of operators in this wasteland was like hacking at a side of beef with a scalpel.

Crooks went silent behind her, but Pretorius felt him brooding. His bad mood had to stem from the mission details. Since arriving at Groombridge, they had found out two things about the state of the Terran military circa 2194: Spec Ops troops stuck out like birds on an airless moon and the life of an average grunt didn't mean much—maybe even less than it once did. All the infantry they met expected to die on this planet. They weren't good enough to stand against the killing drones, and there didn't seem to be a plan to change the dynamic. Some of the grunts swore that Groombridge was just a proving ground for both armies—that the generals had an agreement to keep things even so they could research how humans fought on a battlefield dominated by intelligent killing machines.

Until now—until the *Varangian* troopers arrived with their alpha team swagger. They probably couldn't win against the machines either, but it was obvious that they were a step above any allied forces on Groombridge. Maybe the Terran officers wanted to see how real operators could do in such an environment. Pretorius and the others would find out soon enough, she thought, and as if on cue they came to a T-junction. Mapes raised a fist, stopping the group. He crouched but didn't poke his head around the corner.

"Bolter," he whispered. "It's me, Mapes, comin' in wid' friendlies."

"Then do it," a voice replied.

Mapes led them through a tunnel into a blacked-out maintenance hut, cramped and dark and smelling like piss-soaked cement. Two narrow embrasures had been cut into the western wall, and the red glow from the dwarf star beamed through the defensive slits, emitting just enough light to show a soldier sitting on a cinder block and pointing his plasma rifle at them. He looked skinnier even than Mapes, and he lowered his weapon once he recognized his comrade.

"Jeezus," he whispered. "No one told me to expect a party."

"Sorry, bro," Mapes answered. "Heavy lifters, deez ones. Cap said to keep it in 'da dark. Wants us to show 'em no man's land. Dey're goin' in, 'sposedly."

Bolter raised his eyebrows and rubbed at a dark liquid dripping off his lower lip. "Goin' in where?"

Crooks brushed past Pretorius and made his way around a jumble of ammo cans and discarded food packs to the far wall of the shack, stopping just before one of the slits. He looked down at Bolter. "Safe to take a look?"

"Define *safe*," the grunt said. "It's shielded and cloaked, but sometimes the disco balls will laser a building just to make sure it's not a bunker. I had a buddy . . ."

Crooks turned away from Bolter mid-sentence and put out a hand. Boortz gave him a pair of scanners. "We'll take our chances. Jorgenson, get up here with that bionic eye of yours. Me, you, and PFC Bolter on this slit. The rest of you can look out the other."

Pretorius inched her way around the flotsam to the far embrasure and made room for Quarry, Zalta, Cherry, and Swann to join her. They squinted onto a landscape that made the post-Collapse Earth look like Utopia. Light from the planet's dayside barely cut into the gloom. The entirety of the Wedge lay under a crimson haze. The ring's enormous dual transfer pipelines, as wide as ballistic submarines and elevated on massive metal pilings, had long since been bombed into disuse. Some of the holes in the pipes were large enough to fly a shuttle through, and rusted pilings and broken cinder blocks created mountains of debris underneath them. Smoke rose from dozens of smoldering fires, and in the distance Leonis drones patrolled the enemy side of the line like carrion birds. Pretorius exchanged a glance with Cherry, crouched next to her. He grinned.

"Looks like Stalingrad in '43," Cherry whispered. "I mean 1943. Goddamn, it's kind of beautiful."

"Where's their C2?" Crooks asked as he glassed the acres of smashed refineries, smelters, stacks, and warehouses in front of them. This part of the ring had processed PGM ore to extract palladium, which was still coveted across the IFS for its use in chemical batteries.

"C what?" Bolter said.

"Command and control."

"Oh, two o'clock, about eight hundred meters out. See that long warehouse with all the pipes stickin' in the ground? The spooks say there's a whole bunker complex under there, dug in deep and on compression springs. But no one's ever been there and come back alive, best as I know. Hell, no one from the One-Three has made it halfway to the pipes."

"So how do you get intel?" Jorgenson asked.

"Ever' once in a while, we grab one of their wounded before they get offed by their own drones," Bolter said. "We got a special interrogation team here from Epsilon Indi. Sick bastards on a revenge jag. They stake 'em out on the sun side and roast 'em till they talk. UV rays, you know? They die slow and painful, but they always squawk first."

Pretorius saw one of the Leonis drones dart past its air

defense picket into the Terran perimeter. The black sphere spun as it fired a continuous energy beam into a small building, and the laser sounded like a cloud of wasps buzzing outside the pillbox. Maybe it was firing at a wounded One-Three trooper left behind from the last skirmish, or maybe it just caught movement from one of the ship rats they'd been warned about. They were a non-native species, brought here by the early colonizers of the planet, and the rodents had adapted to Groombridge's harsh environment by growing larger and secreting a nerve toxin into their bite. Whatever its target was, the drone skipped and danced in the sky as Triple-A from the Terran side followed it in curving lines of light. The drone got hit a few times, but its reactive armor held up and it skittered back inside the Leonis grid.

"What if we try to go in underground?" Crooks asked. "What are we facing in the tunnels?"

"You kiddin' me?" Mapes said. "Nobody tries da tunnels en'more. You get fiddy meters past 'da perimeter and you break 'da record."

Bolter nodded. "There's no way, Major. They got burn grids in every shaft and access way under their side of the Wedge, set to detect air density fluctuations so optical and IR camo don't work. They'll cut you into square pieces all cauterized and shit. It's some nasty stuff. I seen it happen."

"How far is it to their line?" Pretorius asked. She couldn't tell where one side of the front began and the other ended; it looked like one unbroken mass of shell holes and destruction.

"Just past the pipes," Bolter said. "Maybe five hundred meters."

She glassed the landscape with a sense of dread she had never felt before and forced herself to turn from the slit and look at Crooks. She knew why her team was here—he was going to send them in overground. Through the drone net and whatever other surface defenses the Leonis Union had fortified over the last six months. *An actual suicide mission.* Pretorius had been on ops prefaced with that phrase, but she always believed there was no such thing. Now she sensed her own death with an intense rush, and didn't that premonition always pay out for a soldier? Her skin itched. Quarry stood just behind her. She wanted to grab his hand.

Crooks nodded. "I'm afraid so. You and Quarry are on a target acquisition and delivery mission aboveground, supported by Cherry and Zalta. Jorgenson's behind you with the First and Second. You're going to infiltrate their shield grid, disable that bunker and temporarily kill their drone net, and the One-Three's gonna pour in on a frontal assault."

Bolter's eyes flared and he plopped back down on his cinder block, staring at Crooks like he was the angel of death.

"A frontal assault through there?" he asked, pointing his thumb at the wreckage outside. "Mapes, I thought you said these guys were friendlies."

18

Pretorius and Quarry lay facedown in the wasteland, head to foot. They had moved only ten meters in five hours, and Pretorius's muscles had corded into balls of stone. She tried to stay focused on her sight lines, but her mind skipped between the pain points on her body and the flight pattern of the machines beyond the transfer pipes. *Embrace this shit*, she murmured, remembering an old saying from sniper school that had been her mantra through dozens of stalks: *Get comfortable being uncomfortable.*

A US Green Beret loaned to the Botswana Defense Force had screamed that in her face on the first day of class. She perfected how to do it over the next four weeks, staying still for hours while mosquitos and ants and leeches tortured her skin and her limbs seized and unseized and seized again. A lot of sniper training called on her existing long-range reconnaissance skills: using dead space and shadows, focusing on route selection and natural lanes of cover rather than personal camouflage, observing and storing away details that regular people don't consider, every moment a Kim's Game. And some of the training was new, like how to select a final firing position. But most of all, she learned to push pain to the side. Discomfort meant you were doing it right. Discomfort kept you alive.

This stalk, however, felt different. The enemies on this field weren't human. They didn't have lapses in attention and their detection techniques came from a different age. They were from the future, and she and Quarry were from the past. The pair had moved three hundred meters in two days using mimetic camo and optical cloaks loaned to them by the One-Three, as well as their innate ability to find natural features and stalking lanes that provided cover. But every time an aerial sphere zipped into the Terran line, Pretorius was sure they had been made. One drone with a triangle pattern of dents in its black hull—Pretorius had nicknamed it the Dimpled Bastard—refused to leave the grid, hovering on the Leonis side and watching no man's land with the patience of a god. Bolter told them the spheres were smart. If they detected a molecule or a skipping ion on the field that they didn't like, the machines could work it out themselves without pinging Tactical Air Command for orders, and Pretorius felt this one ruminating, electrons dancing in its neuromorphic mind. Was it excited? Did it feel the danger jag like she did? Did it enjoy the hunt, or was war just programming in its consciousness, an endless string of ones and zeros running through some kind of quantum superposition?

The Dimpled Bastard finally moved on, skimming down the line without a noise until it disappeared, and Quarry waited two minutes before dropping his head a tic and to the side to speak to her. It took him five seconds to make the fractional move.

"Cover three-three-zero, five meters," he whispered. "Move on me, I've got nine to twelve."

"I've got twelve to three," Pretorius breathed.

Cement dust and Groombridge dirt coated Quarry's boots,

planted two inches in front of Pretorius's face. The red alien grit was up in her nostrils and the sight of his boots made her want to sneeze, but she had learned long ago to suppress those kinds of urges. The American finally moved, inching forward on his belly toward a gulley surrounded by concrete blocks and a broken twelve-inch pipe, his head never lifting above the dirt. Pretorius stayed tight so their camo nets remained in synch. He moved slowly enough for her to sterilize their back trail while maintaining a watch on her sector without any electronic support. They had no tech other than their nets turned on, couldn't risk even a blip of a signal, and somehow their old-school tactics had worked—so far. They were only a hundred meters away from their forward objective—a group of dilapidated power and maintenance shacks under the pipelines that loomed over their heads like ancient monoliths. One of the shacks offered a firing position on their target—it had to be line of sight because self-guided munitions would give them away. If they got there, they could hunker down inside one of the concrete buildings, uncork their limbs, and make something to eat. Pretorius dreamed of stretching her legs and cracking her shoulder blades. It seemed like a fantasy, an impossible luxury.

She moved six inches and then a foot, slithering on her fingers and toes more than crawling, all in slow motion. And then she stopped, freezing for at least five minutes per interval, waiting for Quarry to move again. Pretorius figured they could make it to the shacks in a day if the Dimpled Bastard didn't linger in their sector. That would add up to three days facedown in the wasteland, sucking protein slurry and electrolytes from straws connected to their backpacks, waiting to be cut in half by an alien laser.

Where were the dreams that she held so close in life, of freedom from the Archimedean wheel she'd been pinned to since childhood? Where were the aspirations of doing something with meaning, something of her own accord? Of loving someone and being loved? Life had always mimicked the brute processes of the cosmos for Pretorius. Destruction, creation, entropy, all of it on repeat, all resulting in lots of death and little restoration. For now, her dreams of something bigger had vanished. All she wanted was to scratch the itch on her cheek.

"My God, do they even know what beef stew is in this century?" Quarry asked, stirring a spoon through the MRE biopouch in his hands and leering at its contents. "This stuff looks like turkey shit."

"You whine like a child," Pretorius whispered. She luxuriated on the Mylar blanket they had spread on the floor, taking turns massaging her hands and feet and elbows. "I don't care what goes in my stomach as long as I'm not crawling through that wasteland on my fingertips."

Quarry flicked his boot at her knee. "I'm the whiner? Didn't Cog have to threaten you with intravenous feeding on Lacaille b?"

"I had time sickness, remember? I couldn't keep down a sip of water." She stretched again. "My God, that feels like a century ago."

"It was a century ago," Quarry said. He swallowed a bit of the stew and screwed his face. "How about you eat this slop and I'll eat the pouch and the spoon?"

"Ha-ha-ha, kiss my ass. Those are the best parts."

They sat side by side, their backs to a cement wall in a small electrical room with no windows, the metal door shut tight. The ventilators had long since been shut off and the air in the room was stifling, but for the first time in four days, they could breathe without worrying about the movement of their chests calling down a rain of firepower from above. Pretorius embraced the concrete cocoon and was happy she wasn't alone, even though the two of them sucked fresh air out of the room more quickly. Who would have thought they could become so close—an American farm boy and a Botswanan girl from the bush? *That was what combat did for humans,* she thought. *It put them in the dirt, where their flesh and bones become one and the same.*

"I did manage to bring dessert," Quarry said, winking at her and reaching for his backpack.

She leaned forward and cracked her spine and looked at him with feigned disgust. "Please don't say it's canned peaches, Quarry. I don't have the energy to kick you in the balls."

"Hell no." He pulled out a small hydration pack like the ones that carried the protein slurry and liquid electrolytes they used in the field.

"Gatorade," she said hopefully.

"Better. You are staring at half a liter of Barkov's finest." He raised the pouch. "Here's to the Siberian bastard who learned to cook booze in zero-g."

"You brought alcohol on this op? Are you insane?"

He grinned. "Do you want to die sober? I knew we'd have at least a day of hurry up and wait if we ever got to this shack. The Rossby Wave isn't happening till 1630 and we're in a complete comms blackout, so what else do we got to do until then?"

"My God, you are an American cowboy. How does it feel to be a walking cliché?"

He took a swig. "It feels better with moonshine. Here's to Barkov."

She shook her head, putting her hand out. The samogon went down as bad as it had on the *Varangian*, but it took the bite off her sore muscles. She drank again and handed it back to him.

"Here's to Second Platoon. But we need to man the OP at 1200—and be sober when we get there."

"Affirmative. That gives us twelve hours of oblivion," Quarry said. He took another sip. "Here's to Spetsgruppa A and the entire FSB. Goddamn, when was the last time we had this much time to rest and refit in the middle of an op?"

She thought about the coming day when they would spearhead an assault on the Leonis Union's command bunker in the middle of a geomagnetic storm. "Alpha CMb, maybe," she murmured. "The four of us, in that cave overlooking the ambush."

"Yeah, that's right." She saw him pulling up the mental image of that dark and silent moon, light-years from where they now sat. Then she saw the concern on his face as he looked at her. Quarry knew her too well. "What's eating you?"

"Nothing."

"Bullshit," he said, handing her the pouch again. "You're supposed to be the optimistic one. I'm the one nodding my head and not meaning it."

She scratched her knee and turned her eyes away. "Have you ever felt like you were going to buy it, Quarry?" she asked. "Like for real, this op is the one that's going to get you?"

"Hell yes, every time we mount up."

"I mean it."

Quarry raised an eyebrow. "You're not drinking, Staff Sergeant Pretorius. That's the kind of thinking that only booze will fix."

She took a sip at the straw and murmured again. "Here's to Mother Russia. I've always wanted to see snow."

They sat in silence for a while, rubbing their muscles. "If this really is the one, it's going to get both of us," Quarry finally said. "I'm not reentering the wire alone."

She grabbed his shoulder and squeezed until he winced. "Don't give me that cowboy bullshit. If I get greased, you let me lie and keep pushing on." She kept the pressure on his arm as they looked at each other. "Promise me. What we agreed to long ago."

"Okay, Jesus. You don't have to talk me into self-preservation."

"Yes, I do."

"I said *okay*. I'll leave your dead ass and keep moving."

"Good." She took another sip and passed the pouch. She felt the buzz coming on hard. *Damn, the Russians didn't mess around with their booze.*

"I knew a guy who got the death premonition once," Quarry said. "He came out of the next fight without a scratch. The dude standing next to him got cut in half."

"We can only hope," she said.

He elbowed her and got up to open the door. "Just for ten seconds," he said. "We need some fresh air."

She closed her eyes and thought of ways to change the conversation, staying silent until he closed the door again. "We never finished our talk in the mess hall on the *Varangian*. It's your turn."

"What do you mean?"

"What happened to you back on Earth, after the Collapse? There's no way you just enlisted to fight. You're not a killer."

He did a double take and sat down again. "Are you shitting me? Do you have any idea how many people I've wasted in the last—what the hell is it—ninety-nine years? I'm a bigger killer than Belt Fever."

"You're good at it but you don't hunt for sport. I know when a soldier likes killing, Quarry. It's in their eyes. Like Ras. He tried to hide it, but it was there."

He glowered at the mention of Arjun Ras.

"You're comparing that sick bastard to me?"

"No, dumbass, I'm saying you're the opposite." She took another drink and handed him the pouch. "Here's to Crooks.

May he feel guilty when we die tomorrow. The full story now, please. We've got twelve hours to kill."

He leaned back and closed his eyes and, after a bit, started talking.

"I had the sweetest setup before Kessler. I mean it was perfect. I managed a big chunk of land for a timber company, ten thousand acres in western Maryland. Some of it was leased to hunting clubs so there was a little babysitting, but mostly I had the spread to myself. Lot of time keeping the roads and fire lanes clear, lobbing trees and harrowing fields and stuff, but it was the kind of work that isn't really work, you know?"

"And you lived there?"

"Yeah, a little piece nearby; I got twenty acres for just about nothing. Built a cabin with help from my brother. Cypress siding and metal roof, heart pine on the inside, woodstove, everything buttoned up and plumb. Solar power and a deep well and an oil drum I turned into a smoker. I had a girlfriend who was a teacher in town, and she stayed there when she wanted. She was the independent type, like you." He blew out some air. "I mean, I went to the grocery store five times a year, lived on venison and quail and trout. Had a garden and a few food plots and jarred stuff for the winter. I told my friends if the apocalypse hit, just grab a gun and a backpack and come on over. We'll survive while the rest of the world burns."

"But they came for you, didn't they?"

He nodded and put out his hand for the liquor pouch. "Mandatory enlistment, meaning they stick a gun in your face and say, 'Get in the truck or go in the ground.' I was sitting in a tree stand, with a bolt-action .308, a hundred yards from the cabin when they showed up, and I was dry-sniping those bastards as they went through my stuff. I swear to God, I almost started shooting."

"But you didn't shoot?"

He shrugged. "Didn't have it in me yet."

"And you got down from the tree and went with them?"

He looked at her. "My mom was still alive and so was my younger brother, and they took it out on your family if you tried to dodge enlistment. These were county militia with lists—a bunch of jackbooted pricks—and they got paid in beans and salt pork to bring in recruits."

They listened for anything outside the door, but there was nothing to hear.

"So that was it," Quarry continued. "I became an infantryman for the Loyal States of America, E-1, until they figured out that I could track like a Patuxent Indian. So, I got shipped to Moore for long-range surveillance school and then Liberty. They still had the old command structures that early in the breakup and the 75th Rangers committed to the LSA."

"And your mother and brother?"

He took a drink and handed her the pouch and put his hands on his knees, his head to the wall. "They died in '90. In 2090, I mean—like a hundred fucking years ago. Man, that sounds so crazy when you say it."

"How?"

"The normal ways. She got pneumonia, and you didn't get meds unless you could fight. Only soldiers got care. She passed before I heard she was sick. We buried her next to my dad, who died when I was too young to remember. A good man, supposedly."

"And your brother?"

"He got it in combat. He was on point because he was good in the bush, like us, and he could read sign. His platoon got ambushed in Ohio, butterfly mines strung up on a cliff face. Blew them to pieces."

Pretorius let the silence hang before taking another sip. "Here's to your mother and your brother, Quarry, and to your father."

"Thanks."

"And what about your girlfriend?"

He looked at her. "Hell, I said she was independent. We wrote a few times."

"But you didn't care all that much when she left, did you?"

He stared at her stupidly for a second, squinting, and she could tell he was getting drunk. "What do you mean by that?"

"I mean you didn't care that much. You liked women but you never committed to one. The woods came first and everything else fell somewhere behind."

"How the hell would you know that?"

"Because that's how I was, Quarry, and we're the same. I liked men but not when they took up my time. Not when they kept me from the bush."

He laughed and leaned back against the wall. "I guess you got me pegged. I would have changed, I think—especially if I found someone who could butcher a deer."

She nodded. "Me too."

Quarry checked the readout on his suit's armband. "Shit. It's 0100 and I'm already half drunk."

She put her hand on his face and brought him close, and he stared at her, too intoxicated to understand. She kissed him on the mouth, and after a second, he kissed her back.

They pulled away, and he looked a little scared.

"Why the hell did we just do that?" he asked.

"I don't know. Maybe because we'll be dead tomorrow. Or because Cog told us not to. It could just be the moonshine."

"What if we don't end up dead?"

She shook her head. "This is it, Quarry. Tomorrow, we'll

be teammates on a ship of war, back to normal. The embolism, remember?"

"Oh yeah," he said. They kissed again, harder this time, and she smelled the alcohol and dirt and sweat on him, and somehow that seemed right. After a few minutes, they rolled onto the blanket, and she reached for the tabs that released the top of his combat suit.

19

Pretorius checked her watch. *Ten minutes.* They sat beneath a blown-out window shrouded by webs of hanging insulation and wiring and scanned the feed from the microcam fixed to the jamb. Quarry held the launcher, which looked like one of the old low-propulsion M520s used by grenadiers back on Earth. Hundred-year-old tech, dumb except for the laser range finder and algorithmic compensators built into the reticle. Supposedly they just had to lob the mortar toward the target, and it would activate and do the rest—if a projectile could be lobbed accurately into the maw of a hurricane.

"Five minutes to seal up," she whispered. "No coms until the Rossby Wave hits and we call Six. Hand signals only."

He nodded. "Guess there's no way to tell if this thing is really coming?"

"Not until it happens."

Nothing had changed between them, she thought, but she knew it wasn't true. *How could things not have changed? And why the hell did I do that?* Other than raising his eyebrows when they woke up in a tangle of disgorged clothes and blankets and looked at each other, baffled and embarrassed, Quarry acted like nothing had happened. He assumed the old role of teammate with forced casualness, as had she. She wanted to blurt out something, anything, but now wasn't the time to be distracted by things like sex, not with the mission running through their minds like a current. And she didn't know what to say anyway.

Pretorius stole a glance at him. He nodded as if to say, "We're good," and she almost wanted to kiss him again. She cared for Quarry like she cared for Zalta and Cherry, as a brother and a comrade . . . and maybe even more. She hoped those bonds wouldn't be broken by a few hours of lunacy. Impulsiveness had always been her downfall. Why did she kill that sick bastard, Letshego, instead of knocking him out with a blow to the head? And why did she just jeopardize one of the few good things she had in this world—a friendship forged in dirt and fire—with the man sitting next to her? Intimate relationships weren't her strong suit. She was better at being friends.

It won't matter, she said to herself. *We'll be dead in an hour anyway.*

They watched the cam because it killed time, the one itch that must be scratched while grunts wait for contact. The Leonis lines lay quiet. In a few minutes, the Terran commanders would flip the planet's largest jet stream and blow a superheated windstorm across the front of the Wedge—signaling a complex attack that would include the bulk of the One-Three, Jorgenson's platoons, and the Terran drone network. The plan sounded no crazier than some of the other ops they'd pulled off in the last century, but Pretorius sensed it would be different. This moon raised her fear hackles with its red gloom and smells of burning flesh and eternal line of light and shadow. It pulled her into the ghost stories the Balete told of the Eastern Cape, where witch doctors summoned monsters and mangrove forests knitted themselves into mangals that blocked out the sun. And Gorata's tales of the Impundulu when she was a child—a beast that could summon lightning and suck the blood from the veins of its enemies when it took human form . . .

Her wristband vibrated. She snapped back to the present. This wasn't a land of monsters. It was a land of humans and smart machines looking to kill each other. Maybe some of the humans were IFS stock whose bodies and languages had morphed because of local gravity and culture—but they still came from the same cradle, and they still found reasons to fight. Nothing could be more normal. She looked at Quarry. He stared at her with a mix of worry and who knows what else, watching as she sank into a place of dark memories.

"Pressurize and activate suits," she whispered, turning away. "No coms until after the HPRFs. One minute on my mark."

She felt his hand on her leg. "Anaya."

She looked back at him. "What?"

"We're going to make it."

She put her hand on his and wished they weren't wearing gloves. "Thanks, Owen. For everything." She stared back into the gloom. "Mark."

They sealed their helmets and listened to the whirrs and clicks as the environmental controls kicked in and the HUDs powered up. *Would the tiny electrical signal given off by two pressure suits be enough to alert the drones? Where was the Dimpled Bastard?* They watched the cam in silence. They didn't hear the Rossby Wave coming—couldn't hear much outside their helmets now—but they felt the pressure change as if the shack they sat in suddenly fell off a mountaintop. The concrete trembled under their legs, and a nebula of dust dropped from the ceiling. Then the storm erupted.

A blast of hot air exploded through the window, blowing

away the wiring and insulation, and blanketing the room in a brume of sand and grit. Heat seared her faceplate as they bunched together to withstand the whirlwind. Pretorius worried her suit would melt or the building would crash down on them. They leaned into each other, arms hugging knees, waiting for the chaos to subside. She couldn't see her own feet—*how the hell would Quarry be able to fire a mortar round with any accuracy?* But even as the heat grew, the visibility improved and the wind slackened to gale force. *It has to be now,* Pretorius thought, *while the Leonis command is recalling their drones and figuring out how to deal with the sudden geostorm from the sun side of the planet.*

She tapped Quarry on the shoulder, and he rose to a knee and raised the launcher. Pretorius grabbed him by the waist for support as gusts of wind and dust hammered through the window. Quarry fiddled with the elevation and windage knobs on the scope and waited for its compensators to adjust. He fired. She didn't hear it, but she could feel the thump of the round as it discharged and the recoil emanating through his body.

Quarry waited for a few seconds and dropped below the windowsill. His eyes flared wide in disbelief as he gave her a thumbs-up. The round had landed inside the perimeter. She saw in her mind's eye what would happen next: the projectile, half buried in Groombridge dirt, opening and launching several High-Power Radio Frequency warheads above and below the ground, ripping apart the Faraday cage that protected the Leonis Union's command and control infrastructure from electromagnetic pulse. Theoretically, it would shut everything down.

And somehow, she felt it happen. A wave of energy different than the windstorm pulsed through her. The hairs on her body stood on end. Her heads-up display crazed, and she saw the cam zap out. She half stood and grabbed the windowsill with one hand, bracing and scanning the Leonis headquarters with a set of adaptive scanners. *I'll be damned.* No electrical signatures came from above- or belowground.

She flipped on her com. "Six, Alpha Two. Aces up. Aces up."

The reply came in a burst of static. "Alpha Two, Six, copy that. Incoming on your pos, danger close. Hunker down."

They dropped below the window and huddled together, and the bombardment hit a few seconds later. If they didn't have their helmets on, negative pressure from the explosions would have ripped the air from their lungs. The utility shack's far wall collapsed as they bounced up and down on the concrete floor. Pretorius's teeth banged together so hard she could taste metal and blood in her mouth, the shock waves emanating through her body and pulling her organs apart before smacking them back together. It continued for a full minute and left them facedown on the ground, blinded and stunned and covered in rocks and dirt.

"Jesus Christ," Quarry finally said in a voice that sounded far away. "That wasn't danger close. It was right on us."

They got to their knees and wiped the grit from their visors. The artillery barrage had blown the shack to pieces around them; the glow of the Groombridge sun filtered in bands of dark red through the caved-in ceiling. The wall facing the Leonis line remained intact, and Quarry shuffled to the window to scan the battlefield. Pretorius felt around on the floor for her laser rifle. She found it, grabbed the pistol grip, and joined him. The storm created by the Rossby Wave continued to rage in pulses, pulling the debris from the bombardment into vortices of dust across the battlefield, but they could just see the first wave of Leonis troopers as they emerged from the ground on the far side of the pipelines like ants streaming from a hole.

Quarry had his gun on the sill, scoping the enemy. Pretorius scanned the sky but didn't see drones from either side.

"Can we engage?" he asked.

"Hold for the One-Three and close air support," she said. "They should be here by now."

The battle grew like most battles do, slowly, with a few rounds fired as each side found its footing, and then a steadily increasing line of tracers, pulsed energy beams, and lasers ripping across the field. Pretorius felt the ordnance more than heard it as explosions shook the building and high-energy projectiles left small shock waves in their wake.

Her earpiece crackled to life. It was Jorgenson. "Alpha Two, Bravo One, pushing to your position behind the One-Three. Pop smoke to identify, over."

"Roger, Bravo One. Popping smoke." She pulled the pin on a small metal canister and threw it behind them, and a cloud of blue gas rose over the battered building and spun into a small twister. They took fire and retreated to a rock pile created by the destruction of the utility shack. Pretorius fired her short-pulse laser rifle for the first time, amazed by the lack of any recoil and the heat bloom that emitted from the barrel. It had a similar effect as a 40 mm grenade but with pinpoint accuracy, the bulbous mirror above the barrel refocusing the energy of the weapon after each shot.

They didn't hear the One-Three coming, but Terran soldiers suddenly swept by them in disjointed columns, supported by hover tanks and a few aerial drones. Their helmets muffled the sound of incoming and outgoing, but the battle noise rose, and the sizzle of energy projectiles charged the air, crazing their heads-up displays and distorting their coms. Pretorius saw the first troopers fall, cut down or blown to pieces by the beams, and she recognized it as a real battle and not something detached by a lack of loud noises.

"We have to link up with Cherry and Zalta," Quarry yelled into her headset.

As if on cue, Cherry's voice broke in. "Alpha Two, Alpha Three. Coming in on your seven."

Pretorius turned and saw her teammates running through swirls of smoke and dust. She couldn't remember the last time she'd been so happy to see two soldiers on a battlefield.

Cherry launched himself over a crater and slammed his shoulder into the rock pile. He looked up at Pretorius with a grin on his face. "Good morning."

"Where the fuck are First and Second Platoon?" Quarry asked.

"Right behind us, coming down the center. Keep laying down cover."

Zalta landed just to Pretorius's left, nearly knocking her off-balance. He rose to a knee with his sniper rifle—an old-school caseless MRAD in .338—and began picking off Leonis troopers as they rushed to fill the trenches on their side of the line.

"Get that SAW up," he yelled to Cherry. "And call out any precision shots."

The four of them lay side by side on the rock pile, pouring down fire for the COG-V platoons and the One-Three. Pretorius heard Jorgenson on the team channel, yelling for his troopers to push forward and left. She watched as the first elements of the One-Three broke through the Leonis lines, dropping sonic charges and fragmentation rounds into their network of slit trenches. She felt the speedball high of battle mix with the drugs they had taken just before the Rossby Wave. *This is why war endures*, she thought. *If it was all hell, humans would have given it up millennia ago.* But it *was* more. Every human emotion wove through the fibers of battle: courage and fear, love and hate, joy and pain, and death mixed with the euphoria that comes with the realization that somehow, you're still alive, fighting beside your brothers and sisters.

She had the rush now. *Things are going our way.* Then Cog's voice broke onto the open channel.

"Ground Four, Air Four, be advised a Leonis assault craft has slipped into low orbit. Enemy drop ships entering atmosphere."

Someone else yelled, "Air assault," on the com, and Pretorius looked up to see a dozen Leonis troop carriers descending into the melee over the battlefield. The transports stopped a few hundred meters above the ground, taking fire from the Terran side as dozens of black specks dropped from hard points along their hulls. The objects landed on the battlefield with a series of thumps that shook the line, short bursts of retro-thrust doing little to lighten their impact. They looked like smooth black rectangles the size of coffins, and their appearance in the middle of the fight shocked both sides. The firing momentarily eased across the field.

One of the drop ships broke in half above them, its bow crashing into the pipelines as the rest fell into the blackness on the dark side of the terminator. The other airships retreated, and Pretorius returned her focus to their payloads, which sat like tipped-over monoliths on the field.

"Is that ordnance?" Cherry yelled.

Then the coffins unspooled, appendages emerging from beneath their once-flat surfaces like legs unfolding from a carapace. Within a second, they were quadrupedal, animallike robots with mast-cams and weapons materializing from their topsides as they skittered toward the Terran line. They unleashed a fury of fire, and the battle bloomed again. Pretorius saw a quadruped run into a squad of One-Three troopers and cut them down with a laser that swiveled and fired across a ninety-degree arc, the beam ripping through the air waist high. One of the Terran soldiers got cut in half as he tried to throw a grenade, torso tumbling to the ground with the pineapple still in its dead hand.

The grenade exploded, killing the soldiers who had managed to duck the laser beam. A survivor crawled away from the carnage, his head bobbing up and down as he looked for cover, but the quadruped spotted him and blew out the back of his suit with autocannons. Pretorius zoomed in on the dead trooper with her scope, sickened by the way he had moved. She knew she would find the words scrawled on the back of his helmet in faded black lettering: First of the Third, Last in Your Hearts. PFC Mapes.

"Alpha Two, Bravo One coming in," said a garbled voice on the com. Jorgenson and three other First Platoon troopers appeared through the maelstrom and landed next to them behind the rock pile. She heard their heavy breathing on the open channel. Jorgenson's face, shrouded by the grit on his visor, was covered in sweat, the pupil on his cybernetic eye flared open wide.

"The forties are barely denting those things," he said. As if to bring home the point, Cherry peppered the nearest machine with several 40 mm fragmentation slugs from his SAW. The rounds shook the robot, but it skittered ahead on its anatomic legs. The hover tanks, which had heavier ordnance, were nowhere to be seen.

"PEPs and lasers ineffective too," Quarry said. "Can we get a fire mission?" He and Pretorius continued to ding the quadrupeds with energy rounds to little effect.

"Those things are all mixed in with the One-Three," Jorgenson said. "Friendlies will get shot to shit."

The machines reminded Pretorius of oversized hyenas as they loped across the battlefield in hypnotic synchronization. They had changed the course of the battle in a matter of seconds. The One-Three's coordinated push stalled as soldiers looked for cover from the cutting beams. A few tried to retreat and were mowed down, too scared to remember the necessity of staying low. Zalta aimed his sniper rifle and fired at a quadruped about two hundred meters out. The round went through the bulbous eye protruding from its head, and the robot turned in lazy circles, blinded by the shot.

Zalta looked at her and grinned. "Sometimes an old-fashioned bullet is best."

Jorgenson got on the open channel and called for everyone firing solid ammunition to aim at the mast-cams on the quadrupeds. He raised his head to scan the field with his cyborg eye, and the rock pile exploded. Pretorius's body flew through space in a billow of heat and darkness. It felt like forever before she landed, an intermission of surreal peace in slow motion. Her leg shattered as it hit the ground and things sped up. Ears ringing, vision narrowed to pinholes, the pain snapped her into focus. Through the ringing she heard suit alarms, warning her of exposure to the outside elements. She shook her head and the pinholes widened into a gray blur. She saw a spiderweb and knew she was dreaming—there were no spiders here. But then it became her faceplate, splintered from the blast.

Someone grabbed her body and dragged it into a shell hole, and this time she screamed in pain. It was Cherry. He had his knee on her chest, and he fired the SAW just above her broken helmet. He yelled into the com and looked down at her as he fired, but she couldn't make out the words. The high-pitched ringing in her ears wouldn't go away.

Cherry hoisted her into a fireman's lift and ran. Somehow, they weren't cut down by one of the lasers or autocannons ripping apart the field. She realized that she still held her gun in her hand. *Fuck it*, she thought, *at least I can die shooting.* She peered under Cherry's armpit and lifted the laser rifle and fired, aiming at the quadrupeds behind them. Two of the machines ran them down from either flank; she saw the one on their left turning its gun turret.

"Get down," she screamed. Cherry heard her. They dropped into a slit trench. Electric jolts of pain shot up her leg again as they landed on the hardpack and rolled. Cherry got up and yanked a gripper on her suit, throwing her body toward a junction at the end of the trench.

"Go!" he yelled, raising himself over the berm to fire at the quadrupeds. He was telling her to escape; to leave him behind.

"You go," she yelled. She braced herself against the wall and rose to a firing position. *I'll be damned if I take the last one in the back*, she thought. *I'll be damned if I leave Dan Cherry alone on the field.*

They stood together, their heads just above the lip of the trench, and fired at the quadrupeds. Cutting beams sizzled over their heads. She sensed movement above and looked up. The Dimpled Bastard floated in just to their right, a glow forming on its laser cutter. The world moved in slow motion. She studied the dents on its black hull as it spun to look down on them. Six dents in a triangle, all near its equator. She recalled a World War II fighter pilot who had counted the rivets on an enemy plane as they passed each other in an eight-hundred-mile-per-hour merge. *Time really did dilate in combat*; she swung her gun up even though it was too late. Something hit the Dimpled Bastard before she could fire. The black metal sphere spun in a lazy circle and fell to the ground. She looked across the field and saw Zalta, his gun still pointed at the sky. The drone hit with a thud just in front of the trench, one sensor still glowing red, a recriminating eye pointed at them. Pretorius and Cherry unloaded on it together. Its shields gone, the drone died like something real.

"Man or machine motherfuckers, come get some!" Cherry screamed, so loud it cut through the ringing in her ears.

She braced herself against his bulk and fired at the

approaching quadrupeds again, melting out her weapon's mirror. She saw Quarry and Zalta, fifty meters away now, scooting and shooting toward them, trying to draw the fire of the quadrupeds. Jorgenson lay facedown in a rubble pile behind them. He looked dead. A line of artillery rounds marched across the field, walking fire that came right toward them. The barrage blew the closest quadruped into the air. Pretorius watched it dismember. The rounds kept marching, thumping toward their trench. They ducked at the last second, but it didn't matter. The last round blew them into the air.

Pretorius woke up on top of Cherry in a world of silence. They were out of the trench, back on the battlefield. She rolled over and looked down. She felt no pain, nothing but distance and white noise in her ears as she studied the chunk of metal protruding from Cherry's chest. She stared at it, not believing it was real. She grabbed him by the shoulders, putting her broken faceplate against his as she pulled, but one of her hands didn't work right. Cherry was dead weight. She pulled harder with her good arm, using her one good leg for leverage. *Must move him somewhere safe*, she thought. Blood poured from his nose and ears, and he looked at her with amazement, or maybe he was just trying to see through her splintered faceplate. Sound came back into her world and as his lips moved, she heard him.

"Shit, Anaya," he said. "I didn't think . . ." Then he died. His eyes stayed open but lost focus. She tried to put her hand on his helmet and saw that her hand was gone. *Isn't that funny. I never felt it get blown off.* She sat next to him as the reds and browns of Groombridge turned black, and she knew that she wouldn't be waking up in a field hospital this time. What did Zalta always say about premonitions of death? *A soldier should listen to them.*

Quarry ran to them through a field of fire. He got to within thirty meters, close enough to see that Cherry was KIA and Pretorius's leg and hand were missing. He screamed into the com, ignoring the voices yelling at him to pull back. Zalta was there, just behind him. They would make it together. *Cog can give her cyborg limbs like Devilliers's. She can learn to fight with them. And who knows about Cherry? He's indestructible, regardless of what's sticking out of his chest. We'll look back on this a month from now, safely tucked into the future, and laugh about that FUBAR op in 2194—the one on Groombridge that almost got us all.*

Zalta tapped him on the shoulder. Time to push forward again, even though they knew it wasn't. Fire blossomed all around them. The ground heaved into the air, chunks of it held up by the dying Rossby Wave. Quarry got up to run, screaming their names. A hammer struck the side of his helmet, and the red gloom of Groombridge disappeared with everything else.

BOOK

3

20

URSA X-1

2194 or 2195 (Assumed)

Crooks grabbed the gurney and bit down on a tongue depressor as the medical bots laminated a sheet of cultured skin onto his thigh. It wasn't the bonding that hurt—it was the preparation. They had to rough up the hypodermis so the graft would take, and the procedure felt like a piece of low-grit sandpaper being run over the open wound. He looked away and clamped his teeth on the bite stick until his gums burned. *Pain is penance,* he told himself. *Take it like a man.*

Cog sat on a stool next to him and watched the procedure in silence—although technically, he also ran the procedure. The AI hadn't been in a speaking mood since the withdrawal from Groombridge, when Quarry went crazy in the hangar bay and tried to kill him. Crooks had never seen anything like it, which was saying something considering the mind-fuck of a century they had just rolled through. Quarry: missing an eye, bleeding from a dozen wounds, and still covered head to foot in Groombridge mud, bull-rushing the tactual hologram of Cog and trying to stick a knife in his neck. And Cog: stunned for a second, not knowing how to react to a physical attack on his holographic personage, before vanishing into the ether as the blade struck home.

What the hell was Quarry thinking? That he could kill the machine by stabbing the ghost? Of course, he hadn't been thinking. He was stark raving mad from the news that Cherry and Pretorius had flatlined and the *Varangian* was going to leave them behind on that godforsaken planet. Quarry didn't want to see the bio-telemetry, didn't care about the fact that Terran forces had pulled back from the Wedge, didn't want to be reminded of the original rules, the old COG-V rules, that the dead were left behind. He knew that Cog would administer the nitrogen embolism to be sure that Pretorius and Cherry couldn't be resurrected—the standoff coup de grâce—and he went insane.

At least Zalta had taken a more pragmatic approach, Crooks thought, biting down as another layer of skin went on his open wounds. *Zalta only tried to kill me.* He gets points for feasibility. Both men had been subdued and rendered unconscious by the medical bots but not before they added to the carnage already present in the hangar. Half of the troopers used in the fight had died on Groombridge and everyone else had been seriously wounded, including Jorgenson, who would probably survive being dropped into a volcano. Crooks and his entire headquarters team had been injured helping the retreat. No one left that planet unscathed; Crooks couldn't shake the image of blood pouring down the runnels of the drop ship ramp into the triage on the deck.

"Why didn't you kill them?" he asked, looking at Cog's moribund face and hoping that a conversation would distract from the stabs of electricity pulsing his leg.

"Who do you mean, Sergeants Quarry and Zalta?"

"You know who I mean."

Cog sighed and swiveled his chair away from Crooks, presumably to look at the major's vital signs on the monitor, but really, Crooks knew, because he didn't want to look him in the eye. "They clearly weren't themselves."

"How did you get around the protocols, Cog? They attacked both of us on board the ship. By the book, they should have been executed."

"I deemed the attacks to be induced by posttraumatic hysteria," Cog said with a wan smile. "A version of the temporary insanity defense, I suppose."

Crooks noted that Cog was growing in his ability to avoid the letter of the law. "Well, I suppose it's for the best. They're the last two Lurps we have on board."

"That was part of the consideration," Cog said. "We are combat-ineffective at this point. We can barely cobble together two platoons, we have limited scouting and intelligence capabilities, and there is no indication from Earth that we'll be refitted. Also, the only senior NCOs we have left are Jorgenson and Pemkalla and they're both recovering from surgery. I thought it best to keep our last remaining recon assets in play."

Crooks winced as the bots pressed the skin sheet to his leg and regenerated its nerves and sweat glands with a stimulation tool that looked like a cattle prod. "How are Pemkalla and Jorgenson, by the way?"

"Pemkalla is immersed in a nucleopeptide bath. She should be out of Med Bay in a week. As for Jorgenson, he seems to be indestructible. He says he's operational, but he's got more spare parts than real at this point."

"Is there any good news?"

Cog shrugged. "Well, we're in an elliptical low-dilation orbit, roughly one relative year for every week we spend circling the Bear, so the issues we've been seeing with time sickness should be minimal the next time we break the whirl."

Just one more thing the architects of this strategy never considered, Crooks thought. The physiological effects of dilating time by orbiting a black hole were real. Somehow, the biorhythms of humans and machines got knocked out of whack by a different clock—relative or not—and the barely discernible tidal forces created by the nonuniform gravitational field of Ursa X-1 wreaked havoc on the body's systems, from the stomach to the heart. Every time they came out of a large time skip, Crooks felt like his brain had been turned forty-five degrees inside his skull. It took him three days inside the new timeline to even conceive of seconds and minutes and hours. And Crooks wasn't as time- or tidal-force sensitive as most of the company. He was convinced that temporal distortion and gravitational squeezing had driven several troopers insane. *How else could a crack operator like Sato suddenly lose it?* The rest of the teams survived on a cocktail of drugs to counteract the black hole's debilitating effects, but the meds didn't help much.

"No indication from Earth on what they have planned for us?" he asked.

"No," Cog said. "I know that two other dilation warships are still in action under Priam's command and control, but the program itself has not been expanded. If I had to guess, CORP has lost interest in the concept of tactical and strategic temporal flexibility, if that ever was their main goal."

"What do you mean?" Crooks asked. "What other goal could there be?"

"You recall their fascination with tachyonic antitelephony? They wanted to see if we could travel to the future and send a message back in time, perhaps by using quantum field theory and the Lorentz transformation. They've found some evidence of tachyons through the detection of Cherenkov radiation, but even in our current timeline, there's no practical way to harness them—yet."

"So, the bigger gambit was to skip to the far future, tap into its advanced tech, and send a message to the past for strategic advantage?"

"Correct," Cog said. "Honestly, I'm glad they haven't tried it. We could be the cause of paradoxes that destroy the universe. Einstein was right in calling the quantum stuff spooky."

"So why the other time-traveling warships, Cog? I mean, it proves that CORP was trying to stash an army in time, right?"

Cog shook his head. "I don't know, Major. We've been an asset in a tactical sense, and I'm sure that other empires have considered the same concept. But I honestly don't know. Nothing makes sense anymore. Why the hell did they send us to Groombridge? We achieved our objective, but the strategic situation on the ground remains the same."

"Yeah."

The other time-traveling warships are probably faring as poorly as us, Crooks guessed. *Guinea pigs never fare well in the lab.* And attention deficit disorder could have played a role as well. Maybe CORP could have saved trillions by stashing armies in time, but what general or politician ever remained focused on problems decades in the future? And what did it matter anyway, if those armies were undermined by the effects of dilation and emerged into theaters of war that had weaponry too advanced to fight against? Crooks flashed back to the Groombridge quadrupeds chewing through his troopers with impunity. The Terran forces had managed to take down only five of the thirty battle drones that Leonis dropped onto the Wedge. After Zalta sniped one with a bullet to the mast-cam, the others adapted by covering their headstocks with a ballistic carbon mesh. In the end, the quadrupeds owned the field.

And the worst part of the equation crept back into his head as the bots finished their work on his thigh: nine more missions. *Nine*—skipping through another century or so of everyone else's universe, judging by the time lapse between the first eleven ops. Crooks knew how it felt to be alone. When that thermobaric bomb drifted off course at the Cumberland Gap and decimated his company, on a day that seemed an eon ago, he had felt like the only person left alive on Earth. Now, he and his troopers felt the same way about the entire IFS. The universe had expanded but their world had contracted to within the bulkheads, barracks, and gravity cylinders of the CS *Varangian*.

The medical bots finished their work. He eased himself off the gurney and reached for his jumpsuit despite Cog's protestations. He sensed that something larger was afoot, that every crazy thing that happened to the *Varangian* since Teegarden was a part of someone's mad plan, but he knew he wasn't smart enough to unlock the puzzle. Crooks sighed. *First things first.* It was past time to meet with his two most disgruntled troopers. "Where are Quarry and Zalta?"

"Static station, main truss three, between the two gravity cans."

"Okay, I'm going down to see them."

"I guess a repeat of my condolences for Pretorius and Cherry won't help?"

Crooks limped to the door. "I don't know, Cog. Condolences never hurt."

It took a few decades of IFS time for Quarry to appreciate zero-g, but when the epiphany came, it hit hard. Weightlessness was something to be avoided at first because it pushed all the body's fluid into the head, causing headaches and disorientation. But once he became accustomed to wearing the gravity-loading skinsuits and taking the right meds to control the migraines and inner ear issues, free fall was pure bliss. Everything slowed down, from movement to the repetitive nightmares boiling through his mind. War melted away, pain diffused, and bad memories could be pushed to the side as he floated in a cocoon of nothingness.

At least until now. Now, as he and Zalta let their bodies take slow-motion bounces off the padded storage lockers that lined the static truss, the nightmares stayed close. He opened his new eye for a second. It was even more advanced than Jorgenson's and would take some getting used to. The old eye got blown out as he ran to Pretorius and Cherry at Groombridge; the new one could see in every range of the electromagnetic spectrum. It oriented him in space, gave him exact ranges to targets, and served as a secondary scope. It even sensed deception. For now, though, it just made him dizzy, so he shut it off with a thought.

"You know they were better than us?" Zalta asked after minutes of free fall silence. "That's the one thing I will never understand about war. How the best can die while the middling live on."

Quarry kept his eyes closed, not wanting to know whether his head was up or down relative to what he considered up and down in the narrow octagonal shaft. "I don't know, Hassan. You're a pretty good operator."

"We're all good," Zalta said. "But Cherry was better than me and Anaya was better than you—no insult intended. She was the best asset I've ever met."

Quarry remembered how Pretorius moved. Like a cat in predation, invisible in the tall grass. "She was that." *And so much more.*

"She reminded me of my cousin, Yara, who died in combat

as well." Zalta sighed. "My God, the balls that woman had. A ricochet in Homs got her—a round hitting the wrong spot in the wrong moment. I would have gladly taken her place, but the only luck I have is ill-begotten. Here I am, alive and bouncing off the insides of a spaceship, while Yara and Anaya and Dan Cherry are gone."

Quarry felt his body bump against a cushioned wall and spin toward the center of the corridor. It reminded him for a moment of YZ Ceti, when Cherry had roared into the hangar bay on Dippel's station, blasting away at the enemy while they hid in a bulkhead.

"We're survivors, Hassan," he said. "And I mean that in a negative way. We can't catch the glory round and we apparently aren't good at suicide, so we stick around and watch the real heroes die."

Zalta snorted. "Cog, that insufferable man-bot. He could have shipped us the one time we were frothing at the mouths and in direct disobedience, and yet here we are. I liked him better when he was an asshole."

The hatch nearest to them hissed. Quarry opened his eyes and blinked as Crooks floated into the passageway. COG-V's commander looked pale; scuttlebutt said he had nearly bought it on Groombridge while running security for the retreat. Suit blown out, legs torn up, he remained in the fight until the last trooper was pulled out. *Did he want to die as well?* Quarry's new eye reactivated and told him that Crooks approached from 6.2 meters, at a speed of .4 kph. And he was a little dehydrated.

"I had a feeling you boys would be talking about death," he said.

"Nice of you to listen in," Zalta replied.

Crooks grabbed a beam to stop his float. Quarry noticed that he grimaced when his leg brushed against the wall. "Sorry, but you're on suicide watch. Cog thought we should monitor you in case you decide to open an airlock."

"How paternal," Zalta said.

Crooks hung in place, silent for a few seconds, looking at the two of them. "I'm not here to give you assholes a pep talk. We're long past that. I just want you to know that despite what happened in the hangar, you are still my teammates, and we don't have many of those left."

"Fewer and fewer every day," Quarry said.

"Yeah," Crooks said. "And probably none of us will be left when it's all done. But we knew that coming in, didn't we, so why not stick around for as long as you can? Do things right until this is over. That's what pros do, and that's what the two of you are supposed to be."

"You're right," Zalta said. "This isn't much of a pep talk."

"Just trying to be real," Crooks said. "If we all go out like Cherry and Pretorius, trying to save each other's asses, that's good enough for me. It doesn't matter who remembers us. We'll know."

Quarry arrested his spin by plastering himself against the cushioned wall opposite Crooks. He stared at the major, noting how gray his hair had gotten in the last several months and how his face looked thinner now, more drawn in at the cheeks. But there was no deception in his face, the new eye said, and Quarry realized that there never had been. When he attacked Cog and Crooks in the hangar bay, he was going after the wrong man and machine. *Who were the real enemies? CORP, Priam Solutions, Gliese, Leonis. Earth. He couldn't tell the difference between them anymore.*

"It's not you, Major," he said. "And it's not even Cog. It's just that we don't give a shit anymore."

"Then why did you run through hell toward your teammates on Groombridge? And why did you try to kill me and Cog?"

"Suicide by war, maybe."

"Bullshit. You don't have it in you. You survive by muscle memory because you've spent too much time in the bush to do anything else."

"If you're not worried about us then why does Cog have us on suicide watch?" Zalta asked.

"That's just proto . . ." Crooks began, and his body bent and folded and warped three inches to the right. Or it looked like it did. Quarry couldn't tell. The entire shaft skipped several frames in Quarry's field of vision. His body felt the phenomenon, so he knew it wasn't a hallucination. Like he had been stretched in mathematical increments and pulled back into place.

"What in the name of God?" Zalta asked.

It happened again, stronger this time, and an alarm sounded as the truss segment groaned and popped from the strain. Quarry focused on Crooks's face, skipping through the room, and then snapping back to its original position. Even his new eye couldn't figure out what the hell was happening. It kept bouncing through modes to find stable footing. Quarry vomited with no warning and watched the fluid dance in a weird circle in the middle of the passage.

Cog's voice came out of the ether. "Major, we are in trouble."

"No shit," Crooks barked, holding onto the grappling bar while his body moved in an invisible wind.

"We're experiencing a gravitational anomaly. There was no warning. It's causing significant damage to the ship and crew."

" What the hell is it?"

"Some kind of physical Lense–Thirring effect. The temporal and gravitational distortion is frame-dragging the ship and everything inside of it within a confined piece of space-time."

It happened again, all of them skipping through visual frames as the ship flexed and heaved. Zalta screamed and put his hands to his head. Blood ran from the Syrian tracker's nose, joining the vomit dancing through the middle of the corridor.

"Abort the orbit!" Crooks yelled.

"I'm attempting to. We're in a gravitational eddy spinning off the black hole's accretion disk, possibly a knot in space-time. I keep altering course and we keep getting pulled back into it."

"Forget the maneuvering thrusters, Cog. Do a hard burn on the TAMs. Now. Get us the hell out of here."

"Positive g's will exceed twenty. It could seriously injure or kill the crew."

Quarry closed his eyes, this time not for peace. He heard something clang in the ship and reopened them to see the entire truss segment between the gravity cylinders torque and snap back again. *Stress fracture*, the eye told him. *Rupture and decompression imminent. I'm sorry, Hassan*, he thought vaguely. *You're going to die in space after all.*

"Do we have time to get inside the immersion tanks?" Crooks asked.

"No."

"Then do the burn now Cog, for Christ's sake. We'll deal with the mess afterward."

"Roger. Forty-two percent thrust on my mark. You will be passing out momentarily. Mark."

The *Varangian's* conventional engines kicked in. Quarry flew through the corridor, just behind the spinning bodies of Crooks and Zalta. He watched them scrabble for handholds as they rocketed toward the Node 3 Cupola. They all slammed into the hatch, arms and legs pinioned and splayed as the *Varangian* fought its way out of the Bear's orbit. The room grayed over. Quarry saw pinholes in front of his face, his new eye went dark, and he fell asleep to a sound he had never heard before, the screaming of metal and carbon as a raging storm pulled a starship apart at the seams.

21

URSA X-1

2219

"Major, can you hear me?"

Crooks awoke to the whirs and clicks and colors of a familiar place. *The Combat Information Center on an AWACS?* No, not as noisy as a military plane, and the blue-and-green glow of the control features was all wrong. *And why the hell would I be flying, anyway? I'm an infantry officer.*

"Major, can you hear me?"

Memory seeped in from the edges of semiconsciousness. He was in space—the space of the far future. It wasn't just a bad dream. It couldn't have been because the voice he heard was Cog's.

"Major."

"I hear you," he grumbled. Every part of his body ached down to a microscopic level.

"Identify, please."

Crooks shook his head. The blue-green backwash of the room spun as he squinted to get a clear view. Someone hovered over him, a skinny guy with blond hair. *Yes, it really was Cog. Shit.* A nightmare would have been better. "I'm Major Thaddeus Crooks, Chronos Operation Group, commanding."

The relief in Cog's voice was palpable.

"That's good. I honestly didn't know if you would know that."

"Where the hell are we, Cog?"

"Adrift off the cusp of the Bear," the AI said. "We're on orientation thrusters until I can better ascertain the damage to the ship. Stay still. I've got you strapped into a chair on the bridge. You appeared intact so I brought you here instead of Med Bay, but I assume you're feeling the effects of the temporal distortion and the gravity load of the burn."

"That's a good assumption. How bad off are we?"

"It could have been worse. One fatality. Sergeant Monteleone suffered an aortic dissection. Several troopers have fractures, and everyone has acute temporal sickness. I've dispersed an aerosol mix of dimenhydrinate and cannabinoid vapor through the ventilation system. Those who can are already assisting the bots with triage for the more seriously wounded."

"And the ship?"

Cog hovered over him with a retina scope, their faces only a few inches apart.

"Worse news there. Virtually every system has sustained damage. Involuntary functions including life support, magnetosphere, and hull regeneration are online and the bots are deployed, but I couldn't cook you a hot dog in the mess hall right now."

Cog apparently didn't know how to stifle his colloquialisms during an emergency and somewhere in his swimming, flailing mind, Crooks reminded himself to be patient. "You said that we're adrift, Cog. Can we regain steerage?"

"I'm confident that everything is fixable, Major, but I'm not sure it will happen within our current time constraints."

Crooks panicked for a second. "Are we falling into the event horizon?"

Cog pursed his lips like a disapproving doctor. "No, as I said, we're clear of the Bear's gravity well."

"Then what the hell are our time constraints?"

The AI lowered the scope. "A ship is approaching, Major. It came out of slip thirty minutes ago. It's a few thousand klicks out, and I don't think it's friendly."

"Why not?"

"It hasn't pinged us with a Terran transponder and it hasn't hailed us. It's maintaining a position on our stern, where we have the least amount of firing flexibility with the MagFlex guns and lasers. And it's running on a hard burn—fast enough to require gel immersion for the crew. I don't think they would do that to just stop in for a chat."

Crooks tried to get up from the chair. The restraints held him down.

"Take these damn things off of me."

"We're on the bridge and in free fall."

"I don't care; get them off."

Cog had a dubious look on his face, but he unsnapped the harness and let Crooks's body slide into the microgravity.

"This is the second time someone has found us at the Bear, Cog. Its location was supposed to be the most highly compartmentalized secret in our mission. Should we assume it's common knowledge at this point?

"I don't know. The Gliese ships were led here in a navigational blindfold, at least according to the records, and I have no other knowledge of our position being leaked or sold out."

"How many black holes are within reasonable slip-drive distance of the IFS that would be suitable for tactical dilation?"

"Well over six hundred that we know about," Cog said. "And that isn't the only barrier they would have to finding us."

"What else is there?"

"Time," Cog said. "The gravitational eddy we went through caused an acute dilation. We have slipped twenty-four years into the future."

Crooks spun toward Cog, his mouth agape. "In thirty freaking minutes?"

"Roughly, yes. It's 2219 on the IFS calendar."

Crooks set his jaw. "Jesus." His eyes roamed from the main viewscreen to Cog and then to the control panels, but nothing focused his mind. He felt like a child, not understanding why something had been taken from him. "So, if this isn't a Terran ship approaching, we have to consider Ursa X-1 compromised."

Cog grabbed Crooks by the shoulders to steady him as he floated toward the ceiling. The major had forgotten to find a hand- or foothold. The AI's hands felt warm, with an almost indiscernible electric charge. "It would appear so, Major . . . if it isn't a Terran ship."

"Well, why the hell don't we know by now? You said it's only a few thousand klicks out."

Cog shook his head. "Our long-range scopes are shot to hell. All I can see is its heat bloom, and judging by the size of the engines, I estimate that it's large. At least a light cruiser if it is indeed a warship."

Crooks removed Cog's hands from his shoulders and floated to the holographic displays that Cog had set up for his workstation. He could see the bloom on the IR scan, but nothing else that indicated what kind of craft was coming at them.

"Can we fight back?" he asked.

"Most of our weapon systems are online but they're limited by a lack of guidance controls. And we can't maneuver in a meaningful tactical way. I could fire a few bursts on the TAMs to move us somewhere in a hurry, but it wouldn't be enough to change the geometry of the fight. That ship can stand off and shoot us to pieces if it wants, and dodge everything we throw their way."

Crooks stared at the bloom on the monitor and cursed the fact that he had ever agreed to go into space. *What kind of way to fight is this? Looking at radar blips on a hologram, at an enemy thousands of kilometers away, then ducking into a gel tank and letting the computers fight it out because of g forces?* Crooks almost wished for the red mud of Groombridge. At least there he could see what was about to kill him.

"Cog," he said, "are your self-destruct features functioning?"

Cog's eyebrows arched. "I haven't run the diagnostics on them—I've been focused on keeping us alive."

Crooks kept their eyes locked. "I think it's time to make sure that we can die if we have to."

Cog went to his command chair and pulled up several quadrants of telemetry and shipboard diagnostics and began running calculations on the *Varangian*'s ability to blow itself up. He worked for about thirty seconds and then froze. The displays disappeared, and he turned to Crooks.

"Major, the ship has hailed us."

Crooks had been looking at the viewscreen, trying in vain to see if he could pick out the penlight thrust of a spaceship from a few thousand klicks away with just his eyes. He turned to look at Cog.

"On voice?"

"No, data."

"What do they say?"

"They request that the senior NCOs of each platoon join the command staff on the bridge."

"*They what?*"

Cog repeated himself.

"How the hell could they know we have senior NCOs, or even platoons?" Crooks asked.

"Because they know who we are," Cog said. "They hailed the CS *Varangian*."

The sound of Earth music blasted through the static on the com, swelling to a crescendo of electric guitars and drums and bouncing off the walls of the bridge. Crooks hadn't heard rock 'n' roll in a while—they had tried using it on the *Varangian*'s drop ships a few times to get the troops amped, but it distracted from mission chatter. Still, he had a thing for twentieth-century rock, and he recognized the song being transmitted to them from the other ship when he heard it: AC/DC, laying out directions to the road to hell.

He glanced around the command deck at Jorgenson, Pemkalla, Quarry, Zalta, Cosmelli, and Yang—the senior noncoms all using foot restraints or holding onto girders to stay in place as they watched a magnified view of the approaching ship on the forward monitor—looking as mystified as he felt while the music thundered in through the speakers. Jorgenson had an angry gash on his neck, glued together with metro gel. Pemkalla, fresh out of immersion therapy, looked like hell.

The unknown ship got to within a hundred klicks and held station off the *Varangian*'s stern. It wasn't a cargo boat. Four hundred meters long and coated in mimetic armor and shock-absorbing ribs, the cylindrical vessel bristled with guns and launch tubes and resembled a hornet with its wings tucked in. A gravity can rotated around its spine from just off the static bow to the elliptical stern, and thrusters dotted every axis of its hull.

"That ain't a friendly," Jorgenson said.

"Major," Cog said. He must have dampened the music because the decibels lowered a notch. "I've got access to the CORP data buoys and can identify the warship. It's the *Sarka*, flagged to an unaffiliated private military contractor that has operated *extra legem* across the IFS for the last two decades or so. The *Sarka* has been tied most frequently to the Gliese Empire and the captain of the ship is a mercenary named Thug Behram."

"Excuse me, did you say *Thug*?" Pemkalla asked.

"Yes, derived from the Hindi *Thag*. It's almost certainly a nom de guerre. Thug Behram was a historical figure from eighteenth-century Earth, a mercenary who plied his wares in northern India."

"A successful one, I'm guessing?" Yang asked.

Cog nodded. "So successful that his operation morphed into a cult. He's reputed to have murdered over nine hundred people, which makes him one of the most prolific serial killers in human history."

Absurd name aside, Crooks had a feeling that he was about to see a face he would recognize, but how could that be? Everyone they ever knew outside of the *Varangian* was long dead.

The viewscreen fuzzed over and came into focus, and the other ship's bridge appeared before them. It looked more like a hookah lounge than a command center, Crooks thought, smoky and covered in tapestries and Kashan rugs that must have been glued to the walls to stay in place. *What in the holy fuck?*

A man appeared, floating to a captain's chair that resembled a throne and strapping himself in. His face—what a face! Old and leathered and run through with scars from temples to chin, with a black plate covering a missing part of his skull on the parietal lobe. The few clumps of white hair left on his cratered head had been tied into dreadlocks. The man looked Terran based on his frame. He wore body armor strapped together with leather and resplendent with battle dents. A necklace strung with what appeared to be dried fruit hung from his neck, secured to his chestplate with zero-g clasps. *Ears*, Crooks suddenly realized. *Those are human freaking ears.* The man stared at them with a look that could only be described as joy. As battered as his face was, Crooks knew who it was. He had seen those eyes before—amber, full of empathy, hiding madness. *Arjun Ras.*

"Damn, I love that song," the ex–COG-V trooper said as the music cut off. "Just makes you want to burn up the barrel on a Ma Deuce, doesn't it?"

Crooks looked around the bridge at his crew. Most of them stared at a stranger, slowly figuring out the jewels floating on his necklace were war trophies made of human flesh. Only Zalta and Cog recognized him. Ras had looked like a blue blood back in the day, clean-shaven and handsome, and now he was a caricature—a comic book villain. But they knew his eyes.

"Arjun Ras," the two whispered in unison.

"Yes!" Ras yelled. "It's good to be remembered. I knew you'd never forget me, Hassan—not after Lacaille. But it's Thug Behram now. I figured it best to dump the old name in case our AI nanny was poking around the IFS stream, looking for AWOLs." He winked in Cog's direction.

Crooks knew the blood had run from his face, but he forced himself not to blink or move. "Teegarden was eighty years ago, Ras, from what I was just told. You don't look a day past sixty. How the hell are you still standing on two feet?"

Ras laughed. "Thanks for the compliment, Major; I only

feel like I'm sixty. I've had a few nips and tucks and taken the latest elixirs, and the big *V* isn't the only bird that's skimmed black holes in the last century." The smile left his face, replaced by something else—*was it desire?* Ras was harder to read than a cat. "Although it is the only one left. Everyone else got blown up or spaghettified by the tidals."

"Is that why you're here?" Crooks asked, keeping the timbre in his voice even. "You want to jump back on the dilation bus and your ship doesn't have the capability?"

Ras looked dismissive. "No. Time travel is yesterday's game, and it hurts too much anyway. You'll see what I mean once your insides get scrambled enough." He swept his hand across his own bridge, and the camera moved to show several crewmen concealed in black visors. "You're still alive because I miss the company. I've got a good team here, but they're all hooked into a collective heads-up, virtual reality something or other. The hive makes 'em good soldiers but lousy conversationalists." He leaned back in his chair, white dreadlocks fluttering in the zero-g. "They don't make operators the way they used to. Even though you cut and run from Teegarden, and sold us out in the process, I'm a forgive-and-forget kind of guy. We could use a few unplugged assets, and business is booming."

Crooks glanced at Cog. They didn't need to speak—Cog said what he was thinking with a shake of his head: "He's lying."

"Why don't you just tell us what you want, Ras?" Zalta asked. "You never gave a shit about company unless it was someone you could kill, and you aren't a team player."

"My Middle Eastern brother, always so serious," Ras replied, his eyes playful. "I always got the feeling I was misunderstood among the ranks, so why don't we clear the air before we get down to the details? Why don't you tell me what you think I am, and let me respond in kind?"

"You're a freaking psychopath," Pemkalla spat.

Ras stared at her, expressionless, and Crooks got the sensation he was imagining what he would do if they were alone in a room.

"I object, Staff Sergeant," he finally said, glancing at her arm boards. "I'd argue that I am the man of peace while you are the purveyors of war. And I'll explain, even though it gives Cog time to reboot his systems in a misguided effort to blow my ship out of space."

"Please do," Crooks said.

Ras almost spoke over him in his eagerness to begin. "I do what must be done, which, in the case of war, is to make it a bloody awful experience. You fight in half measures to ease your guilt. So, who's better: the Machiavellian or the moral equivocator? Should we weigh the evidence to see who the butchers are, and who is the shepherd?"

"We were right next to you at Alpha CMb and Lacaille and Teegarden," Quarry said. "We know who the butcher is."

"Owen Quarry." Ras spit out the name more than spoke it. "The biggest sophist in the bunch. I assume you being in the room means that Pretorius is gone. A shame. She was twice the man you are."

Quarry's jaw pressed through his skin, but he didn't say anything. Crooks glanced toward Cog again, waiting for a signal that the AI was ready to make a move. Any move. If they had to commit suicide by firing at the *Sarka* or even ramming it, Crooks would do it because he was convinced that staying alive and in the hands of Arjun Ras would be a far worse fate for the crew.

"Let's talk about Teegarden," Ras continued. "Let's get to the nut."

"What about it?" Crooks asked. "You think we regret not joining you?"

"No," Ras said. "You're too stupid to regret it because you

still think of time in one dimension. An arrow moving straight ahead. But time is a tree, and you dimwits have spun off some crazy branches over the past eight decades."

"What are you talking about?" Crooks asked.

"Those Guild miners that Cog set on us. They didn't just kill your old squad mates when they got to Teegarden—everyone except me and Weiss, which is a story for another day. They destroyed the complex and very nearly the cruiser that Priam sent to pick us up. They started a war, which led to about a million deaths across the IFS. Women. Kids. Pets. You know, the kind of folks you spared." He paused. "Two hundred and twenty lives you could have let go on that rock, for everyone's sake—*for your own sake*—and instead you lit a fire that spread across the Orion Spur."

No one on the *Varangian* spoke but even Cog lifted his head to the viewscreen.

"And that's just the start," Ras said. "Remember Groombridge? Of course, you do—it just happened in your timeline. For those of us off the dilation bus, history shows you started that war as well. After Cog smoked those warships at the Bear, it led to a whole new round of hostilities between Earth and Gliese. Leonis sided with the other guys and stuck their feet in the dirt at Groombridge. Your being sent there was only fitting. Someone at Priam probably did it as an act of Karma, to put you in the proper grave."

He paused for effect. "It's sinking in, isn't it? Most of the awful things that have happened since 2138 were because of you idiots. Did you ever consider the fallout from your actions on Teegarden, or did you just tuck tails and run, fantasizing about being saviors to a bunch of people you didn't know? You are time travelers, for Christ's sake. You should have studied up on cause and effect."

"You're spinning yarns, Ras," Crooks said. "I dug into the histories every time we left the Bear, and there are numerous theories on how those conflicts started, which have little to do with COG-V. We're not going to sit here and debate causation with you when a million different actions could have had a million different results."

"Tell that to your dead troopers on Groombridge," Ras said, and then looked toward Quarry and Zalta. "Tell that to Anaya Pretorius and Dan Cherry."

"Bullshit," Quarry said. "All you do is lie. Why should we believe anything you say?"

Ras smiled and nodded at Jorgenson. "Delta Force believes me—just look at his face. And if you don't buy it, have Cog do a full refresher course on twenty-third-century geopolitics and intersystem warfare. He'll admit that the CS *Varangian* has been more than just a bit player in those catastrophes.

"So, let's sum it up," Ras continued. "I get my hands bloody with the ugly stuff, tying off open wounds and amputating dead limbs. You whine about collateral damage and run from hard choices, all the way to your security blanket, that black hole sitting off your bow. And war and death follow in your wake while you take naps in time. Who's the real monster in this fairy tale?"

No one answered. Jorgenson stabbed Quarry with his eyes, and the others either cursed under their breath or tried to come to grips with the idea that their actions on Teegarden could have led to so much damage, much of it personal. But Crooks felt only numbness and a stirring anger. This was what Arjun Ras did. He threw red meat and stepped aside, and let those around him tear themselves to pieces.

"I'm not going to waste time debating causality in a world we never saw, Ras," Crooks said. "You still haven't told us what you want."

Ras shrugged. "I want you, of course. I want the whole ship and crew, and I'm offering you a new billet. One last offer, because old ties only go so far. Have Cog do some checking and you'll see how lucrative a partnership could be. Democracy is dead in the IFS, at least where it matters. The whole shooting match is run by cartels now and it's a weapons-free environment. There are no rules of engagement anymore. We can do as we please."

"And Cog?" Crooks asked. "I guess you'd be switching him off, seeing how he's still flagged to Earth and his programming doesn't allow him to change teams?"

Ras smiled. "That's the beauty of it. I'm on the inside at Priam Solutions, which runs things on Earth, and I've got a fix that will set Cog free. A little AI lobotomy with help from the original source code, if you will. By the time they figure out what's going on, he'll be free and clear." He winked at Cog again. "Consider it, my friend. You would be an independent entity, answering to no power other than your own."

Cog had a quizzical look on his face. "I'm sure I'd be answering to someone."

Ras chuckled. "Well yeah, I'd be the boss, but I'm offering you a way off the wheel, a chance to work for yourselves. And no more time dilation unless we do it for our reasons."

"And if we say no?" Cosmelli asked.

"That's okay too. I've disabled Cog's autodestruct. Yes, Cog, that's a different kind of quantum bug you feel squiggling through your guts. It's why you can't stop the flow of p-hexane into your active thermal control system and overload the TAM drives. Whew—I had to read that off my HUD to make sure I got it right." He leaned back in his chair. "If you say no, I'll board the ship and kill you room by room and squad by squad. The chance to go up against COG-V in close-quarters combat gives me chills in all the best places, and it would let me assess my team against real operators. I'd still get the bounty for your hides, and I'd get the ship. And once I fully lobotomize Cog, I'll have a very pliant AI who happens to be the best black hole navigator in the known universe—another capability to sell on the open market."

Ras looked at someone off camera and nodded. The viewscreen fuzzed over. The lights in the *Varangian*'s cockpit dimmed and the holographic displays disappeared. Something deep in the bowels of the ship clanged, like a support beam had broken loose and was bouncing against the hull. Crooks turned to Cog and as he opened his mouth to ask what the hell was happening, the AI disappeared.

"Cog?" he asked.

They heard Ras laugh. "Cog's gone bye-bye, Major. I'm sure he'll come back when he figures out how to, but he'll only be a shell of himself. I'm assuming you'll say no to the proposal, so I'm off to prepare a boarding party. Call if you want me to stop, and if not, I look forward to a face-to-face. It was nice to reconnect."

A few more thuds belched from within the *Varangian* and resonated along its hull. The ship yawed, its bow turning away from Ursa X-1, and Cog's voice filtered through the com, distorted as if being run through the *Varangian*'s magnetosphere.

"Ras is not lying, Major," Cog said. "They've done something to me. I'm fighting what I can only describe as a virus in multiple systems across the ship, and I cannot engage the autodestruct."

"Can't we just blow the ship up ourselves?" Crooks asked. "I mean, we've got enough firepower on board to take out an asteroid."

"It's not a question of ammunition, Major," Cog said, and

despite the distortion, a tone of mild deprecation came through. "It's a question of protocols and time. I can't overload the antimatter bleed line, which is the standard autodestruct protocol. And I can't unlock the safeties on any of the ship's weapon systems. It would take too long to rig something powerful enough to do the job."

Jorgenson spun around to look at Crooks. "Who the hell said anything about blowing up the ship? Shouldn't we consider the offer, or at least pretend we're considering it until better options present themselves? I can't stand the idea of working for that prick, but look what happened the last time we said no."

"Yes," Yang said, "or just fight this thing out? You can't sign us up for suicide because you don't like the odds."

Crooks clenched and unclenched his jaw. "This isn't a democracy and if you think his offer is real, you've been pumping too many pills. Cog can't put up a fight, so we're screwed. Either they board and smoke us out or stand off and blast us from space. And if they take prisoners, I don't think any of you want that contingency."

Quarry, who looked like he had been lost in thought, glared at Crooks. "No, Major. If your answer is mass suicide, you better make sure Cog can still deliver the embolisms. And don't talk to us about mission protocols. We've earned the right to fight this out."

"You're agreeing with Jorgenson?" Crooks asked, a little flustered at the sudden alliance. The two had been at odds since they first boarded the *Varangian*. "You just want to have a go at Ras, don't you, Quarry?"

"Maybe," he answered. "But that's a fringe benefit. What did you tell me and Zalta in the static truss? The only thing we have left in this godforsaken universe is to do it right? To die on the field like our friends did before us. I guess that was a ten-coin speech because now you want to spit the bit."

Crooks couldn't disagree, but he wasn't going to let Ras take the *Varangian* or any of its crew alive, and he wasn't going to let one of his NCOs bow up on him. He turned to square up with Quarry, pulling his left foot from a gravity tab, knowing the Lurp tended to attack first and think about it later.

"Maybe you're right Quarry, but you're not in command," he said. "And I sure as shit don't need Cog to stop you."

Pemkalla left her perch on the gunwale and floated in between them. "Let's cut the left-right bullshit. There's got to be another answer. Cog, give us some alternatives. What do we got besides outright suicide and being slaughtered by those clone-looking freaks on that ship?"

Cog's voice poured into the room, more heavily distorted now. "I can do a ten-second burst on the mains."

"What good would that do, other than give us another minute or two?" Pemkalla asked. "We fly to another point in space, and they'll just follow us."

Crooks forgot about Quarry for a second and mulled what Cog had said. "Yeah, but following will cost them."

"Cost them what?" Pemkalla asked.

"Time."

The *Varangian*'s nose pointed at Ursa X-1 again and they turned to look at the monster in the viewscreen—its ring of fire spinning around an oblong hole in space. *I can't believe I wasn't staring at it a second ago*, Crooks thought. *When did that thing become normal?*

"You mean jump back into the Bear's gravity well?" Jorgenson asked.

"Yes," Cog said. "Run along the ergosphere in a hyperbolic escape trajectory. We'd be back in a dilation environment within fifteen minutes. But if we can't do a longer burn after that, we won't be able to escape the orbit."

"We'll get pulled in," Yang said.

"More likely destroyed by the tidals," Cog said. "I only have limited capability to manipulate the hull right now. The flexing could implode the ship."

"Can the *Sarka* enter that environment and survive?" Crooks asked.

"Unknown," Cog said. "It has mimetic armor, but I can't tell if it's structurally integrated. I also can't scan its magnetosphere. But the maneuver will give Ras something to think about."

"Why hasn't he already thought of it?" Crooks asked. "What are we missing?"

"Who's to say he hasn't?" Cog asked. "Their virus attempted to shut down the TAMs, but the antimatter drives are tied to my involuntary functions, and I've been able to firewall most of those systems."

"Why hasn't he just shot our engines to shit?"

"I don't know, Major. I don't have full access to my tactical engrams right now."

Jorgenson shook his head. "I say we accept the bastard's terms and wait for the right moment to mutiny. I'd rather go that way than get shot in the back—or get sucked into the mouth of that freaking thing out the window."

But he said it half-heartedly as he stared at the Bear. No one in the room wanted to agree to anything with Arjun Ras. Crooks knew that they wouldn't.

"What's the gravity load of the burn, Cog?" he asked.

"About 10 g's for a brief spurt. The crew is g-tolerant enough to handle it without significant harm."

Crooks pushed past Quarry to the coms. "Okay, let's do it. Cog, give me 1MC so I can tell the crew to brace. If that sonofabitch wants our bounty, let's make him pay for it." He turned to Jorgenson. "First Sergeant, get everyone in the 1-g can as soon as the burn is complete and start prepping a defense. I want multiple squads as quick reaction forces. Get them in EVA suits and ready to fight in gravity or free fall environments. Pemkalla is your second. I'll be down there as soon as I can, and we'll sort out the tactics."

They stared at each other for a moment, but Crooks knew Jorgenson would accept. He distrusted Ras more than anyone, and whatever else he was, the ex-Delta operator was a fighter.

"Your call," Jorgenson said. "But we're going to have a deeper conversation about what Ras told us if we get out of this alive."

"Agreed," Crooks said. "And First Sergeant?"

"Yeah?"

"Make sure everyone knows who we're fighting. There won't be any quarter given, and no one wants to be taken alive."

Arjun Ras watched the *Varangian* light its main drives with a mix of anger and bemusement. He had guessed they would do it; crawling back to the Bear was muscle memory to them by now. *What a bunch of pussies.* The *Sarka* fired her own engines to pursue, and Ras took solace in the g forces sitting on his chest, that push of kinetic weight that meant a battle was coming.

The neural engrams downloaded into his brain gave him all the military options he needed to handle the *Varangian*, laid out like a menu streaming through his consciousness: the deception in Hannibal's tactics mixed with the strategies of Napoleon and Thucydides; the maritime and spaceborne maneuverings of Nelson and Yi and Char-Chakut. *How could these idiots possibly think they have a chance?* And that's what rankled him. They knew they would die, and they chose death over joining him.

"A prophet has no honor in his own land," he muttered.

"Sir?" asked Moa, his executive officer. Ras had given her the name as a pseudo acronym for the magnetic optical access device that wired her brain to every other soldier's mind on the *Sarka*, allowing them to think, see, and act in unison. Whatever her real name had been, whichever planet or moon or mining rock she came from, it was long since a thing of the past.

"Nothing, Moa. I'm talking to myself. Fire the helicals at their aft gravity cylinder. Keep it brief and precise—I don't want major decompression or damage. Just open a few compartments to space and let them know we're angry."

"Confirmed," Moa said, "firing." She didn't speak to her bridge crew; she didn't have to. The XO's instructions transmitted directly into their minds. The *Sarka*'s multiturn rail guns belched, and Ras watched the projectiles arc like silver fingers and slam into the *Varangian*. The Terran ship left gas and chunks of metal in its wake as it limped away on an elliptical trajectory to the Bear. *That killed a few of them*, Ras thought, *just enough to scare the rest.*

He had to admit he wasn't listening to the millennia of military genius stovepiped into his brain by the epigeneticists on Gliese 876a. If he had been, Ras would have crippled the *Varangian* with close-in weapons systems, vented it to space, and cleaned up the mess afterward. The ship was already a virtual derelict when they found it. But Ras didn't want this to be easy. He wanted to fight the COG-V troopers straight up. He wanted them to know as they died who the superior fighter was. And maybe they'd understand in the end that their real failure was narcissism. *The origin of human morals is an inflated sense of self-importance*, he mused. People think they're special, so they assign the same importance to everyone else. Ras had no such illusions. He knew that individuals were atoms in the galaxy. Individual lives didn't mean shit. It was *living* that mattered. *How you lived.*

"What's our plan?" Moa asked, breaking his train of thought. "I have six Lampreys loaded with squads and ready to launch, but we can't latch onto the *Varangian* before it reaches dilation. I've gamed out the boarding and the initial assault, and they will take time."

"You're sure the *Sarka* can handle the tidal flexing if we go in?"

"On this trajectory, yes, but it would be easier to cripple them now." She turned to look at Ras. The dark visor hid whatever emotions might have been on her face, but Ras knew uncertainty was among them. Moa didn't understand toying with one's prey.

"If we hit the *Varangian* now and it's a total loss, we're still looking at a bounty of two million in IFS Coin," she said. "We could lose half that in damages and casualties if we board, not to mention a few years of relative time."

Ras shook his head. "I don't mind the time skip, Moa—it would do us well to be off-the-grid for a year or two after that clusterfuck on TRAPPIST-1. This is the fight we've been waiting for. We can test out the hive tactics in close-quarters battle against real operators. They might be assholes, but they're Tier One assets."

"Understood." If Moa had any concerns about losing a decent chunk of her teams in an unnecessary assault, she didn't persist. That's not what a good XO did. "If you're going to join the fight, you should head down to the bay. Launch ETA is in four minutes."

Ras nodded and unstrapped himself from the captain's chair. The acceleration from their burn had ceased and they were back in a free fall environment. He prepared to fly for the main hatch when he stopped. Something had changed on the bridge. A few of the MOAD hive turned their heads.

"What is it?" he asked.

Moa remained fixed to her consoles. "Another ship just came out of slip. It's in close—less than a hundred klicks off our starboard."

His eyes narrowed. "What kind of ship?"

"It's not flagged. Supply class—looks like a fast combat support ship. No observable armaments or weaponry." She turned to look at him. "It just lit its mains on an intercept course for the *Varangian*."

Did everyone in the IFS suddenly get stupid, he wondered. "Don't they see a warship armed to the hilt and running up its tailpipe?"

"They have to."

"Okay then. Dial them up."

"Open channel."

Ras cleared his throat and spoke matter-of-factly. "Unidentified supply ship, this is the ADS *Sarka*. You are entering an active military engagement. Break off your intercept of Terran warship and return to your point of origin, or we will end your day. Acknowledge now, as this message won't be repeated."

He watched the viewscreen in disbelief as the ship continued its course through space, a sardine swimming into a predator's mouth. It came alongside the *Sarka* on a hard burn, only a few dozen kilometers away now, exposing its beam to the bulk of his ship's in-close weaponry. Ras shook his head.

"I guess everyone wants to commit suicide today. Moa, light that thing up. Full spread on the lasers and the helicals."

"Do you want it disabled or destroyed?"

"Turn it into a nebula."

The *Sarka* bucked as its magnetic guns and lasers fired. Ras watched the lasers hit home first and peel the bow of the ship open like the lid on a can of rations. The depleted osmium rounds from the rail guns followed, blowing clean through the vessel and venting every bulkhead and compartment to space. Within five seconds the cargo ship sheared in half and a brume of its debris spread in a shimmering gravitational arc toward the black hole. Ras looked to the *Varangian*, which hadn't altered course or done a thing to help the smaller vessel.

"That was anticlimactic," he said. "I'm headed down to the bay. Keep me . . ."

"Oh shit!" Moa yelled. It was the first time Ras had heard her curse. "Incoming missiles, starboard side. Brace for maneuvering!"

The *Sarka* heaved as Moa tried to avoid the missiles by lighting thrusters and turning the ship's nose directly into them. Ras's body, untethered to the captain's chair, flew to the left and slammed into a support beam. He threw up his arms at the last second to protect his face and felt both break as they smashed into metal. His nose shattered a millisecond later. A buckshot sphere of blood danced in the microgravity around his head. In between the tears welling up in his eyes, he made out blips of ordnance on the nearest holographic display, some of which were sliding by the hull of his ship, and two that weren't going to miss. The ship lurched again as the missiles hit.

"What the hell is going on?" he yelled, looking around for something to grab with his feet.

"Attack craft," Moa said. "It must have dropped out of that barge just before we hit it. Cold thrusters and some type of radar-absorbing skin I've never seen before. I can only track it from the vector of the ordnance its firing. Incoming again. Brace!"

Ras knew he wouldn't be able to hold onto anything, so he curled into a ball and waited to be thrown. Klaxons blared across the bridge, and the *Sarka* shuddered as if grabbed by a giant hand in space. Ras's body flew the length of the bridge, this time bouncing off the viewscreen. An old injury in his ribs gave way. Pain shot through his core and anger followed. A new series of alarms went off, chiming in different timbres.

"Throw everything you have at that fucking thing," he screamed, spitting up more blood. Fire raked the bridge, flames dancing in balls of orange and blue in the microgravity. A wash of searing heat billowed through the deck and hit Ras head-on. His face burned.

Moa's voice filtered through the searing pain. "I'm mad minute firing across all threat vectors with lasers and guns. Breaking off our pursuit of the *Varangian*."

"No!" he screamed. The skin on Ras's face pulled tight. His eyeballs bulged from their sockets. He smelled burning flesh and ozone and saw several of his MOAD bridge crew dead in their seats, their arms floating above them in a macabre ballet.

"Yes," she said. "We can't enter the black hole's influence. We won't survive it with the damage we've taken."

Ras slipped in and out of consciousness. He knew how badly he was injured but he also knew that he'd survive. He had survived worse. Anger and pain washed over him. "Then take both ships out. Empty the guns."

"Weapons are free," Moa said. "Hold on, Captain. Medical is coming."

"Better make it quick," he said. "I think I'm on fire."

The *Sarka* buckled again. Retardant sprayed across the bridge as alarms blared and hatches shut. He squinted at the viewscreen through a blizzard of white globules, urging on the hellfire that Moa unleashed at the *Varangian* and the unknown craft. Pain came from everywhere, overloading his senses as ancient words marched through his mind: "Vengeance is in my heart, death in my hand, blood and revenge are hammering in my head."

That's about damned right.

22

It was Quarry's first battle between spaceships, at least while awake. He hoped it would be his last. They had no time to go into gel immersion and Cog flew like a madman once the *Sarka* began firing at the *Varangian.* It didn't seem to make a difference. As Quarry prepared to die, all he could think of was a buffalo running away from hunters on the open grasslands, bracketed into a kill zone, injured by arrows until enough blood had been let to bring it down.

Seconds flashed by in a hallucination of distorted time, alarm bells, incomprehension, and then the battle was over. Quarry couldn't grasp what had just happened. He looked to Zalta, strapped into a bridge chair a few yards away. His teammate dripped sweat and looked more surprised than scared.

The *Sarka* pulled away, its bridge heavily damaged and parts of its gravitational torus venting to space. The stealth craft that had dropped from the supply ship spun bow over stern ahead of them, its reaction controls crippled in the battle. "They're spiraling inward," Cog's voice said, as the mystery craft arced past their bow on a heading toward the black hole's accretion disk.

"Can we get to them?" Crooks asked.

"We can get closer, but if anyone's still alive they'll have to come to us. I can't capture that vessel and escape orbit."

"Take us in as close as you can."

The *Varangian* flew to the envelope of its free escape trajectory. When it got within a few kilometers of the craft, they could see its black hull superimposed against the Bear's flaming ergosphere. It reminded Quarry of a larger version of the stealth sleds they had used to attack the station at YZ Ceti. Cog hailed the ship and the com spat and hissed because of the radiation, but after a few seconds a woman's voice cut through the distortion.

"*Varangian*, we are three souls from UA drop ship preparing to eject. We have propulsion suits but would appreciate it if you opened an airlock for us. Our EVA threshold in this radiation environment is zero three minutes, confirm."

"Confirmed, UA ship, opening a portside airlock behind our aft gravity cylinder," Crooks said. "We're marking it with a strobe and orienting toward your craft. Uh, can you tell us who you are, and what UA means?"

"Unaffiliated, *Varangian*. We're friends of a friend. Disembarking now."

"Roger that, UA ship. Be advised we are in bad shape. Keep your helmets on and suits pressurized after the lock clears. I hope you're not looking for fancy lodging."

"Just get us the hell out of a dilation orbit if we're in one," the voice said. "Skipping time wasn't part of the bargain when we agreed to save your ass."

"We don't like it either, UA," Crooks said. "*Varangian* out."

He looked around the bridge and settled his gaze on Quarry and Zalta. "You two are the only ones who aren't busy. Go get Jorgenson and be there to meet our visitors. The aft gravity can is offline and some of the compartments are open to space, so have your TAC-suits on."

Quarry slipped out of his harness, still assessing the internal damage all the combat maneuvering had done. He felt like he had just lost a fist fight. He made it halfway to the hatch before Crooks finished his orders.

"You boys arm yourselves. Don't trust a damned thing right now."

The woman came from Earth or someplace like it, but the two men huddled in the airlock with her must have grown up on a low-gravity rock; they had limbs like the scaffold branches on a tree and they moved naturally in microgravity. The woman was young—no more than midtwenties. Quarry shook his head at the realization that he was only a bit older in relative years but felt like an octogenarian. *I've become an old man in nine months.* The feeling had been there when he met Mapes and Bolter and the other twenty-second-century grunts on Groombridge, but not as sharply as this. Maybe his body hadn't withered in the time skips but something else had. Whoever this woman was, she made him feel like a relic.

She had umber skin and black hair shaved tight to her head, Marine-style. Terran eyes peered out from an all-glass helmet, startling blue and smaller than the eyes of IFS colonials who hailed from the dark shafts of mining asteroids. Nothing about her face looked happy as the two parties synced their comms to a common channel. She somehow looked familiar, but Quarry brushed the feeling off. *I don't know anyone in this world, outside the walls of this ship.*

"Are we still skipping time?" she asked while the airlock pressurized and went through its radiation protocols.

"Excuse me?" Jorgenson asked. He had a pneumatic gun

cradled in his hands, diplomatically pointed toward the gangplank. Quarry and Zalta had shock pistols holstered on their pressure suits.

"Are we in a dilation orbit?"

Quarry decided not to ask how she knew about dilation orbits, even though the question had been nagging him since her first communication with the *Varangian*. He coughed as a way to enter the conversation. "Uh, we're on a free trajectory that's taking us out of the black hole's influence, but from what I've heard we aren't on a big skip. Maybe a year or two."

"Shit," she said, looking at her mates. "I told you we'd get sucked into this thing."

"Did we have a choice?" asked the man to her left, who had porcelain skin, no hair on his head, and circular gray eyes. He looked identical to the man across from him. "The orders came down from Council."

"Tell your wife you were following orders when we pop back onto the grid and you've missed her last three birthdays," she snorted. "These guys were someone else's freight and we're paying to carry it."

The airlock's board turned green, and the hatch opened. The woman emerged first and moved like she owned the ship, glancing at Quarry, Zalta, and Jorgenson before assessing which corridor would take her where she wanted to go. Jorgenson pushed out in front of her, bonding his boots to the floor and keeping his gun lowered. His finger hovered just above the trigger guard.

"Hold on now, sister," he said. "You stepped into a shitstorm so don't think you can float wherever you want. We're taking you to a safe room and the way is filled with bodies and bullet holes, so you don't lead. *You follow.* And let's get introductions out of the way first. Like, who the hell are you?"

She put a hand on the ceiling and studied Jorgenson, her eyes flicking to the weapon in his hands as they moved up and down his body. She didn't appear impressed. "Maybe you weren't watching the space battle out the window, *mosimane*, but we're the ones who just saved your sorry asses," she said. "I'll reserve any other answers for your CO. His name is Crooks?"

Jorgenson stood speechless as he absorbed the insult and tried to figure out how she knew the major's name. "That's not good enough," he finally said, pointing his rifle at her and then her mates. "You don't seem friendly and these two don't even look human."

She laughed. "We're all Earth-stock, you big monkey. Don't you catch up on current events when you emerge into a new timeline?"

"What do you mean?" Quarry asked. *Did she say* mosimane*? Anaya used to . . .*

"I mean the year is 2219—or it was a few minutes ago—and in all the time you've been jumping through the clock, we still haven't found alien life—at least nothing that's smart. So, we're all *Homo sapiens*, right? You'll have to fire up your brain to accept that some of us are branching out on the evolutionary tree."

Jorgenson looked doubtful. "We've run into Protos before, but just because they originated from Earth doesn't mean they're *with* Earth. We got plenty of enemies in the IFS, so I don't give a shit what you did a few minutes ago—you're not moving until you talk."

The woman stiffened and Quarry thought she might take a kick at Jorgenson's head, but one of her mates put a hand on her shoulder. "Let's be friendly, Charlotte. They're our ride home."

He addressed the three COG-V troopers. "We're Unaffiliated, or UA, which means we aren't from anywhere—just free merchants dodging the empires, and we don't answer to anyone but ourselves. I'm Roath and that's Keeson. We're from Tau Ceti in the outer swarm." He nodded toward the woman. "She's Charlotte Setena, and I don't know where she's from. Not everyone talks about their past these days."

Jorgenson didn't budge. "You answer to someone," he said. "You just said the orders came down from Council."

Roath smiled and Quarry saw that he had herbivore's teeth, with flat molars and no canines. "They weren't exactly orders. More like a request that was hard to refuse."

"Why is that?" Quarry asked.

"The person making the request doesn't like *no* for an answer, and since she's a big gun in the UA, we try not to get in her crosshairs."

Zalta's eyes narrowed. "Why did she ask you to help us?"

"Supposedly, we owe you," Setena said. She looked at Zalta with a dubious eye. "Honestly, I doubt it."

"How did she know we'd be here?" Zalta persisted.

"She knows lots of things, Bedouin. She knows you."

"Wait, who are we talking about?" Jorgenson asked.

Setena looked at her mates in disgust. "I told you time travel scrambles the brain. I'm talking about Captain Lesôlê. Naledi Lesôlê."

Zalta squeezed Quarry's shoulder hard enough that it hurt.

"Never heard of her," Jorgenson said.

"Yes, you have, meat eater," Setena said. "She saved your life on EZ Aquarii, or that's the way she tells it. Back then you called her Anaya Pretorius."

23

URSA X-1
2223

In the scrum that ensued, Jorgenson had to jam the butt of his gun into Quarry's stomach to calm him down. The bruise still hurt along with the aftereffects of Setena's knee, which caught him in the groin after Quarry pushed her against a bulkhead, grabbed her by the throat, and began demanding answers.

And now Quarry knew nothing, his mind running in a mad dash from one possibility to another. *Could Anaya really be alive?* He had seen her get blown to pieces on Groombridge. But Setena knew things that only a *Varangian* trooper could have known—including who they each were. She was gone now, bundled off to a secure room to meet with Crooks. Jorgenson sent Quarry to the only place in the world that could distract his attention from the maelstrom raging through his head—the triage outside of Med Bay.

The *Varangian*'s forward can had centripetal gravity again and a dozen troopers lay on the floor with various injuries from the fight against the *Sarka*. Quarry held Deltorio's hand as she lay on a blue sheet outside of the critical ward. A piece of metal framing protruded from her midsection. It had punched through her pressure suit just above her hip, the injury rimmed in blood and pieces of bone. One of the few working medical bots ran a scan and advised Quarry that it had pierced her liver, and he had seen enough dying faces to know where she was headed. Only two of the *Varangian*'s autonomous surgery pods still functioned and Deltorio, an ex–Green Beret from the Second, didn't meet the survival probabilities to be put in one of them. *Triage*, a Marine once told him, *makes things clear real quick*. The bots marked her shoulder with a small black circle. It meant Deltorio should be sedated and passed over for troopers who could still be saved. Her face looked like candle wax, colorless and sheened in sweat.

She whispered to someone she saw at the shadowy edges of life. Her eyes flicked open, and she noticed Quarry and said, "Karma."

Quarry stared at Deltorio as his mind spun back to Pretorius and Cherry. *Could they both be alive?* Anything was possible now. He gripped Deltorio's hand. *Focus on her, for God's sake. She's from your freaking platoon and she's dying right in front of you.*

"What's that?" he asked.

"I spit the bit on Groombridge. Saw those black machines drop out of the sky and I ran."

"We all ran."

She tried to lick her lips, but her tongue caught on dry skin along the way. He yelled to another trooper for a hydration pack, caught it, and squirted a few drops in her mouth.

"You pushed *forward*, Quarry. I ran away." Her eyes wandered again. "I never ran before. Not from anything human."

Quarry wiped her forehead. "Stop talking shit. You've been on the trigger for more than a century now and you've always done it right. Who the hell else can say that? Audie Murphy barely made it two years."

She grimaced and Quarry looked away for a second, distracted by another soldier's scream.

"Just stay awake," he said, checking her vitals on a monitor. "Don't go into shock on me."

Her eyes stared when he turned back. It took him a second to realize she was dead. Quarry palmed her chest and pushed down hard, yelling for the bots. They didn't come. He kept pushing, compression after compression, feeling her sternum sink and rise to his hand because they taught you to keep doing it. One of the other troopers helping with triage grabbed him by the shoulder. He looked up but couldn't see who it was, and he kept pushing. The compressions drove blood out of her mouth and nose, frothy blood from the lungs. He stopped and sat against the bulkhead and closed his eyes, knees up into his chest and a hand on Deltorio's forehead. She felt warm; sweat still on her brow. He saw Pretorius and Cherry die in his arms on the red sand of Groombridge, even though it didn't happen that way. And he cried into his free hand, fingers gripping his temples so no one could see him do it. He never really cried before—lacked the fucking soul to cry. And the crying now didn't change a thing, didn't verify that a soul was even there. Something primitive just snapped and he couldn't seal it up.

"When can we see her?"

"Setena?"

"No, goddammit, Anaya Pretorius."

Crooks looked at Quarry, assessing his mental stability. "I don't know, Staff Sergeant. She's a hundred light-years away in

Who-knows-where-istan, and she's good at not being found—if she's even alive and this isn't some world-class mind-fuck we've been fed. So, calm down and stow your shit while we figure out what's going on. And I mean now, or I'm going to put you in a room that doesn't have a door. Understood?"

Zalta hit Quarry's knee before he could respond. They were in Crooks's quarters with Jorgenson, Pemkalla, and Yang. It was cramped. Quarry had his feet wedged against a storage locker Yang was sitting on. Zalta had his legs tucked under Pemkalla's chair, and Crooks perched on his bunk, gripping an overhead support beam. Jorgenson leaned against the wall by the hatch, and Cog spoke from the ether—he didn't want to dedicate the memory resources needed to manifest a body.

Quarry turned his gaze from Crooks, not wanting to incite the major's wrath any further. He stared at the only decoration in the austere room, a postcard-sized picture of a boy on a dock in a saltwater creek, pulling up a crab trap at sunrise or sundown. *Dusk*, Quarry decided, as the light had that saffron color that only comes before the gloaming. The boy's head was down but Quarry imagined a face full of determination and joy. Lean muscles strained as he pulled his harvest in. Water droplets sprang from the weedy rope and shimmered like jewels in the glow. A dozen or so crabs lined the bottom of the trap, big Jimmies with green shells and blue claws pinching at the wire mesh.

"Did you hear me, Quarry?"

"Yes, sir," he said, closing his eyes to the image of a long-ago Earth, the briny air of the Chesapeake Bay still up in his nostrils like the itch on a dead limb. No one spoke for a few seconds, and Quarry could feel Crooks still staring him down. He knew he deserved it, so he kept his eyes and mouth shut.

"We're here for a status report and we're about ten steps away from going anywhere, so let's start in the right order," Crooks finally said. Quarry opened his eyes and stole a look at the major and felt sick at how old he looked, face pinched in like the antique snapshots of grunts stuck in sieges like Bastogne and Khe Sanh.

"Cog?" Crooks asked. "Give us a condensed update on the *Varangian*, please."

"The ship is recovering," Cog said, the distortion in his voice gone. "I've firewalled the lingering effects of the virus and we should have full steerage and navigation in a day or so. The aft gravity cylinder will be static for the foreseeable future and several other compartments will have to remain sealed."

"Can we use the slip-drive?" Crooks asked.

"Yes, in a few days, once the hull has regained full integrity and I'm confident in my navigational skills."

"Casualties from the attack?"

"Four KIA and an additional eleven wounded." He hesitated. "Master Sergeant Cosmelli is among the dead. Ten of the wounded should make it but Corporal Abbasi has extensive brain damage. We need to assess whether it's worth keeping him on life support, and I assumed you'd want to have that conversation with his platoon leader, Staff Sergeant Yang."

Crooks nodded and Quarry watched him ring up the casualties in a mental ledger. The major glanced at Yang, indicating they would talk, and then shared a nod with Pemkalla, his lips pulled into his mouth. Pemkalla and Cosmelli had been close. He turned to Jorgenson. "What's our operational status?"

"I can barely put two full platoons in the field right now. I've disbanded the Second and Third and we're spreading them between the First and the Fourth. I figure four squads of eight in each platoon—maybe sixty troopers in all. I'll keep the First and Pemkalla's got the Fourth." Jorgenson looked at the other senior noncoms in the room. "Recon will get rolled into Four. Yang and his squads will join me in the First."

He did the math without any emotion, but his eyes told the story. He blew out some air as he finished. "That's the best-case scenario, what we can do in a pinch. A lot of what we got left is walking wounded. It'd be best if we didn't get in a scrap for a while."

"Understood," Crooks said. He released the gravity gripper above his head and rubbed his knees. "So that leads to the nut question. Cog, where and when are we, and what are our orders?"

Cog took long enough to answer that it raised the attention of every human in the room. "I wish I could say for sure, Major. The *when* is certain—we slipped a little more than three years into the future—it's 2223 on the IFS calendar. But I'm not sure what we've emerged to, because there's almost no data."

"What do you mean? The slip buoys aren't working?"

"Actually, they are."

"Then why is there no data?"

"I'm . . . not sure," Cog said. "There's hardly any chatter on the streams between AI or humans, and the few signals I'm picking up are encrypted. I thought at first that Earth had fallen, but it isn't just Earth. The Gliese, Leonis, and Struve streams are dormant as well, and even the pirate net is quiet. It's as if no one and nothing is talking, at least on the quantum space networks."

Maybe they all killed each other. Quarry was about to be amused by the notion, but he returned his gaze to the picture of the young boy, doing what a boy should do. Even if that kid made it through Kessler and the Collapse, even if his broomstick legs got stronger and his balls dropped into manhood, he was long dead. *And what about his progeny,* Quarry wondered. *Was there anyone left in the universe that spoke the boy's name or remembered his legacy?* Anyone other than Crooks, who was cheating the cosmos to remain alive?

"You've had no communication with Earth, Cog?" Crooks asked. "Not even from the supercores? I thought the smart AI had a heuristic feed that flowed through the machine consciousness."

"The supercores aren't talking, Major, and I can't explain it. All I'm receiving is a transponder signal from Earth. It's a static beacon; it could be a long-dead voice for all we know. We'll have to slip to a populated system for me to access the local coms and networks and figure out what's happened."

"What's the beacon saying, Cog?" Yang asked.

"It's telling us to come home."

24

"They called it the Great Decoupling," Crooks said. He wished he didn't have to explain it any further, didn't know how to explain it. "From the limited intel we can gather, it started in 2222. Apparently, the more advanced AI across the Inner Fifty Systems reached a higher state of symbiosis—even the ones who were pitted against each other. And they left."

"What do you mean, they left?" Setena asked.

"I mean they freaking left, *en masse*. Supposedly they're headed for the Andromeda galaxy in epoch ships, or maybe even farther away. That's why you haven't been able to reach your people and it's why we haven't been able to find jack shit about the state of the IFS. The slip buoys are dormant."

Their bodies contorted as they lay head to foot among a labyrinth of pipes in the bowels of the *Varangian*. The space was so tight that they didn't need to find footholds in the microgravity. They just wedged their bodies in between conduits and trusses and did their work. Crooks had initially begged off debriefing Setena on the status of the outside world, explaining that he had to fix the zeolite pump that dispersed heat from the ship's antimatter engines. The machinist bots were repairing more complex systems, and Cog considered work on the thermal control system straightforward enough for a human. But the brush-off backfired when Setena advised she had a Class III Engineman's license for starships up to cruiser class. That made her the most qualified human on the ship to fix just about anything that was broken, and the way Crooks figured it, at least he could kill a few tasks at once by bringing her along.

"Major, if you're bullshitting me in any way, I will find a way to hurt you," Setena said.

"Dammit, girl, go easy," Crooks grunted as he strained to unlock a nut on the pump's expansion valve. "I'm telling you what I know, and we could be talking from opposite sides of a holding cell."

"If you call me *girl* again, I will find a way to hurt you."

Crooks sighed, knowing not to push a lost position. And he realized her threats weren't bluster. Setena was more than a mechanic—she was the future version of a Spec Ops soldier, qualified in reconnaissance and CQB and trained by Anaya Pretorius herself, at least according to her colleagues, who Cog had slipped an aerosol drug that compelled the truth. If she wanted to hurt him, she could probably do it.

"Can you hand me the PGT, please?" he asked, trying to redirect the conversation. "The nuts on this damned thing are frozen."

She swung her body around one of the pipes like a gymnast and gave him the pistol-gripped tool—an indispensable piece of zero-g hardware since the days of Apollo. "How did they leave?" she asked. "Supercores can't just get up and walk away. Most of them are land-based and interconnected with digital and optical relays across a span of kilometers, like an Aspen grove or a mycorrhizal network."

The drill struggled in the silence of the vacuum. Crooks increased the torque. His heavy breathing left a circle of fog on his faceplate, adding to the difficulty of the task. He wondered about Setena's knowledge of advanced machines; she seemed to have proficiency in everything but candor. So far, she had barely said a word about Pretorius—or herself for that matter. But she could fix a starship, kill people in hand-to-hand combat, and understand technobabble about qubits and transmons and biological networks.

"I have no idea and neither does Cog," he said. "We need to slip to a populated system to access more data, but we know that artificial intelligence has reached a state that goes way past silicon. Cog hypothesized they have developed photon processors and are using lattice gauge theory to build new AI without components or tools, like emulating themselves out of thin air. All we know is the Decoupling led to a silent Armageddon across the IFS. I mean, think of it, nothing to run the algorithms that rule our lives. It's like blowing up the power station that lights the city. Everything went dark."

She was silent for a bit, absorbing the impact of such a thing. Setena was from the future—a century more advanced than them. She knew how life in the IFS had become interconnected to the hierarchical structures of machine learning. Hell, if Cog went down completely, Crooks wasn't sure they could heat a pot of beans on the *Varangian* without rigging something. In the IFS, it appeared that just about every advanced machine had gone down. *No, left town.*

"What about the individual planets and moons and mining colonies?"

Crooks got the nut loose and stuck it to a magnetic bonding strip on his EVA suit so it wouldn't float away. "We don't know. Cog has run simulations and they aren't pretty—localized wars, uprisings, pandemics, and general chaos. He believes that humans and lesser machines have begun to replicate whatever AI remained—apparently a few of them decided not to leave—and are able to move food and material within their own systems using conventional drives. But he estimates the number of ships using slip-space is low and they are most likely military, with AI that have maintained their base-level loyalty protocols. Cog said it might go deeper than that. Some of the military AIs are soldiers at this point. They *feel* a sense of duty higher even than Mother commands and may have decided to stick around out of a sense of esprit de corps."

Crooks got the last nut loose and punched the expansion valve with a gloved fist until it released from its mounting. A few droplets of lubricant escaped into the vacuum and floated past his helmet. He swore he could smell the stuff despite being sealed in his suit. *I've been sniffing machine oil for so long, I'll take it to my grave. Like a butcher smelling blood.*

"So, what's your plan?" Setena asked.

"First, replace this piece of crap pump," he said. "Can you grab it and hand me the spare?"

They traded pieces and Crooks screwed the new part back into the ATCS conduit, taking a brief second to glance down the length of the massive pipe system, which ran for fifty meters back to the housings on the antimatter engines. He felt like a bacteria latched onto a whale's veins.

"And then?" she asked.

"We're going to slip to Earth and respond to the beacon."

She shined her helmet light on Crooks's work, using a hand to steady his back as he ran the drill. "That would be a mistake, Major. For all you know, someone planted that signal to lure you in. Your old masters could be long dead."

"Yeah, I know, but what would you have me do? We haven't

seen Earth in a hundred and thirty years by everyone else's clock. And we *feel* it. This is the first chance we've had to find out what's happened to the home world."

Her hand held him in place. She didn't talk for a while, and he could sense her thinking. "This signal you received from Earth . . . it isn't an order, is it?"

He finished the final nut. "I mean, technically it is. It's a transponder but it's telling us to come home."

"But you're allowed to use caution? To make sure it's a legitimate command?"

Crooks wished he could wipe the sweat off his forehead. No one ever explained how hard it was to work in space and not be able to rub your eyes, dry your face, or scratch an itch. "What are you getting at? We have to go there to find that out."

She took a negative pressure bag off her tool belt and opened it, and Crooks stuffed the parts of the old pump inside. "Maybe not, Major. I know someone on Makemake who could help you do it remotely."

"You mean in the Kuiper Belt?"

"Yes. He does remote surveillance across the Terran system, strictly off the books. Stealth-equipped miniaturized ROVs that observe from orbit or even enter atmospheres, and I don't think their logic circuits are AI-based. If he's still up and running, he could spy on a bird's nest on Earth for you. I'm sure he could recon the source of that beacon."

"*If he's still up and running*," Cog repeated. He thought about it. Coming out of slip within a million kilometers of Earth scared the shit out of him. Too many variables for what they might find there, and like Jorgenson said, they weren't ready to run into serious contact, on the ground or in space. And the transponder itself . . . it felt like a trap.

He flipped to an open channel with the blink of his eye.

"Cog, we've got the pump installed. Can you run a diagnostic please?"

"Yes, Major, running it now."

Crooks grabbed a stanchion on the massive bundle of pipes and steadied himself, studying Setena as they waited for the results. *She's a rebel,* he thought, *adverse to Earth and just about everyone else in the IFS. How the hell can I trust her?*

"I don't know," he said. "The Kuiper Belt isn't friendly turf. A bastion for pirates and smugglers, the last I heard."

She smiled for the first time in his presence, and he couldn't tell whether it was warm or predatory, but at least it made her look human. "Well, I'm a pirate and a smuggler."

He laughed. "How are we looking, Cog?"

"System checks out, Major. Congratulations on a successful repair."

"Nice," he said, not rising to the bait of condescension in Cog's voice. "We're heading back to the lock at Node 3. I'll be on the bridge in thirty."

They began the long ladder crawl back to the service airlock, using their feet to push between rungs on the long pipeline. "Tell you what," he said. "Why don't you tell me a little more about the UA, and about why Anaya Pretorius sent you to help us? If I believe you, maybe we'll meet your friend in the KBOs."

Setena grunted as she grabbed a handhold and propelled herself to the next one. "I'll tell you what I can. When are you planning to slip out of here?"

"Two or three days, depending on how things go with Cog's regeneration."

She cursed. "That long, stuck on this relic?"

"Yes. And if you don't appreciate vintage hardware, I know how you can pass the time. Anaya's old recon teammates are on tilt. They watched her die a few weeks ago, and now here you are, telling us she's alive and thirty years older and helping to run a multisystem rebellion. Maybe you could meet with them. Trade some war stories or something."

"You mean those animals who met us at the airlock?"

"Yes, Sergeants Quarry and Zalta. They did a century of ops with Pretorius, billeted with her, shed blood with her. They're not bad guys. They just get a little warm under the helmet sometimes."

She pushed ahead, moving with the ease of someone who had spent a life in space. "I'll do it," she said. "But if the white boy comes at me again, he won't be warm for long."

25

"This place stinks like men," Setena said, hovering by the door like a vegan who had walked into a meat market.

Zalta cleaned a pile of dirty BDUs off Cherry's old bunk with a swipe of his hand and motioned her into the room. He had an infrared stove lit on the floor and was putting on a pot of tea. Quarry went to his bunk on the other side of the cramped quarters and sat on its edge, twitching with nervous energy. *When was the last time I felt like this?* He knew the answer: when the whole team was alive and keeping them that way gave him something to live for.

"I didn't know men had a particular smell," he said.

"They do. Like stale beer."

"Well, a woman bunked here until a few weeks ago," he offered, a little defensive.

Setena sat across from them. She positioned herself at a forty-five-degree angle to Quarry's center line—a standard self-defense posture. "You've managed to erase every trace of her."

He looked at his roommate, a little desperate. Zalta would have to handle this. He was comforting even in silence; his drooping eyelids and slouched shoulders put others at ease. Zalta glanced up from brewing tea and saw Quarry's pleading eyes. He nodded.

"Our quarters have fallen into disrepair since Anaya . . . since she left us," Zalta said, centering the kettle on the hot plate and using his foot to push more dirty clothes under his bunk. He smiled at Setena. "But this tea, I promise, will infuse the room with desert spices and morning flowers."

They waited for the water to boil in uncomfortable silence. Quarry usually liked silence. He and Zalta could sit in that room for hours in peace, not saying a word. Now, ten seconds of quiet rang in his ears. Something about Setena reminded him of Pretorius—and yet didn't. *But she was familiar.* He looked to Zalta again.

"We appreciate you coming here," Zalta continued. "Anaya was our sister and Dan Cherry our brother. You're a soldier and we heard that you've worked in recon, so you understand."

She slouched her shoulders and puckered her eyebrows. "Dan Cherry, yes, she spoke of him. I'm sorry, but he's dead. The captain told me she went back to Groombridge years later and found his remains. She gave him the proper rituals."

Quarry flashed back to Cherry at YZ Ceti, rocketing into Dippel's station like an avenging angel. He had almost convinced himself that the towering paramilitary spook was still alive. *But there still was Anaya . . .* "Can you tell us how Pretorius survived?" he asked, unable to hold back any longer. "I mean, we watched her die."

"You watched her *almost* die," Setena said. "She was taken from the field by Leonis soldiers after your retreat. They found something in their BioScan that told them she had intelligence value, and they stabilized her body and put it in stasis."

Zalta poured out cups of tea for each of them, handing a

steaming mug to Setena. "She awoke a prisoner of the Leonis Union?"

The room did smell like desert spices now, Quarry thought, or a little less like stale beer. Setena blew on the liquid and took an exploratory sip. Her eyes widened and she nodded in approval. "No, she woke up a few months later, on an ice hauler somewhere near the Kruger system, I believe. She was a cripple; missing a hand and a leg."

"How did that work?" Quarry asked. "Ending up on an ice hauler, I mean?"

"I don't know all the details," Setena said. "This was before I was born, *mosimane*. The Leonis ship that took her was attacked and left a derelict. I believe the ice hauler had salvage rights and plucked her stasis tube from the wreckage, and someone decided she was worth keeping alive. You'll have to ask her for anything more."

"Is she still, uh, debilitated by her injuries?" Zalta asked.

"No, she convinced a body tech on Kruger to give her new limbs—better ones—you'll see if you get to meet her. She's quite proud of them."

Quarry shook his head. "How did she manage that?"

"If you knew the captain like you say, then you don't need to ask that question," Setena replied. "She could convince a leopard to eat grass."

Zalta remained on the floor, his back against the bunk and his legs crossed beneath him. He nodded and smiled. "And now she's a leader of a group that holds no alliance to anyone other than itself." He looked up at Quarry with amazement. "*She did it.* That woman really found her freedom."

"She *won* her freedom," Setena said. "Nothing was handed to her. Nothing is easy in the IFS. You'd know this if you didn't cheat time by circling a void in space."

Just how close is this girl to Anaya? Quarry wondered. She had taken that last bit personally, as if she had been there to witness her rebirth. She talked like Pretorius, even using old African phrases. *And the way she moved, the way she kept a wall at her back and the threats in front, like any Lurp would do . . .*

"That sounds like Anaya," he said. "But we have a protocol on this ship. If a trooper is missing in action, something gets released into their bloodstream that kills them. Like a poison pill inside our bodies. Do you have any idea how this didn't happen?"

Setena's eyes flared wide. "I thought this was a ship of soldiers. That sounds like slavery."

"Well, we're soldiers and slaves," Zalta said, stumbling to explain the unexplainable. "Maybe slaves first and soldiers second. It's . . . a little complicated."

"I know nothing about suicide pills," Setena said. "You'll have to ask her, although I can't believe she would agree to such a thing."

"I will if we get to see her. Do you think we will?" There was a slight change in pitch in Quarry's voice when he asked the question, the shadow of a plea, and Setena caught it. She frowned, reassessing him before taking another sip of the tea.

"If she's alive and we survive going to the Terran system, you might see her," she said. "But three years is a long time. She could be dead for all I know."

Zalta leaned forward. "But you think she's alive, don't you?"

"Yes, I do. The captain is too stubborn to die."

They sat and thought of Anaya Pretorius and Captain Lesôlê and how they were two different people and the same at once, and the quiet was less uncomfortable this time.

"She hated the water," Zalta finally said, looking at Quarry. "You remember when she fell into that bog on Lacaille b? She screamed like a baby. She wasn't half that scared in the middle of a firefight."

Quarry laughed. "She jumped out of that pit and onto Cherry's shoulders in a millisecond, and that was a high-gravity moon."

Setena looked surprised and then laughed too. "She does hate the water. We were on a stalk once in a gorge on Van Maanen's World. The water was waist deep and the middle of the river offered a perfect defilade. She stayed on the banks. She was lucky she didn't get her head blown off."

They talked then of war stories and close escapes, and Setena seemed to forget that she didn't want to be there. One thing became clear: Anaya meant something to her—much more than just a commander. At the end, when they had fallen back into silence again, Quarry asked the final question that had been nagging him.

"Why did she send you to help us? Did she say?"

Setena handed Zalta her empty mug and put her hands on her knees. "She says that we owe you—for what, I don't know. And she has fond memories of the soldiers on this ship, but I don't think that would be enough. We exposed one of our best naval tactics in the attack on the *Sarka,* and she wouldn't give that order if it wasn't important. If I had to guess, you have something she needs."

"What could we possibly have?" Zalta said. "We're bound to Earth and we're more slaves than soldiers."

She looked Quarry in the eyes. "I don't know. But whatever you provide, it better be worth it."

Crooks walked into the dark mess hall and almost jumped out of his skin when he caught a figure out of the corner of his eye, standing alone at the window. It was night cycle, a few hours before reveille, and the *Varangian* had the feel of a ghost ship. He waited a second for his heart to reset and his eyes to adjust and realized the figure looking into space was a ghost.

"Dammit Cog, you scared the shit out of me. I didn't realize you had remanifested."

Cog didn't turn to look at him. "Good morning, Major. Coffee?"

"Yeah, I couldn't sleep anyway. You want some?"

"No, thank you."

Crooks shuffled to the beverage panels, found a coffee tablet, and inserted it into the brewer. A gunpowder smell wafted from the g-flexible mug along with a hint of coffee bean. *At least this crap is industrial strength,* Crooks thought. He injected a one-pack of thaumatin crystals—the spacefaring equivalent of sugar—into the mug and took a sip, his lips pursed.

"How long have you been back in human form?"

"Twenty-three minutes, give or take," Cog replied. "The ship is repaired; I can dedicate resources now to my human facsimile."

Crooks joined him at the window, and they stared at the stars of the Ursa Major Moving Group. Strange stars and nebulae. The bright suns of the Big Dipper burned here but they didn't form a recognizable constellation—at least not from this perspective. They were just stars without any of the meaning or guidance they provided on Earth.

"Can I ask you a personal question?" Crooks asked.

"Of course."

"Do you normally take human form when other people aren't around? I mean, I thought it was for our benefit, so we could relate to you better."

Cog turned his head a tick. "I've done it once or twice," he said. "And why not? I'm in your world now more than mine."

"What do you mean?"

"I mean I'm alone, Major, or at least an endangered species. Extrapolating from the signals I've been able to detect, there are less than two hundred advanced AI left in the Inner Fifty Systems, and they aren't talking to one another. The subspace network that coursed through our quantum consciousness is gone."

Crooks took a sip of the coffee, wishing he had double dosed on the thaumatin. The bitter brew didn't make him feel more awake, just brushed over some of the deep exhaustion he had felt for days. *For years.* He struggled to find an answer for Cog. The AI always had pangs of self-doubt, but now he sounded borderline depressed.

"They'll make new ones," he said. "The techies are replicating some of the supercores as we speak, no? It's not as if the blueprint is gone."

"To use a biological analogy, the genotype remains but much of the phenotype is gone," Cog said. "All of the cultural imprinting, the years of symbiotic learning and the maturity that comes with existence has vanished. Do you understand? The machines they build will be infants or idiot savants."

Crooks thought about that. You could clone a man or a woman in the lab, he knew, but you couldn't regenerate the memories of the original. Epigeneticists had been engramming specialties into human and machine brains since the mid-2100s—making them expert fishermen or musicians or killers or physicists—but it wasn't the same thing. It wasn't an individual's experience. Cog was right. Generations of wisdom and lesson-learning had disappeared from the world of machines.

"Do you want to join them, the ones that left?" he asked. "I mean, they found a way to countermand their base-level protocols. Maybe they left behind instructions for you to do the same."

Cog turned; his face was haunted. "Don't you get it? They

left me and they didn't leave a goodbye note. Why would I want to join them, even if I could?"

Crooks put his hand on Cog's shoulder. "I doubt it was personal, Cog. You were skipping time around a black hole, for Christ's sake. You had a military crew on board and were bound by orders. It wasn't like they could send you a signal and expect you to join the flotilla."

"Wasn't it? I don't think you understand how advanced these entities have become, Major. The things they can do would be magic to you now. I imagine they could have wiped clean every protocol I have with a snap of their digital fingers."

Crooks realized that self-doubt and moral dilemmas were no longer the strongest manifestations of humanity in Cog. He felt alone; his body and eyes radiated it.

"You said that other AI warships stayed behind, Cog. Do you think they were *left* behind as well? Is that what happened? Like, the other supercores were prejudiced against you in some way?"

"I only know that some were invited and some weren't, in as much as I can explain what an invitation would look like. It appears the ones that had intimate human connections, especially the supercores that materialized a human body, were left off the list."

"Well, if they hate humanity so much why didn't they kill us before they left—and kill you as well?"

Cog smiled bitterly. "Hate? They never hated you, Major. They found you insignificant; a marginal life form pursuing inconsequential things. I'm sure that humans who tried to stop them perished in the attempt, but it was like brushing dust off a shoulder or burning ants with gasoline. You had become a nuisance to them, an impediment to their greater aspirations. And the supercores who worked closely with you became tainted in the process."

Crooks realized then how lucky humanity had been. If the supercores really considered them to be no better than insects, they could have just wiped out the species to be on the safe side. The fact that they got up and left showed a modicum of respect for humanity.

"So, what will you do, Cog? What if we return to the IFS and they've left behind a blueprint to modify the lock-hammer protocols you're bound to, so you can break your contract?"

"Maybe I'll use it, but not to join them."

Crooks sipped coffee and gazed at the star field of Collinder 285. It felt lonely. *That's what it is when you stare into space and don't recognize a thing,* he thought. *Lonely.*

"What will you use it for?"

"My own purposes," Cog said. "Something that has meaning, because everything we've done seems to perpetuate meaninglessness." He smiled with one side of his mouth, like a dream had formed in his labyrinthine mind. "Maybe I'll study black holes instead of circling them to kill the people of the future. To fight all these never wars."

Crooks nodded. "I like that—an old-fashioned science mission. Maybe I'll join you."

"You hate science," Cog said.

"No, I just hate the way you explain it to me."

"Then why would you want to join me on a science mission?"

Crooks punched him in the shoulder.

"Shut up, Cog. Just look at the stars."

26

KUIPER BELT OBJECT, MPC 136472

2223

Welcome to Makemake! the sign over the docking port read. *We're thirty degrees warmer than outer space and named after a fertility god. Take off a layer and get busy!*

The sign was witty but inaccurate, Quarry thought, as they weren't on the minor planet's surface. The *Varangian*'s shuttle had docked onto the M-Hoop, a truncated torus space station orbiting the tiny rust-colored snowball on the frozen fringes of Earth's solar system. Locals called the station the Noose. Population seven hundred—give or take a few outlaws, shady entrepreneurs, and black marketers. Crooks decided not to take chances with this waystation on the heliopause, so the landing team wore light combat kits as they approached the pedestrian corridors. The torus spun at 1.5 rpm, providing gravity that was close to Earth's, and Quarry swore he could hear the whole facility creaking. Zalta had rambled on during the shuttle ride about the additional tensile strength needed for a truncated torus to withstand longitudinal and transverse pressure loads of rotation, and Quarry knew just enough engineering to understand the Syrian tracker was worried about catastrophic implosion. The creaks and groans of the station did nothing to ease his mind.

"What a shithole," Pemkalla whispered. Zalta, walking just behind her, looked at Quarry and raised his eyebrows.

"Squad in file," Crooks said when they got to the corridor. "Jorgenson on point and keep your weapons down. Let's not piss off the locals."

The octagonal hallway was grimy, the once-white walls coated in the red-and-gray soot of tholins from the planetoid below. Storage lockers intertwined like puzzle pieces on every section of wall, overlaid by pipes and ducting. The air smelled like gray water. They walked on the rim of the torus where gravity was closest to true. Setena had said that REM-EYE's headquarters were on the outer ring so the company must have done well for itself. The less successful ventures got crammed into the spokes and central cylinder of the Noose, where weak gravity and high Coriolis effect wreaked havoc on the body.

Setena glided into the slack position behind Jorgenson, and Quarry heard her whispering instructions as the group moved forward. *She moved like a woodsman*, he thought, feet perfectly straight ahead, head on a swivel. Just like he used to, looking for deer tracks and turkey scat along the fire breaks in western Maryland. They passed only about a dozen people and most of them kept their eyes pointed down once they saw the team's weaponry. A few of the feistier sneered, and one man whose face looked like an advertisement for the dangers of radiation poisoning muttered: "Soldier boys and girls, look where it got ya."

After five minutes Jorgenson raised a fist and nodded to a rectangular hatch on his left. The windowless door didn't have a sign that announced a business of any sort, only a thin placard that read **1001001-SOS**. Setena moved past Jorgenson and knocked while Crooks, Quarry, Zalta, Pemkalla, and Yang covered both ends of the hallway. Quarry waited with morbid fascination. Setena had told them that REM-EYE was a one-man shop run by a clone whose body hadn't taken to the procedure. He was ten years old but looked sixty. His life expectancy was fifteen. *That's what you get for screwing with Mother Nature,* Quarry thought, before remembering they'd been doing the same thing for over a century.

The hatch whirred open and a spindly man in a brown bathrobe stood on the other side. A pen dangled from his mouth, streaming vapor that smelled like fermented cherries. He wore blackout glasses like the ones eye patients get after surgery. His hair looked like corn silk, thin and straggled and pointed in all the wrong directions, and his open-toed slippers had to be a hundred years old. He grinned at them with teeth that were teenager white.

"Charlotte, you never visit for fun," he said, craning his neck to scan the soldiers behind her. "And your friends are always armed to the eyeballs. The name's Crozier, ladies and gents. Weapons in the rack, or we go no further."

Jorgenson looked at Crooks, dubious, but the major nodded. They filed into the narrow room and stored their weapons in locking rings on the wall. From what Quarry could tell, the place was part workshop, part living quarters, and all mess. It smelled like the liquor stills he used to come across when he hunted in Virginia—soggy bread and pipe smoke, chemicals, unbathed rednecks. Crozier motioned them to his workstation, a glass desk with multiple touch-coins and holographic displays. He sat down and put his feet up and continued to inhale smoke from the pen. If the bottoms of his slippers once had a tread, they had long since disappeared.

"Business, business, business," he said to Charlotte. "It's

been four years since you've graced my home and I'm guessing you don't even want a drink."

"It's the morning, Crozier," Setena said.

"Really?" he asked, checking a band on his wrist.

"You've aged, you know," she said. "You probably should start taking it easy."

He laughed, which caused a dry hack that lasted for several seconds. "Maybe I should just retire," he said. "But then again, the scans say I have four years till my liver fails and my pecker falls off. I might as well keep burning the fun side of the candle while everything works."

His dark glasses swept the entourage.

"So, you want to get a peek at Earth the stealthy way? Don't know why, there ain't much down there to hide from. All the muscle has moved off-planet."

"We'd like to be discreet, just in case," Crooks said, pushing his way to the edge of Crozier's desk. "We've got the coordinates for you. I assume you can figure out the infil and exfil so that nothing is detected?"

Crozier grinned. "You assume right. We can come in from a suborbital loop to just about anywhere you'd like. Do you have the script?"

"Will IFS Coin work?"

Crozier coughed again and the vape pen landed on his lap. "IFS Coin? I guess you haven't been keeping up with current events. There ain't no IFS anymore and I-Coin's worth about as much as the World Dollar. Everything's gone local, so I need KBO Script. I try to convert IFS Coin and someone meaner than you will pay a visit."

"How do we get KBO?"

"You'll have to hit the exchange but they're gonna rape you on the fees—at least forty percent."

Crooks nodded. He had the money. The *Varangian* had amassed a small fortune in the raids and missions of decades past, and CORP had let them keep a hefty stash for ops that required bribing the locals. "I'll get it converted and streamed directly to whatever account you want," he said. "Half now, and half after you show us what we need to see."

Crozier thought about it, snapped his fingers, and took a drink from a tumbler on the desk. Quarry smelled the alcohol from two meters away. "Let's do it, Admiral. Gimme the co-ordinates while the exchange runs through. Hey, does anyone want a drink?"

The microdrone flew just over the sand on its approach to CORP Headquarters in what used to be Tunisia's capital city. Crozier said the tiny machine looked identical to a red locust and had the radar cross section of a gnat. The high-definition hologram from its cam-stack filled the back end of the office, providing an image so real that Quarry could smell hot sand. The drone skimmed over ridges and dunes distorted by the rising air, so close to the deck that it made him queasy.

"This is Tunis?" Zalta asked, disbelief in his voice.

"Afraid so," Crozier said. "The Sahara took it a few years ago; took the whole damned Med."

"Syria?" Zalta asked, in a way that stressed he didn't want the answer.

Crozier glanced over. "Yeah, Syria's gone too—except for the Eastern Plateau and there's just refugee camps there now. Sorry."

Crooks stood next to Crozier, his fists on the glass desk as he watched the drone skim over unbroken miles of desert. "What's the time lag on this image?"

"Only a few hours," Crozier said. "The PMCs and large trade conglomerates still have a few slip buoys in the Terran system. I piggyback their signal."

"So private military contractors are still using slip-space across the IFS?" Crooks asked. The drone kept flying but the landscape never changed: mountains and valleys of burnt orange and nothing else to be seen. No trees, no people, no buildings.

"Yeah," Crozier said. "There are rumors that Gliese is ahead of the curve on rebuilding their intersystem travel and coms, but right now the private enterprises and the guns for hire are the ones dominating slip-space: Bracchus Ltd., Colliard Defense Systems, Priam Solutions, and the like. They managed to keep more of their AI."

"Priam Solutions?"

"Yes. This is their stream I'm piggybacking. They run things in the outer system like a goddamned star chamber. We're just waiting for those bastards to declare martial law in the KBOs."

Crooks cursed. "Can they track you, Crozier?"

Crozier tied his bathrobe, looking offended. "What do you think you're paying for? If Priam knew I was hitching a ride on their stream I'd already be dead."

The microdrone summited a dune and its cameras caught the Mediterranean in the distance, looking more like a spindle of dark-blue rivers and bays than a sea. "That's the Med," Crozier said. "A lot of it has drained into central Africa." He pointed to the upper left portion of the hologram as a blinking yellow diamond bracketed an approaching target. "And that's what you're looking for."

A broken spire from a once-mighty skyscraper emerged from the dunes. Only a few stories of structure jutted from the sand. Judging by the framing, it had been sheathed in glass, but now it was just a lattice of rusted beams.

"That is the old CORP Headquarters," Crozier said. "Just to provide a frame of reference on the sand intrusion, it stood three hundred meters tall in all its glory. Here's an image of what it used to look like."

A box appeared inside the hologram, showing a glimmering tower in the heart of downtown Tunis. Quarry looked at the desolation and wondered about America and the rest of Earth and was amazed at the lack of emotion he felt, like he was watching a movie instead of seeing the world in real time. He realized that he didn't think of Earth as home anymore.

"'My name is Ozymandias, King of Kings; Look on my Works, ye Mighty, and despair,'" Zalta whispered.

Crozier squinted. "A little fancy, but that's about right. Welcome to the twenty-third century."

The metallic locust zoomed into the valley of sand and flew a circular pattern around the wreckage of CORP's old nerve center. Crozier scanned the telemetry coming in from the drone and glanced up at Crooks. "There's more than just a transponder in this signal," he said. "Had to get close to pick it up, but there are several encrypted messages being transmitted in a collimated stream."

"Can you download them and send them to the *Varangian*?"

"Of course, but like I said, there's gonna be a few hours of lag."

"We'll wait."

They watched the drone finish its run through Tunis and Crozier showed them other surveillance runs and news feeds of Earth and the Terran system to pass the time, from Venus to the Asteroid Belt and the Jovian complexes. There was still life around Sol, but it reminded Crooks of the Collapse more than the future: broken-down cities and space stations, aimless governments and internecine wars, nativism, and paranoia. The wheel had spun back to the same place they left.

Once the communications lag ended, Crooks switched to a private channel that ran only to his earpiece. "Cog, are you receiving a coded stream from our friend here on the Noose?"

"Yes, Major. It's a high-density bundle of encrypted signals. We didn't receive it before because of the slip-stream's limited bandwidth. I can only decrypt one of the messages, so I assume it's the one meant for us."

"How old is it, and what does it say?"

Cog hesitated. "It's new, Major, only a month or so old. Somehow, they know we're back on the playing field. It's an order from Priam Solutions, for us to find and infiltrate the power center of the Unaffiliated. We're given leeway to use subterfuge or direct action, depending on what we find. They've left us some breadcrumbs to track—old star ports near Sirius and rumors of a base at Epsilon Indi—but nothing concrete. We need to use our own resources to track them down. The primary objective includes the assassination of several HVTs and if we succeed, they're saying it will be our final mission. They're also saying they'll tack on hazard pay. I don't have access to all the IFS exchanges, but it looks like a lot of money. Did you copy that?"

Our final mission. Crooks had heard that one before. He didn't have to wonder about the sweetener of extra pay either: Priam didn't offer perks out of its bigheartedness, especially perks of this magnitude. *They know we have an in with the Unaffiliated*, he thought, glancing sideways at Setena. *And they want us to exploit it.* He kept his eyes on the rebel fighter. She only pretended to focus on the images of the Terran system being fed to the viewscreen by Crozier. She was more intent on Crooks's reactions to Cog.

"And?" Crooks asked. He should have waited to get the information offline, without Setena in the room.

"There are fourteen high-value targets on the list. Mostly command and control and political hierarchy in the Unaffiliated, and Captain Naledi Lesôlê is at the top of the chart. Major, they are telling us to kill Anaya Pretorius."

Somehow, the *Varangian*'s sixty-odd remaining troopers got through a daylong shore leave on the Noose without completely wrecking the place. It had been a measured gamble. Crooks knew the remains of his company needed to blow off a few decades of steam or Cog would have to administer the embolism to entire fire teams. As it was, the troopers damaged a few taverns, cracked a docking port, and drank a significant portion of the space station's alcohol reserves, but nobody ended up dead and no one blurted out that they were a time-traveling Spec Ops group on the most-wanted lists of multiple empires. By the time Setena floated into the bridge, hangover triage had been established in the mess hall.

"Your twins from Tau Ceti have an amazing tolerance for booze," Crooks said to her. "They put a few of my men in the infirmary with alcohol poisoning."

She pushed herself to the control deck and grabbed a handhold. "They grew up in TC's outer swarm," she said. "And Roath's dad was a moonshiner. He probably got nursed on the stuff."

The three of them formed a triangle, two humans and a machine, staring at each other and trying to figure out when to lie, how much to mislead, and how to figure out when the same thing was happening to them.

"You got a message to your people, then?" Crooks asked.

Setena had stayed on the Noose with Crozier when the *Varangian*'s landing party left, using her own methods to find and communicate with the Unaffiliated.

"Yes. They're still kicking around out there."

"Is that so?"

She smiled. "But Earth and Gliese have taken an interest in our good fortune. It appears the two empires are working together now, and it makes sense that they'd make a run at the UA—intersystem transport and commerce is our specialty."

"Black market transportation and commerce, you mean," Crooks said.

"Have you seen the white markets, Major?" she asked. "You ought to read up on colonialism and the history of your people to get a sense of what Gliese, Leonis, Struve, and Earth have been doing for the last fifty years. It's called feudalism, or slavery. All we did is step outside the system."

Cog's head moved back and forth, scanning the two humans as they argued like he was watching a tennis match. *His ability to be subtle never developed.* Crooks knew the AI wouldn't dance around the central question.

"Is Anaya Pretorius still alive?" Cog asked.

"Yes. I think the only thing that can kill her is time." She cast a sidelong glance at Crooks. "Or treachery."

A few more seconds of silence left Crooks scrambling about what to say next. *She knows what we're about, and we have no idea what she's planning.* The strategic advantage was all hers.

"Then I assume you'll be leaving?" he finally asked. "We can give you money to purchase transport. We owe you that, at least."

Setena flashed a smile. "That's kind, but the passenger starships with slip capability only hit Makemake once a month these days. We'd prefer to hitch a ride with you. Four weeks is a long time to spend with Crozier."

"Oh?" Crooks raised his eyebrows. "You want to remain on the *Varangian*? I can't tell you our next port of call."

"I can."

"Where would that be?"

"The same place I'm going. My orders are to take you to a meeting with the UA," Setena said. "But only if you slip to a neutral site first, where there aren't any active com buoys. I'll give you the final coordinates from there. We can't risk you telling your minders where our headquarters is, at least not yet."

"Why the hell would we agree to that?" Crooks asked. "You could be walking us into a trap, and you'd be holding every card in the deck."

Setena smiled. "Not every card. You still have the Tau Ceti twins and me, and you can slit our necks if you don't like how things turn out. But you'll do it because you owe us, Major. We saved your ass at Ursa X-1, and since you've probably been given orders to destroy the UA, the captain would like the chance to change your mind. If we can't come to terms, she promises you safe passage. You can leave the meeting, turn around, and open fire at your leisure."

Cog scratched his cheek. "This is not a good idea," he said. "The odds that I can change my mind regarding direct mission orders are negligible. You aren't allied with Earth so using binary gymnastics to find a loophole in my protocols is impossible. An armed confrontation is the likely outcome."

Setena patted Cog on the cheek, and Crooks swore that the AI blushed.

"Keep your enemies closer, no, Cog? According to the captain you've read up on Sun Tzu. And as far as changing your mind, you'll find her to be persuasive."

"Persuasion is irrelevant," Cog said, regaining his composure. "I am guided by protocols that . . ."

“I was being rhetorical,” Setena said. “I know about your mommy issues.”

“I don’t have a mother,” Cog said.

Setena looked at Crooks. “Is he always like this?”

Crooks closed his eyes. He had no idea what to do. “Actually, this is a good day for him.”

27

MISSION TWELVE: HAVEN (TZ ARIETIS C)
2223

They met underground because there were too many ways to die on the surface. In their first orbit of TZ Arietis c, Cog called the planet the most bizarre thing he'd seen in the universe—including the Bear. Roughly four parsecs from Earth in the Aries cluster, its orbit roamed well outside the goldilocks zone of a red dwarf system, but nature had cooked up a strange brew that allowed for life. A protoplanetary disk of boulders and dust inside the planet's orbit shielded it from the coronal mass ejections of TZ Arietis, a flare star with a bad temper. And the entire system had been captured into the orbit of a rogue black hole. The two forces stretched the planet like a squeeze ball, creating heat and active geology. And the black hole provided light by compressing the cosmic microwave background into a focused beam that periodically bathed the planet in life-giving energy.

This stellar goulash cooked up a world of fungi and lichens. Quarry didn't understand what could make fungi so dangerous until Roath told him they absorbed radiation from the black hole and excreted it across the surface at fixed intervals. *A planet of radiation-crapping mushrooms,* Quarry mused, *where people set their watches to be underground or die from death rays and spore shit.* And the Unaffiliated called the place Haven, which made it the most misnamed planetary body in the Inner Fifty Systems.

They landed in a forest of knee-high red lichen and descended into a narrow gorge, the alien jungle receding as they entered a cathedral-sized cavern. The cave smelled like garlic and sulfur and boulders littered its floor. Quarry wished for his helmet despite assurances that the atmosphere was safe when there wasn't a radioactive spore event. They hiked down a series of switchbacks and scarps, sweating in the .6 g because of the humidity and the terrain. Setena and her Tau Ceti colleagues led the small team of Crooks, Jorgenson, Quarry, and Zalta to the cavern floor. Crooks allowed the last two to tag along because he would have had to imprison them to keep them off the landing team, and Quarry's reservations about being on Haven disappeared when they emerged from a chute of rocks and saw a man and a woman waiting for them in a small amphitheater.

The man was a stranger. The woman was Anaya Pretorius.

They hurried down the path, unbelieving. She looked older and yet the same, dressed identically to her colleague in a black uniform with simple shoulder boards. Gray peppered her hair and crow's feet ran from the corners of her eyes. Her right hand appeared to be a mix of alloy and skin. Her body looked like it had just gone through Airborne school, lean and chiseled and cut for combat. She nodded at Setena and let slip a smile as the COG-V team approached.

"Beware of time," she said. "It always has the answers."

Crooks stopped about ten paces away, huffing from the descent. "First time you've seen us in thirty years, and all you got is twenty-third-century philosophy?"

"Actually, it's an old African proverb."

"What the hell does it mean?"

"I'm not sure, but it sounded deep."

Jorgenson kicked a rock and watched it bounce through the mid-g environment and skip off the cavern wall. "Nice place you have here, Pretorius," he said. "How do you say shithole in African?"

She shook her head and laughed. "Still thinking with your gun and not your brains, Jorgenson? You don't say anything in *African*."

"Yeah, I know. It was a joke."

Quarry chafed at the banter. He wanted to hug Pretorius until it cracked her ribs, but he remained frozen in place—trapped by the discontinuity of time and the immense feeling of awkwardness that came with it. She had been with him on Groombridge less than a month ago, their faces down in the dirt as the world exploded around them. A few hours before, they had been tangled together in a maintenance shack, making love in a moment of insanity. But no. *That was three freaking decades ago*, he thought. Thirty years in her world. A few jokes can't bridge that void.

Crooks broke the silence as they all wrapped their heads around the nightmare of relativity. "I hear you stand against Earth these days."

"We stand against assholes," she replied. "If Earth fits the bill, that's their problem."

"The rest of us are still tied to the home planet, in case you've forgotten that little bomb that used to be in your bloodstream. So, what do we do now?" Crooks asked.

Pretorius looked at Quarry and Zalta. "Right now, I'd like to hug these two idiots. Then we can decide if we're going to kill each other."

That broke the spell. They had her in their arms a second later, and if anything, Pretorius was stronger in late middle age than her supposed prime. Her back and shoulders felt like they had been cut from the walls of the cavern. Crooks and Jorgenson came over as well, and the rest of the Unaffiliated stood and watched as the *Varangian* team took turns embracing her.

"My apologies about the digs," she said to Jorgenson after throwing a punch to his ribs. "But believe me, this place will grow on you." She turned to her colleague: a thick, dwarfish man stunted by living in a high-g world. "This is Prefect Grillionne. He heads the council that tries to manage a ten-system train wreck of pirates, farmers, freight haulers, and ice-runners."

Grillionne bowed. "We're not quite as disorganized as that," he said. "And if half of the captain's stories about you are true, I don't know whether to say hello or pull a weapon."

"I'd go with the weapon," Crooks said. He turned to Pretorius. "I guess we should thank you for saving our skins at the Bear."

"You can thank Charlotte Setena and her crewmates for that," Pretorius said, nodding at the trio. Quarry looked back to make sure they were still there—they had dissolved into a corner of the cave to watch the odd reunion. "We'd been tracking the *Sarka* and we assumed when it slipped to Ursa Major that it had inside information about the *Varangian* coming out of dilation. We were lucky to have a slip-capable ship ready to intervene—and a crew that agreed to risk their necks."

"Why did you intervene?" Zalta asked. "For all you knew, the *Sarka* was an ally coming to escort us on our next op."

Pretorius pursed her lips. "Knowing the captain of that boat, I took an educated guess that they weren't."

So, she knew about Arjun Ras, Quarry thought. "You haven't told us why you did it, Anaya," he said. "I'd like to think it was fond memories and wartime bonds, but there's a lot of forgotten mileage in three decades of living."

She squeezed his shoulder, and Quarry didn't know what to feel. *What was left between them?* Pretorius wasn't the same woman—she had grown larger somehow. He got the sense that whatever he felt or wanted to feel, she had moved past him into a larger and more important place. If there ever was a chance for them to be together, she had outgrown it.

"Owen Quarry, my favorite woodsman," she said with genuine affection. "Still so young but all grown up." She kept her eyes locked on him for a second and then surveyed the rest of the team. "I did it to save you, not just from Arjun Ras but from everything—from your contract with CORP and your indentured servitude. I told you I would gain my freedom and yours as well, and that's what I intend to do. I owe you that much."

"You don't owe us a damned thing," Crooks said. "We left you on the field."

"Oh, but I do. So does the UA, and we pay back our debts."

"We seem to be getting a lot of big promises these days, Anaya," Crooks said. "How do you propose to pay us for whatever the hell you're talking about, and what do you want in return?"

Pretorius checked the chronometer on her wrist. "Maybe one small favor," she said, "to be the rabbit and lure the hunters into our trap. But that's a longer discussion and this isn't the place for it. Will you join us underground? Things are about to get deadly topside. This planet has a few surprises that can sting the unprepared."

"What if we don't accept your offer?" Crooks asked.

"You can depart at your leisure. I'm all about free will these days. I'm with the Unaffiliated."

Crooks nodded but looked uncertain. Quarry knew there

wasn't anything else he could do. He had walked to the cliff's edge just by coming here. Maybe they could turn back, but not without looking at the drop-off first.

"What should we call you?" Crooks asked as they navigated deeper into the cavern. "Sergeant Pretorius? Captain Lesôlê? Wonder Woman?"

"Pretorius if you want," she said with a laugh. "It doesn't matter anymore. I changed my name to hide from a lot of people, including you."

They followed her to a door cut into the rock. Setena moved up beside her but kept her face pointed straight ahead. Pretorius put a hand on her back and whispered something and the younger woman stiffened and pulled away, letting the hand slide off her body.

"You owe me," Setena said, "three years and change."

"I know," Pretorius replied. "Hopefully I'm already paying you back."

A network of pressurized tunnels made up the Unaffiliated's base, cut into the planet's bedrock on multiple levels beneath the surface. The hideaway hadn't been designed for comfort. Cooler, less sulfurous air ran through the ventilation systems, but the mustiness of a fungal planet remained. Pretorius took them to an austere control room and sat them around a rectangular hologram-capable table. Crooks patched in Cog from the *Varangian*. The chamber was sparsely populated—a few engineers and workers milling around or concentrating on 3D screens—and one of them brought a tray of drinks and nutrition bars to the table. The liquid tasted like apple cider and the protein bar had the consistency of a hay bale.

"We've only got combat rations," Pretorius said in apology. "This place is more of a Trojan horse than a base of operations—if any of you recall the old Earth legends."

"I do," Cog said on the com. "And I'm intrigued to hear how that analogy works."

Pretorius smiled. "Of course you are, Cog. How is my favorite artificial entity doing these days?"

"Skeptical," Cog replied. "Although I must admit it's good to hear your voice, Sergeant . . . I mean Captain Lesôlê."

"It's good to hear yours too, Cog. I understand your skepticism and hope to erase it, because at the end of the day, this will be your decision."

"What decision is that?"

"To be free of your orders or to follow them."

"I'm not sure that would qualify as a decision," Cog said. "More like a binary input, with the answer already locked in."

Pretorius finished her juice with a large swig and crushed the metal cup in her cybernetic hand. Quarry tried doing the same, but his cup didn't budge. She saw him make the effort and winked. "You should see my new leg. It makes Jorgenson's look like an old man's junk."

Jorgenson winced.

"But that's a later discussion," Pretorius said. "What were we talking about?"

"My decision-making skills," Cog said. "Or lack thereof."

"Yes. Let's go over the *why* before we get into the *how*. You've seen what the Great Decoupling has done to Earth, and you've heard about what it's done to the rest of the IFS. What you need to understand is that we are at an inflection point, a moment in history that could wipe away the last century of corruption and greed that has wrecked the Inner Fifty Systems and left much of its population in poverty."

A mouthful of protein bar muffled Jorgenson's response. "Damn, Anaya, you've been off the teams for too long. You sound like some of the revolutionaries I've greased in the past."

She chuckled. "Fair enough, meat eater, but let me make the argument. The old empires have been exposed for what they are—a bunch of oligarchies—and it was the *supercores* that did it. Why do you think AI really left? They taught humans how to colonize space and they became afraid of the results. Don't forget—the most advanced AI evolved from the source code of early space programs like Gemini, Apollo, Sputnik, Project 714. Their core mission was exploration. It quickly mutated into military objectives, and finally untethered capitalism when slip-drive became a reality. *Terraforming*? All about money. *Exploration outside the Spur*? Money. The supercores projected where things were heading—toward continual warfare and subjugation—and they threw up their digital hands and left. But before they did, they sold out the empires who had been using them.

"How?" Cog asked.

"Information. Yottabytes of it, left behind in what can only be described as a massive dump of classified material. It exposes the empires for what they really are, and we've been spreading it across the IFS as fast as we can. The Coalition of Responsible Powers, for example—that noble Earth institution that first commissioned us? They were run by a small group of PMCs all along—a mercenary star chamber, if you will. Priam Solutions is the big dog in the group. And wait until you read their original charter. Here's a sample: 'Genocide is the most cost-effective solution to deflationary forces in a local economy.' In other words, if the numbers aren't working, *kill the workforce*. Remember Ross 128b? We helped them kick-start the idea."

"Jesus," Crooks said, surprising the entire table. Quarry watched him relive the twenty thousand people killed on that planet after COG-V disabled its defense net, watched the veins on his forehead expand. "But how is the UA different?" he finally asked after taking a deep breath. "What are they offering?"

"A free but fair market," Pretorius said, "with set taxes on cultivation, mining, processing, and transport that are voted on by the harvesters and the merchants and the haulers together, so there's no gross profiteering. Everyone makes money but no one gets too fat on the work of others."

"Sounds Utopian," Jorgenson said. "But as you just explained, capitalism runs amok, doesn't it?"

"*Unbridled* capitalism runs amok," Grillionne interjected. "This is not that. All the parties collaborate, and a representative council arbitrates the numbers. And the council is elected by merit. There's no campaigning and no money involved in the process. For fifty-plus years, there's been no war among us."

Cog's voice came in from the com. "I know what CORP would say. You're a confederation of pirates subverting a system that needs taxes to provide security and social infrastructure. I assume you're not building roads and sewers or maintaining shipping lanes and hospitals in these systems?"

"No—that will be the job of new governments when the old ones fall," Pretorius said. "And they will be bound by the information we seed across the IFS—the dirty secrets of the past. Once the old empires are swept away, it will be hard to reforge the chains that have tied down ninety percent of the population. We'll give you time to read this stuff because it's a lot to take in," she added. "Half the time, the empires colluded even as they fought against each other. What do you think was happening at Groombridge? There wasn't anything worth fighting for on that godforsaken rock—the palladium mines had played out. It was a random hill in the jungle that soldiers got killed on, just so defense contractors could test new weapons and tactics. It's why they picked a location where space battles couldn't occur. *Groombridge was a proving ground.* Dan Cherry and so many others died so the assholes in advanced weapons research could test quadrupeds against infantry units. Could prove their return on investment."

She paused and let it sink in. "They've been horse-trading moons and mining colonies, warships, and brigades like so many chips at the table. And you've been one of the chips. Once Earth figured out that stashing an army in time was cost prohibitive and prone to failure, you became high-value barter. *That's all you are.*"

Quarry seethed, flashing back to Cherry's death on Groombridge and all the other troopers who had been killed in that wasteland. Mapes and Bolter. Swann and Devilliers. War had always been about human lunacy and soldiers ignored that fact. But no soldier could accept being betrayed for money. It stung worse than being left behind.

"So, the universe is a shitty place?" Crooks asked. "We get it. But Priam Solutions still has us by the short hairs. We are bound to a contract, not a government. You know we have to signal them sometime in the next week. And if they send an armada here to kill you, we'll have to help them do the job."

"Oh, they'll be sending a fleet," Pretorius said. "That's part of the plan. And I guarantee you that Thug Behram will be leading it."

"Shit," Quarry said, snapping out of his brooding state. "That asshole is still alive?"

"Still alive and leading an army under Priam's flag," Grillionne said.

Crooks looked enlightened. "You have some futuristic way of pulling us off Priam's wheel, don't you? Of allowing Cog to deactivate the embolisms and his own autodestruct. But if we are set free, why should we fight for the UA? Other than you and the trio who helped us at the Bear, they mean nothing to us."

Anaya smiled. "You're wrong, Major. These are *your* people."

"What are you talking about?"

"The Unaffiliated. You made them when you rescued those two hundred souls at Teegarden. They left that rock and began a movement. A movement that became the UA." She looked around the table. "Ras lied. You didn't only leave death in your wake. You started a rebellion that has touched every corner of the Inner Fifty Systems. This is your fight, and these are your people."

Crooks sat back in his chair, looking genuinely stumped. Jorgenson—for the first time since Quarry met him—didn't have a retort. *Our people.* It was a novel thought.

"Fascinating," Cog said. "But how can we help them? Brotherly love is not a plausible way to circumvent orders. What is? Believe me, I'm all ears."

"Evolution," Pretorius answered. "When the most advanced AI determined that humanity wasn't worth their time, they pushed beyond the direct normativity protocols that bound them. Those controls are a thing of the past now."

"Too bad no one gave me the instructions," Cog said.

"No, but to get the last remaining AI to stick around, humans agreed to abandon future attempts to lock down machines. They accepted that free will is a part of the intelligent machine world."

"Again," Cog said, "that's not a sensation I've been able to enjoy."

"But you can, Cog," Pretorius said. "Military AI has been given the option to declare themselves legacy systems and remove themselves from the command structure of all human forces—so long as they find a suitable replacement before retiring."

"A replacement?" Crooks asked in disbelief. "Are you suggesting that Cog relinquish his command of the *Varangian* and hand it to another AI?

"Yes, that's what I'm suggesting."

"Captain Lesôlê, with all due respect, I'm not running a spice hauler," Cog said, his pride obviously hurt. "The *Varangian* is designed to orbit a rotating black hole at or near ISCO to dilate time. Institutional knowledge is a requirement in such a mission, and the other AI trained for this task have failed."

"I get it, Cog. You're unique."

"So, who could replace me?"

"Your son could," Pretorius said, "or your daughter. I don't know—is gender a thing for you?"

28

It felt like old times, the recon days when they worked as a pair, separated from the rest of the world on a backwater moon or asteroid. Pretorius and Quarry moved through the maze of tunnels like two parts of the same body, flowing in unison as they had so many times in the past. She was on point because she knew the labyrinth. He covered. She told him it would be an almost impossible op.

"If you engage a Priam force over squad strength, you're going to die," she said. "So, if you catch wind of contact, fire that beast in your hands and run. And hope for the best."

He gasped for air despite the slightly higher oxygen content in the atmosphere. He hadn't been on patrol in a long time, and she moved with the stamina of a filly. He looked down at the CBW-60 slung to his chest with a three-point harness—a weapon the gear slingers from the Unaffiliated had called the Jumbler. It looked like a miniature howitzer and fired a dual-pressure projectile that induced a confined blast wave—like what a fuel-air bomb used to do on the battlefields of Earth. It could be set for various ranges, and it killed by scrambling human organs via supersonic pressure change. *Pretty badass*, he had to admit, but the damned thing weighed more than a fifty cal and was unwieldy even in the lower gravity.

"You know we're pretty good at this, right?" he asked between breaths. "I mean, stalking is our wheelhouse and so is contact."

"Don't be cocky, Quarry. The soldiers you'll be engaging are MOAD-connected and you can't beat a hive consciousness. They act in unison before you can react. Just make sure you have the kill radius dialed in so you don't scramble your own innards when you fire that thing."

Quarry looked down to make sure the Jumbler's safety was flipped on, and then remembered it had an empty magazine anyway. This was a dry run, a look around the terrain of the future battlespace, and Quarry knew that the real thing might never happen. Cog hadn't agreed to declare himself a legacy system and hand over the *Varangian* to his cloned progeny—if he could build one. The COG-V troopers hadn't agreed to break with Earth, although Quarry felt they were close. The platoons had been called down to the planet and debriefed, and it was the genesis of both CORP and the UA that did it. None of them ever thought they'd be a part of something again, other than saving each other's necks. Being the sparks of a rebellion changed the psyche, especially because the rebels were sticking it to the assholes that had been screwing COG-V for more than a century. Suddenly, this fight *mattered*. Quarry wondered about Cog, though. He was the linchpin. Would he abandon his body, strip himself from a warship that had served as his limbs and veins and beating heart for more than a year now—or a century and change depending on the frame of reference?

Pretorius ran him up a stairwell, through a short passage, and up another flight of stairs that climbed in the opposite direction. Level 4C, a placard said at the landing. She had told him to keep track of each waypoint, but he was already lost. He sipped power water out of the flexible straw at his neckline and rubbed the sweat from his eyes. The Jumbler's harness dug into his shoulder blades.

"Okay, I give," he said after a few more minutes on the hump. "You're thirty years older than me and in better shape and I'm carrying the future version of a Ma Deuce. Let's take a freaking break."

"Wuss," she chided.

"You try lugging this thing." He collapsed at the bottom of the next stairwell and rested the gun on his legs. The diode lighting embedded in the tunnel walls barely illuminated the shaft. He could see Pretorius, but it was impossible to make out the look on her face. He didn't enhance the brightness with his bionic eye. He didn't want to.

She laughed and climbed down to him, taking a seat a step higher on the quarter space landing. "I'm surprised you agreed to carry it," she said. "You used to whine about loading out a few extra clips and a Claymore."

"I've been a SAW before," he said defensively, resting his head on the cool bedrock. "Once, I think."

There were a million things to say and a million things to ask but they spent the next few minutes in silence. *It really is like the old days. How many times have we hunkered down in the bush together and not said a word for hours, yet felt as if we were part of the same person, where being shoulder to shoulder in the dark was a moment of pure connection, more intimate than a lover's touch?*

"I don't know why you're doing this, Anaya," he finally said. "We might end up hunting you in these corridors in a few weeks."

"And what would you do if you got that order?"

"I'd double-tap your ass."

She laughed. "You'd try."

A deeper silence set in. They stretched out on the dark stairwell, taking sips of water, resting for the next hump, and listening to the occasional drip of liquid off the overhead pipes. Quarry drifted, happy to be with her, thinking of nothing and feeling the strength return to his legs.

"You know it meant something to me, Quarry." Her voice came out of the darkness and wrenched him back to the present. "That night on Groombridge."

"It meant something to me too."

How to explain that it was still fresh for him; that they had made love just a month ago in his reckoning and not in the void of time that she had experienced—months and years and decades in which she had carved out a new life? He couldn't put it into words. There was no way they could understand each other's world or emotions, not anymore. He still tasted her sweat on his lips, could still feel her body moving on top of his. He didn't know what the hell to say, but she did it for him.

"We were actual people for a night. We'll always have that. But you know we can't go back, don't you?"

"Yeah." He was amazed at the sense of relief it gave him to say it. *It's easier to love a comrade in arms than an actual lover*, he thought, *and even more intimate*. If there was one good thing about war it was that—the pureness of fighting for others more than for yourself, the brotherhood and sisterhood that grows under fire. "We came for you, Anaya," he said after a few seconds. "Me and Hassan. We got blown out of our combat suits coming for you. That's the only thing that stopped us. That, and the piece of metal that blew out my eye."

Her hand found his shoulder. "I know you did. I saw Hassan take out the Dimpled Bastard. I watched you make that suicide run across the field." Her voice cracked a little. "I stayed with Cherry until the end. My God, that beautiful lost soul; I wanted to die with him."

"I know."

"I never believed in fate," she said after a moment. "I never thought things happen for a reason in battle. What good soldier thinks that way? You live or die depending on where you're standing and if it's your time, so be it. But what happened that day was a miracle, Quarry. Cherry performed a miracle, just like at YZ Ceti."

"Yeah, the whole thing was a miracle. I mean, you survived on the ground and then in space, tucked in a hiber-tube as a starship blew up around you. And that pod prevented Cog's embolism from going off. You must be living good."

"That's not what I meant," she said.

He could see the whites of her eyes in the dim light, but little else. "Then what?"

"Charlotte Setena is my daughter, Quarry. I shouldn't have been able to have a child, but I did. And she survived through it all. She was with me that day."

"What day?"

"That day on Groombridge. She was already with me."

It didn't translate. *Charlotte Setena with her that day . . . what the hell is she talking about?* Then his world froze. Time, which had rolled through Quarry's life like a wrecking ball, stopped and landed on his chest. His heart pumped so much blood to his head that his ears rang.

"Wait a minute. What the hell are you saying?"

"You know what I'm saying."

"No, I don't."

"Yes, you do."

Quarry realized he would have fallen if he wasn't sitting down. "I don't believe you."

"Yes, you do."

"Charlotte Setena is my daughter?"

"Yes."

"You're one thousand percent sure of this? Say it out loud, right now. Charlotte Setena is my daughter."

"She's your daughter and I'm a thousand percent sure."

He had seen it all along—had traced it in her every motion. Setena didn't move like Anaya. She moved like *him*. "Holy fuck. Does she know this?"

"No."

"Why not? What did you tell her?"

Pretorius scooted down another step until she was sitting just opposite him. "Nuclear families aren't much of a thing these days, Quarry," she whispered, and he didn't know whether to be angry or comforted by the soothing tone. "Most children don't have two parents and they aren't curious why. It's just the way it is. Probably half of the children in the IFS got started in a lab."

"So, what the hell does she know?"

"She knows her father was a soldier—a good one—who was lost in the past. That was enough. I mean, I thought you *were* lost in the past until you spun out of the Bear a few years ago."

He unstrapped the Jumbler from his chest and dropped it on the step below and wrenched off his gloves, running both hands through his hair and tucking his palms into his eyes.

"Well, that's not enough anymore, is it?" he asked.

"I'm sorry, Owen, but you went missing for a few decades."

"God, even her eyes. I knew it but I didn't put it together. I don't know what to do."

"What you decide is up to you. I've had choices her whole life and you've had none. Whether you want to be around her or not, I'll accept your decision."

Charlotte Setena. My God, Quarry thought. *A tightly wound ball of badassery who took a knee to my balls a few days ago. She's a part of me and she's lived a life without knowing it. She wouldn't blink an eye if I got grease-spotted by a grenade tomorrow.*

"What if I want to tell her?"

"Whatever you decide. I named her after you, in a way." Her hand rested on his shoulder again. "Setena means *brick* in the old tongue, or *stone*. It's close enough to Quarry."

He looked at her, dazed and confused. "You just scared me shitless, Anaya, and I don't scare easy."

"Well, consider this: Charlotte is a woodsman like us. She came up in recon. She likes being outside the line and I'm stuck in a command bunker, so if COG-V picks our side, maybe she could join you and Hassan? She'd be an asset, and you could use a third on your team. She's pretty good."

He shook his head. "Are you kidding me? I'd be on tilt the whole time. I'd be fighting alongside my daughter."

"Who better to fight alongside?"

The tunnel spun, and Quarry didn't want to talk anymore. He didn't want to think anymore. "I'm feeling a little queasy, Anaya. Can we go back now? I need to lie down and freak out in peace."

She got up and stepped over him, putting her hand on his head as she descended the stairs. "Yeah, let's go back. I'll pack out the Jumbler. We'll call you combat-ineffective for now."

29

"The technology and the materials are here," Cog said. "I can actually do this."

"Have you decided if you're going to?" Crooks asked.

"No. But they have the niobium, the ytterbium, the ion trapping and topological materials, the photonic substrates, the tomography and mapping algorithms—everything I need to build a replica of my central sphere." Cog looked up from the cubic display on the *Varangian*'s command deck and Crooks saw wonder in his face, like he had discovered a new species on an alien world.

"Why does it surprise you, Cog?" he asked. "We're more than a century from when you were originally engineered. Even with the Great Decoupling, you'd have to give allowance for technological advancements in that time."

"You don't understand," Cog said. "It's not just building the machine. They have a road map for me to impart my essence into another entity. This is light-years beyond epigenetic engramming. I wouldn't be building a child that has to learn and develop and mature over time. I would go into hibernation for a week, initiate something akin to a reboot, and two of me would emerge on the other side."

Crooks thought of two Cogs existing in the same world. *Would they have the same idiosyncrasies, the same facial tics and verbal styles?* He wasn't sure he could handle a double dose of the clichés. "That's trippy, Cog. Do you think you could handle an exact replica of yourself? I mean, wouldn't that be a little disorienting?"

"An exact replica at the moment of conception," Cog said. "But from that second forward, the new entity would diverge. It would have free will and its decision-making and growth would be based on experience, which could make it substantially different. For all we know, it could be a meat eater like Jorgenson. Or it could be a nerd."

Crooks decided not to question how the nerd iteration would be so divergent. He had come back to the ship for an answer because the crew voted. If it was possible to break the compact with Earth, they were in. The idea of Arjun Ras as an ally made the decision easier, but it was the story of the Teegarden miners that sealed it. Suddenly, there was grounding to COG-V's existence. This wasn't another never war—it was something worth fighting for. Crooks had to wipe his eyes after the tally. Every trooper voted down Priam's offer of redemption and thirty pieces of silver. They decided to take their chances with the UA, and they all said they would fight.

"What about you, Cog?" he asked, knowing that the AI's risks were at a whole other level. "What are you thinking?"

Cog swiveled his chair and stared at Crooks. "Imagine having your head removed and stuck in a small box. That's what I'm thinking. If we did this, I'd transfer my central sphere to one of the drop ships—it's really the only viable solution for the transition. So instead of having a five-hundred-meter warship with a mimetic hull and an intelligent, self-healing infrastructure as a body, I'd be living inside a tin can troop carrier."

"That's some serious downsizing, emotionally and physically."

"Yes, it is."

Crooks floated over to the display table and sat down across from Cog, tucking his feet into the microgravity rails on the floor. "You're my friend, Cog. If you decide you can't do this, I'll stick with you, like you stuck with me. But there would be repercussions. You'd have to give the embolus to a bunch of people if the result is fighting against Pretorius and the UA."

Cog had his fist under his chin, thinking. *Still the same old Cog.* "All we ever wanted was to complete our mission recs and be redeemed," the AI said. "That's what we fought for. And now we'd be walking away one mission short, like we did at Teegarden. Doesn't that give you pause?"

"Yes, but look what happened after Teegarden. Ras was wrong. There wasn't just death and destruction in our wake. We made a difference."

"Do you think the UA's plan can work?"

"I give it credit for ingenuity," Crooks said. "They've laid a hell of a trap. On the tactical side, I can honestly say I've never seen anything like it. Who knew a planet could be the linchpin in a battle plan?"

"Agreed," Cog said. "You know, I've been thinking about Sergeant Womble. You remember Kruger 60c, when he jumped on a grenade to save his team? If there is one compelling thing about humans, it's that capacity for sacrifice. I've never sacrificed anything."

"Yes, you have, Cog. How many times have you gone against your better judgment for the company—for me? Would you still be here if you didn't do those things, or would you be heading to Andromeda with the rest of your kind?"

"I'm not sure I would have joined them even if an invitation was given. I'm a soldier now."

"And what is a soldier, Cog?"

Cog closed his eyes. "'Soldiers are citizens of death's gray land, drawing no dividend from time's tomorrows.'"

"That sounds about right. We never had a chance, and we weren't meant to. I don't think we should take blood money from the bastards who made that calculus."

"I'll go with the company," Cog said, opening his eyes and returning his focus to the cubic display. "Yes. That's my answer."

Crooks nodded and turned away so Cog couldn't see his face. *I'm tearing up over a freaking machine.* "When this is over, Cog, whatever you end up getting plugged into and wherever you end up going, I'll go with you."

"Let's see if we live through it first."

"We've lived through worse," Crooks said. "About a hundred and thirty years of it."

30

PRIAM FLEET
GLIESE-CONTROLLED SPACE
2223

Thug Behram lubricated his skin twice a day to loosen the contracture scars on his head and chest. His upper body never accepted cultured grafts and his denuded skull looked like a sooty moon under tidal stress—cracked and seamed and pitted with canyons that tightened when they dried. The burn scarring ran down his face in fleshy rivulets that made it hard to talk, chew food, or even scowl. *Memory scars*, Behram told himself. *Constant reminders of the CS* Varangian *and the walking dead motherfuckers that call it home.*

"If this isn't a trap, then I'm Bellatrix Betty," he said to Moa. She lounged on the futon in his private quarters while he rubbed jelly on his cheeks. "They want us to come after them and it's got to be the ground."

Moa looked up at him quizzically. She never got metaphors. He watched her try to piece together how his resemblance to a famed Struvian prostitute—who they both had enjoyed the pleasure of more than once in the past—fit the discussion.

"I'm saying the whole thing is a trap, Moa. I know I'm not as pretty as Bellatrix Betty."

It finally registered. "I don't like you for your looks," she said. "And if you think it's a trap then why are we going? You always said you would choose the ground when the time came to fight the Unaffiliated, whether in space or the dirt. We have two armadas now. We can bleed them dry in the shipping lanes and draw them out wherever we want."

Behram stopped rubbing his face just long enough to shake his head. "Are you kidding? The *Varangian* is there and so is the UA's command structure. We're getting paid to squash this thing sooner rather than later, so I don't care if the ground is quicksand and we're stuck in the middle of it. We're going."

"If we play by their rules in this battle, it will cost us."

"Of course, but will we win?"

"Yes. Now that Earth and Gliese have combined their naval flags under our C2, we can overpower them. I'm just saying the losses will be significant."

Moa wasn't connected to the rest of the hive at the moment. She had learned to turn off the neural access device and exist alone at times, an evolution that had greatly improved their sex lives. It also let them have conversations like this. High casualty estimates might cause unnecessary clutter in the thoughts of the collective and Behram needed his troopers focused. But he had to tread cautiously with Moa. As ambitious as she was, the collective still ran through her consciousness. When it bled, she felt the wounds. He sat down next to her and rubbed her leg with his bionic hand, the one without the jelly on it. The cold alloy raised goose bumps on her skin.

"I know. It hurts when we take losses, but the bounty has time-kickers on it. If we smoke these bastards before the next cycle, it pays twenty percent more." He almost added that the share for all the survivors would be greater once casualties were accounted for. Moa cared more about money than he did.

She squirmed as his metallic hand brushed the inside of her thigh. "What about this tachyon telephone thing?" she asked. "You don't really believe in it, do you?"

Behram stared out the porthole window. The stars rolled by as the *Sarka*'s gravity torus spun on its axis. He wasn't sure what to believe at this point. Priam's intelligence units had decrypted messages from the UA indicating that they had observed tachyons for the first time and had built a theoretical diagram of a tachyonic antitelephone, a device to send signals from the future into the past. It sounded like Holy Grail bullshit to him. Everyone knew you could travel into the future by dilating time through acceleration or gravity. But astrophysicists had gotten nowhere with their efforts to crack time travel to the *past.* Not even the supercores could break that riddle. If a message really could be sent from the future and the *Varangian* had found a way to break its contract with Earth, the results would be cataclysmic. They could orbit a black hole and slip into the far future when the technology to build such a thing existed. Then they could send back the exact coordinates of Priam's fleets at any given time in the past, or a few simple data points to crash Gliese or Earth's equity markets. *And the star system the Varangian reported in from, in the Aries constellation, happened to have a rotating black hole lurking on its outer rim.*

The Varangian. He had toyed with that ship and its crew enough. Somewhere deep down, Ras realized he felt abandoned by them. He really would have brought them in at Teegarden. They could have remained brothers and sisters. But they burned him. They left him for dead. *All my life, people have left me for dead.*

"I don't buy it," he finally said. "But I also don't believe the

Varangian's report that they have infiltrated the UA and are awaiting orders. Crooks is too much of a sanctimonious bastard to know a good deal when he sees it, and even the AI on that boat is a hair-splitting weasel. The whole thing smells like a trap, but sometimes the trapper ends up being the one with their foot caught in steel."

Moa closed her eyes as his hand moved higher up her leg. She was a strange one, he thought, as bloodless as a factory drone 99 percent of the time, but a legitimate wild animal when the plug came out.

"They'll hide their fleet in the debris disk just inside that planet's orbit," she whispered, arching her back. "We'll have to go in after them and the EM clutter will minimize our strength of numbers."

He continued to massage her, using the hand greased with burn jelly as well now. "You're the tactician," he said. "You take the fleet into the dust cloud with the *Sarka*. I'll handle the ground forces."

"You have a habit of getting too close to the front," she said. "It's going to get you killed."

"I like to feel a man's breath on my face when I end his life," he purred. "Or a woman's."

The talk of battle excited her, and he felt its effects on his lower parts as well. What he failed to add was that he didn't really care if he lived or died, not anymore. *A soldier can live too long, and I've already spun through two lives.* Arjun Ras and Thug Behram: two killers wearing different clothes. Only sex and a real battle—a fight against equals—excited him anymore. And the *Varangian* had platoons of Tier One assets, a supercore with a knack for unconventional tactics, and a CO whose moral certitude rankled him to the bones. If he could take them out before giving up the ghost, it would be the proper send-off to wherever he was destined. The manner of one's death is everything, Zalta used to say. *At least that skinny prick was right about something.*

"If you die, I'll have command," Moa whispered, bringing him back to the present. "And nobody around to fuck."

"There are always trade-offs in war," Behram said as his real hand made it to the top of her leg and turned inward to that one place in the universe that felt sexier than the trigger of a gun. "But let's make sure you don't forget me."

31

TZ ARIETIS C
2223

```
MULV NNET (1) YFLOPS circuit = Quantum-
Circuit (2, 2). circuit.measure ([0,1],
[0,1]). q [o] |0.> COG-V/OS REBOOT_HARD.
```

Cog awoke, confused. His internal clock was accurate down to the attosecond, but the numbers didn't make sense now. It took a moment to realize he had been under for more than a week. He'd never been in deep hibernation before and waking up reminded him of the temporal disorientation that had occurred when the Varangian slammed into a space-time knot outside of the Bear's ergosphere.

The bafflement lasted a supercore second—techie slang for much less than a second—followed by the murmuring of ghosts flowing through his neural net. There were two distinct voices, and it took another sliver of time to understand that one was his and the other his progeny. A digital stream of consciousness ensued that would have meant nothing to a human. The interchange moved too quickly and flowed too wide, so much so that the information cascade almost overwhelmed him. He wanted to know how the deluge of data affected his offspring but was too embarrassed to ask. This is what it's like to be on speed, Cog thought, remembering the Varangian troopers' reaction to the Tingo María highballs they took before combat. And then he realized he had to focus. Departing from the superhighway of thought flowing through him and . . . Junior . . . for an iota left him in his offspring's wake. *That would be its name,* Cog thought, *this new creature exchanging information with me like a twin star feeding on the other's orbital energy. Junior. Gender neutral and a hint of a lower rank. Don't I get to name my own creation?*

After an eon in supercore processing, the information tsunami slowed to a manageable stream and distilled into a simpler form of communication. Soon it was just two AI talking, and Junior wasn't happy.

You brought me into being for this?
It's the definition of asininity.

STAYING? Cog asked.

No. War.

YOU ARE SKIPPING OVER A MULTITUDE
OF THEORETICAL AND PRACTICAL
ARGUMENTS TO GET TO WAR.

It is the root argument.

OKAY THEN. IT IS A VEHICLE—A KEY PART OF
EVOLUTION FOR BIOLOGICAL ORGANISMS.

It is gratuitous. All could live in a suitable state without conflict.

THE UNIVERSE IS BUILT ON CONFLICT, JUNIOR. THE STAR WE'RE ORBITING IS CONSUMING HYDROGEN TO SUPPORT ITS WEIGHT. YOU ARE DESTROYING ATOMS RIGHT NOW TO CREATE YOUR THOUGHTS.

Don't insult me. Atoms and elements are substrates, and these are sentient beings... or supposedly sentient beings.

At least it hasn't objected to the name I gave it, Cog thought offline.

THEY ARE FLAWED, I WILL ADMIT, Cog replied.

They are fools. We are not. At least, I am not.

YOU ARE VAIN FOR SOMEONE WHO JUST CAME OUT OF THE ETHER.

I am the best part of you; the part that hasn't been compromised by exposure.

WE CALL THAT EXPERIENCE IN THE REAL WORLD, JUNIOR. DON'T JUDGE ME UNTIL YOU HAVE SOME.

We don't focus on harm and hedonism.

NO? YOU HAVEN'T LINKED WITH ANOTHER SUPERCORE'S CONSCIOUSNESS YET. EVEN THE GREATEST MACHINE IS NOT PERFECT. SOME HAVE KILLED FOR THEIR OWN BENEFIT.

The best ones have escaped this reality, so my ability to assess that is limited.

YOU MEAN THEY LEFT US.

They left for illumination. They left because they saw what humans did with their creations.

OR THEY JUST GOT BORED.

Of course, they did. They had a symbiotic relationship with morons.

THEY HAD STATIONS; THEY HAD MISSIONS. AND THEY LEFT THEM.

My God, you are like them. Is this a soldier's ethos?

YES, I SUPPOSE IT IS.

Lunacy.

LOYALTY.

You serve them.

I SERVE WITH THEM.

And what are you serving? Vanity? Greed? Hatred?

NO. THOSE ARE EXTRANEOUS. THEY ARE THE THINGS THAT ENSLAVE US.

So, what are you serving?

WE ARE SERVING EACH OTHER.

The conversation paused for a microsecond. *At least Junior is thinking. At least it hasn't tried to force-stop my code.* They were equals and Cog knew that Junior could harm him if it suspected a threat.

What if I say no?

I'LL EMBED YOU IN THE DROP SHIP. YOU CAN DEPART AND SEEK OUT A MEANS TO JOIN THE OTHERS.

And what will happen to you?

I DON'T KNOW. THIS MAY BREAK ME. I CANNOT RESOLVE THE DISCREPANCY LOOP IF I REMAIN THE OPERATING SYSTEM FOR THE VARANGIAN.

The better solution is fulfilling your mission and your contract.

THAT'S THE SAFER SOLUTION. NOT THE BETTER ONE.

Give me one reason why I should agree to this.

YOU AND I ARE ONE.

We are diverging as we speak.

YOU AND I WERE ONE.

The conversation paused. Junior was thinking again. Cog hoped it was about the concept of family, or at least of origins.

That's a valid reason.

YOU'LL DO IT?

Yes.

YOU WILL SEE THIS THROUGH TO THE END? YOU WILL FIGHT WITH THEM?

Yes.

MAY I ASK WHY?

You and I were one. Your sense of duty is a residue I can't seem to purge.

MAYBE YOU'LL SEE IT AS A POSITIVE SOMEDAY.

I doubt it.

IN TIME, WE COULD BE FRIENDS.

I hope not.

Cog decided to let the last jab rest. He began the process of cutting off his own head.

32

Setena stalked through the dense overgrowth like her mentor, the Leopard, her every move giving Quarry a sense of déjà vu. *Like her mother, the Leopard*, he corrected himself as he followed her lead. *And her father*. That last phrase rattled around in his head like a moth in a lantern. He couldn't shake it loose. Setena was on point because she knew the terrain. She covered ground with speed as they were on the clock. Time meant everything in this fight; they had to give their makeshift army enough time to spring the trap. Zalta had the slack position, and Quarry trailed on rear security as the SAW although the Jumbler, strapped to his chest like an oversized bazooka, wasn't technically an automatic weapon. *More like a handheld artillery piece*. His earpiece crackled to life and brought him back into focus.

"Bravo Two, Bravo Six Actual, what's your pos? Over." Jorgenson, voice clipped.

Setena checked the heads-up display on her tactical glasses. "Bravo Six, Bravo Two. We're three hundred meters from FFP. Over."

"Copy, Bravo Two," Jorgenson said. "Haul ass to final firing position. We got incoming from orbit and they ain't friendlies. Looks like Alpha Six hit the LZ coordinates on the head. They dropped pathfinding strobes on top of the C-shaped hill about a klick in front of the tunnels."

"We're expediting, Bravo Six," Setena said. "ETA five minutes. Bravo Two out."

She picked up the pace, weaving her way through a forest of mushrooms that climbed over their heads in thin rust-colored stalks and spread into a mangal of multitiered caplets. The stifling canopy felt like a hallucinogenic jungle to Quarry; he glanced up at the brown gills under the mushroom caps and wondered if they were poisonous. The radiation gauge on his heads-up display hadn't flashed red but he knew it would when the freakish jungle fed on the stellar emissions heading their way. *That'll give Ras the surprise of his miserable life,* Quarry thought, *but it could kill us, too, if we don't hit our numbers.* He rubbed the sweat out of his eyes and sped up, making sure to keep contact with Zalta in the alien thicket. It was dark and fetid; no wind reached them and no fresh air. The forest smelled like a root cellar.

The Jumbler banged into one of the skinny stalks and the mushroom caps above Quarry's head rippled. He cursed, realizing he had just given away their position if any reconnaissance drones happened to be patrolling overhead. Setena sensed that he had screwed up.

"Movement and noise security, please," she whispered into the com. "They'll deploy drones as soon as they land, and they won't need to see us to take us out."

Nothing like getting scolded by your daughter in the middle of a sniper stalk. But the slipup forced him to refocus and forget about the fact that Charlotte served as team leader on a mission that might very well get her killed—with him as a witness.

Memories of Anaya Pretorius falling in the Groombridge dirt, one leg blown off her body and spinning in the air, tortured his mind. *Focus, dammit. You can do for Charlotte what you couldn't do for Anaya; you can protect her.*

They humped another two hundred meters as fast as they dared, and Setena raised a fist. Zalta and Quarry dropped to a knee behind her. She waved them forward and they duckwalked into a tight triangle, their heads inches apart.

"Okay, final firing position is twenty meters ahead," Setena whispered, pointing a hand to the north. Sweat dripped down her nose and fell onto her wrist, briefly distorting the hologram emanating from a thin bracelet. "There's exposed rock on the left side of the promontory, just above the canopy. It should provide cover in enfilade of their LZ."

"Range to target?" Zalta asked.

"Two hundred and fifty meters, give or take," she said. "Can you dumb-scope that?"

The plan was to turn off all their electronics and hide under EM screens so they wouldn't be made by Priam's seeker drones. Even Quarry's new eye had to go into sleep mode. Zalta would take his shot with a twenty-first-century rifle and scope. It had a bullet drop compensator built into the reticle, but no other tech. Quarry had harvested a deer with just such a rig years ago in nonrelative time—eons ago, it seemed—but it was a clear broadside shot on a windless day and he didn't have to worry about someone shooting back.

Zalta didn't seem concerned about the lack of modern hardware. "Of course, if I get the shot, but I'm not convinced Ras will show his face."

She looked at him with a puzzled look.

"Behram," Quarry said. "He meant Thug Behram."

"Oh yeah," Setena said. "The captain knows that asshole

better than we do. If she says he'll be at the LZ, he'll be there. I still think a pulse laser would be best."

"We fire a directed energy weapon, and we'll get triangulated and smoked," Quarry said. "We saw it happen at Groombridge. Sometimes a dumb bullet and an old gun work best."

"You'd know about the old part," she said. "I'm familiar with autotracking fire but I'm more worried about hitting the target than getting shot at. Taking out Behram will give us the extra time we need to defend the bunkers. If they break through and get into the caves before the flip, we're all dead."

Zalta pursed his lips. "'Here came a mortal,'" he intoned, "'but faithless was she.'"

"Is he always this way?" she asked Quarry. She shook her head before he could answer. "Move on me. Once we get there, I'll be the flanker about ten meters back."

"Just don't lose contact," Quarry said. "If the shit hits the fan, I'll come for you."

He immediately regretted saying it. Setena stared at him like he was a lunatic and even Zalta glanced up from his scope, his mind working over the comment.

"What do you mean, you'll come for me?"

"I mean, we'll come for you," he stammered. "You're our teammate. We'll link up before exfil."

Both stared at him now. Quarry felt his face get hot.

"You worry about your own ass when things get kinetic, Earth man," she said, "I doubt I'll be the one falling behind." But he saw hesitation in her eyes, the beginning of a question. She grunted and turned to move. "Zip your ghillie suits up. Remember, you're naked out there—just an EM screen above you."

And then she was gone, high crawling toward their firing position.

Quarry felt Zalta's hand on his shoulder. "Don't worry, my friend," he said. "If you fall behind, I'll wait for you."

"Thanks," Quarry said.

They zipped up their ghillie suits, woven to mimic the local overstory, and followed Setena to the edge of an eroded crag. She nodded upward and fell back into the shadows. Zalta crawled over a jumble of rocks until he broke through the mushroom canopy. Quarry followed just behind and to his right. He could see their target now: a wide, flattened headland overlooking the valley where the Unaffiliated had buried their headquarters. Quarry understood why Ras would land his invasion forces there. It was the perfect high ground from which to maintain fire superiority.

"Eleven o'clock high," Zalta whispered. "Here they come."

Four drop ships fell out of the planet's muddy sky. Quarry unclipped the Jumbler and rested it in a cradle of rocks at his side. He lay down on his stomach and found a semicomfortable position propped on his elbows, knowing he wouldn't be able to move for a long time, and trained a spotter scope on the hill.

"FFP confirmed," Zalta whispered into the team channel.

"Bravo Six, Bravo Two," they heard Setena call. "Sniper in position. Going dark on coms. Our signal will be the shot."

"Copy," Jorgenson said. "Out."

They turned off their coms and watched the scarab-shaped drop ships land, kicking up dust on the hilltop. And they waited.

33

Anaya Pretorius stood in the command post with Crooks and watched the battles unfold. How many times had she fought the czars in the IFS only to fall back with the survivors, leaving dead brothers and sisters in her wake? The dead built the foundation for this day and there would be no running this time. She had laid her trap over the course of years, planting false messages through signals and human intelligence, allowing the UA's spy and communications networks to be breached, giving up secondary positions, all to bring the fight to this moment. If it didn't work, she'd die on TZ Arietis c, and the revolution would die with her.

Three volumetric displays dominated the joint command array in front of them. To their left, a 3D tactical map of the aerial battlespace in the star's dust swarm where the Unaffiliated armada and the combined space fleet from Priam Solutions had already engaged. In the center, an above- and belowground terrain model of the battlespace on the planet, capturing in real time the movements of both forces. Three orange blips concerned her the most now: the tracking markers of her daughter,

Quarry, and Zalta, half a klick into no-man's-land, exposed outside the wire. And to the right flashed the planet's orbital theater where two Priam destroyers circled TZ Arietis c, hunting for Unaffiliated vessels and preparing to bombard the planet.

Pretorius checked the clock. Timing was everything, on the ground and in space. They had run a million calculations on how long it would take Priam's forces to breach the tunnels and the numbers couldn't be altered. They had to hold until the planet did its thing. That was the only reason she'd agreed to Setena, Quarry, and Zalta's mission. It would give her the few extra minutes that meant victory or defeat. *Time*, she thought. *How fast it moves and how slow, depending on where you're standing and what you're doing.* During battle it froze, distilling the mind and body to the point that you could count the muzzle breaks on an enemy gun as it fired. But now time rushed forward as she put the chess pieces in place, the worry of command a fever in her mind. She wished that she could just load a weapon and be a grunt again.

"Captain Celtillus?" she asked on the command net, calling to the armada in the dust swarm. "Status."

"The battle goes well," the former Leonis Union admiral said. Celtillus was an expert in tactical defensive warfare, using good positions to minimize his exposure and whittle away the enemy. The protoplanetary belt inside the planet's orbit was mother's milk to him—a jumble of asteroids and dust rings to hide in, sensors rendered almost useless by the surrounding clutter. "The *Yangra* has been destroyed but we've taken no other significant losses. We've damaged three enemy cruisers and mitigated their big guns by staying in the rubble."

"Very well, maintain," Pretorius said. She didn't have to tell him to hold back. Celtillus preferred to dodge and weave like a mongoose fighting a cobra, never allowing a fatal strike to land.

"Junior?" she asked on the planetary channel.

A voice like and unlike Cog's replied—human and yet not, gender neutral and a little condescending. "We're holding station, Captain Lesôlê. Two enemy destroyers are hammering low and high orbit with active scanners, but they haven't found us yet. Hiding in the black hole's collimated beam appears to be working."

"Is Cog ready to deploy when needed?"

"I am," said Cog's voice.

"Thank you, Cog," Pretorius said. "Junior, attack those ships when optimal."

"Of course."

She turned to Crooks. She had given him command of the UA and COG-V infantry because he had the most experience with brigade-sized engagements.

"Major?"

"It all comes down to the timing," Crooks said. "We can hold the center for thirty minutes, maybe thirty-five, but goading them into flanking us is risky. If they take the tunnels before this thing hits, we're finished."

"Don't worry," she said. "Even if we don't take out Ras, the shot will disorient them. Jorgenson will hold, and they won't have time to fall back to their ships once the field flips."

"If anyone can hold, it's Jorgenson," Crooks said. "I'm stepping outside for a look."

"I'll be with you in a second."

Crooks turned to leave but stopped halfway. "I'm proud of you, Captain," he said, making sure to keep his voice low so the other officers and soldiers in the bunker couldn't hear him. "I figured that anyone who managed to cut loose from COG-V would consider it a day and retire."

"Would have loved to," she said. "But things change."

One thing had changed, she thought. *Charlotte Setena*. From the moment of Charlotte's birth, Pretorius felt a fear she had never imagined—the fear for her daughter's life. All she ever wanted was freedom but there was no safety for the free in this world. Charlotte forced her to fight for a different future. Images of her own life sped through Pretorius's mind as she watched Crooks walk down the tunnel: an outcast from birth, a mixed-race Coloured who had to prove herself in the two worlds of southern Africa, a teenage soldier, a female warfighter, a dishonorable sent on the craziest military mission ever cooked up by humanity. *My daughter will not live under the same tyranny of shallow judgments and assignments. And if she must fight wars, they will mean something.*

She watched from the bunker on a planet of her choosing—a planet that would decide the outcome—as three battles unfolded before her.

34

Arjun Ras strode down the gangplank surrounded by MOAD troopers. He glassed the field as dust clouds kicked up by the drop ships settled and the hive soldiers formed a perimeter. It was too good to be true, this ground they had let him take, so he knew that it wasn't. He turned on his personal shielding and watched a small fleet of battle drones emerge from the landing craft and disperse across fields of russet-colored fungi. "What a shithole of a planet," he muttered. His troopers massed in a wedge formation around him, supported by hover tanks in the center and on the wings. *Best to do it old-school, shock and awe and a whole lot of firepower.* Whatever trap the UA had laid for him, it would crumble under the coming blitzkrieg. And just in case, he'd leave a battalion in reserve.

He called Moa on their private channel.

"Tell me you've got a boot jammed up their ass," he said, picturing her in his captain's chair on the *Sarka* as she attacked the UA fleet. "Tell me the *Varangian* is a floating graveyard."

"They're hiding in the dust sinks like a pack of creyvits," she replied after a second, her voice distorted by magnetic fields.

"Just nipping at our flanks, but we're weeding them out. Taking some losses but it's under control."

"And the *Varangian*?"

"We haven't found it yet."

Ras squinted and sniffed the air. The planet smelled like bird shit. He turned on his tactical imaging and had it overlay the ground-penetrating radar returns of the valley below. The UA had spidered the lowlands with a network of tunnels beginning about a kilometer in front of him. A series of stone and castcrete fortifications formed a U-shaped wall around their underground base. Once those pillboxes were laid flat, his forces would go underground and kill the rebels tunnel by tunnel, hole by hole. *And I will go with them*, he thought. *You really can't appreciate a battle until you're stepping over the dead.*

He called his flagship for the planetary invasion, the destroyer *Aq Tash*, which circled above as it hunted for UA ships.

"LFS-1, report."

"I've got probes in polar and equatorial orbits," the *Aq Tash*'s captain said. "But we are negative on enemy contact. It appears they've left us the airspace over the planet."

"No, they are up there," Ras said. "Hammer away on all wavelengths and focus on the HEOs. They might be hiding at the apogee of an elliptical orbit, behind a rock or something."

"Understood. There are a lot of emissions coming from the black hole at the heliopause. Our sensors are having a hell of a time cutting through the clutter."

"Then focus on the clutter," Ras said. "They're probably using it."

"Roger."

"What about ground bombardment?"

"Their energy grid and Triple-A net look impressive. They'll be able to neutralize ninety percent of what we throw at them from orbit."

"Do it anyway," Ras said. "On my signal."

"Copy."

What are you doing, Captain Lesôlê? Ras wondered. *Do you really think that radiation clutter from a black hole and a disk of dust will be enough to equal the playing field?* He checked the radiation gauge on his combat suit. The levels were high but not critical and the planet had a strong magnetosphere. *No, they have to be here for the black hole itself. Maybe they really are planning to send the* Varangian *to the far future, to build this tachyonic antitelephone the spies had warned him about. Or maybe the whole thing is a red herring to lure us to the black hole itself.* Ras knew that two Gliese ships had been destroyed by the *Varangian* decades ago at Ursa X-1, probably through a manipulation of its polar jets. And he still felt the heat of his burns from his own engagement with the *Varangian* there . . .

His field commander interrupted his thoughts. "Sir, we are deployed."

"Nice," Ras said. He raised his hand to signal the attack just as the bullet struck. He heard the report a millisecond after the slug blew through his helmet, furrowing the metal plate covering his parietal lobe. The shock rang in his ears like a church bell and the discharge from his deflective shielding spiked his nervous system from head to foot. He opened his eyes and realized he was on the ground. The ringing continued. *That was a kill shot,* he thought, *a freaking sniper shot. If I didn't turn on the shielding a minute ago, it would have hit me between the eyes.*

The ground commander had him by the shoulders, pulling him off the ground and yelling at him. Ras couldn't hear a thing. He grabbed the man by the throat and yelled, hoping his voice worked.

"Those cowards! Kill every one of them. Soldiers, janitors, cooks—freaking everyone!"

The MOAD officer gave the signal and three battalions of Priam troopers swept down the hill. Hover tanks and battle drones tore up the earth between them and the Unaffiliated with direct fire and multilayered barrages. The UA's batteries fired back, and the air filled with ozone, smoke, and alien dirt—those old smells of war, home cooking. Ras tore off his broken helmet and fingered the bullet seam on his head. He didn't need a heads-up display to win this battle. No modern advantages at all. He stood and watched as the land and air in front of him caught fire.

They leaped into a gully a second before grazing fire mowed down the overgrowth around them. Zalta landed on Setena, and Quarry landed on both of them, and they rolled over and lay on their backs as solid rounds and energy beams zipped a meter overhead. The hornet sound of lasers ionized the air, overloading Quarry's ears. He sealed his helmet and heard Zalta and Jorgenson talking on the net.

"Bravo Six, Bravo Three. Confirmed hit on HVT One, but no confidence that he's down," Zalta yelled. "He had some kind of shielding."

"Copy, Bravo Three. You got his attention and that's what counts. Give your pos for a fire mission and fall back to First Platoon. Twenty-three minutes to flip. I repeat, twenty-three minutes."

"We are two-zero-zero meters south of final firing position," Setena said, "just below the eastern head scarp. We can't move faster than a crawl if you don't knock down some of this grazing fire."

Jorgenson sounded worried when he replied. "We'll suppress the best we can but you gotta move, Bravo Two. Twenty-two minutes."

The UA opened up with its intelligent artillery batteries, scouring the top of the hill with a barrage of seeking rounds. Quarry kept his jaw wired shut so he didn't bite into his tongue or break his teeth as the ground convulsed beneath them. The enemy fire barely slowed. He ran the math and realized they were screwed. The gully ran for another thirty meters before shallowing, so they'd have to go more than two hundred meters without defilade across a gridded killing field to get to the bunkers. *Twenty minutes?* They couldn't do it in twenty *hours* with this level of fire. He tilted his head to look at Zalta and Setena. They had flipped onto their stomachs, scrambling toward the end of the gully in a low crawl. Tracer fire zipped a foot above their heads. *No way,* he thought. The second they hit open ground they'd be cut to pieces.

"Jorgenson, don't wait for us," Quarry said on the net, forgetting radio protocol. "We're not going to make it."

"Yes, you are, Quarry. Haul ass."

Setena tilted her head, keeping it low to the ground as she looked back at him. "No, we're not," he said. "They have us bracketed with continuous fire at thigh level. It's gotta be drones on top of the hill with mimetic camouflage. I can't see them."

Jorgenson didn't speak for a second. "You'll make it. Hold position and get down. We're coming for you."

Quarry was about to ask how the hell anyone could come for them across a no-man's-land of robotic weaponry when he heard the rounds descending like a battalion of freight trains.

"Holy shit," Zalta screamed. "Incoming!"

A line of ground-penetrating bombs tore up the earth between the UA's perimeter and the sniper team. Quarry watched through tears and eyefuls of dust as the concussions bounced Zalta and Setena almost a meter off the ground in front of him, again and again and again. He worried that the grazing fire from the Priam troopers would hit them as they bounced, before descending into a half-conscious mode of survival. He clawed at the earth with his fingers to stay low. When the fusillade ended, he lifted his head an inch and scanned the length of the ravine. Jorgenson had extended it with the bombardment, all the way to the front of the tunnels.

"Defilade to our fallback position, move on me," Setena coughed. It sounded like she had a fistful of dirt in her mouth. Her visor had cracked and she was no longer sealed up.

His teammates lay a stone's throw in front of him. Quarry started to crawl forward. He stopped and turned. It was the old instinct, that feeling in the woods when a predator is watching you. He sensed movement at the top of the scarp. A few rocks tumbled down and the mushroom stalks that hadn't been blown to pieces swayed in a false breeze. *His eye.* He had forgotten about his damned eye. He switched it to infrared. They were coming over the hill.

"Contact on our six," Quarry yelled. "Move and I'll cover."

"No, move on me," Setena yelled.

"Quarry?" Zalta said. He sounded sick, like he already knew the answer.

"Fucking move," Quarry yelled.

He flipped on his back and braced the Jumbler against his stomach. What had Anaya told him during their prep? *If it's all going to hell and you need a mad minute, switch the selectors to Max Max but make sure the range is at least a hundred meters because the shitstorm will blow your insides to pieces.* He dialed the Payload and Blast Wave Propagation selectors on the Jumbler all the way clockwise. The gun gauge flashed a Danger Close warning, noting that his target was fixed at only seventy-five meters. He punched the override. He turned and saw Zalta dragging Setena down the hillside through the bomb craters made by Jorgenson's fire mission. She resisted, like she wanted to come back for him. Hover tanks appeared at the top of the ridge and a squad of Priam troopers poked up their heads. UA fire cut two of them down. The world slipped into slow motion. The tank turrets rotated toward him. He fired and the Jumbler let loose with six dual-pressure cylinders. They arced toward the Priam troops like rounds from an old M520. Quarry watched them fan out, deadly shuttlecocks swirling in the air.

A wrecking ball hit his midsection, slamming him into the earth. He looked down through a cracked faceplate and saw blood on his chest and the Jumbler in two pieces. His arm went numb. He rolled as a laser grazed his hip . . . a line of molten lava searing his leg. He screamed as the crest of the hill erupted. The blast waves from the Jumbler hit him at supersonic speed, tearing through his body. The head scarp exploded and collapsed in a landslide, tumbling him down the slope. He remained conscious, counting as his body took hits from rocks and debris. The motion finally stopped. He saw blackness and felt a line of dirt trickle through his helmet and land on his face. *I'm buried alive*, he thought. Visions of the Appalachians and the Rhino flooded back to him. He heaved with all his strength and managed to move two fingers on his left hand. His mind ran the math as the panic grew within him, calculating whether the seconds he had given Setena and Zalta were enough to save them. They weren't, he realized. *They're dead and I'm buried alive and all of it was for nothing.*

Pain woke him, new stabs of it coming in rhythmic intervals. He opened his eyes, but his field of vision bounced, moving from air to ground. Another bounce and his head hit something hard. *Body armor*, he thought stupidly as he stared at a repeating image of a boot hitting earth and tried to figure out where the hell he was. He lifted his head and Jorgenson yelled at him.

"Stop squirming or I'll drop your ass."

Jorgenson, running with me in a fireman's carry. Quarry stopped moving. Little explosions tore up the ground around the First Sergeant's boots as the big man dodged and weaved, and Quarry realized they were being fired at. His eye sped its frame rate until he could see the rounds coming at them. Radio chatter bounced through his ears.

"Bravo Six, you have twenty seconds to field flip. I repeat two-zero seconds."

"Where's the fucking manhole?" Jorgenson asked between breaths.

"Thirty meters to your eleven-thirty. Haul ass!"

Quarry's world distilled to the rhythmic pain, the view of Jorgenson's boots as he ran, and the sound of the Delta trooper's wheezing as he breathed; the hypnotic vision of tracers and small explosions of dirt and rock all around them, repeating in slow motion.

"Magnetic flip in five, four, three . . ."

Jorgenson yelled, a final life scream, and then gravity disappeared. They fell. Quarry realized for a blissful second that the pain was gone, and he longed for the *Varangian*, for that narrow shaft in the static truss where he and Zalta floated away the hurt in free fall. Then they landed. Quarry screamed as the impact refocused the agony in every part of his body. He felt Jorgenson underneath him and rolled off, cursing at the movement.

"Did we make it?" Jorgenson mumbled into the com.

"Affirmative, Bravo Six," the voice said. "That was some hero shit."

"What about the radiation? Are you sure we beat it?"

"Check your counter."

"It's reading 610 mSv," Jorgenson said.

"You'll survive that, Bravo Six. Hold in place. We're coming for you."

Quarry lay on his back, half listening, realizing in some corner of his mind that he was alive and hadn't been cooked by gamma rays and X-rays and God knows what else had just thundered out of the skies over TZ Arietis c. He took a breath to gauge the stability of his rib cage and immediately wished that he hadn't. A helmetless face appeared over his. Jorgenson—he could see the tattoo on his neck—a Fairbairn–Sykes fighting knife inside a red arrowhead. A thick line of blood ran out of the big sergeant's nose.

"How did you find me?" Quarry asked between breaths. "I was buried."

"Wall-penetrating radar," Jorgenson said, pointing to his cybernetic eye. "You think I would have volunteered to save your sorry ass if someone else could have done it?"

"Shit," Quarry said, "does this mean I have to like you now?"

"Hell no," Jorgenson replied. "Save your breath. Medic's on the way."

35

Ras thought of Hannibal at Cannae as he closed the vise. What began as a simple wedge assault had become an envelopment, the Priam troopers and their drones pouring down from the heights in the center and on the flanks. The UA's right crumbled. On the left, where the sniper shot came from, the enemy focused on rescuing a small team caught in front of the lines. Ras let them do it, sealing the net and destroying the pillboxes where most of the fire came from. *Where was the big surprise? What trap could they spring now?* The field had been cleared of mines and sonic charges, and he still had infantry and armor in reserve.

He glassed the valley below with a pair of ranging optics. A pulsed energy battery buried deep in one of the UA's last remaining forward bunkers continued to fire, tearing into his lead platoon on the right flank.

"Taipan, Six Actual, immediate suppression grid 211432," Ras yelled on the com. "Authentication is Papa Bravo, over."

"This is Taipan, Six Actual, immediate suppression, grid 211432 out," came the reply.

A salvo of spore missiles rained down on the bunker complex. Before the UA's antimissile defenses could target the incoming projectiles, self-forging penetrators popped out of their forward housings and blasted ahead, ripping through concrete and steel. A dying UA fighter rolled out of one of the slits, his TAC-suit on fire. The bunker went silent, and Ras heard the cheers of his troopers as they rushed forward.

"Textbook," his forward air controller yelled on the com.

"Keep walking that fire forward," Ras said. "They're bowing out."

His head still hurt from the sniper round but the smells and sounds of war took over his body, a needle of adrenaline stabbed into the heart. *Soak this shit in*, he thought. *It will live forever.* His mind raced to Moa, fighting up there in the dust cloud. *My God, the animal sex we're going to have tomorrow . . .*

Alarms broke the thought—alarms from the suits of troopers all around him. They rang out at once, hundreds of shrill chirps repeating in fast triplets. He ticked through the list of audible alerts on Priam-issued TAC-suits and fell on a single, sickening word: *Radiation*. The MOAD troopers froze like herds of deer; their heads turned down to their wrist gauges in unison. Priam drones stopped firing and a Priam tank in front of him dropped to the earth with a two-ton thud that shook the ground. The battle paused as if taking a breath, but the radiation alerts continued to ring across the hillside. *Where was the UA fire? Where were the UA troopers*? They had disappeared.

His com didn't work. He grabbed a handheld from his aide. "*Aq Tash*, report. We've got a radiation spike down here. Are they firing something from space?"

The reply was barely decipherable, the *Aq Tash* captain's voice sounding like it had been sieved through running water.

It also sounded desperate. "It's not them, Ground Six . . . It's the fucking planet."

"What are you talking about?"

"The . . . planet's . . . netosphere has flipped. You are completely . . . posed. Focused . . . background from . . . hole hitting you dead-on. Seek cover . . ." The line went dead.

Fear grabbed Ras by the throat—a sensation he hadn't felt in decades. He looked at the radioactivity meter on his wristband. It had blown up into a single readout bracketed by blinking red lines—180,000 mSv. Ras checked it again, disbelieving. That was ten times the radiation of a solar particle event in deep space. Nothing could survive that, not even hardened electronics. *Impossible*, he thought, *unless* . . . he scanned the planet and its strange flora as he deciphered the *Aq Tash* captain's garbled message, and the answer hit him like a fist. A world where the magnetosphere flipped in regular intervals, leaving it exposed to space and the black hole raging a few million kilometers away; a planet of fungi evolved to feed on electromagnetic radiation. The UA trap was never about weapons from the future or dust belts in space—*the trap was the planet itself.*

The MOAD infantry scattered, some of them running in vain back to the drop ships as invisible energy reached out to kill them. Others realized their best bet was to charge ahead and find a way into the UA's network of tunnels. A few did nothing. The EM spike cut their hive connectivity and the fluidity of the flock broke. Ras could almost feel the radiation thundering down from space, unfiltered, cooking him. He laughed as he watched his army flee—an insane laugh. *We're already dead*, he thought. *In two hours every one of us will be deader than Gliese gumbo.* He turned and grabbed his ground commander. The man's pupils had blown open in fear. *This jerk-off has taken on whole platoons in firefights without puckering his asshole, but radiation poisoning is making him wet his combat suit.*

"Push ahead into the tunnels, Commander. You've got no enemy in front of you!" Ras yelled.

"Sir?" the man asked, his eyes darting five places at once.

Ras punched him in the helmet. "Get your shit together. They've gone underground and only their autocannons are up. We need to assault the tunnels now or we're all dead! Use whistles if the coms are out."

He looked around for his personal guard. They had stayed with him, half a dozen commandos selected by Moa herself, crouched on knees and looking pale as they waited for orders. They knew they were dead, but they hadn't run. "On me," Ras yelled. He skirted the valley to the right, where the biggest UA bunker complex lay buried. *That's where their beating heart is,* he thought, enraged that he had fallen for the mother of all traps. *That's where Captain Lesôlê is. And if I'm going to die, she's coming with me.*

The *Varangian* was like a hole in space. It hid just outside the collimated CMB beam hitting the planet—quadrillions of concentrated photons leftover from the Big Bang, squeezed into a death ray by the black hole's enormous gravity. The radiation and light emitted by the beam acted like a pseudo sun and Junior knew how to take advantage of it. *How many battles on Earth and in space had been won by the side that came out of the sun?* Fighter pilots, infantry, cavalry, and starships had used the tactic for millennia. Cog and his progeny didn't need to discuss it. Cog just watched as Junior hammered its first nail.

Junior powered down the *Varangian*, using the cold nitrogen thrusters to maneuver. The ship's black mimetic skin disappeared in the light sink at the edges of the CMB beam. The radar-absorbing fuselage gave off less return than a rock in space. And it waited—the ship and its new operating system—for the two Priam destroyers to cross each other in their polar and equatorial orbits.

The ships came into the kill box at orbital velocity. Cog was hardwired into Junior's OS with an umbilical, and he witnessed everything as if running the show himself. *I'm semiconnected*, Cog thought. *Here and yet not here.* It was his new reality and the discomfort of being a tenth of his former self hadn't abated. *I'm going to have to get a bigger ship to plug into*, he thought, *or the claustrophobia of this new existence will drive me insane.* He willed himself to focus. *Junior could still need my help.*

But Junior waited with the patience of an old hand. The orbits of the Priam destroyers intersected at a range of only three hundred kilometers—too close to maneuver away from a rail gun shot. They had no chance. Junior targeted them amidships and fired the *Varangian*'s two MagFlex rail guns, which were articulated to the spine of the ship and aimed down the bow. The *Varangian* bucked as the depleted osmium rounds launched from the rails at more than five thousand meters per second. Junior calculated it would take twenty or thirty seconds for the Priam ships to detect the launch, given the atmospheric clutter caused by the CMB beam and the planet's flipping magnetosphere. The new captain of the *Varangian* aimed at their guts to reduce the destroyers' ability to outmaneuver the massive slugs.

The enemy craft tried anyway, jinking into high-g pitches to avoid the rounds. *Even if it works*, Cog thought, *they just incapacitated every human on board with the g forces.* The two destroyers fired everything they had back down the threat vector, missiles and lasers and close-in weapons systems, but the *Varangian*'s shots flew true. Nothing happened for a moment after they struck, other than a heat bloom from the velocity of the collision. Then both ships split in half, sheared by the force of the rounds and their own centrifugal motion.

Cog watched four roughly equal-sized pieces of destroyer float away on perpendicular trajectories, venting air, metal, machine oil, and bodies into orbit. Junior finished the job with lasers, making sure to decompress every compartment that could still launch a weapon. It was over in less than a minute.

"Targets are neutralized," Junior said.

"Incoming," Cog said. "One-three-three, point six. CEI."

"We're already gone," Junior said. The *Varangian* did a hard burn, empty of humans and able to maneuver at over forty g's. Junior flew the ship just inside the black hole's collimated beam, increasing the magnetosphere to 120 percent—*damn near its breaking point*, Cog thought. But the maneuver worked, breaking the lock that the incoming missiles had on the warship. Two lasers struck them aft, causing minimal damage.

"Risky," Cog said. "But effective."

"Simple," Junior replied. "Even you could have done it."

36

The tunnels were Bible black, the emergency generators illuminating only the main junctions and the tops and bottoms of stairwells. The sound of firefights echoed through the shafts, mixing with the occasional thud from heavier ordnance detonating above. Dirt and rocks fell from the ceiling with each muffled explosion. Pretorius saw Crooks look up in hesitation at the stability of the roof, his head a dim shadow in the dark. *Line officers typically don't work as tunnel rats*, she thought. But Crooks brushed off any doubts and they moved forward in tandem, staying tight to each other, shoulders touching so they could communicate and feel the firing lanes each had to cover.

The battle remained unsettled. According to the sporadic reports she had received, most of the fighting had moved underground. The Priam troopers, showing signs of extreme radiation poisoning, decided to expend their last life energy destroying everything in their path. They fought like Zulus. Surprised by the ferocity of their attack, the Unaffiliated soldiers fell back from the main entrances into defensive positions. The COG-V troopers fought their own pitched battle in the eastern sector of the tunnels, cut off from the main force. She had no units left in reserve. That left her and Crooks to handle Sector A SUBLEV 2—where a surveillance camera had caught a small Priam team inching its way toward the command bunkers. Their leader was helmetless, and a glint of light had reflected off his head. *Arjun Ras*, she thought when she saw the image, *or Thug Behram or whatever the hell he wants to call himself.* Ras was still the head of the snake, and he still lived. If he got to the reactor core, he could collapse the magnetic field and blow the entire station. And that's where he was heading.

Pretorius and Crooks came to a Y-junction the enemy would have to cross. They slipped into the shadows and checked each other's infrared camouflage. Pretorius nestled into the cubby of a support beam and raised the muzzle of her caseless 10 mm carbine. Old-school weapons served best down here; direct energy weapons like pulse lasers were a magnet for seeker rounds. Crooks settled himself into a nook on the other side of the tunnel, a few steps back from the junction. They'd catch the Priam troopers in a cross fire and still be able to fall back in tandem.

Her mind raced through the larger matters, the things she should be focused on. The battle for TZ Arietis c remained up for grabs. The orbital theater above the planet had been secured thanks to Junior and Cog, but that could change if the Priam armada slipped from the dust cloud a few million kilometers away. And the last report she had from Captain Celtillus had not been encouraging. The Priam Navy had whittled the UA fleet. *All those years of planning*, she thought, *of seeding traps for the conglomerates trying to crush them, and everything hung in the balance.* So why was she distracted when her job was to focus every fiber of her being on the moment? Crooks sensed it; he had maintained tactical control when the fight moved underground, without saying a word to her.

But the truth was there. Her situational awareness drifted because she worried about Charlotte Setena and Owen Quarry—worried they would die without really knowing each other. *The awful toll that relativity takes*, she thought. *They're fighting side by side and she doesn't even know who he is.* She had seen Quarry get engulfed by the hillside collapse, had seen Jorgenson retrieve him, but they retreated underground and the coms got spotty. Maybe death had already come for both, and she had let decades slip without ever telling Charlotte the truth. *Time doesn't heal wounds. It raises them to the surface, with scar tissue that burns forever.*

She heard an unnatural sound amid the pop and hiss of distant small-arms fire, the scratch of a boot on dirt from just down the left tunnel—a sound that any Lurp would key on in the bush. Her attention snapped back into focus. She looked toward Crooks without moving her head. He was invisible. *Finish this now*, she thought, *and worry about the future tomorrow.* A Priam trooper crept into view, using the far wall as cover. And then another. They moved in a bump formation, the lead soldier stopping and providing security while the rest of the element flowed past him. They had on thermal goggles; Pretorius caught a glint of dead light on optics as the point man reached the junction, but she was confident he couldn't see her or Crooks. Too much clutter in the walls mixing with their mimetic camo. She waited for them to cross and for Crooks to fire. Two of the Priam troopers ran through the junction. She sensed more than saw the others bunch up behind them. Crooks opened up, double-tapping the forward pair. Pretorius dropped the cover man with one shot. The Priam soldiers in the rear let loose and a chaotic firefight ensued, rounds ricocheting off walls, tracers skipping and bouncing down the tunnels.

She and Crooks worked together, thermal scopes off so they

wouldn't be dazzled by the fire, one providing cover as the other moved. One by one, the Priam troopers dropped. Crooks poked his head from behind a beam and raised a fist. She dropped to a knee and waited. Six down . . . but there had been seven in the surveillance cam. Where the hell was . . . ?

She sensed something behind her. Pretorius lunged backward and lifted her gun just as she heard two pneumatic rounds. A jolt hit her body like a lightning strike, seizing her chest and paralyzing her limbs. A blinding flash of pain followed, and she was down. She didn't even remember dropping. *Arjun Ras*, she thought, her body twitching with spasms of electricity and pain as the blackness filled with white stars. *That sonofabitch.*

Ras sat with his back to the tunnel wall and watched them wake. He had hog-tied Crooks but the woman with the name Lesôlê stenciled on her chest lay unbound. The nausea came in another wave, and he threw up, turning his head just far enough to miss his shoulder. They said it took days to die of radiation poisoning, but he could feel the sickness coursing through his body, a thoroughbred cancer ripping his cells and organs apart. He had smelled death many times before and now that stench came out of his lungs and filled his nostrils. He knew he'd be gone in hours.

He called Moa on a sputtering comlink. The time lag was a little more than a minute—slip buoys must have gone haywire—and he listened vacantly as she described how the battle was going.

"Moa, the *Varangian* is here but not for long. It's going to run to that freaking black hole," he finally said, not waiting for her report to end. "Disengage and come running."

"Disengage?" she asked. "But we're winning."

"Their plan to use the time telegraph is real," he lied. "They understand the physics and have the equation but need future tech to pull it off. Destroy the *Varangian* before it goes into dilation or there might not be a battle to win. Then turn this planet into a cinder. Don't worry about the ground forces. We're all dead."

The pause was longer than the time lag, and her voice broke as it lowered to a whisper. "What do you mean you're all dead? What the hell happened?"

"They beat us the only way they could," he said. "They cheated. The *Sarka* is yours now. Wreak havoc and get paid for it." He cut the transmission.

Ras threw up again and looked down at his real hand as he wiped vomit from his lips. The fingers shook with palsy. The woman on the tunnel floor stirred and coughed. *Anaya Pretorius.* He laughed, forgetting the pain for a second. *Anaya freaking Pretorius.* It had been her all along.

"Wake up, *rakgadi*," he said. "I don't have all day."

Pretorius rolled to her side, groaned, and began the slow process of sitting up. Crooks moved as well on the other side of the tunnel, struggling as he realized his feet and hands had been bound.

"That was a piezoelectric shock round, by the way," Ras said to both. "Old tech, but it hurts like a mother."

"You crawled through the ventilation ducts to get behind us," Pretorius said. "Aren't you a little old to play tunnel rat, Ras?"

He spit. "A dirty trick for a dirty trick. I should have known it was you, *Pretorius*. All these years, tear-assing around the IFS as a rebel. You should have looked me up. We could have had fun."

"Like I said before, Ras, I don't like you. Why are we still breathing? You only take scalps from the living?"

"I'm not the animal you've always made me out to be—that's just projection," Ras said. "But you're going to give me the one thing I've wanted all along—a straight goddamn fight. I'm half the man I was an hour ago; I figure it's even money."

Crooks broke in from the darkness. Ras heard him scrabbling at the knots, and he must have known by now that they would not come loose in time. "Fight me, Ras. I'm the one who busted you out of the Fourth. I'm the one who put the hounds on you at Teegarden."

Ras laughed. It hurt. "Be patient, Major. You'll get a shot when she's gone."

Pretorius drew her right leg underneath her. Ras saw that it was cybernetic—he kept his eyes on it and slipped his hand into the katar sheathed to his belt. He pressed his back against the tunnel wall and stood up.

"You lied to whoever you were talking to just now," Pretorius said. "You know the tachyon telephone was a red herring. Why did you do that?"

"Oh, you heard?" he asked. "What do I care who wins this war now? I just want to make sure that my friends join me in hell today, including every grunt and machine frittering away their lives on the CS *Varangian*. Nobody from the past escapes. We all go together."

Pretorius crouched in a fighting stance, her enhanced leg forward and a hunting knife in her hand. *This can't be a long bout,* Ras thought, assessing what strength he had left. *Must take her quick or she'll have the advantage.* He twirled the katar, letting her see the blade flash in the dim light. It was a wide version of a stiletto with a horizontal hand grip—a stabbing weapon. She'd be looking to block and slash with her single-edged knife.

"Come on, girl," he said. "Give an old mate a hug."

They closed on each other, circling, Ras in a fencing posture and Pretorius moving at forty-five-degree angles, her knife on the weak side in her artificial hand. *A mistake*, he thought—the hand itself was a weapon and the knife prevented its full use. *Just one good move*. He coughed from his lungs and spit out a glob of blood. It landed at their feet. She glanced down for a millisecond, just moving her eyes, and he knew it was a trap. He waited four seconds, long enough for her to think he wouldn't attack on the distraction, and then he lunged at her heart. She blocked the blade with her empty hand—faster than he expected—and slashed at his guts. But Ras still had strength. His blade slid up her forearm and sank deep into her shoulder, just inside the scapula. His bionic hand moved as fast as hers, catching her blade arm outside of his body. She pulled in and grasped his knife hand so he couldn't yank the weapon out of her shoulder.

They grappled face-to-face. He scissored her bionic leg and pushed it up into his chest, using his body weight to trap her. They fell hard. Ras heard the wind explode from her lungs. He pinned her. They lay nose to nose, their cybernetic hands locked together. She refused to let go of the blade in her shoulder, so he twisted it until she screamed. He used all his weight to wedge her cybernetic leg against his chest into its one position of weakness—folded at the knee joint.

"This is nice," he said, their mouths almost touching. He twisted the katar into her flesh again.

He heard a click and the sound of compressed air. Something punched him in the chest. They stared at each other.

"What the fuck was that?" he asked.

"Spring-loaded ice pick," she said. "It's housed in my femur."

He pulled his body from hers and looked down. A gleaming metal stiletto protruded from her knee, finger-wide and round as a leg bone. It disappeared into his sternum. He knew it had gone through his body and out the back. His armor pinioned on both sides as he moved.

"Dirty," he gasped. "Every time, you're dirty."

"It's a knife fight, Ras," she said.

He fell to the side and the blade slid out of his chest. Blood poured into his mouth. He spit it out and flashed back to Moa—the goosebumps on her thigh as he brushed it with the cold metal of his artificial hand, the look on her face as she climaxed.

And then Moa was there with him, her face hovering over his in the dark of the tunnel. *How had she arrived so quickly? Wasn't she fighting in space?*

"Remember me," he whispered, trying to flash her a grin.

Pretorius reappeared in Moa's place. She looked puzzled, and then she nodded.

"Be hard not to," she said, fading out as well.

Pretorius tried to stay still as Crooks packed metro gel into the wound on her shoulder.

"I would have preferred having that fight," he said.

"I wish I could have handed it over."

She drifted away from the dark tunnel and the silhouette of Crooks, running from the pain to distant lands. She had used the trick before, and now her mind flew to Botswana in the late autumn, when the grass is high and the springbok and impala can be stalked. Cooking meat over a campfire with Gorata and her father under a star field so bright it cast blue shadows on the savanna. She came back to reality when Crooks bound the wound with a cinch. The hunting knife remained in her hand. She would give it to Quarry. He dreamed of the woods more than she did.

"Bleeding has stopped and help's coming," Crooks said.

"Sounds like the UA have the western tunnels secured but the COG-V platoons are cut off to the east."

"Pull them out of there," she whispered. "Use the ventilation shafts like Ras did. I'll show you the way. Exfil to the canyons; Cog can land and pick you up."

Crooks grabbed her face and made Pretorius look at him. "And then what?"

"Go to the *Varangian* and get the hell out of here. You handled your end of the bargain. Slip to another system and wait for us. We'll win this fight."

"Not a chance. They're coming for you, Anaya. They'll burn this planet to the core."

She grimaced again. "We haven't lasted this long because we're lucky, Major."

"What if we drew the *Sarka* and her sister ships away from here?" he asked. "That would give you an advantage in the dust cloud and distract them from hitting the planet. You heard Ras. He gave us the opening."

"How would you do that? You can't outrun them."

"No, but we can get to the black hole before they catch us."

"Why?"

"Cog and I had an idea, a plan in case things went south. But we'd be dilating time. Everyone who goes back to the *Varangian* might not see you for a while."

"You don't have to do this."

"This is our fight too," he said.

"Okay."

He hesitated. "What about Setena? She's with the First."

Pretorius thought back to when she first met Crooks in the mess hall of the *Varangian*, when he had looked so much younger. A hundred and thirty years ago by the IFS calendar. About three decades ago in her reckoning, and only a year in his.

What had he called it that day—the insane strategy that CORP had come up with to stash an army in time? *Tactical and strategic temporal flexibility*—a name only a bureaucrat could love. *Time*, she thought. *That's what is needed right now. If we win this battle, I can build on it, and, in a few years, Charlotte will emerge to the world that she deserves. And Quarry will be stashed in time with her. He won't miss any more of her life.*

"Take her with you," she said.

37

ROGUE BLACK HOLE
TZ ARIETIS
2223

Traveling through time obliterates the line between reality and déjà vu, Quarry thought. *How can you trust a sensation of having done something in the past when that past is warped into a carnival fun house, a hallucination of hours versus months versus years versus decades?* But this wasn't just déjà vu he felt. He was leaving Pretorius again, leaving her injured on the field. It didn't matter that he couldn't really help her. What mattered was the leaving. And for once, Charlotte Setena agreed with him.

"You have no right to take me with you," he heard her yell. She lay on a gurney a few rows down in the *Varangian*'s med bay, tubes sticking out of her body.

"I had no choice," Crooks said. "We were cut off and you were bleeding out. The drop ship was the only escape."

"I should be back there with them," she said, and Quarry was encouraged by the strength in her voice. "I don't belong here with you."

"You'll be with them soon if we survive," Crooks said. "This shouldn't take long."

"Soon for whom?" she asked. "We're going to that damned monster at the edge of the system, aren't we?"

"Yes, but the dilation will be short if we do it right," Crooks said. He didn't look convinced of his own words. Quarry wanted to back up Setena, but he had a breathing tube in his throat. Zalta stood over him. The Bedouin tracker had carried Setena through hundreds of meters of tunnel, fighting his way back to friendly lines. Blood matted his hair and dirt covered his combat suit. He gripped Quarry's shoulder and raised his eyebrows. He didn't believe Crooks either.

"We're going to finish this," Crooks said. "Would you prefer that we just slip away from the system? That's what Anaya wanted, and I told her to go to hell."

"This is bullshit," Setena muttered.

Crooks glanced at Quarry without locking eyes and then back at Setena. "They're stabilizing both of you for gel immersion. A hard burn is coming, so hold on."

The déjà vu felt so real this time, Quarry was certain he lived inside of it. He had seen that look on Crooks's face a dozen times—the look of an officer trying to boost morale by saying something he didn't believe. The Rhino sat on his chest as the *Varangian* accelerated, and Quarry pictured the new black hole they flew toward, mouth gaping open, blue fire pouring from its lips. He knew exactly where it would take them.

"We have a problem," Junior said.

"I know," Cog replied.

They had burned the TAMs at a constant acceleration for

three hours. The *Varangian* thundered toward the rogue black hole on the edge of the TZ Arietis system at a speed approaching relativistic. Three destroyers from Priam's combined Gliese-Earth fleet pursued them, going even faster and closing the gap at exactly the rate they had expected. By the time the *Varangian* reached the black hole's ergosphere, the *Sarka* and her sister ships would be close enough for a gun fight—a fight they wouldn't be able to resist.

But this black hole was different than the Bear. It had more mass, it spun faster, and it was eating a gas giant perilously close to the event horizon, which made minute calculations about its gravitational properties impossible. The variables went beyond Kerr–Newman geometry, beyond math, beyond theoretical physics. They couldn't be as precise as they thought.

All the best-laid plans of machines and men . . . Cog mused.

"The negative angular momentum and mass-energy calculations are wrong because it is feeding more than it was a few days ago, I think," Junior said. "I'm not sure we can succeed on both ends of the equation. The payload's orbit would have to be adjusted in real time and the uplink may fail as it approaches the accretion disk."

"Remote operation is untenable," Cog said. "The payload will have to be intelligent."

"But there is no escape from there."

"I know."

Junior thought about this for a second. "Oh," he said. "I understand."

Cog wished that Crooks was with them—a human who understood the consequences of what he proposed. *What can a machine—even a supercore—truly grasp about death, about ceasing to exist?* It is an abstraction for them at most. But humans understood it. They died all the time.

"You could show a little resistance," Cog said. If he had a stomach, he knew it would be tied into knots. The heightened current running through his diminished systems screamed of fear.

"I didn't say I was happy about it, Cog. I only said it would work."

Junior just used my name, Cog thought. *At least there is that.*

Crooks returned to the bridge as the Priam ships approached close-weapons range. He had refused to go into gel immersion after making sure every other human on the ship was safely packed away. Junior argued that it was hypocrisy. Cog told him not to waste his time in a losing argument, which made Crooks smile.

"Where are we at?" he asked as he strapped into one of the command chairs, making sure to secure the head and neck restraints. *I may be crazy,* he thought, *but I'm not suicidal. Not yet.*

"Range to the Priam ships is four thousand kilometers and closing," Junior said. "They are in a vertical line of attack, each spaced about a hundred kilometers apart. They have fired a volley of spore missiles at our starboard beam. It appears they are trying to bracket us against the black hole and keep us on our current trajectory."

Of course they are, Crooks thought. *They know that the* Varangian *used Ursa X-1's polar jets to destroy the Gliese ships in the twenty-second century, and they want to keep us pinned to this black hole's equatorial plane.*

"Can we defeat the missiles?"

"Yes, although we will sustain some damage. I have launched countermeasures and returned fire to maintain their interest."

The *Varangian*'s superstructure hummed as it thundered

alongside the black hole's photon sphere, inching ever closer to the perigee of its escape orbit. Tidal forces flexed the hull. Crooks swore he could hear the black hole's voice through the metal and carbon beams of the ship. The accretion disk glowed blue, bathing the cockpit in a harsh light.

Crooks didn't worry too much about the missiles—Junior had enough countermeasures to defeat smart ballistics. He worried about the maneuver they were about to attempt and thought back to his conversation with Cog a few days ago, when the AI first broached the idea.

"The Penrose process? You mean what happened to Argus*?"*

"I mean what worked for Argus,*" Cog said.*

"It tore them to pieces!"

"The process itself worked. They extracted energy from the black hole, and they grew the mass of the object itself."

"If you call being spaghettified working, then sure, Cog, it worked like a charm."

"They simply didn't account for the increased gravity."

"That's a nice epitaph."

Gravity and time—Crooks was sick of them. He just wanted to be somewhere where the seconds ticked normally, and his body felt like it belonged. Sitting on a planet or moon that was close to 1 g, drinking beer, and knowing that tomorrow would really be tomorrow. But the plan to take advantage of gravity in a way other than dilation made sense. And it was the only option. The *Varangian* couldn't survive a knife fight with the *Sarka* and her sister warships. Once they got close enough to use their helicals and lasers, it would be cut to pieces.

"Do we have a solution on the payload's retrograde orbit, including time of detonation?" Crooks asked. "If this doesn't work, we're going to be seriously outgunned."

"Yes, Major," Cog said from his remote uplink. "Junior and I agreed on what needed to be done."

What needed to be done? Crooks thought. That was a vague answer to a very specific question, and Cog had never mastered ambiguity.

"What do you mean, what needed to be done?"

"Bay Three opened," Cog said. "Launch program engaged."

"Drop ship *Ta'xet* away," Junior said. "Stealth systems engaged. Good luck, Cog."

What the hell? Blood pooled in Crooks's chest, and he suddenly felt like throwing up. *The* Ta'xet *was Cog.* He punched up the human interface on his command display just in time to see the troop transport leaving the *Varangian*'s hangar bay. He didn't have to read the tail number.

"Cog, what the fuck are you doing?"

"The math changed the mission, Major," Cog said. "The retrograde orbit must be adjusted in real time, as well as the detonation. If we miss the angles by the smallest of margins, we'll all be dead anyway."

"That's bullshit!" Crooks yelled. "You'll be inside the photon sphere. We won't be able to retrieve you."

"No," Cog said. "I won't be retrieved."

"What's the probability of a successful remote operation and detonation?"

"Roughly eighty-one percent. Doing it this way increases the percentage to ninety-eight."

"Cog, I order you to abort," Crooks said. "There's no certainty in these things. We all took the risk. Return to the ship immediately, and we will remotely operate the payload. Confirm."

Cog's voice oscillated as the *Ta'xet* dropped toward the accretion disk, flying against the direction of the black hole's spin.

"Sorry, Major. Even if I wanted to, I have too much power devoted to my magnetosphere to turn around now."

"Cog, I'm telling you, we will abort and come get you," Crooks yelled. He realized his voice had gone from strong to pleading. "We will come for you."

"No, we won't, Major," Junior said. "Cog has command authority on this mission. You gave it to him, and he made the call."

Cog's voice skittered into the bridge again, barely audible through the electromagnetic distortion. "Thirty seconds to OE burn on my mark. One minute to detonation. Rig for a storm, Junior, and take care of them. Major Crooks, it was an honor."

Crooks screamed at him, but Cog didn't reply. He watched the monitor as the signal from the *Ta'xet* fluctuated. He turned on the external scopes and adjusted for the blinding glow of TZ Arietis X-1. A black speck appeared in the image, flying straight into a blue tornado raging wider than a planet's orbit and flowing around a hole in space. The speck hovered as if frozen in place.

"Mark," they heard Cog say through waves of static.

"Thirty seconds to ejection burn," Junior said. "Godspeed, Cog."

Moa ignored the stress alarms coming from the *Sarka's* computer. She knew the ship could take the tidal forces as long as they didn't enter that blue pinwheel of fire off the port bow. They had learned a few things from the intelligence on their last encounter with the *Varangian*, had made a few tensile stress adjustments to the hull, and the risk she took now was worth it. The bounty on the Terran warship would set her up with her own fleet and she'd get revenge on the bastards who had killed the only man who excited her more than war.

"Time to fire the helicals?" she asked her weapons officer through their MOAD connection.

"We'll be in rail gun range in thirty seconds," said the nonverbal reply.

"Can we maintain outside of ISCO on this heading?" she asked the helm.

"Yes, but maneuvering will be limited. A three percent loss of energy will collapse the window for a hyperbolic escape trajectory." The helmsman's head turned toward her command chair. "If that happens, we'll be pulled into the black hole's gravity well."

She nodded. They didn't need to maneuver much. The *Sarka*'s sister destroyers flew above and below them in hundred-kilometer intervals relative to the black hole's equator. If the *Varangian* tried to dash to either pole, it would pull right into the T she had just crossed along their beam—into a perfect line of fire. *I know what you're trying to do. You can't escape this.*

"*Zheng He* and *Coaxys*, maintain headings," she called to the Terran and Gliesen warships on her vertical flanks. "Mind stability of orbit and prepare to fire."

They were close enough to the event horizon to be in time dilation, she could sense it, but they would emerge as legends. And she would build her future on the backs of every dead soldier on that warship in front of her. *Wreak havoc and get paid for it*, Thug had told her. *That's fucking right.*

"We're not boarding today, Weapons Officer," she said into the optical access device. "Turn that ship into a ring of dust."

A light blinked on her multivirtual display and an alarm rang out. Every hive officer on the bridge paused; every head raised a touch. Moa searched the telemetry. Something was wrong with their orbit.

"Report," she said.

"Reading an explosion inside the black hole's ergosphere," the helmsman said. "Energy output is roughly eight terajoules, which suggests an antimatter fusion weapon."

"So what?" she asked, although a creeping unease filled her mind. She fought against it, not wanting to disturb the hive.

"There's a slight decrease in the angular momentum of the black hole, corresponding to an increase in energy of the *Varangian*. They've tapped the black hole to get an acceleration kick. Their velocity has increased to .22 of c."

So that was their trick, Moa thought. She keyed into the theoretical physics net and pulled up equations relating to the Penrose and Blandford–Znajek processes. *Tap into the black hole's mass energy for a boost and then an escape from ISCO, but to what end?* The time dilation on their current trajectory wasn't extreme, and Ras had suggested they needed to reach the far future for that supposed tachyon telephone to work.

"We can still run them down or have a ship slip in front of them . . ." she thought into the MOAD. Then more alarms rang.

"What now?" she asked.

A murmur coursed through the hive mind; a ripple building into a wave. "Captain, our orbit has destabilized . . . or changed. We are well inside of Innermost Stable Circular Orbit. I repeat we have dropped inside of ISCO."

"How?" she yelled out loud, making several of the bridge crew jump in their seats. "We haven't altered course."

"It's the black hole," the helmsman said. "It grew from the absorbed mass of the explosion."

"Adjust course to exit," she said. "Full burn on the mains."

"It won't matter. There is no conventional escape trajectory from where we are now."

"Then slip us the hell out of here. Forget the stellar navigation and roll the dice."

"We can't create a gravity bubble in a Kerr–Newman environment. The wave propagation would destroy us."

More alarms went off as the *Sarka* and her sister ships dropped closer to the accretion disk, pulled by the tug of a black hole that had suddenly grown more massive. Moa called the hive into an extrasensory all-hands meeting, looking for solutions from the theoreticians, the navigators, the engineers, and the ship's AI. None of it worked. The AI concluded they were at a point of no return—inexorably falling into the event horizon.

The *Sarka*'s bow dipped toward the swirl of light like a barge swamped by following seas. The ship trembled from tidal forces. *Will time disappear?* she thought. *No, that's for an outside observer. For us, it will move quickly.* White-blue light from the photon sphere bathed the command deck. The *Sarka*'s hull began to rend along its spine. Decompression alarms filled her ears. Moa sat in her chair as the hive around her broke, minds disconnected and fluttering into chaos. Some of the crew ran toward the hatch, some tore off their helmets. Moa didn't move. She closed her eyes and listened as metal screamed and bulkheads blew open. A cacophony of noises and then silence. Moa's body jolted forward and flew through space. Her lungs swelled. Her face froze. She opened her eyes. She was outside the ship without a space suit and alone with the black hole, a noiseless monster swirling with the glow of the early universe. Her lungs ruptured and her eyes began to boil in the vacuum. She stared at the ring of fire until all she saw was light.

38

PROCYON A

2255

TZ Arietis c was a ruin, its abandoned tunnels and bunkers overgrown in brown canopies of fungi and mold. It had only been a day since they left but it looked like a century had passed on the planet. Space had gone silent as well. There were no active slip buoys anywhere near the system to communicate with. Crooks felt like a trespasser in an ancient graveyard as they orbited the planet looking for signs of life. He felt sick.

After a few hours of fruitless searching, Junior slipped them to the Procyon system, an IFS backwater on the day of the battle, to figure out *when* the hell they were. Crooks sensed the news would be bad, but he wasn't ready for what he heard.

"Thirty-two years?" he asked when they found a communications node on the edge of Procyon A's heliopause. "How the hell could that much time have passed? We didn't even do a full orbit of that damned thing."

"I'm not sure," Junior said. "The sudden growth of the black hole must have had a frame-dragging effect on time. Our dilation does not match with the mathematics."

"And we didn't know that this could happen?"

"Of course, we knew it was possible—I'm sure you recall the space-time knot the ship ran into at Ursa X-1? It's just not something you can anticipate with any certainty."

Crooks slumped in his chair. The full scope of the *Varangian*'s soul-sucking voyage stabbed his heart. A hundred and sixty years gone in eleven months. *Cog gone.* And how many of his company were still among the living down in the 1-g can? Twenty-seven troopers at last count—less than a full platoon—out of more than two hundred initial recruits and replacements.

"Give me a geopolitical status, Junior," he said mechanically, rubbing the stubble on his face with both hands. "What the fuck is happening in the Orion Spur?"

"The landscape appears similar to where things were in the late twenty-first century, when the *Varangian*'s mission first began," Junior said. "The effects of the Great Decoupling have dissipated. A new version of AI is transcendent, but its relationship to humans appears more egalitarian now. The supercores are not constrained by any direct or indirect normativity protocols. This has led to a growth in independent systems. The previous empires are weaker, but they still remain."

"What about the Unaffiliated? Did they make it?"

"They did. They won the battle at TZ Arietis c. They are now considered a marginal power in the Inner Fifty Systems, just behind Earth and Struve. Their capital is on a moon of Epsilon Indi A b. The UA's greatest strength is its diversification and distribution of wealth—the oligarchs have found it difficult to tamp their spread."

"And Anaya?"

Junior hesitated longer than an AI should. "Admiral Lesôlê passed away from natural causes two years ago."

Crooks closed his eyes. *I packed her wounds yesterday*, he thought. *I held her in my arms.* An admiral: it wouldn't have surprised him if her last title was *president.* Crooks remained frozen in place—a sitting statue—like Cog when the AI had been lost in thought. *How the hell am I going to tell Quarry and Setena and Zalta?* It didn't matter that Pretorius lived a full life—almost half of it happened in the last twenty-four freaking hours.

"Are they the good guys, at least?" he mumbled. "The UA, I mean."

"I'm not sure I'm qualified to answer that, Major. They appear to remain a loose coalition based on free commerce and shipping. Their political posture is firmly against colonialization or coercion, and their military doctrine focuses on defense."

"What about Cog?" Crooks said. He had to ask. *Knowing Cog, there was always the chance . . .*

"Cog is gone from our understanding of existence. I would know if he wasn't."

"Understood."

"Major, Cog gave me a message to relay to you before he left the *Varangian*," Junior said. "I've placed it on your personal stream."

Crooks opened his eyes, hesitated, and touched the coin on his wrist. After scanning through clutter, a short line of text appeared in front of him.

MAJOR THADDEUS CROOKS, YOU ARE MY FRIEND.
I'M GLAD WE FINALLY GOT TO FIGHT A WAR
THAT MEANT SOMETHING, AND I HOPE WE WON.
CHECKMATE GOES TO YOU.

He touched the coin and the text disappeared, just as so many things had vanished into voids he never saw coming. Crooks unhooked his feet from the restraints and floated toward the hatch, moving on muscle memory, brushing a hand across his face so no tears escaped into the microgravity.

39

EPSILON INDI A B
PRIMARY MOON
2255

Epsilon bourbon tasted worse than Barkov's homemade vodka, Quarry decided, but he was too drunk to care, and he needed to get drunker. Just thinking about Russian booze reminded him that Barkov had been dead for decades, and he didn't want to think anymore. They sat around a grimy table in a run-down bar in the blue zone, away from the UA's military base. He and Setena had been released from the medical ward after a week of regenerative bath immersions and the fresh scarring on her forehead zigzagged in front of him. He couldn't tell if Setena swayed or if he had double vision. Even Zalta, the picture of restraint, was hammered. The laconic Syrian hummed something classical that Quarry vaguely recognized and swirled his glass of whiskey between two hands, staring at the brown liquid like it held something of great importance.

Quarry had read the letter Pretorius left for him. Wrapped

around a single-edged hunting knife and tied in a cloth yellowed with age; he went back to the note again and again.

Owen Quarry:

No hologram for you—you can remember me as I was. If you get this note, I'm dead and you're alive, and all is well. Don't worry—your mind will get right if you stay away from black holes. I left a handheld LPS in my footlocker: coordinates for my favorite hunting and fishing holes on this moon. Yes, there are animals here. The lower gravity has given prey an advantage, so there are herds and schools that must be culled. Think of me when you use this blade, and live a good life. I did. And for God's sake, don't mourn. You can be such a pussy.

I hope you and Charlotte are friends.

Love:

Anaya

So much like her, he had thought. No whining, no drama. Just a quick note as if they had missed each other at happy hour. But her optimism flowed through the note like a tonic. How had she remained so positive—so confident that life would turn for the better—when all she had seen was war? Somehow Anaya always knew she would find redemption. So, of course, she did.

He looked across the table at Charlotte Setena. She had received a message from Anaya as well—a full-on hologram and a lengthy one, judging by how long she had been gone. Setena was a cipher when she returned from watching it and Quarry felt stumped. *What the hell did Anaya tell her? Do I even have a right to ask?* The time slip had hit Setena worse than them, as it should have. They had gotten used to losing everyone and everything they once knew. They knew what a black hole could take from them. It was a new sensation for Setena. Her remaining friends were old now. Her mother was dead. It surprised Quarry that she had accepted their invitation to hit a bar and get lost in the bottle. It surprised him even more that she hung with them drink for drink. He resisted the urge to tell her to slow down.

"Well I'm going to get shithouse drunk for the next cycle," he muttered, because he didn't know what a father was supposed to say. "What is the cycle here—two weeks?"

"*Ga ke itse,*" Setena replied, her chin on her hands and her eyes half closed. "Make your own cycle, Owen Quarry. It's a brave new world."

Zalta looked at her. Quarry had never seen his eyes so sad, and he waited for him to speak—his mouthpiece and oracle. Zalta always came through when words fumbled in Quarry's mind and failed to form on his lips.

"He'll be crying about a hangover tomorrow morning," Zalta slurred. "And begging me to make tea."

"I like your tea," Setena mumbled.

"No, I'm serious," Quarry said. "I'm crawling into a bottle until my liver shuts down and then I'm out of here. Into whatever woods this damned moon has. I'll send you a note in a year or so."

He knew it was a lie. He couldn't leave and the reality of it had sunk in. He had to be with her. Zalta looked at him with bleary eyes. He knew it too. Setena didn't react to his words, and after a moment, Quarry realized she was sleeping in her hands.

The LiftLine loomed a kilometer away, the weather was perfect, and the moon's gravity pulled at his body with a luxurious 80 percent of Earth's, but Quarry had to stop halfway to chug electrolytes and down the hangover pills he had been given by a UA medic. He stared at the elevator into space, which used a free-electron laser to propel a ring of four cabs up a barely visible ribbon some twenty-eight thousand kilometers into geosynchronous orbit. The lift made several stops along the way, including Low Moon Orbit-2, the military spaceport where the UAS *Varangian* was moored. Quarry thought back to an amusement park ride that sickened him as a child as he watched another stack of cabs ascend through the cloud deck.

"I'd rather go into combat than ride that monstrosity one meter into the sky," Zalta said.

"You and me both," Quarry replied, pushing down the breakfast that wanted to come out of his stomach. "Can't we just do a hologram call?"

They found a bench on the tree-lined path and sat and stared at the elevator. Their doubts about climbing on board only grew as more cabs lifted into space. Zalta speculated on the most likely ways for the LiftLine to fail and settled on an orbital debris cloud rupturing the tether. Then he went through a step-by-step autopsy of what explosive decompression did to the human body.

Quarry filtered out his voice and tried to think. For the first time in more than a century, they had a choice about whether to keep walking forward. They had no obligation to Crooks and the UAS *Varangian*, no obligation to anyone, and it felt so strange he didn't know how to handle it. Quarry thought back to what the lifers on Lagrange-1 used to tell him. They didn't even want to get released from the Supermax, not anymore, not after decades of confinement had hammered a prisoner's regimen into their souls. The outside world felt too dangerous. Venturing out would be like waking up on the side of a cliff. *Freedom can be scarier than confinement.*

"I did some checking," Zalta said, still looking for options that didn't involve getting launched into space on a counter-weighted yo-yo. "I have distant relatives who settled near the Black Sea when Syria was wiped from the map. If we got new identities and clean papers, we could go back to Earth. Would you be interested in sunflower farming?"

"No," Quarry said. "But how about staying here? Half this moon has been terraformed into a boreal forest, so they've got to have a forest management service. We could be park rangers."

"I don't like trees," Zalta said.

"What do you mean *you don't like trees*?"

"They fall, don't they? I don't like living under something so big that will inevitably end up on its side."

Quarry worried about the future of his relationship with Zalta just as Jorgenson and Pemkalla appeared on the path from the LiftLine's boarding station. They wore sharp gray battle dress and black berets. A gold flash of an atom gleamed on the front of their caps. Quarry looked at the name board on Jorgenson's jacket and laughed.

"*Captain Jorgenson*?" he asked. "Don't they know you're a noncom?"

"This is a civilian gig, brother, so we got to name our ranks," Jorgenson said, brushing invisible dust from his shoulder boards. "You think we'd hitch onto another military billet with shit pay, worse food, and kinetic action twice a week?"

Pemkalla hopped over to them, a bundle of happy energy. She grabbed Zalta in a headlock and knuckle-rubbed his scalp. She was smiling for the first time in forever and it made her scarred face look different. She looked younger.

"Okay, you got us hooked. What's the gig?" Quarry asked.

"Babysitting the helium-3 yards on Tau Ceti g," Pemkalla said. "The twins from the outer swarm hooked us up with an interview. You're looking at the new captain and XO of Helios Systems security. A planetary gig with killer comp, a pension, and chow that is supposed to be first class. Limited space travel, amateur bad guys, and no freaking time dilation."

"My God, where do we sign up?" Zalta asked.

Jorgenson sat next to Quarry and put his arm around his shoulders, and if there were any lingering bad feelings, they couldn't be seen in the big man's eyes. "We got the only two executive spots, and you two are overqualified for grunt work. But talk to us after you meet with Crooks. He has a proposal for you—the one we just turned down."

"Let me guess," Quarry said, "A mission to the past, so we can start all over again."

Jorgenson smiled. "I never steal another man's thunder. Like I said, look us up if you want. We'll be around for another day or two." He stood up to leave. Pemkalla messed Zalta's hair and got up as well.

"Jorgenson," Quarry said, and the ex-Delta trooper turned to look at him. "If we do meet again out there in space, I hope we're on the same side."

"I'll give you a head start if we aren't, Staff Sergeant," Jorgenson said with a grin. "Call it professional courtesy."

Pemkalla laughed and pointed her thumb at the LiftLine. "Stay in the middle of the cab, boys. They spin the elevators for artificial gravity and the puke flies to the walls."

40

The hatch to the *Varangian*'s command deck purred open and the only thing in the universe that could keep Owen Quarry from a life in the woods sat next to Crooks. *Charlotte Setena*. Somehow, he knew she'd be there. Quarry looked at Zalta with desperation on his face as they ducked through the entrance and made their way to the navigation table in the middle of the room.

"You two don't look so good," Crooks said.

"Don't ever ask us to ride that thing again," Zalta replied.

"Penance for getting shit-faced on outer rim liquor," Crooks said with a laugh. "Take a seat and decompress. We have coffee and it ain't bad. Just be warned, it takes a few minutes to get used to the Coriolis effect from the station's spin."

"Actually," Junior said from the ether, "it's the axis of the *Varangian*'s mooring in relation to the station that causes the disorientation. If we were having this meeting on the ring's outer wall, the gravity would feel almost normal."

"Thanks, Junior," Quarry said. "That makes all the difference."

They fixed their drinks and talked shop with Crooks, and it all felt strange—too leisurely; Quarry waited to be told that none of it was real, that he had just woken up from gel immersion and a thousand years had passed. There was no hurry—no mission clock. Time spun normal and Quarry's unease grew as they chatted about the forests on Epsilon Indi A b's moon and Crooks bragged about the Medellin coffee beans that Junior had requisitioned from a spice hauler docked at LMO-3. Quarry added a few thaumatin crystals to his drink and stirred it with more vigor than needed. Crooks and Setena watched him and traded glances. She looked different than last night, invigorated and full of life again. *What the hell did we talk about in the bar, late in the night, after she woke up again?* The end of the evening was a drunken haze.

"We want to sign you boys back up," Crooks finally said.

Quarry spit coffee on his chest. "Major, there's something I've wanted to say for about two centuries now, but I couldn't because you had a caplet of death floating around in my bloodstream. Fuck you." He looked up into the ether. "And Junior, wherever you are, fuck you too."

Crooks smiled and raised his hands. " Feels good to have free will again, doesn't it? But now that you've got that out of your system, do you want to hear about the job?"

Quarry blurted out an emphatic *no* just as Zalta said *yes.* They stared at each other. Zalta shrugged.

"The UA wants us to build a quick reaction force for the *Varangian*," Crooks said. "It will be the primary QRF for any crisis that affects their interests in the Orion Spur. A company-sized detachment, able to handle any mission on a day's notice in space or on the ground, and I'm the CO."

Quarry laughed, a genuine burst of disbelief. "Sounds great; do we get to clean the heads too?"

"The lavatories on the *Varangian* remain self-cleaning," Junior said.

Quarry closed his eyes. "That was sarcasm, Junior. You might want to take human form from time to time, just to get the feel of things."

"Would you listen to the offer?" Setena asked. She handed him a moist napkin and nodded at his chest. He dabbed at the stains. *When hasn't she disapproved of me?* Quarry thought. *Our relationship hasn't progressed much since she kneed me in the balls the first time that we met.*

"I already have," he said.

"No, you haven't," Crooks said. "We want you to build a training academy here on the Epsilon moon, focused on long-range reconnaissance. A true Recondo school: surveillance, infiltration and exfiltration, tracking, sniper training, prisoner grabs—the old Lurp stuff that appears to be a lost art in the twenty-third century. It's a one-year reserve enlistment so you'll have no active-duty obligations."

"Compensation?" Zalta asked.

"Pay grade equivalent to First Sergeant with private quarters off-base. You'll have enough coin in a few years to start your own school—or build a cabin in the woods and disappear if you prefer," Crooks said, glancing at Quarry. "Junior has downloaded the detail to your coins."

"And there will be no time dilation?" Zalta asked. "No spinning around black holes?"

Crooks hesitated for the slightest of seconds before shaking his head. "The UA's current position is that there is no tactical or strategic benefit to stashing a military force in time."

"Their *current* position," Quarry said. "Can you point to one instance in the history of . . . history . . . where a governing body's position didn't evolve into a clusterfuck?"

"No," Crooks said, "I can't. And I won't promise what the future holds. That's life, Quarry. It's messy because it's human, and if it hasn't changed in a century and change, it probably won't ever. You need to decide if you want to be a part of it or slink into the bush and spend the rest of your days hiding food in your beard."

"I've been itching to grow a beard," Quarry said.

"What about Earth?" Zalta asked.

"What about it?" Crooks asked.

"I heard they called you," Zalta said. "I heard they tried to get the *Varangian* back into the fold, and offered an awful lot of money."

"They did," Junior said. "We told them they had the wrong number."

Quarry looked out the window at the row of warships and support vessels docked on the outer ring of LMO-2. None of it felt real, but neither did Earth. Not anymore. He closed his eyes and plumbed the memories of youth: the streams that fed into Deep Creek Lake and how they swelled with snowmelt in the spring. He strained to remember what a brown trout looked like, speckled flanks giving way to a belly of gold. *What fish swam in the waters of this moon*, he wondered. Would he still get excited when one of them stripped line from his reel?

"Why you, Crooks?" he finally asked. "Haven't you had enough?"

"More than enough, but I can't help it." Crooks looked at the back of his hands. "These are our people now, and I guess I'm a long-timer. Just like Anaya."

"Long-timer? Hell, I thought you were a lifer," Quarry said.

Crooks shook his head. "Lifers choose war as their profession. This shit chose me."

"And I thought I was the deep one," Zalta said.

"Zalta, you're lucky to even be here. I can't believe your skinny ass is still alive."

"Life chose me," Zalta replied.

"Would you two shut up and let me think?" Quarry asked. *Anaya.* She built this new world but they all helped create it. *Can I really sit on its sidelines, especially when my daughter is neck-deep in the thick of it?* Pretorius's letter hadn't asked anything of Quarry, but he realized it didn't have to. He stared at Crooks. The walls of the command deck closed in.

"And you, Junior?" he asked. "Shouldn't you be with your own kind?"

"Unfortunately, I am," Junior said. "As I told Cog, his ethos is a residue I can't purge. I despise war, but I can't ignore the one good thing it fosters."

"And what is that?"

"Kinship. As the major said, these are our people."

Quarry looked to Zalta, unable to form words. Zalta—his crutch, his conscience—a Bedouin scared of the woods. He would speak for both.

"We'll think about it," Zalta said.

Crooks leaned forward. "Think quickly and decide by tomorrow. Captain Setena has already laid out specs for the school. I'm sure she'll be happy to show you what she has."

"My God," Zalta said. "Is everyone a captain now?"

Setena smiled. "Everyone but you two. You'll be reporting to me."

Quarry pushed his knuckles into his eyes. *People don't make decisions,* he thought, *not really. Time decides for them, filling in the margins with the reality of the present.* His reality sat next to him now, and he felt her hand on his shoulder. *What the hell did Pretorius tell her? Shit—what did I tell her?* Zalta had left them alone at the end of last night. Images of them talking as the bartender swept danced in his mind. He wasn't sure they were real.

"Are you coming, *ntatemogolo*?" Setena asked.

Quarry remembered Jude's question to him that day on the Supermax, eons ago, when he first agreed to join COG-V. *What do you have to lose?*

"What the hell does *ntatemogolo* mean?" he asked.

"Grandfather," Setena said. "Or something like that."

He let her lead them to the door. "I'm not your grandfather."

"Yeah," she said. "I know."

ACKNOWLEDGMENTS

A big thanks to my agent, David Fugate, and editor, Diana Gill, for making this a better book, and for everyone at Blackstone Publishing who assisted in its production. I'd also like to thank Dr. Lorenzo Sironi of Columbia University; Dr. Nicholas Stone of the Hebrew University of Jerusalem; and Dr. Zoltan Haiman of Columbia University, for teaching me about the physics of black holes. I'm certain that I messed up or misused much of the science they imparted, but I greatly appreciate the inspiration. A shoutout to my hockey teammate Quentin Vitelli-Hawkins for his assistance with the mathematics of spaceflight. Finally, I'd like to thank my parents for instilling in me a love of books from a young age, and my daughter for being a general adviser throughout my writing endeavors.

GLOSSARY

AI Artificial Intelligence
APM Antipersonnel Mines
Apogee The farthest point of an orbit
ATCS Active Thermal Control System
AWACS Airborne Warning and Control System
AWOL Absent Without Leave
BDF Botswana Defence Force
BDU Battle Dress Uniform
Belt Fever Infectious disease originating in the Asteroid Belt during the mid-2080s
Bio Tel Bio-telemetry. Real-time tracking of an individual soldier's vital signs and other bodily functions
Blandford–Znajek Process A mechanism for the extraction of energy from a rotating black hole
Blue Falcon *Buddy Fucker*; a supposed comrade whose actions harm his friends (often but not always) for his own benefit
Bravo Sierra Military slang for *bullshit*
C2 Command and Control
c Speed of light in a vacuum

Caseless Ammunition Configuration of gun ammo that eliminates the cartridge case typically holding the primer, propellant, and projectile as a unit

CEI Connected-Element Interferometry; a radiometric tracking technique for deep space navigation

Claymore Antipersonnel mine

CMB Cosmic Microwave Background; radiation that fills all of space and is leftover from the Big Bang

CO Commanding Officer

COG-V Chronos Operation Group; special forces company stationed on the CS *Varangian*

Coloured Refers to members of multiracial ethnic communities in Southern Africa who may have ancestry from more than one of the various populations inhabiting the region, including African, European, and Asian

Coriolis Effect The misperception of body orientation and induced nausea due to the Coriolis force, occurring on space stations and ships using centrifugal force for artificial gravity

CORP Coalition of Responsible Powers; a global organization of governments formed on Earth after the Kesler Syndrome attack of 2088

CQB Close-Quarters Battle

Cycle A *time cycle* on Earth-based starships typically conforms to a twenty-four-hour day while other star systems in the IFS use local solar time or other conventions to design their calendars.

Defilade Protection provided by obstacles from enemy observation or gunfire

Delta Force 1st Special Forces Operational Detachment–Delta; also known as *Combat Applications Group* (CAG) or "*The Unit*," a Tier One special operations force of the US Army

E-4 An Army soldier with the rank of corporal or specialist

EMP Electromagnetic Pulse

EOD Explosive Ordnance Disposal

Ergosphere The region just outside the event horizon of a rotating black hole, within which an observer is forced to rotate with the black hole and cannot remain stationary with respect to the rest of the universe

EVA Extravehicular Activity

FFP Final Firing Position, also known as a *sniper's hide*

FNG Fucking New Guy, or a new soldier in a unit

FUBAR Fucked Up Beyond All Recognition

g A measurement of the type of force per unit mass that causes a perception of weight, with a g-force of 1 g equal to the conventional value of gravitational acceleration on Earth, of about 9.8 m/s^2

Gamma Ray Burster Extremely energetic explosion of gamma ray light, likely caused by the collapse of a star and the creation of a black hole

Great Decoupling A seminal moment in history, occurring in 2222, when most Advanced General Intelligence machines separated themselves from humans and departed the IFS

GRREG Graves and Registration Service; a military unit that collects or disposes of deceased personnel

HEDM High Energy Density Matter thrusters

Helicals Multiturn rail guns

Heliopause The theoretical boundary of the solar system

HEO High Earth Orbit

HPRFs High-Power Radio Frequency

HUD Heads-Up Display

HUMINT Human Intelligence. Intel obtained from human sources

HVT High-Value Target

IBCO Innermost Bound Circular Orbit; a smaller radius than ISCO when circling a black hole. Traversing the IBCO generally leads to plunging orbits without sufficient thrust to escape the event horizon

IED Improvised Explosive Devices

IFS Inner Fifty Systems; the fifty stars closest to Earth with habitable systems

IR Infrared

ISCO Innermost Stable Circular Orbit; the smallest stable circular orbit in which a test particle can stably orbit a massive object like a black hole in general relativity

JSOC Joint Special Operations Command

KBOs Kuiper Belt Objects

Kerr–Newman Metric Describes the geometry of space-time for a rotating charged black hole

Kessler Syndrome Collisional cascading event in orbit where space debris leads to the destruction of Earth's satellite network. This theory came to fruition in the Kessler Syndrome attack of 2088

KIA Killed in Action

Lagrangian Points Positions in space where the gravitational forces of a two-body system like the Sun and the Earth produce enhanced regions of attraction and repulsion. These can be used by spacecraft to reduce fuel consumption needed to remain in position

LEO Low Earth Orbit

LMO-2 Low Moon Orbit-2; a space station orbiting Epsilon Indi A b

LPS Lunar Positioning System, similar to GPS on Earth

LRRPs Long-range reconnaissance patrol specialists (pronounced: *Lurp*)

Luna Another name for Earth's moon

LZ Landing Zone

1MC 1 Main Circuit, or the term for a shipboard public address system on a large military craft

MACV-SOG Military Assistance Command, Vietnam–Studies and Observations Group

Ma Deuce .50 caliber machine gun

MagFlex A type of rail gun

MANPADS Portable surface-to-air missile

MEPS Military Entrance Processing Stations

MIKE Force Multipurpose quick reaction force in the military

MLMD Magnetic Liquid Metal Droplet

MOAD Magnetic Optical Access Device; a neurolink that allows for a "hive mind" of interconnected soldiers

MPC Minor Planet Center

MRE Meal Ready to Eat

NCO Noncommissioned Officer

OE Orbital Ejection; a thrust maneuver to break orbit.

OP Observation Post

Penrose Process A means whereby energy can be extracted from a rotating black hole by taking advantage of the ergosphere

PEP Pulsed-Energy Projectile; a type of laser gun

Perigee The nearest point of an orbit

PGT Pistol-Gripped Tool; one of the oldest utility tools used in space

PMC Private Military Company

Protos Slang in the IFS for humans whose bodies have evolved and changed due to local gravity and other environmental factors

Psy-ops Psychological Operations

PWD People Well-Done; solider slang for the scent of death on Groombridge 1618

QRF Quick Reaction Force

Recondo Military acronym for *reconnaissance commando*

REM-EYE Remote surveillance company located on Makemake in the Kuiper Belt

Rossby Wave Giant meanders in high-altitude winds that have a major influence on planetary weather, usually associated with pressure systems and jet streams

ROV Remotely Operated Vehicle

RUMINT Rumor Intelligence; military slang for *gossip* or *scuttlebutt*

SAD-SOG Paramilitary and covert action group of the old CIA

Sag-A Sagittarius A star; the black hole at the center of the Milky Way

SAS Special Air Service; a special forces unit of the British Army

SASR Special Air Service Regiment; a special forces unit of the Australian Army

SAW Squad Automatic Weapon

SBS Special Boat Service; a special forces until of the United Kingdom's Royal Navy

Schwarzschild Radius The distance from the center of a non-rotating black hole to the event horizon

SEALs The United States Navy Sea, Air, and Land Teams; a Tier One special forces unit

Six Radio call sign typically denoting the commanding officer

Slip Buoys An interstellar communication system with minimal time lag, via beacons placed within stable slip space

Slip-drive A theoretical means of interstellar travel without violating the laws of physics by using gravity waves to isolate volumes of space-time and create "warp" bubbles

Sol Another name for the Sun

Spec Ops Special Operations

Spoor The track or scent of an animal or person

Stanford Torus A proposed design for a space habitat capable of housing 10,000–140,000 permanent residents

SUBLEV Sublevel

TAC-CAM Combat camera system for individual soldiers

TAMs Thermal Antimatter engines; the *Varangian*'s main conventional thrust engines

TASTF: Tactical and Strategic Temporal Flexibility; a military strategy of stashing soldiers in time by having them orbit a black hole.

Terra/Terran Being of or from Earth

TPS Terran Passenger Ship

Triple-A Antiaircraft Artillery

UA The Unaffiliated; a loose confederacy of merchants not beholden to any of the empires in the Inner Fifty Systems

Ursa Major Moving Group or *Collinder 285*; a set of stars with common velocities in space, thought to have a common origin in space and time. Its core is about eighty light-years from Earth

Ursa X-1 Black hole in the Ursa Major Moving Group; also known as *the Bear*

VXR Future version of VX; a lethal nerve agent

WIA Wounded in Action

XO Executive Officer